Lizzie Lane was  toughest areas of Bristol, all born before her parer her, who had endured both natural-born story teller, eriences of the tumultuous twentieth century that Lizzie gets her inspiration.

Lizzie put both city and rat race behind her in 2012 and moved on to a boat, preferring to lead the simple life where she can write and watch the sun go down without interruption.

Also by Lizzie Lane:

LIZZIE LANE
Home Sweet Home

EBURY
PRESS

3 5 7 9 10 8 6 4

Ebury Press, an imprint of Ebury Publishing
20 Vauxhall Bridge Road
London SW1V 2SA

Penguin
Random House
UK

Ebury Press is part of the Penguin Random House
group of companies whose addresses can be found at
global.penguinrandomhouse.com
Copyright © Lizzie Lane, 2015

Lizzie Lane has asserted her right to be identified as
the author of this work in accordance with the Copyright,
Designs and Patents Act 1988

This novel is a work of fiction. Names and characters
are the product of the author's imagination and any resemblance
to actual persons, living or dead, is entirely coincidental

First published in 2015 by Ebury Press
This edition published 2016

www.eburypublishing.co.uk

A CIP catalogue record for this book is
available from the British Library

ISBN 9781785036095

Typeset in India by Thomson Digital Pvt Ltd, Noida, Dehli

Penguin Random House is committed to a sustainable future for our business,
our readers and our planet. This book is made from Forest Stewardship
Council® certified paper.

MIX
Paper from
responsible sources
FSC® C018179
FSC
www.fsc.org

Printed and bound in Great Britain by Clays Ltd, Elcograf S.p.A.

PROLOGUE

Sumatra, September 1942

John Smith eased over on to his side, wincing as he did so. Every bone in his body, every wasted muscle, cried out from the effort. Oh, for a bed with proper springs! Just a dream. Something he'd once enjoyed and nothing like he slept on in this hellhole!

A proper bed! Even a mattress! What he'd give for a feather bed or even a mound of moss in the middle of an English field. Or a Scottish, Irish or Welsh one. A place where the air was cool and his bed soft. Not like this bloody thing, no more than wooden slats banged together with iron nails. And only a few slats at that.

Thanks to burrowing insects and the skin-soaking humidity, the slats rotted quickly and needed frequent replacing. Where slats had not been replaced, only the iron nails remained on the struts sticking up to trap the slack skin of the man who lay on it. It took a great deal of effort to pull them out. Iron nails provided currency, a poor currency maybe, but anything one could barter or sell was like money in the bank. Taken out and hammered straight, they could be exchanged for food, a cigarette, or an extra ounce of rice. You needed a lot of nails to barter for anything like that.

Even here nails had a use: they were needed to form secret compartments in an inmate's bed, or used to form a box which was then buried deep in the dirt floor – anywhere hidden from the Nips – their slang for the Japanese and Korean guards. Everyone kept a little cache of something precious that could be bartered or merely treasured: jewellery, watches – anything that hadn't been taken off them.

Johnnie had originally been interned in Changi – heaven compared to this place, which was surrounded by hot, humid jungle, the air a perpetual swamp of sticky heat.

Leather boots fell to bits, the stitching that had fastened the uppers to the soles rotted away along with the rough bits of string that had long since replaced army issue boot laces.

Men rotted here too. Their uniforms, once proudly worn, were either a mass of ragged patches or completely gone, replaced by a sarong knotted at the waist and obtained in exchange for the last precious item a man might own – a cigarette lighter, a wedding ring, a lucky coin – not so lucky here.

Photographs were vulnerable to both insects and humidity. And photographs were the most precious of all: each photograph contained a memory, a reminder of a life once lived before ending up as a prisoner of war on the other side of the world.

After making sure nobody was watching, John eased the photograph of Ruby Sweet from the tobacco tin he kept it in. The sun was going down and there wasn't much light left. What with the stink of sweating men and the crowded surroundings, it was hardly the most romantic setting in the world. However, he'd made a habit of studying her photo before he fell asleep. In that moment he forgot his dire surroundings. Looking at her kept him sane, gave him hope. He'd received no letters from her since he'd become a POW, but then, he conceded, it wasn't her fault. None of the other blokes had received letters either. The only one he had was the one he'd received before Singapore had fallen. He'd read it until the folds broke, the paper softened with moisture. Still he kept it; and kept reading it, even though he could recite it almost word for word by now.

The letter contained a recipe. He'd read that recipe over and over again, salivating as he did so. In his mind's eye, he could see her giving one of her cooking demonstrations. Those memories always made him smile.

The photograph had been taken by an official of the Ministry of Food for propaganda purposes. He'd been lucky enough to persuade the photographer to make an extra copy for him. He'd forgotten to tell Ruby about it, but he was glad he had it.

Gazing at the photograph, he remembered everything about their time together. In fact, he went over each occasion in his mind as often as he could just so he wouldn't forget that he'd once known her in another life.

Another life. In this one, fear had become a tight band around his chest. Hopefully, he would return to that other life. He held on to the hope that he would survive his incarceration, that the war would end and Ruby would be waiting for him. He imagined her cooking an evening meal, just for the two of them, husband and wife. The future he imagined with her might be a leap too far, but a future in which they would be together was the only thing keeping him going.

What would she say about that? he wondered, and couldn't help smiling. They'd never expressed anything definite. They'd just flirted. Sometimes they'd argued, but they'd been slowly getting closer. And then there was that day in the field close to the railway station. I mean, you can't get much closer than that, he thought to himself.

He sighed, rolled on to his back and held the photograph to his chest with both hands. If it wasn't for his memories of Ruby, he would go mad. If he didn't cling to the hope of better things to come, he would give up and die.

Hope had surged in his chest a few days ago when the Japanese guards had come round with postcards for them to fill in. It was whispered that the cards would be passed to the Red Cross, who would in turn send them to their loved ones. The camp commandant confirmed it. The prisoners, starved, despondent and abused, had received such promises before. But then no cards had materialised. The conclusion had been that their captors had been playing with them, giving them hope in exchange for them behaving themselves.

But this time the cards had actually materialised. They dared to hope that it wasn't just a ruse. Hopefully, the postcards really would be handed over to the Red Cross and sent home.

Like the other blokes, John had avidly filled his in. There had been a fight over the few pencils they'd been handed and he'd made the mistake of getting involved. The butt of a Japanese rifle had connected with his forehead. His eye had been half-closed as a result of it, blood trickling down his cheek. It wasn't the first time he'd been beaten. Everyone had. Bleeding was a consequence of being a prisoner of the Japanese.

He'd ignored the blood and kept writing what they'd told him to write:

I am well. I am being well treated. The Japanese are winning the war.

Nobody dared deviate. It stuck in his craw that he had to write the lies dictated to them. He so wanted to tell Ruby the truth about how cruel their captors could be. But how?

In the past, early on in the war, he'd got round the army censors by adding a cryptic note in his letters that left her in no

4

doubt of where he was and what was going on. That was what he wanted to do now, but it wasn't easy, not here. The guards were watching him closely. The camp commandant and his aides were carefully scrutinising each card. Those whose English was poor merely counted the words, comparing one card with another.

How to let Ruby know the truth?

A droplet of blood had fallen on to his hand from the cut above his eyebrow where the rifle butt had split the skin, and for a moment he had stared at it as though surprised there was any blood left in his body, he was that thin.

A number of flies began to buzz around the spilled blood. Another droplet fell on to the card as an idea formed in his mind.

He glanced swiftly around him. The coast was clear. The prisoners were concentrating on writing their cards, the guards on collecting the finished articles and reading what they had written.

Nobody saw him press his thumb into the droplet of blood that had fallen on to the card. Was it too obvious? He didn't think so. No more than a smudge, almost like mud – unless one looked very closely.

It was done! Now all he had to hope was that nobody would notice it.

His heart had been in his mouth as the postcards were snatched and flicked like a pack of cards by an officer who could read English. He might see the right number of words, but he was holding them at the corners. The imprint was hidden. After that they were placed into a box marked with the Red Cross insignia. The cards were taken away for despatch – at least he hoped they were.

Now John lay back on his hard bed. From outside the tent he heard the chattering of monkeys, the droning of insects; and inside there was the sobbing of a man a few beds down from his. Groans, murmured prayers and whispering voices were background noises he'd grown used to.

Despite everything, he still felt incredibly elated. His message was there on the postcard, printed in blood. Never mind the reassuring words that he was well and being taken care of. The bloodied fingerprint would tell the truth. But would Ruby see it and understand? He sorely hoped that she would.

CHAPTER ONE

England

On the day Mary Sweet finally left Oldland Common for good, the train journey to the east of England seemed to take for ever. It had been bad enough the first time round when she'd fled in haste to visit Michael in hospital. Fear and apprehension had travelled with her, and the dull weather had done nothing to raise her spirits. She had left early in the morning in autumnal darkness, a darkness that had only lightened to grey thanks to the gloomy sky and pouring rain.

Just like now, the train had passed acre after acre of ploughed-up fields, the monotony intermittently relieved by a green oasis of pastureland where cattle or sheep still grazed. Even though they passed close to Newmarket, the heart of British horse racing, she didn't see any horses. Grassland was precious; horses were a luxury, though they were also a valuable alternative to cattle. Horse steak wasn't dissimilar to beef, though she hadn't tried it herself.

Leaving home for good had left her with an empty, cold feeling inside. It wasn't just leaving her family and the village she'd grown up in; the prospect of what she would have to face at the other end of her journey also concerned her. She'd seen Michael's bandaged hands and torso on her last visit. Now he was due to have his bandages finally removed.

She'd thought herself prepared for the event, but still her stomach rolled nervously at finally having to face the extent of the injuries that Michael had endured.

Michael's job was necessary to the war effort, but extremely dangerous. She had to face that. But how injured was he? She'd been told he would fly again and not to worry, but what did that mean? People would say anything to help her get over the shock. She didn't blame them for doing so, but despite their reassurances she couldn't help imagining it being worse than they admitted to.

They'd explained all this to her on her previous visit. Only some of it had sunk in. Questions remained. How badly scarred would he be? Could he still walk? Yes, he must be able to walk otherwise they wouldn't have said that he would still fly once he'd recovered. But his hands? His beautiful hands? Would he be able to feel her when he touched her?

All those questions still hung in her mind on this journey through the flat Lincolnshire countryside. Before she'd left, her father had taken her to one side and reminded her of where she needed to be. 'Your place is with him. By his bedside.'

'I should have moved there when he asked me to,' she'd replied.

Her father had looked a little sad at the prospect of losing her, but had said, 'He's your husband, Mary, and it's only right that you should be living with him, not here with us.'

It was dark by the time she'd alighted from the train at a branch station. The sound of a whistle screeched before the name of the station – the one she'd travelled to on her last visit – was shouted out. A dim blue lantern, similar to the dim bulbs they used in the railway carriages nowadays, cast just enough of its cold, blue light so people could see where they were going. Apart from the lantern, the unfamiliar surroundings were as black as a coal pit.

Shouts and laughter fell on to the platform as a whole battalion of army privates bundled out of the train carriages making jokes and laughing, their burning cigarettes glowing red in the deep black night.

On the train, one of them had told her that they were on their way to important east coast bases. The south and east coasts would be the front line should the enemy invade and had been packed with troops since the outbreak of war – more so now the Americans had arrived.

She had looked at the faces of the private and his companions, bright and cheerful despite the gloomy compartment, young faces that would soon turn old and worldly wise once they'd experienced what a war really was.

What the station lacked in light it made up for with other noises besides those of the men in uniform. Their boots clattered over the platform and clouds of steam hissed from the underbelly beneath the locomotive and the funnel on top.

In her heavily pregnant state, Mary's sense of smell was extremely acute, sickeningly so sometimes. Damp wool, men's sweat, cigarettes and smoke smelling of cinders from the steam engine formed an acrid brew that made Mary gag. Swaying slightly and closing her eyes, she placed her hand over her nose and mouth.

The crowd pressed on around her, a human tide surging towards the ticket inspectors and the exit, the former only serving to slow the flow but determined to do their job.

Once the throng had largely dissipated and she had room to breathe, she placed her case between her feet, took a deep breath and looked around her. Last time she had come here, Mike's friend Guy had been waiting for her and taken her straight to the hospital, where she had stayed until it was clear Mike was out of danger. Then she had returned to the only home she'd ever known, to pack up and return.

The light from the lantern threw a pool of light immediately in front of her. Whoever had been sent to pick her up would see her here, picked out by the poor light and close to the station clock. She looked up at it, saw its Roman figures. Nine o'clock. It had indeed been a long day, though according to some on the train, fifteen hours to cross from one side of the country to the other was quite normal.

Emerging from the gaping blackness of the exit, a figure paused to flash his identification at one of the ticket inspectors. Like a shadow that had come to life, he made his way to her, the only woman still on the platform. It wasn't Guy.

'Mrs Dangerfield?'

The light played tricks with his features, but his uniform was that of a member of RAF ground crew. He was of average height and build, not a prepossessing man at all, though there was something odd about one side of his face. At first glance, she put it down to the dark shadows thrown by the blue lantern. On second glance, she knew the cold light was not to blame.

Fear and a creeping sickness tightened her stomach. The skin on one side of his face resembled a mask, a cruel mask that made it seem as though his face had been torn apart then reassembled from the wrong pieces. The skin of his right cheek looked paper thin, one eye slanting downwards, his mouth uneven from a silky patch of skin that seemed to have been sewn on to his upper lip.

Her mind raced and her blood ran cold as the man in front of her saluted smartly and offered to take her case.

'Yes . . . yes . . . of course.'

'My name's Sergeant Paul Innes. It's a bit late to go straight to the hospital, so I have strict orders to make you comfortable tonight and take you to the hospital tomorrow.'

Mary tried not to let her mouth hang open, but it wasn't easy. It was difficult to take her eyes off the damaged side of his face. Suddenly she became aware of her bad manners.

'I'm sorry,' she said apologetically and tried to sound light-hearted, as though nothing was out of the ordinary and his face was unblemished.

My voice sounds shaky, she thought. My smile is too stiff, and as for my hands . . .

She curled the fingers of one hand into her perspiring palm. Luckily she was wearing gloves otherwise she would have left red crescents behind. Her teeth ached with the effort of smiling and pretending that nothing was wrong.

Sergeant Innes didn't appear to notice, or if he did, he hid it well. It was no good. She just had to apologise properly.

'I'm sorry. I don't mean to stare.'

He smiled a lop-sided smile. 'Oh, don't you be sorry about that, Mrs Dangerfield. I'm afraid it's a legacy of a burning Hampden bomber. I'm still alive. That's all that matters. The wing commander sends his apologies, Mrs Dangerfield. He would have collected you himself, but he's on Ops tonight. I've been ordered to take you to your cottage. I've got you some food in and lit the fire.'

He was affable and kind, but she shuddered as she wondered how many times he'd had to carry out this duty.

After placing her luggage on the back seat, he helped her into the car. They moved off, away from the town and into a dark, flat landscape. It took about an hour travelling along unlit country roads before they finally arrived at Woodbridge Cottage.

Once out of the car, he grabbed her luggage from the back seat, helped her out from the front seat and switched on a torch. They followed the flashlight's circular beam the length of the garden path.

'Where are you from, Sergeant?' Asking a question helped to keep their conversation light and friendly, away from the taboo subject of Michael's injuries.

'Birmingham.'

She couldn't help remarking that he was a long way from home, simply because she felt she had to say something, however innocuous.

'We're all a long way from home, Mrs Dangerfield.' Sergeant Innes didn't seem to have noticed her anxiety. 'But that's the nature of war. All hands to the pumps, no matter where they come from. Right. Open sesame.'

The beam from the torch picked out a bird box on the right-hand side of the cottage door. She couldn't remember it from her last visit but then she'd spent so little time here. It had been just somewhere to sleep after spending most of her time with Mike at the hospital. A huge iron key hung on a hook just below it.

'Here it is,' he said. He took the key and swivelled the torch ahead of them to pick out the keyhole. Now she noticed that the cottage had a sweet little front door. The key clunked as it turned in the lock.

Although the sergeant wasn't that tall, he had to duck to enter, and the top of her head barely missed the frame too. She smiled at the thought of Michael hitting his head on its low oak lintel. A pang of regret clutched at her heart. If only she'd come here sooner. They could have enjoyed some time together, talking about the baby, walking through the surrounding countryside. On the first visit she had stayed here all alone. Hopefully on this visit she wouldn't be alone for too long.

Precious as it was, some time together was all it would have been if she had come up earlier. Nothing she could have done would have prevented what had happened.

Because it had been dark, she hadn't seen much of the garden and had been too preoccupied to notice anything on her first visit. Tonight she smelt damp green leaves and fertile earth and imagined that in summer it was a riot of smells and colour thanks to sweet-scented stock, honeysuckle and lavender. Although the countryside was flatter than at home, the smells at least were the same.

The door opened directly into the living room, where a welcoming fire glowed in the grate. Once the blackout curtains were pulled, Sergeant Innes switched on a table lamp. The room echoed the look of a summer garden with its chintz-covered armchairs and flowery curtains. Despite the fact that the seats of the chairs sagged a little, they looked comfortable.

The sergeant offered to take her suitcase upstairs for her.

'There's no need. I can manage.' She wanted him to go. Her legs felt terribly weak. She reached out and grasped the back of a chair.

Sergeant Innes reached out as if to steady her. 'I think you need to sit down, Mrs Dangerfield. You've had a long journey in your condition.'

'Oh, don't worry about me,' she said, attempting a light laugh. 'You surely have more important duties with the air force.'

'Not at all. That's what I'm here for, Mrs Dangerfield. Would you like me to make you a cup of tea before I leave?'

'No,' she said, managing a weak smile. 'I'm quite fine now.'

There was kindness in his eyes. 'Now this here's the kitchen,' he said. The door he opened was almost a mirror image of the front door, planks of pine nailed to two cross braces.

'I remember,' said Mary.

'Ah, yes. Of course you do. Well, there you are. It's small but cosy. I've got you in a few tinned things, your bacon ration and some eggs. Had a hard job getting those,' he said to her. 'But where there's a will there's a way – and a farmer over the back field willing to gamble just about anything in a game of cards.' He winked. The corner of his damaged right eye drooped downwards, giving him a strange, almost roguish look. 'Trouble is he isn't much of a gambling man. Oh, and I persuaded Mrs Catchpole, who does a bit of cleaning for the officers, to make a nice toad in the hole. Not that there's likely to be many toads in it, but I guarantee it'll be tasty.'

For the first time since seeing his injured features, Mary controlled her fear and looked him directly in the face.

'Thank you, Sergeant. I think I'll be very comfortable here.'

'No bother, Mrs Dangerfield. Not sure what time I'm to pick up your husband, but don't count on it being too early.'

'Whatever time is fine. It gives me a chance to settle in.'

Once the door had closed behind him and the big iron key was hanging on yet another nail to one end of the fireplace, Mary sat down and thought about things. Just as she'd composed her expression to face Sergeant Innes, she'd have to do the same for her husband when she saw him tomorrow. It wouldn't be easy and she thought about it long and hard, so long that she hardly noticed that the only light in the room was from the glowing fire and the meagre table lamp. Dancing shadows played over the walls, but they didn't worry her. Today was almost over. It was tomorrow she was worried about. How would she cope?

She took a deep breath. Control yourself. Be calm.

The words popped into her mind and she took instant notice. The best thing to do is to keep yourself occupied.

Determinedly, she got to her feet. Sergeant Innes had gone to a lot of trouble. It was only right that she should enjoy what he'd arranged for her. She recalled Michael telling her that although far from town, the cottage had some degree of electricity downstairs.

'Upstairs it's candles or oil lamps,' he'd told her.

Her first stop was the kitchen. Besides the eggs and bacon Sergeant Innes told her about, she found bread and cheese, tinned meats and fresh vegetables set in the middle of a simple pine table. She couldn't help wondering whose ration card had been used.

A covered pan containing the toad in the hole was keeping warm on top of a cast-iron range. The coals in the fire bed glowed hot and red. Despite the iron cover, the smell escaped, made her nose tingle and her stomach rumble. However, eating could wait. This was the cottage Michael had earmarked to be their home for the duration of the war – or at least as long as he was stationed here.

There was no gas stove. Not surprising, really. They were in the midst of fertile agricultural land, some of the best in England. She guessed there was no gas for miles. As long as she kept the kitchen door open, the range would heat the house and cook the food. Hunger hadn't been much of an issue the first time she'd been here as she was so worried about Michael. But now he was coming home and she had it in mind to make sure the house was well presented. In the morning, she would explore the garden and pick some flowers, even if she had to put them in jam jars around the house.

After placing the tinned things on to a dresser and the rest into a metal meat cupboard, she wandered back into the living room.

Downstairs, the cottage had only the two rooms, the kitchen and the living room. The large inglenook fireplace took up one third of a wall, and while the furniture was shabby and the carpets worn, the atmosphere was warm and cosy. The smell of polish lingered in the air, evidence that someone cared for the cottage and was doing what they could to make the old furniture last that bit longer.

Armed with a wax candle she'd found in a kitchen drawer, she made her way upstairs. The candle flame flickered in the draught as she explored the two bedrooms. The front bedroom, the largest, held a double bed with a plain wooden headboard and smaller, matching footboard. The floors were of bare wood, a rag rug in pink and red to one side of the bed, a smaller green one close to the window. The curtains were of a Paisley-patterned fabric in matching colours. A wine-coloured satin eiderdown sat on top of a faded candlewick bedspread that might once have been yellow but was now a very pale lemon.

The second bedroom had a small square window, a chest of drawers and a single bed with a patchwork cover. She opened the window at the exact same time as the moon chose to emerge from behind a navy blue cloud. The air was crisp and cold. The flat land of Lincolnshire was spread out before her like a patchwork counterpane.

The blackout curtains were not drawn. She wondered at that, then recalled that Michael had said something about the pilots using the escaping light from this cottage as a kind of marker buoy, situated as it was at the very end of the runway. 'Against blackout regulations and all that, but we don't get many enemy bombers up here. Too far and not too much for them to bomb when they get here. Except us, that is.'

He'd laughed at his own joke, at least she'd thought it was a joke. Perhaps that business about bombers being able to see a light from ten thousand feet was rubbish.

The sight of the moon stirred a vein of anger inside her. She slammed the window shut and pulled the curtains, blotting out its silvery light. She didn't want to look at the moon, the bomber's moon, as Michael had described it.

'It's great for navigation,' he'd told her. 'The moon shines on a river, the water reflects light so we follow water or a river all the way to our target. Once we get there we can see everything.'

He'd been more reticent about adding that because they could more easily see the ground, those on the ground could also see them. After she'd challenged him, he'd admitted that there was a greater chance of being hit by an anti-aircraft gun on a clear night such as this.

Just for once in her life she found herself hating the moon, yet there had been a time when she'd loved it. She didn't know for sure whether the moon had been shining on the night Michael had been hit, but she couldn't help hating it in case it had aided his plane being shot down.

She managed to eat some of the toad in the hole, and left the rest for the next day. In the morning, she ate only a slice of toast and drank a cup of tea, and even had trouble keeping that down. Yes, there was the usual feeling of nausea, but this morning it was coupled with a sickening fear that lay in her stomach like a bag of rocks.

Closing her eyes, she willed it to pass and uttered a heartfelt prayer. 'Please, God, don't let him be too badly scarred. Please!'

CHAPTER TWO

It was a day in autumn 1942, not long after Mary had left to join her husband Michael, when something happened that made her cousin, Frances, determined to find her mother. Perhaps it might never have entered her head if it hadn't been for her cousin Ruby's hand-me-down red dress and her friend Pearl – suitably armed with her ration card – insisting on calling in at 'Mother' Powell's for a packet of Woodbines before they went to the dance that evening at the church hall.

Gertrude Powell's shop meant a bit of a detour, but Pearl had been insistent. 'I can't go without a smoke, Frances. Sure you don't want to join me?' Smoking didn't appeal to Frances. The taste was bad enough; the smell of people who did smoke was even worse. 'I've no wish to smell like an ashtray,' she'd countered.

Pearl was seeing a freckle-faced boy named Ty. He was from New York and kind of boastful because he came from the 'Big Apple', as he called his home city.

'He wants us to go the whole way before he heads for France,' Pearl whispered as they tottered on three-inch heels down Court Road to the village store.

Frances sucked in her breath. 'Are you going to?'

'I don't know. I want to, but . . . well . . . my mum would kill me if I got pregnant.'

'So you won't let him.'

'I didn't say that. I might. I mean, you know how it is. There are times when you just can't help yourself.'

Frances thought about Ed, his sweet words pouring like honey into her ear, the feel of his body against her, the boyish face and the touch of his hands . . . Although she was fond of him, she wasn't sure whether she was inclined to give in.

Mrs Powell looked up when they entered, her black eyes fixing them with a dull glare, her nostrils flaring. Her face was white and her hair and clothes as black as her eyes. She wore no discernible expression, said nothing and stood stiff as a poker. If they didn't know better, they might think she was made of wax, not real at all.

'Five Woodbines, please. There's my ration book.'

Pearl slammed her mother's ration book down on the counter.

While Mrs Powell stamped her ration book and reached for the cigarettes, Pearl held her skirt some way above her knees and asked Frances if her stocking seams were straight. Not that they were real stockings, of course. Real stockings were hard to come by these days.

'My little brother drew them with the brown from the box of crayons he had for last Christmas. The trouble was he wasn't wearing his glasses.'

Frances fancied that one seam was a little crooked, but not enough to worry about. 'They're fine. Did you use gravy browning?' Gravy browning turned white legs a more subtle shade of brown, almost like stockings but not quite.

Dropping her grip on her hem, Pearl shook her head. 'I got some of that natural brown stuff in Woolworths when I last went to Kingswood. I heard it doesn't go all streaky in the rain like gravy browning. What did you use?'

'Bisto. But I think I'll get some of that stuff you've got when I'm in town next.'

'Bisto does run something terrible. That stuff I got in Kingswood works okay.'

Pearl said 'okay' with an American drawl that Frances found quite fascinating. It was as though Pearl was readying herself for a life with her American among the skyscrapers of New York.

Mrs Powell, who had progressed from wax-like stiffness to outright impatience, began tapping her fingers on the counter. 'Anything else?'

Pearl didn't hear her, busily whispering in Frances's ear about her freckle-faced American. 'He has such a nice body—'

'Excuse me!' Mrs Powell's voice rattled into their conversation. 'I have other things more important to do than wait on a couple of young floozies out to throw themselves at anything in trousers!'

Pearl's mouth dropped open.

Frances was taken aback but rebounded swiftly. 'There's no need for that, Mrs Powell. We're paying customers!'

Glowering, Mrs Powell snatched the cigarettes back and threw the ration book across the counter, where it slid off the edge and on to the floor.

Pearl turned bright red. 'What about my cigarettes?'

'You'll have to do without,' snarled Mrs Powell. 'Get some off your American friends. I dare say you'll be giving them something in return.'

'I don't like your insinuation,' declared Frances. Although she was seething inside, she lifted her chin high and spoke with cold precision.

'Insinuation? Insinuation?' Gertrude Powell, a middle-aged woman who looked older than her years, laughed, though not jovially. It conveyed nothing but contempt. 'There's no

20

"insinuation" about it! You come into my shop and keep me waiting while you hitch up your skirts and show your knickers!'

Pearl looked horrified. 'I was only checking my seams . . .' She sounded as though she was about to burst into tears.

'That's a disgusting thing to say,' snapped Frances. 'She was just showing me her stocking seams that her brother drew on her legs. So let's have the Woodbines.'

'I've told you, no,' said Mrs Powell. Her pointed features jutted forward over the counter, reminding Frances of a gargoyle on a church roof. 'Now get out of my shop.'

'No,' Frances said, her expression just as adamant as that of the shopkeeper.

Eyes unblinking and without sparkle, Mrs Powell ignored the ration book Frances was holding out to her.

'As for you,' she said, looking Frances up and down, 'you're no better than that fancy cousin of yours. Always with a different feller. Is that a red dress you're wearing beneath that coat? Yes, I can see it is. Well, that's no big surprise, is it? Given what your mother was like – a scarlet woman if ever there was one. I hear tell that she liked soldiers too, and the more the merrier!'

Up until this moment, Frances might have treated this whole affair differently. She and Pearl would probably have laughed about it all the way along the road. But she'd slighted Ruby and her mother. Frances could barely remember her mum, but she couldn't stomach the older woman's insults.

'Take that back, you evil cow!'

Pearl gasped. She'd never heard Frances swear before – not in public, anyway.

Mrs Powell's coal-black eyes glared at Frances from deep sockets. Her spidery fingers gripped the counter top as though she were using it to keep herself upright.

'I'll do no such thing! Your mother was a Jezebel! A scarlet woman. A whore, a slut and any other name you can think of that means the same thing . . .'

Tears stinging her eyes, Frances ran out of the shop, the strident words ringing out behind her, Pearl at her side.

Once outside, Frances took deep breaths and told herself to calm down, that they were just cruel accusations, that Mrs Powell was unhinged. She'd never used to be quite so bad, but that was before her daughter Miriam had gone away to live with her grandmother.

Their hurrying footsteps echoed on the chill night air, the light from Pearl's torch picking out the uneven stones that made up the pavement.

'Frances? Do you think she's mad?'

Pearl's breathless tone interrupted the thoughts that Frances was trying to set into some order. As a child, she'd entertained the notion that someday her mother would come back for her. She'd grown up since then and her life at her uncle's had been mostly happy. Her mother had never figured prominently in her thoughts. Now, thanks to Mrs Powell's nasty comments, things had changed.

A yearning to know the truth had suddenly emerged like a buried spring bulb coaxed from the earth by incessant rain. Mrs Powell's words had brought all those old wishes back to the surface.

'Do you think she's mad?' Pearl asked again.

'As mad as a March hare!'

They had sped on in silence towards the village hall, Frances wondering how much Pearl had taken in and what she thought of the outburst. Even though she'd barely known her mother, it pained Frances to have her maligned. Surely she can't have been that bad? She didn't want Pearl to think so.

22

But Pearl had noticed. 'Those things Mrs Powell said,' Pearl began, her voice hesitant. 'Were they true?'

'No,' snapped Frances, glad of the blackout. Pearl must not see that her eyes were moist with hot tears. 'My mother was wild, but she was not a whore. She was not!'

The music was loud and the village hall was hot and stuffy. Just for a heartbeat, Frances looked down at her dress once her coat was hung up. Scarlet. The colour was scarlet.

She took Pearl by surprise, grabbing her arm. 'You won't say a word,' she hissed. 'Promise you won't repeat what that old cow said about my mother. I don't want the whole village to know.'

Frances's tone was insistent. She didn't realise how much her fingers were digging into Pearl's arm until the girl winced and asked her to let go.

'I won't say anything. I promise. It's a secret. Right?' Pearl smiled nervously before trotting off to meet her soldier boy.

'Can I share this secret?'

A handsome stranger – a Yank at that – emerged it seemed from nowhere. He had black hair, an inquisitive expression and held a cigarette in his right hand. His smile was an odd mixture of self-satisfaction and amusement.

Frances felt her cheeks warming. She couldn't be sure whether he'd heard or not. 'It's none of your business!'

'I was close by. I couldn't help it.'

His smile annoyed her. Was he just teasing her or had he heard what she'd said? 'Then you should have made your presence known.'

'But overhearing secrets is such great entertainment.'

'It's rude!'

His smile grew wider and he raised his eyebrows.

Frances snatched her scarf from off her head. Her hair fell in a glossy veil about her shoulders.

'I've heard tell a woman's hair is her crowning glory,' he said to her. 'I was undecided up to now, but after seeing yours . . .'

'Stop teasing me.'

'I'm not. I'm being my usual most sincere self.'

Tonight had started badly and she was in no mood to cope with this. She was about to tell him to get lost when she caught sight of the look in his eyes. His expression had changed. Frances realised he meant exactly what he'd said.

'Frances! I see you've met my friend, Declan O'Malley. Declan, meet my cousin, Frances.'

Ruby Sweet, Frances's cousin, looked a dream in a blue dress cut down from the bridesmaid's dress she'd worn at her sister Mary's wedding. Her hair was bundled into a black snood scattered with sequins. Ruby had crocheted it and Bettina Hicks, their father's dear friend, had sewn on numerous sequins from what seemed to them a secret haberdashery that she kept in her loft. Ruby had an elegance and confidence beyond her years. Becoming a Home Economist had a lot to do with it. Speaking in front of a room full of strangers had caused her to grow up quickly. She still looked her age, but there was something more commanding about her.

Ruby slid her hand possessively through the crook of the American's arm and smiled when he bent to kiss her cheek. So this was Ruby's latest beau! Frances knew there was one but hadn't met him until now.

Declan O'Malley's demeanour was warm and courteous. His smile was all embracing.

'I should have known,' he said, shaking his head and adopting a doleful expression. 'Two beauties like you had to belong to the same family. Tell me: how do the guys around here cope with their fluttering hearts?'

Ruby nudged him in the ribs. 'Declan! Stop that.' She turned her attention to Frances, her gaze running down over the red dress that had once been hers. 'You haven't spilt anything on it already, have you?'

Frances shook her head. 'No. I've only just arrived.'

'You look flustered. Are you a little peeved?' asked a smiling Ruby, still clinging on to the American's arm.

'Of course not,' Frances responded hotly. 'Why should I be?'

In the presence of the good-looking American, Frances held back from telling her what Mrs Powell had said.

Ruby was not fooled. Looking her cousin in the eye she said, 'Frances! I can tell, you know.' She turned and smiled at Declan O'Malley. 'My cousin has always worn her heart on her sleeve, even when she was a child.'

Declan's expression was inscrutable. 'But she's not a child now. That much is obvious.'

Frances had been simmering at being referred to as a child. 'That's right. I'm not.'

Ruby apologised. 'It's just that you seem a bit off.'

'I'm fine. I was just wondering whether red suits me.'

A small frown puckered Ruby's forehead. 'Of course it does. Actually, it suits you better than it suited me. Red is your colour. Don't you think so, Declan, my love?'

Declan, a knowing smile on his lips, added his opinion. 'I have to agree with Ruby. You look like a movie star. Perhaps I can have the pleasure of dancing with you later on?' His very black pencil-thin eyebrows rose with quizzical amusement.

'Perhaps you can,' returned Frances, unable to stop herself from blushing.

His smile was warm and full of the confidence every American seemed to have in buckets.

'I'm not the best dancer in the world, but I promise not to step on your toes.'

Wishing her face didn't feel so hot, Frances tossed her head so that her hair fell around her shoulders in the seductive way it had earlier. 'Oh, I don't think you're being honest, Declan. I bet you're a really good dancer.'

'I try to be.'

'There!' Ruby said in breathless exclamation. 'My good friend Declan is in agreement with me. You look good in red. It's been confirmed.'

Frances thanked them both, at the same time wondering that Ruby had called Declan a good friend, not 'my sweetheart', 'my boyfriend'. Though she had referred to him as 'my love', earlier. But that was without meaning, Frances decided. Ruby tended to use the same endearments for customers, for everyone.

Ruby flitted from one man to the next, never staying too long in the company of any of them. Except her driver, thought Frances. Johnnie Smith, the corporal from the Royal Corps of Transport, had been assigned to her by the Ministry of Food. It had been his task to drive her from one baking demonstration to another. Ruby had spent more time with him than any other man, even if only in a working capacity.

But Johnnie Smith had been taken prisoner when Singapore had fallen to Japanese invasion. If it hadn't been for that, who knew what might have happened between the pair of them.

Frances said nothing until Ruby's friend Declan was out of earshot on the other side of the hall ordering fresh drinks. He'd been cornered by George Gibbs, an old farmer who was out tonight dressed in his Sunday best which, unfortunately for him, smelled of mothballs and mouse dust. Frances took advantage of being alone with her cousin to ask about her mother.

'Ruby. Do you remember my mother?'

Ruby frowned. 'No. Not really.'

'Do you know where she is?'

Ruby appeared agitated. At the same time she surveyed the dancers on the floor as though their steps were slightly out of sequence and needed a severe frown to bring them into line.

'I'm not sure. You need to ask my dad.'

Ruby's eyes continued to search the dance floor. Her lips were sucked inwards. 'You mean Uncle Stan knows?'

Ruby shrugged and still didn't meet her cousin's look. 'I don't know. Not for sure. What's brought this on?'

'I would like to meet her.'

Ruby's frown returned. 'Meet her? After all this time?'

'She's my mother. I want to know what she was like.'

Seeing the desperate look in her cousin's eyes, Ruby reconsidered. 'Well, I suppose it's only natural that you would want to meet up with her, but—'

The time seemed ripe to change the subject. 'The spread looks good. If you hear what seems like thunder, don't worry! It's just my stomach rumbling!'

Ruby pretended to treat the matter in a light-hearted manner. At the same time, she eyed Frances with nervous apprehension. She had not expected her cousin to ask something like this. What with that and the way she'd seen Declan look at Frances, the night had not turned out exactly as she'd hoped. Turning the conversation to food was an acceptable alternative to discussing more serious matters.

'We're not allowing anyone to indulge until the interval or there'll be nothing left. I think the apple cake will go well, don't you? Did you know that dried apples are fetching nine pence per pound?'

Frances replied that she didn't know. Quite frankly, she didn't care, but if it took discussing the price of dried fruits to stop Ruby's questions, then she would do it.

'Dates are the cheapest. Seven pence a pound.'

Declan still hadn't returned from fetching drinks for himself and Ruby.

Ruby carried on talking about the price of provisions until he'd signalled from the other side of the room, raising the two drinks he'd bought.

'I'd better go.' Ruby paused, her expression one of concern. 'You will be all right, won't you?'

Frances nodded. 'Why shouldn't I be?'

Ruby stroked her cousin's arm in a gesture of sympathy. 'We'll talk about it later. Is that all right with you?'

Frances nodded again. Ruby was not to know that she had already made her mind up: she was going to find her mother. Nobody would stop her. She wouldn't let them.

On the other side of the room, Declan handed Ruby her drink. 'Does your cousin want something?'

Ruby lay her hand upon his arm. 'With regard to your comments to my cousin and the way you looked at her, Declan, can I remind you that Frances is only fifteen years old?'

His smile gave nothing away. 'I don't know what you mean.'

Ruby was not fooled. Her jaw was set, her eyes hard. 'Oh, yes, you do. You know very well. Leave her alone, Declan. She's too young. Leave her alone or you'll have my father to answer to. And me. I promise you, it will not be pleasant!'

CHAPTER THREE

Ruby was up early the following morning, preparing for a talk she was giving to St George Housewives Group. St George was a suburb of Bristol and thus most households were more dependent on shops rather than farmland for their food. With that in mind, she'd devised a pie made from vegetables and Spam. Tins of Spam were becoming quite commonplace on the shelves of grocery stores, thanks to the American allies.

She'd also devised a pie recipe using snoek – a variety of dried fish imported from South Africa.

The last items were loaded into the wickerwork hamper just as her father came in from the bakery.

'I'm parched. Is that a fresh brew?'

Ruby reached for the pot. 'I'll pour one for you.'

'I thought you had to be off?' Stan Sweet knew his daughter's schedule off by heart; in fact, he made a point of being well informed about all his family.

Ruby placed the cup of tea in front of him. 'Dad. It's our Frances. I wanted to warn you before she gets up.'

It was not yet six thirty. Stan Sweet regularly got up at five to bake bread. Ruby or Frances would take over once the bread was baked and cooling, ready to be transferred to the shop.

Stan looked at his daughter over the rim of his teacup. He took a big slurp. 'What's wrong?'

Ruby took a deep breath. 'She wants to find her mother.'

Slowly and thoughtfully, her father placed his cup back into its saucer. For a moment, he was totally silent as he mulled over what Ruby had said.

'That's bad news. Come to that, her mother was always bad news.'

'I told her I had no idea where her mother was. I told her to ask you.'

Still silent, eyes downcast, Stan nodded in his usual thoughtful way. 'I suppose the day had to come.'

Ruby eyed her father, wondering when it was that he'd began to look old, when his hair had started thinning, when the loose skin of his jowls had become so wrinkled.

She hesitated before finally asking whether he really did know the whereabouts of Mildred Sweet, Frances's mother.

'Yes. I do.'

A wary look came to Ruby's face.

Pushing his teacup away, Stan asked, 'Why now? She's never shown much interest before.'

Ruby shrugged. 'I don't know, but as you've just said, the day was bound to come.'

Her father got up from his chair. 'Leave it with me. Say nothing about this until I've thought it over.'

Ruby nodded, then glanced at her watch. 'I have to go. Will you check the post for me? Just in case there's a letter . . . or something.'

Her father's smile was sad but understanding. He knew his daughter was asking him to check if there was anything from Johnnie Smith. Ruby checked every day, hardly giving the mail a chance to fall through the letterbox before pouncing on it. So far, in all this time, there'd been nothing.

* * *

Later in the morning, leaving Frances to run the shop, Stan and his grandson Charlie made their way to St Anne's church.

The weather was dull and overcast, droplets of rain sprinkling from bushes each time the north wind blew. Once they were in the churchyard, Stan used both hands to draw his coat collar up around his neck.

Finding he was no longer constrained by his grandfather's firm grip, Charlie broke into a tottering run, gleefully laughing as twigs and leaves blew across his path.

Stan headed for his wife's grave, pleased to see that Michaelmas daisies were in flower. As was his habit, he settled down beside his wife's headstone, just as he might if she'd been lying in the marriage bed they'd shared for such a few short years.

This was where he came to speak his mind, gather his thoughts and ask questions he wouldn't voice to anyone else – even to his good friend Bettina Hicks.

He called out to Charlie not to wander off before voicing what was in his mind.

'Sarah. The war goes on. All our family are safe and sound, at least for the present. Mary rang me yesterday from Lincolnshire to say that Michael is doing well and that it won't be long before he's home and maybe flying again. I get the impression she's hoping the war will be over before that time comes. I can't say I blame her. Anyway, I think she'd like him to be there when the baby is born, any day now.'

He looked up to see Charlie chasing a baby rabbit round and round a stone guardian angel.

'You won't catch him, Charlie,' Stan called out.

Charlie stood still, turned and regarded his grandfather with a cheeky grin, his cheeks pink and wisps of black curly hair escaping from beneath his balaclava.

'Bunz,' Charlie shouted, pointing to where the baby rabbit had been. 'Gone,' he said on looking back to the bare spot.

'It's not Bunz,' Stan corrected him. Bunz was Charlie's favourite toy. 'It's a real one.'

His grandson looked quite mystified. 'Bunz,' he said again, more emphatically this time.

Stan chuckled as he shook his head. 'My, my, Sarah. If only you were here. If only you could see our first grandchild.' He fell to silence as a thought hit him. 'If only his parents could have too.'

His son Charlie, after whom the little boy had been named, had been lost at sea, thanks to an enemy torpedo. Gilda, the boy's mother, widow of a man who had died in a death camp in Nazi Germany, had been killed in a bombing raid on London. Both events had saddened the whole family, but at least they had young Charlie, a little boy born out of wedlock but conceived from love.

Stan focused on his wife's name carved on the headstone. A frown furrowed his brow. 'Young Frances has asked about her mother. She wants to meet her. She hasn't asked me as yet, but she told our Ruby. Ruby told her she must ask me, that I'm the only one likely to have her mother's address.'

Stan rubbed his hands together, feeling their powdery roughness. Baking was not quite the soft-handed option that people tended to think. Flour could roughen hands; in fact, flour could be downright flammable.

'The thing is, Sarah, I would prefer that she didn't meet her mother. You only knew Mildred briefly and although you cautioned tolerance for her flighty ways, even you accepted that she could be her own worst enemy. And that was putting it mildly! So, until she asks me, I won't broach the subject. I had a letter from Mildred a while back when she asked me for money. Not how her daughter was, but money! That is Mildred all over. Totally selfish.' Stan sighed. He'd thought the past was all over as far as his niece was concerned. It wasn't so. 'I should have known better. Call me a coward, but I can't face giving Frances the information she needs to find her mother. She's only going to get hurt. But I guess if she asks, I will have to tell her.'

He looked up at the sky. A pillow of grey cloud had settled over the church steeple. Just then it seemed to break in two, sliced through by a beam of sunlight. For a moment, he thought he saw Sarah's face, smiling and shaking her head in admonishment.

'Stan Sweet, you're a fool,' he murmured. 'Charlie, come down off there,' he shouted at his young grandson, who had managed to climb halfway up the stone angel.

CHAPTER FOUR

It was seven thirty in the evening. Dr Foster was sipping his whisky very carefully. Although he had a supply at home, buying a shot in one of the village pubs was something he liked doing in order to find out the local gossip. He'd also just come from delivering a baby, so the tipple was by way of wetting the baby's head. Not that he'd been treated by the grateful parents. He just liked congratulating himself on a job well done.

He was also here in the hope of seeing one person in particular who could help him out with a certain problem. The problem had been playing on his mind.

When Stan Sweet came in they greeted each other cordially. Being of the same age they tended to view the world with a sense of shared experience and also, when it came to the war, déjà vu.

This evening, Stan Sweet had the distinct impression that the good doctor was aching to ask him something. The man was fingering his glass, turning it round on the bar top as though something was worrying him.

'Jim,' said Stan, addressing the doctor by his first name. They'd known each other since the end of the Great War. 'Is something wrong?'

The doctor drained his glass and accepted Stan's offer to refill it. 'It's me that's supposed to ask you that.'

'You usually do, but now it's me asking you,' said Stan.

'I need a favour.'

'If it's extra bacon you're after, there's none available until we've got the approval to slaughter,' said Stan, who still kept a few pigs in partnership with an old friend.

Dr Foster shook his head. 'Nothing to do with pigs and bacon, Stan. It's Mrs Gates. She's had another baby . . .'

Stan's eyebrows rose like hairy wings above eyes that saw more of people than he sometimes wanted to see. 'Another?'

'It's her sixth. It makes me feel like contacting her husband's superior officer and suggesting he gives him less leave. If she doesn't get some rest, she's likely to become very ill, perhaps be unable to care for the baby—.'

Stan took a sip of his beer, relishing its dark oaky flavour. 'I hear what you're saying. She needs a break from the rest of those kids.'

'Quite right.' Satisfied that the subject he'd broached had been well received, the doctor took a sip of his whisky and prepared to put forward the rest of his plan. 'The trouble is she's got no relatives in these parts, so I was thinking now's the time for her children to be evacuated, that way she doesn't have to find the money to keep them, money she hasn't got and something extra to worry her.' He took another sip of whisky then wiped his bushy moustache with two long fingers.

'That seems the best solution,' commented Stan.

'I think so too, except that she won't have them sent anywhere the evacuation people send them, and she won't have them split up. So I was wondering . . .'

Stan Sweet was ahead of him. 'Ada Perkins. Our Frances loved being over there with her.'

Dr Foster peered at Stan, owl-like wisdom shining in his eyes. 'Can you get in touch with Mrs Perkins? I did ask Mrs Powell, but you know what she's like. Told me that both her mother Ada and her daughter Miriam were dead to her. Shouted at me that people who lived in the Forest of Dean were followers of the devil, burrowed into the ground like rabbits and . . . did other things that rabbits do.'

Stan's hand holding the beer mug stopped halfway on its journey to his mouth. He smiled and shook his head. 'Poor Gertrude. Telling us all that we're on our way to hell is about all she's got left.'

'Can you get in touch with Ada?' the doctor asked again. 'I would do it myself but it might be better coming from you, seeing as your niece was evacuated into her care.'

Stan nodded. 'I dare say I can. Frances was very happy there and I'm sure she can be persuaded to take the Gates kids there, get them settled in, like. I expect she wouldn't mind staying with Ada if it came to that. It's just a case of getting somebody in the shop to help when our Ruby is off doing her war work.'

He conceded at least to himself that it wouldn't be that easy getting somebody to cover in the shop on those days when Ruby was demonstrating her baking skills. But if Frances could be persuaded to go back to the Forest of Dean, it would put off the dreaded moment of her demanding to see her mother.

'So you think Ada will be willing to help out?'

'I can write to her and ask.'

Dr Foster frowned. 'The only problem is that writing can take a while. I wish there was some quicker way of finding out.'

Stan upended his glass. 'There is. Leave it with me.'

* * *

36

The red telephone box stood only yards from the door of the post office in the village of Bentley in the Forest of Dean. A red pillar-box stood next to it.

Most people in the village – at least those who could read and write proficiently – used the pillar-box. Few used the telephone box unless it was a dire emergency, mainly because they knew nobody with a telephone. Another reason was that the whole procedure of putting pennies into the slots, pressing buttons A or B, dialling a number and speaking to a person they couldn't see, could be rather frightening for some.

The man who ran the village post office was just as daunted by the telephone box as most of the village. He did not want anything to do with the contraption the red metal box contained, but because he ran the post office, and the telephone was outside his premises, he was the one through whom messages were relayed. It was to this man that Stan Sweet sent a message for Ada Perkins.

To Stan, the doctor and Mrs Gates's great relief, Ada said that she would be happy to have the three girls and would arrange suitable accommodation for the boys.

'Your only problem's going to be transport,' she said when she'd managed to call Stan back. 'They've cut the amount of train services coming through, thanks to the shortage of staff. Men prefer to fight in a war rather than drive a steam train, which only serves to strengthen my belief that men are mad!'

Stan had chuckled at her comment while trying to work out how to get round the transport problem. He could use the bakery van – as long as he could get enough petrol to drive all the way around Gloucester and down into the forest.

He voiced his reservations to Ruby. 'I've still got a bakery to run. I can't really spend a lot of time driving over there and shepherding the Gates kids.'

Ruby stopped running the hot iron over one of her dresses and frowned. 'There has to be something we can do, though it's not just a question of transport. Someone has to accompany those kids. I can't do it. I've got baking demonstrations to prepare for.' Her face brightened. 'The only person who knows that area well enough is Frances. She can help Ada settle the children in suitable accommodation that's not too far from where Mrs Perkins lives. I assume she won't have much room, seeing as she's taken Miriam in.'

Stan agreed with her, 'Yes, I'd already thought our Frances would like to go with them.' Though he didn't admit that he'd also been hoping spending time in the country would help Frances forget her foolhardy plan to find her mother.

Frances didn't hesitate when her Uncle Stan asked her to shepherd Mrs Gates's children to Ada's. If there was one person who could advise her best on finding her mother, it was Ada. There had been a number of occasions when she'd attempted to ask her uncle Stan, but she'd chickened out at the last minute.

Neither Stan nor Ruby appeared to notice the look in her eyes. As far as they were concerned, everything was going to plan and she'd forgotten about finding her mother.

Stan voiced one particular problem that still remained. 'We still have to work out how to get everyone there.'

Ruby was ready with an answer. 'How about I ask Declan if he can arrange something?'

'Do you think he could?' Stan's face brightened. All he knew about the military policeman was that Ruby went out with him. As long as the man didn't marry her, he was all right with him. He really did not wish his remaining daughter to marry an American and move to the United States. It had already been suggested that Mary would eventually move to Canada with her husband Michael. But not yet, he counselled.

He sorely wanted to see his new grandchild before that happened.

'That doesn't mean he can just borrow a truck and a driver to take a gang of kids out for the day. He'll have to get permission,' Ruby pointed out.

'Of course he has to get permission. I understand that.'

'And he'll need to work out how to get there. Maps and things.'

'That's no problem. Frances, you can show Ruby's friend the way, and if he's got any common sense at all, he should be able to find his way back by himself – otherwise I fear the US Army will never find France, let alone Germany!'

Although Frances looked forward to seeing Ada again, she had no intention of staying there. 'I'll show him the way back too! Ada won't have room for me and the Gates family. Anyway, you'll need somebody in the shop and to look after Charlie. I have to come back.'

Stan saw the defiance in his niece's face. His plan had backfired. He'd have preferred her to stay over with Ada for a week or two at least, just long enough to forget this madcap scheme of finding her mother. Still, a day out might do her good.

'Let's hope your friend can arrange things,' said Stan.

'I'm sure he will,' said Ruby with a smile. 'I'll explain it all to him when I see him tonight.'

Ruby returned to her ironing. On hearing the crack of her father's newspaper as he prepared to read it, she knew instantly that there was something he wanted to say, but he was holding it back.

'Are you serious about this American?' he asked suddenly.

Ruby laughed and shook her head. 'I knew you were going to ask me that.'

Her father's confident expression faltered because she'd actually read his mind. 'There's nothing wrong in it,' he responded with a grumble to the edge of his voice. 'I'm only concerned for your welfare and happiness.'

Ruby kept on ironing. 'I know, Dad. But we're only friends. I'm not about to run off with him. My home is here.'

He asked the question that had been on his mind for some time. 'What will you do if you never hear from Johnnie? What if he never comes back?'

She stopped ironing. Without raising her eyes from the pillowcase, she said, 'I think of him every day, of what he might be going through – if he's still alive, that is. I . . . I might marry him when he gets back.'

She purposely didn't use the word 'if'. She had to believe that he would come home.

CHAPTER FIVE

Mary Sweet was getting used to life with her husband in the flat Lincolnshire countryside.

'That's why there are so many flying fields around here,' Michael had told her when she'd voiced her desire to see a few hills. 'Aircraft need flat land.'

Mary had been amused. 'And there was me thinking it was because Germany was a shorter flying time from here!'

September was proving to be very mild, although a fierce gale had blown through the countryside at the end of the first week.

Not that Mary had cared about the rain hammering against the windows or the draught creeping through the gap at the bottom of the ill-fitting front door. The seventeenth of September was a milestone in her married life: it was the day Michael came home from hospital. His bandages had been removed the day before. Up until that date, his damaged hands and torso had been bathed in a saline solution and the dressings changed regularly.

Mary had wanted to go to the hospital and bring him home, but he'd refused, saying it was bad enough that he would smell of antiseptic without her smelling of it too.

After taking off his cap, he'd ducked his head beneath the front door lintel. Sergeant Innes had fetched him and his effects in an official car and followed him through the door. The sergeant had placed a brown paper carrier bag on the floor. It didn't contain much, just two pairs of pyjamas, underwear, shaving soap and a face flannel.

'Is there anything else I can do, sir?' Sergeant Innes asked.

Michael shook his head. His gaze was fixed on his wife. 'Everything I want is here, Sergeant.'

'Then I'll wish you good day, sir. Good day, Mrs Dangerfield.'

'Good day,' Mary said softly. 'And thank you.'

The front door had closed softly on the nasty weather and the discreet RAF sergeant.

Her heart racing, Mary had covered her cheeks with her hands. This was it! Michael was home. She could hardly believe it. Her legs would still have been weak even if she hadn't been pregnant. She had waited for this all morning, wanting to go with the sergeant to fetch her husband, but had been advised to consider her condition. Not that she'd been able to rest – she'd cleaned, dusted and polished to distraction, darting to the window every half hour to see if the car was in sight. And now he was here.

She'd baked a rabbit and mushroom pie for their lunch, and made a cake from stale breadcrumbs and stewed apple. She'd also rehearsed what she was going to say to her husband, words of love, of welcome and telling him how much she'd missed him. But all she had been able to say was, 'Michael!'

There was triumphant glee in his smile and the way he flung his cap on top of the rest of his things. 'Honey, I'm home.'

Mary tried to say something in response, just a few of the words she'd rehearsed; surely she could do that? It was no use. The words just wouldn't come. Instead her mouth had opened and closed like a goldfish. As though I'm drowning in happiness, she'd thought.

'Do I look good to you?' he had asked.

Mary had flown into his arms and buried her face against his shoulder.

'Whoa!' he cried out, spreading his arms to take the impact before folding them around her. 'You almost knocked the breath out of me.'

There were no words that could express what she was feeling. Mary burst into tears. 'Michael, Michael, Michael!'

'Is that all you're going to say?' His arms were around her, his hands caressing her back.

Her face safely hidden against his jacket, she squeezed back the tears. He was home. He was safe and he wasn't nearly so badly disfigured as she'd thought he might be.

He held her at arm's length and laid his hand on her stomach. 'So how's my family coming along?'

'You didn't say "son".'

'I'm learning to be diplomatic. I know there are two possibilities.'

'Would you prefer a son?'

'I'll settle for a girl if she looks like you.'

'I've made a pie.' Shyly, Mary changed the subject.

'Does it have any meat in it?'

'Yes. Paul knows somebody with a shotgun who knows where there's a warren bursting with rabbits.'

'Sounds good. Spotted Dick for afters? With custard?'

'Apple cake.'

'I like apple cake. As long as it's sweet. Like you.' He kissed the top of her head.

She laughed, but one thought nagged at her. 'I wish you didn't have to fly again,' she murmured against the warmth of his shoulder.

He winced when he read the fear in those eyes he loved so much, so blue, so clearly showing her love for him. 'That's like saying you wish I never drew breath again. Anyway, the final decision isn't down to me.'

Mary closed her eyes and said a silent prayer. She knew very well that he ached to get back into action. What was it about men and war that drew one to the other? 'But you've done your bit. You've been injured. Your plane caught fire and you were almost killed. Surely that is enough?'

She could tell her argument was dismissed. He shook his head, his fingers combing her hair back from her forehead. 'I was injured, but not incapacitated. My hands are healing. My arms and legs still work and my brain is still in my head. Or at least I think it is.' He tapped his head. 'Sounds as though there's something in there.'

'I wish you wouldn't tease me like this.'

His amused expression became serious. 'I'm not teasing. I'm telling you how things are. I'm a serving officer. I have to fly. It's my job.'

Mary had hung her head. Deep down she had known it was useless, but she had had to try. She almost hated him for being so devoted to his job and to the war against the Nazis. Of course he couldn't promise, and he didn't deserve her hatred. She transferred it to the enemy instead. The war was not over and her husband would remain in danger until it was. Until then, there would always be the fear, but she knew better than to voice her fear. She had to support him. She had to have faith.

Another storm occurred on the twenty-sixth of the month. A torrential downpour turned roads into raging torrents and strong gales brought down trees. The cottage creaked and groaned under the onslaught, windows rattling and water overflowing from guttering and pouring down drainpipes.

Around midday, Mary went into labour. Michael managed to telephone the midwife before the single table lamp went out and the telephone went dead.

'The lines are down.'

He pulled back the blackout curtains and looked out of the bedroom window with one thought in his mind. What do I do if she can't get here? The answer was obvious, if daunting: he would have to deal with the birth himself.

Mary caught his mood. 'It's quite easy, really—' Another pain racked her body, forcing her to bend from what little waist she had left. 'You won't be the first husband to do it—'

Astonished that she had read his mind, he looked at her helplessly, thinking how brave she was and how scared he was. Battling the enemy was not nearly as frightening as the prospect of bringing a child into the world.

'Do I need to get some water boiling? Isn't that what they do?'

'Who?'

'In films they always send somebody to boil water and fetch towels.'

Mary's laugh was short-lived as another pain made her draw her legs up to her middle.

Michael felt so helpless. 'What do I do?'

'Make me a cup of tea.'

'I can't leave you.'

'The kitchen is only downstairs,' she declared somewhat sharply. The pain was increasing.

'Tea I can manage, but actually . . .'

'Michael. She'll get here. Sister Monica is indomitable. The weather means nothing to her. She'll fight her way through it.'

'Sounds as though she should be on the front line,' Michael murmured and wished to God that she would hurry up.

A lull in the pains gave Mary the chance to turn her head to one side and close her eyes. The one thing she did know about having a baby was that it took a lot of energy. Sleep was the best way to conserve that energy for when it was needed.

While she slept, Michael paced the room, sat down, got up, went downstairs, put more coal in the kitchen range, and came back up again. Seeing her still sleeping, he went back downstairs. Between peering out around the blackout curtains and willing somebody to hammer on the front door, he checked the wall clock. The thin black hands ticked from one Roman numeral to the next, though to him time seemed to be standing still.

When would the midwife come? He was terrified that he would have to bring the baby into the world himself. 'What do I know about babies?' he muttered.

The wind chose that moment to blow down the chimney, sending a shower of sparks from the burning logs and on to the hearth-rug. There was a smell of singed wool.

'Oh hell!'

Michael stamped on the sparks then pulled a wire fireguard in front of the glowing embers. Bombing raids were scary enough, but this waiting for a baby to be born on a night as tempestuous as this was taxing his nerves.

He was just about to dash upstairs again when a heavy thudding sounded from the front door. He opened it to a round-faced woman wearing a broad-brimmed hat and a sodden woollen cloak.

'I'm Sister Monica. Sorry to be late, but it's a filthy night. My bicycle and I have been blown all over the place. Besides which I'm soaking wet and on a night like this I really should be able to put my headlamp on full beam.'

She breezed into the house with more force than the wind was blowing outside, leaving a trail of water behind her, her bulldog expression reminiscent of Prime Minister Winston Churchill.

Michael closed the door, though a scurry of leaves managed to enter with the midwife.

The midwife took off her hat and shook it. Michael helped her off with her waterlogged wet cloak, which weighed a ton.

Sister Monica continued to complain. 'How they expect me to see on these dark roads, I don't know. And the wind nearly blew me off my bike! Did I already tell you that? I think I did. Well, I'm here now. However, I think I shall write to someone. Just because there's a war on doesn't mean to say that babies will stop being born! I need to use my headlamp on full beam. It's imperative!'

Michael stood dumbstruck, the midwife's hat in one hand and her cloak in the other. This was it! They were about to have a baby! Suddenly, with the midwife standing here before him, it all felt very real.

Sister Monica fixed him with an expression almost of contempt. 'Right! Well, once you've finished doing a very poor imitation of a coat stand, perhaps you wouldn't mind shaking my things dry and hanging them up.'

Michael leapt into action. 'Right.' Everything was quickly hung up. Relieved the midwife was here, he rubbed his wet palms on his pullover, beginning to feel excited at what was about to happen.

'Hot water,' Sister Monica said to him when he attempted to follow her up the stairs. A stout arm barred him from going any further.

His expression reflected his anxiety. 'Hey! That's my wife up there and I'm not used to taking orders.'

'Well, get used to it,' the midwife retorted, her bag clenched in a meaty fist and her feet plodding heavily up the stairs.

'Anything else?' Michael called after her.

'Tea. Sweet tea. Oh, and whisky if you've got it.'

'Whisky? For my wife or for you?' Tea he could understand, but surely it wasn't routine to dispense alcohol.

'No. For you. To keep you occupied and out of my way.'

The slamming of the bedroom door made the windows rattle and brought an empty bird's nest down the chimney.

He boiled water for the midwife and made a pot of tea. She came tramping down the stairs to pour a cup for herself and one for Mary. She didn't bother to offer him a cup and he didn't ask.

Once she was back upstairs again, he went to the sideboard and got out a bottle of whisky and a tumbler. 'Two fingers should do it,' he said to himself. He added just a splash of water then sat down in his favourite armchair to await developments.

He didn't know how many times he went over to the sideboard or at what time he'd fallen asleep. His dreams varied between a burning aircraft, acres of Canadian prairie and a riotous evening in the bar of a local pub. A curly-haired tot accompanied him in all those scenes, which was ridiculous because the baby hadn't been born yet.

He was still dreaming when a strong hand shook his shoulder so roughly it felt like it was being jerked out of its socket.

'Rise and shine!'

He blinked his eyes open, half expecting he'd been woken up by a particularly loud sergeant-major. He found himself face to face with the midwife's Churchillian features.

Assured he was fully awake, she plucked her hat and coat from off of the chair in front of the fire where he'd spread them out to dry.

Michael leapt up from his chair, then groaned and ran his hand over his aching head. 'Has it happened? Has he been born?'

The midwife glanced at the half-empty bottle before throwing him a disdainful look. 'Yes. She has.'

The moment Michael saw the baby he felt totally inadequate.

'I'll break her,' he said when Mary suggested he hold her.

'You won't.'

'She's so small. What if I hold her too tight?'

Mary smiled. 'You won't,' she repeated.

'What if I drop her?'

Mary was tired after the effort of giving birth, but still she couldn't help chuckling at her big brave husband's inadequacy. The tiny bundle not only scared him but filled him with awe.

'But my hands . . .' he said, looking down at them.

Mary understood now why he was so worried about picking the baby up. He was well on the way to recovery, but the damage to his hands had been significant. 'You'll be fine,' she said reassuringly. 'I know you won't drop her.'

As though sensing his nervousness, their daughter began to cry.

'Wow! I can't believe such a small thing can be so noisy. She's got the lungs of a sergeant-major.'

'The boys at the base said babies all look like Churchill,' he said, after a while, gazing into the tiny face peering out from the folds of a white shawl. He shook his head. 'I don't think she does. I think she's the most beautiful female I've ever seen.'

'You do realise you're making me jealous?' Mary's face shone with amusement.

He looked up and grinned. 'It can't be helped. Perhaps I should just say that she's just as beautiful as her mother.'

Once persuaded that babies were pretty durable, he couldn't put her down.

Sister Monica, who also happened to be the district nurse, popped in every day for a fortnight, checking the baby's weight and on-going development. Beatrice was pronounced fit and well.

'A bonnie baby indeed,' Sister Monica stated with the air of a woman who's seen a great many ugly ones.

'I bet you say that about all the babies,' Mary said.

The midwife had a cryptic look in her eyes when she told her otherwise. 'If a baby is pretty, I say so. If it's ugly, I say nothing.'

Sister Monica warned Mary to stay in bed for two weeks. 'It's standard procedure. You have to regain your strength.'

Mary nodded meekly and promised that was exactly what she would do. Veronica, the wife of another pilot at the base, popped in each day to keep an eye on her and was also putting out feelers for a woman to come in and do the cleaning. But after a week, Mary couldn't stand it any longer. She was out of bed and keen to get on with her life, though she made sure she was in bed on the days when Sister Monica was due to call.

Only Michael and her friend Veronica knew she wasn't obeying orders.

'I can't stay in bed all day. I didn't have too bad a time during the birth and I'm bursting with energy,' she complained.

Veronica was impressed that Mary wasn't taking advantage of an enforced stay in bed. 'I'm glad to hear it, but take care.'

Michael found every excuse he could to grab time to come home and see her, or more specifically to see baby Beatrice. The moment he came home, he picked the baby up even if she was fast asleep. Mary ticked him off for doing it, but he just couldn't help it. His argument was that there would shortly be a time when he couldn't get away from his duties and so he had to make up for lost time.

Mary smiled when she recalled his initial concern and clumsiness when picking the child up. His worry that with his damaged hands, he would fumble while holding her. Bit by bit his handling of the child improved.

'I'll be real skilled at being a dad by the time we have our sixth.'

Mary looked appalled. 'Six? Who said anything about having six?'

He put his arms round her. 'I like kids.'

'I like them too, but there are limits. Let's settle for two – one girl and one boy.'

'Okay.'

Settling in to the area and her new role as a mother turned out to be easier than Mary had expected. Even though she missed her family, she was happy and glad she'd come here, though she would have preferred that Michael hadn't been injured.

There were signs that the injuries disturbed him more than he let on. Sometimes he woke in a cold sweat in the middle of the night, screaming that the flames were coming closer, that everyone had to bail out.

Mary tried to calm him down, shushing him and speaking as softly to him as she did to Beatrice when she cried.

The secret, so the doctor at the hospital had told her, was not to press him, to treat him as normal, regardless of the cruel marks that remained on his hands and torso. This she promised to do.

By the beginning of the new year, Michael still came home, though not so often and not with the same spring in his step. His mood changed, a deep frown permanently creasing his brow. There were also long silences as though he had heavy thoughts on his mind. Only the sight of his daughter seemed to chase the haunted look from his eyes. Something was going on at the base, but he wasn't letting on what it was and Mary knew better than to press him. However, what with lonely days and weeks at the cottage when nobody called, she could do without the morose silences that Michael fell into nowadays when he was at home. She guessed some important mission was in the offing but knew better than to ask him for details.

Much to her annoyance, he did not respond to other subjects of conversation. She needed somebody to talk to after being left with only a baby for company. One evening, Mary finally snapped. 'Michael! You haven't been listening to a word I've said.'

He was staring into the fire, elbows resting on his knees, hands clasped tightly. 'Don't nag, darling.'

Mary was stunned and it took a great deal of self-control to keep her voice calm and level.

'I wasn't nagging, Michael. It's you. You're not listening.'

'Of course I was!' His tone was sharp and totally out of character. 'It's you, keeping on. You have to understand I have things on my mind.'

'So do I!'

'Not the kind of things I have on *my* mind. The demands of war weigh a darn sight heavier than the demands of a housewife.'

'How dare you! You're the one who wanted me to be a housewife. If I was still back in Oldland Common, I would be doing a great deal more than baking bread! I worked for the war effort, Michael. I did my bit then and I could do the same now. If I could have a nanny—'

'Our daughter is not to be left with strangers . . .'

This was the first time Mary had voiced the possibility of returning to her work with the Ministry of Food, travelling around to local towns and villages just as she had back home.

'Well, I'm not sure I want to be just a housewife. Obviously you consider it a pretty worthless job and—'

'This is ridiculous!'

Their first proper argument was interrupted by the sound of Beatrice crying.

Mary eyed him furiously, her fists clenched and her eyes blazing. 'Now look what you've done!'

'Me? What have I done? I merely said—'

Mary ignored him, marching to where Beatrice was lying in her pram. 'There, there,' she cooed, lifting her out and laying the little mite over her shoulder.

Michael followed her. 'I'm sorry. It's just the tension . . .'

Mary turned her back on him, but Michael wasn't to be fobbed off that easily. Drawing his wife and child against his chest, he kissed the top of Mary's head and laid one hand on that of his child's.

'I'm sorry, sorry, sorry. Call me an ill-mannered pig, if you like.'

'You're an ill-mannered pig – but I still love you.'

The tension between them was broken. Mary allowed herself to smile. She wasn't one to hold grudges and didn't believe in prolonging a confrontation. It was over. They were one again.

Michael sighed heavily. 'I shouldn't be telling you this, but something special is being talked about.'

'I guessed.'

Mary became tense. Michael hadn't been on any missions since coming out of hospital. His commanding officer firmly believed in having his men fully recovered before they became operational again. However, Mary knew that the time would come when he would be required again, but she'd pushed that fear to the back of her mind. Stupidly she'd told herself that perhaps the war would be over before he had to go up again. It was a faint hope but one she'd clung to. The dreaded time had now arrived and the fear she'd resisted facing was unavoidable. However, she mustn't let Michael see that. She had to be strong for him, dependable and supportive.

She looked down at Beatrice, who was snuffling around her breast. 'Hungry again,' said Mary, biting her bottom lip to stop herself from crying. She sat down on a chair, opened her blouse and put her child to her breast.

'Can I ask what it is?' Even to her own ears, her voice sounded thin, almost frightened. She kept her gaze on Beatrice, unable to meet Michael's eyes until the wave of fear had flowed over her and was manageable again.

'I've told you more than I should have done.'

'Which isn't very much.'

'I'm sorry. It's top secret.'

Mary felt full of wonder as she watched the rosebud mouth sucking on her nipple. It was at times like these that she missed her family the most. Michael had his duty and although she'd made friends with a few air force wives, it would have been lovely if Ruby or Frances could visit. But the distance was too great and they couldn't leave the bakery.

She knew from Ruby's letters that she was managing to fulfil quite a number of cooking demonstrations; the Kitchen Front Economists were still thriving. She'd even passed on some recipes in her letters.

I think you and your lovely little family will like these. Coconut cakes made with breadcrumbs and coconut. Mix with just a little butter and a good dollop of treacle. I do hope you can get the ingredients up there.

Frances sends her love. She's shepherding the Gates children shortly over to the Forest of Dean. They're being evacuated in order to give their mother a rest. Mrs Gates has had another baby.

Dad says he can't wait to see baby Beatrice, and neither can I. Charlie is growing straight and strong and is tiring of Bunz, his toy rabbit. This is because he's discovered the real thing in the churchyard – not that he's managed to catch one yet.

Give our love to Beatrice and also of course to Michael. We miss you.

'I hate war,' she said to her husband.

As she looked down at the sleeping Beatrice, she wished very much she could be like her baby, completely oblivious of it all.

Michael shook his head mournfully. 'I'm sorry you're left here alone,' he whispered against her hair. 'I shouldn't have dragged you up here.'

'You're my husband. You were injured. I had to be here.'

Michael sighed. 'All the same. Don't think I don't know how much you're missing your sister and the rest of your family.'

Mary managed a smile. 'We write to each other and we telephone.'

The telephone was a necessity for all the pilots and senior officers in case they were needed urgently. Mary was extremely thankful they had it. Her family in Oldland Common never let a week go by without ringing her. Although she made a point of sounding bright and breezy, she was always glad when somebody telephoned and didn't let on how bored she was and how much she was missing everybody. It wouldn't do to have them worried about her.

*

The time for Michael to fly again came too quickly.

'I'll be away for a few weeks on this next mission. Don't worry if I'm not home quite so often before then too.'

'No. I won't.' She beamed up at him with a cheerfulness she didn't feel. She would worry about him. She couldn't help worrying about him.

On an April morning, following a breakfast of porridge and farm fresh eggs, she watched him leave the house. She wondered what he was up to and whether she would ever see him again. The last thought was the one that was best ignored and thus quashed immediately. All the other air force wives agreed that they had to think positively. But it wasn't easy. All of them feared being widows only a short time after they'd been brides.

His visits home had become briefer, as he'd said they would. During those first weeks of the new year, when he was at home, he was secretive and looked tired. He'd also spent time poring through books from the groaning shelves, though on reflection she realised it was the same book every time.

It was on one such occasion, just after she'd put Beatrice down for her post-feed nap, that she found him sound asleep in his favourite chair, his scarred hands resting on an open book. Gently she took the open book from his hands. Before putting it back on the shelf, she glanced at a fuzzy photograph and descriptions of Derwent Water in the Lake District.

She frowned, her fingers tapping the cover as she tried to work out why he would be studying the book so often. Did he have it in mind to surprise her with a short holiday? She hoped not. Surely the north of England was chillier than the south at this time of year, and besides, if they were to have some time away, she'd prefer to go home. She pined for her family and guessed that Michael's aunt, Bettina Hicks, would love to see them too.

'What?'

Michael jerked into wakefulness. On seeing the book she was holding, the look on his face was one of alarm.

'You fell asleep,' said Mary attempting a weak smile.

He snatched the book from her hand. 'I'll take this. I might need it later.'

'Was it a surprise?'

He frowned. 'Surprise? What the hell do you mean?'

Mary ignored the sharpness in his voice and tried again even though it looked as though she might have made a mistake. 'Have you got any leave coming up? I mean, after this next job is over – whatever it is?'

His weary eyes blinked. 'I don't know. Probably.' He sounded thoughtful.

'Have you arranged for us to have a holiday in the Lake District? Only if we are, I'll need to make arrangements for Beatrice. She's too young to travel and Derwent Water is a long way away and—'

She saw the look in his eyes, confirmation as if she needed it, that she was very much mistaken.

'We're not going to the Lake District?'

He hugged the book to his chest, rose from his chair and stuffed it back on the bookshelf. 'No. We are not!'

Mary felt hurt. Michael didn't usually snap at her. The way he spoke was usually calm and collected unless he was really riled. A sudden knot of alarm started deep in her stomach and her skin prickled with fear. His attitude was confirmation enough that something big was on the cards, something that would put him in danger.

She took a step closer and looked up into his face, reaching out to touch it.

He jerked back as though her touch had stung him. There was a hooded, secretive look in his eyes. She realised that she was right. The big thing he'd hinted at some time before was on. What was it and, more to the point, how dangerous was it?

She knew she shouldn't ask, but couldn't help herself. 'Michael. What is it?'

'Ask no questions; you'll be told no lies.'

She ignored the childish rebuke. Michael was obviously under a lot of pressure.

Her eyes swept the spot where he'd put the book back. The books to either side of it were red. The one relating to the Lake District was green. Somehow it seemed very appropriate, the Lake District being a watery area of both natural and manmade lakes surrounded by lots of green trees and grassy hills.

'I don't think I deserve this,' she said, shaking her head. 'Trust me, Michael. Please trust me.'

He had his back to her. She sensed his reluctance to share what he was involved in, which of course meant it was dangerous.

'Michael. You can trust me.' There was pleading in her voice even though it was little more than a whisper.

She saw his shoulders heave in a huge sigh before he turned from the bookcase, his head turned slightly to one side. He attempted a smile. 'It's nothing to concern yourself about. We've been doing some training exercises up there. I just wanted to check up on the details, you know, see how the land lies. Literally. Still, who knows,' he said with a smile that came swiftly and did not reach his eyes. 'We might go there one day. When Beatrice is older.'

She instinctively knew that wasn't the reason why he'd been reading the book, but she wouldn't press him. He'd been more secretive than usual, lately; this was just one more step to convince her that something very special was going on. The fear still prickled her skin, making her feel as though she'd been plunged into icy water. Needing to feel warm and needing his strength, she flung her arms around his neck. 'Michael. Hold me. Tightly! As tightly as you can.'

'Hey!' Although taken by surprise, he recovered quickly, his hands running up and down her back before he wrapped his arms around her.

She leaned her head against his chest, closing her eyes as she listened to the sound of his heart thudding against her ear.

She clutched his upper arms tightly. 'Promise you'll take extra special care of yourself. Promise me!'

His lips brushed her hair. 'How could I refuse?'

Michael had closed his eyes, silently praying that he would survive the dangerous mission in a few weeks' time. The heights they were required to fly at were ridiculously low. No matter what anyone did to reassure him, he suspected the casualties would be high, not that the man with the codename Geoff seemed aware of that fact. The professor – he couldn't be anything else – was adamant that his bouncing bomb would work. It was just a case of delivering it to the right depth and the right distance, he'd assured them. As yet they had not been told the probable target, but Michael had guessed that it was over a stretch of water with a similar layout to Derwent Water, the area they'd been practising over.

'Do you have to go on this mission?'

Michael remained silent until he could find the guts to lie, which was all his reassurance would be. 'Don't worry. I'll be fine.'

He couldn't tell her anything, let alone the worst bit: that no matter how skilful their flying, they also needed the right night, as little enemy flak as possible, and an enormous amount of luck.

CHAPTER SIX

The Gates children tumbled out of the door of their cottage wearing the best clothes they had, all hand-me-downs from other families in the village. Baggy coats and cardigans of ill-matched colours were coupled with knitted balaclavas for the boys and berets for the girls. Even their hats looked too big for them – as a consequence most were held on with thin scarves or string and fastened under the chin. All of them were carrying scruffy-looking canvas satchels or brown paper carrier bags containing the requisite clothing for their time on the other side of the River Severn.

Ruby had arranged for the children to eat a hearty breakfast at the bakery before somebody from the US base arrived with the necessary transport. Feeling sorry for the Gates kids, the villagers had donated eggs, bacon and cheese. Although everyone was on rations, Ruby had persuaded a lot of people to give a little – and a little, certainly in this case, added up to quite a lot.

Stan had marvelled at Ruby's power of persuasion.

'I just stated the facts. That's what the army does too. Declan did the same with the supplies people at the base. They've been amazing.'

Stan admitted he was impressed. 'I take my hat off to them all.'

'That's the way Declan is. He's a generous guy, and before you read anything between the lines again, we just enjoy each other's company. We're not in love, Dad,' she said with a sidelong smile. 'One member of the family marrying a man from the other side of the Atlantic is quite enough, don't you think?'

She refrained from saying anything about her fears that Declan was smitten by her young cousin. She might be wrong, so for the time being at least it was best to say nothing.

For his own part, reference to Mary, her sister, made Stan wonder how long it would be before she moved to Canada with Michael. He nodded sadly as he tousled his grandson's hair. Young Charlie was enjoying the company of the Gates children, watching as they cleared the porridge and the villagers' bacon and egg rations from the table, before attacking the homemade jams and preserves, liberally spreading it on slices of toast already smothered with margarine.

Ruby had drawn the line at giving the kids their butter ration, predicting rightly that they wouldn't notice the difference once the toast was piled with jam.

The smell of freshly made loaves of bread being piled on to the shelves persuaded the kids to eat more than they should have. Ruby worried they would be sick if they went on the way they were going. 'Perhaps I should call a halt.'

Stan told her not to. 'They've been scrabbling about for food since their mother's been ill. Let them eat what they want.' The sight of so many cheery faces tucking into breakfast with gusto bucked him up no end, and even young Charlie joined in, cramming a crust of jammy bread into his mouth.

A loud honking on an army transport horn sounded from outside. Ruby, who was serving in the shop for the day, saw it pull up. 'It's here,' she shouted over her shoulder.

Frances had been looking forward to her visit to the forest and shepherded the children out, though not before she had made sure everyone had been to the lavatory.

'Right! Everyone get your gas masks. Those of you with carrier bags can carry them too. I'll take that,' she said to one little girl who was struggling with a bulging carrier bag.

The children followed her out, chattering and wiping away the jam they had smeared around their mouths.

Ruby followed behind Frances while her father stood waving by the door.

'Now you're sure you'll be all right?' he asked Frances. She looked happy enough and, thank God, she hadn't mentioned anything about finding her mother while waiting for the trip to come together. It had taken quite a lot longer than they'd imagined. Perhaps she had already changed her mind.

Frances told him she would be fine before doing a swift head count of her charges.

'I just want to make sure that I have the same number of children at the end of the journey as I do at the beginning.'

She noticed one of the Gates boys wiping his nose on the sleeve of his jacket. 'Peter, isn't it?'

'Paul,' came the shouted reply.

'Right. Do you have a handkerchief?'

He shook his head.

Frances sighed. She'd never expected this to be easy, but neither had she expected the whole exercise to make her feel so happy. She went back to counting and reeling off their names.

'Paul, Patricia, Ellen and Maggie, and Patrick?'

The boy shook his head. 'Lancelot. My name's Sir Lancelot.'

'No, it isn't. It's Patrick.'

'No. I'm Sir Lancelot!' The smallest boy was adamant that he'd been named after a knight of the Round Table.

Frances exchanged a brief glance with Ruby and sighed. 'Okay. Be Sir Lancelot if you like, but just get in the back of the truck here. Unfortunately, we can't supply you with a horse.'

The driver's door of the small truck, a Jeep with a canvas-covered rear, opened and the driver stepped out. 'Here. Let me help you kids get in.'

Ruby was taken aback. 'Declan! You didn't say you'd be driving.'

Frances stared. She hadn't expected it to be Ruby's friend Declan either.

Declan shrugged in that casual, obliging way of his. His uniform looked to be newly pressed, and his boots shone to within an inch of their lives, as if he was going on parade or somewhere special, not shepherding a bunch of evacuees.

'There was nobody else. The kids need help, so me and Uncle Sam are giving it. All I need is for somebody to show me how to get there!'

Stan Sweet shook the American's hand. 'Frances knows the way.'

Dr Foster had also dropped by. He too took Declan's hand in both of his and gave it a hefty shake. 'Glad to hear it. We really appreciate this.'

'No problem, Doc. Happy to oblige.'

Frances couldn't help but be drawn to Declan's smile. It was the kind of smile that spoke a whole volume without the need for words. She had the impression that it was for her alone. That, and the roguish look in his eyes. She blushed.

Ruby was alarmed when she saw who was driving. If she could have called it off, she would have, though that was impossible. Everyone would think her mad and want to know a reason why. She was loath to do that. Nothing had happened between Declan and her cousin, but that didn't mean it wouldn't. Was she the only one who could sense the attraction between them, or was she just imaging things? She didn't think so.

Frances made a big effort to look unconcerned, as though she really didn't care much that she would be travelling for hours with a man who puzzled and unnerved her. She also had a sneaking suspicion that he had purposely arranged to undertake this journey, not only out of the kindness of his heart. She could feel something radiating from him, something that made her tingle from the top of her head to the tips of her toes; something she could not ignore.

'We'd better get going,' she said, trying not to sound flustered.

'Sure. I understand we've got a ferry to catch.'

Although his smile was controlled, she almost flinched at the challenging look in his eyes.

Ruby opened her mouth, about to say that they might not be able to get on it. The transportation of war commodities and military personnel had priority.

Uncle Stan voiced the possibility before she did.

Declan was a picture of confidence. 'No need to concern yourself, sir. The army's made arrangements for us to be taken aboard. We *are* priority transport.'

Frances felt Ruby's eyes on her. Then Ruby was pulling her to one side, out of earshot of everybody else. 'Frances, I think it might be better if you serve in the shop today and I go with the children.'

Frances eyed her accusingly. 'My, my! Are you that jealous?'

Ruby winced at the comment and the defiance in her cousin's eyes. 'No. Of course I'm not,' she hissed, keeping her voice low. 'It's just that . . . well, a man like Declan . . .'

'I can cope with Declan. Anyway, I know the way there better than you do. I know the forest and I know Ada. I want to see her. I *have* to see her. I'm going.'

Ruby leaned closer. 'Sweetie, you don't understand. Declan is not like one of the boys you're used to, he's a man . . .'

Frances could barely keep her temper under control. 'What you are saying is that he's *your* man. You want him for yourself!'

'No,' Ruby hissed back. 'That's not it at all. He's a man, Frances, and you're only a child!'

Frances shrugged off her hand, her manner indignant. 'I am not a child!'

'Frances, that isn't exactly what I meant to say!'

Declan O'Malley and the Jeep were surrounded by children. Fuming at being told she was still a child, Frances flounced away from her cousin. The bold smile she gave Declan was returned just as broadly.

'Are we all ready?' She beamed up at him, no longer caring what anyone might think. Ruby might not want Declan for herself, but she was clearly jealous because Declan preferred her. That's all there was to it.

'Come on, you kids. Here's the supplies for the journey.' He proceeded to hand out bars of chocolate into outstretched hands. Squeals of delight erupted from all concerned. The kids had already been furnished with rucksacks containing thickly cut sandwiches spread with margarine and jam, and a slice of cake made by Stan Sweet and an apple. The bars of chocolate disappeared into hungry mouths, though not before Ruby had instructed them to thank Declan.

Mouths full of chocolate, they all mumbled a muted thanks.

'You should have saved the chocolate for the journey,' Ruby remonstrated. Her glare was enough to silence Hitler, but Declan ignored her. He was where he wanted to be, and despite Ruby's cross features, he was enjoying himself.

Deliberately playing to the crowd, both adults and children, he picked up a box from the vehicle's dashboard and waved it around. 'Like any professional army out on manoeuvres, I brought reinforcements.' He handed out more chocolate bars to the children and threw a few more to the adults watching the event.

'Very clever of you, Captain,' Ruby said. 'Just don't make them sick. The River Severn can be very choppy.'

Frances laughed dismissively, though she knew Ruby was right. The River Severn that divided most of Wales from England could be quite choppy when the wind was blowing against the tide, and the tide itself was the second highest in the world. Frances had learned that at school, but she wasn't thinking about it at this moment in time. Still seething at being called a child, she resolved to be good company for Declan and for the children.

'So let's get going,' said Declan. His first job was to help Frances into the front seat of the Jeep. The warmth of his hand on her elbow sent a bolt of electricity up her arm.

I will not blush, she thought to herself. I will act like a grown-up. I am no longer a child, after all.

After thanking him, she settled herself in the front seat, purposefully looking ahead through the windscreen, anything rather than stare at his chiselled features. Working out exactly how she felt about Declan wasn't easy; all she did know was that she felt comfortable if not entirely safe in his company.

Declan took his place behind the wheel, his thigh only inches from her own, making her heart tick like a time bomb.

Unconcerned that they were leaving their mother and the tumbledown cottage they lived in, the kids waved furiously, shouting and laughing at the start of their big adventure.

Frances covered her ears and shouted for them to be quiet. It didn't work.

'Come on, kids. Settle down.' Declan had more luck. The noise subsided to a reasonable level.

'They're just overexcited,' said Frances. She waved one last time before they pulled away. After that she didn't look back but knew beyond doubt that her cousin Ruby was stone-faced and probably about to voice her fears to anyone who would listen that something was happening between her cousin and Declan O'Malley.

Declan drove down on to the main road that would take them through Hanham Village, St George and Lawrence Hill, finally into the city centre where they would pick up the road to Avonmouth and ultimately the Aust ferry.

The noise that had dissipated for a short time resumed, though more loudly this time.

'I don't think they'll settle down until we get to the ferry,' Declan pointed out. 'Do you think you can keep your hands over your ears all that way?'

Frances had to admit that he had a point.

'Right,' she shouted out. 'Who knows the words of "Old MacDonald Had a Farm"?'

A raucous chorus indicated that they all knew the words, though Frances couldn't believe the very youngest of the Gates brood was actually telling the truth.

All the way into the city, heads turned to stare and smile at the singing children, the handsome American officer and the pretty young girl with the long dark hair sitting beside him.

'Old MacDonald', 'Daisy, Daisy', 'Knees Up Mother Brown', 'Ten Green Bottles', and a whole host of nursery rhymes and favourite hymns from Sunday School were sang at the top of their young and very loud voices. None of the children had ever strayed far from the village, except for an occasional trip to Kingswood where there was a greater variety of shops than in a country village.

Lulled by the motion of the Jeep, as they got closer to the ferry the younger children had fallen asleep or at least were resting their voices. Those left awake were playing I Spy, in between marvelling at the changing landscape.

Now the singing had finished and Frances could no longer join in with the songs, she fell to silence. Like the children, she viewed the passing scenery, the shops, the bomb damage, the green parks planted in Victorian times for the general populace to enjoy. At one time they'd been surrounded with iron railings – all gone to be smelted down for the war effort.

The route through the city was not as she'd expected it would be. Declan purposely avoided the heart of the city, which had suffered the worst bomb damage. They headed southwards and then followed the River Avon through the Avon Gorge and beneath the Clifton Suspension Bridge. In peacetime, the bridge was lit at night with over a thousand electric light bulbs. But not now. It seemed a reasonable enough subject for conversation.

'They say this bridge won't be lit up until the war is over.'

'Is that so?'

'Yes. And the blackout will be over. The streetlights will come on too. And all the young men and women in the forces will be coming home. And you'll be going home too,' she added after a short pause.

'I will indeed. What will you do when this war is over, Frances?'

His question threw her off guard. 'I . . . I . . . don't know . . . not really . . .' It embarrassed her to hear herself stammering.

'Ruby seems to think that you'll marry your Ed. Is that so?'

The question surprised her. 'She told you that?'

'Uh huh.'

Thinking he might be making fun of her, she chanced a quick glance.

Declan's eyes were narrowed and fixed on the road ahead. There was a firm set to his jaw, as though he were concentrating very hard, but somehow she felt that look was deceptive. He was only pretending to be serious; his sharp wit and sense of humour bubbled just below the surface.

Frances shook her head. 'I don't think we're getting married.'

'Has he asked you?'

'Sort of.'

'What does that mean?'

'We've talked about what we'll do after the war. Nothing's set in stone.'

'Has he proposed or hasn't he?'

Frances turned sharply to face the front and the road ahead. 'I'm not sure it's any of your business!'

'Has he told you what he intends to do when the war's over?'

'Yes. He's going to open a hamburger shop when he gets home.'

It was something Ed had mentioned to her that she hadn't really thought about until now.

'So you are going to marry him? Run it with him?'

'I . . .' No words seemed to come out. She saw him glance at her, saw the mocking smile that he only just managed to keep under control.

'Okay,' he finally said. 'So it's none of my business.'

'You're right. It isn't.' He'd managed to make her feel flustered when she'd least expected him to.

'Do you think I should marry your cousin Ruby?'

This was not a question she'd expected to be asked. 'Ruby?'

'Yeah.' He nodded. 'What are her good points? Tell me the reasons you think I should marry her.'

Frances found herself lost for words. At last she said, 'You want me to tell you Ruby's good points?'

He nodded. 'That's about it. List them by number. First: number one reason she'd make a good wife.'

Frances laughed. 'That's easy. She's a good cook.'

He nodded again, his eyes still fixed on the road ahead. 'Okay. She can bake a cake. What else?'

Frances thought hard. 'She can sew and do housework. And she's very pretty . . .'

He seemed to think about this before nodding as he had done before. 'So she's an all-round homemaker and easy on the eye. Is there any other outstanding reason you think I should marry her?'

It came to her that he was enquiring about more than Ruby's homemaking skills.

'Do you love her?'

Although only knowing a little of his nature, she'd expected him to laugh. He didn't. He seemed to be considering his answer very carefully.

'I like her. But I don't think I love her.'

'How sad.'

'No, it isn't. It's honest.'

'Will you ever love her?'

'No. I don't think so. There's no passion between us. I don't know why, but there isn't. It's love and passion that go together before love and marriage. Tell me, is there any passion between you and Ed Bergman, our young friend in the catering corps?'

It was impossible to stop her cheeks warming up. 'I think so . . . I don't know . . .'

There had been passion. They were both young and he would soon be going away to fight a war. Not that she would let this self-assured, incredibly magnetic man know that.

'If you only think so, then there isn't.' His lofty, slightly caustic tone was as evident as ever.

Not willing to be outdone, Frances adopted that same know-all manner and made a statement intended to knock him off that high perch of his. 'Then that's it! I can't marry Ed and you can't marry Ruby. Do you think we should marry each other?'

'Hey!'

His concentration wavered and the Jeep swerved from the centre of the road to the verge.

'Steady, Mr O'Malley!' Frances smiled. Her eyes laughed.

'That was one hell of a curve ball,' Declan declared.

'Which is what?'

'A baseball expression. Baseball is a sport we play. I thought you used the same term in your game of cricket.'

'I wouldn't know. I don't play cricket.'

On the surface, she tried to seem detached and unaffected by his incisive charm; inside, she was both confused and intrigued. This mature man, older even than her cousin Ruby, had the power to turn her legs to jelly and make her feel her blood had turned to red-hot lava.

Ed had never made her feel that way. Ed was dependable, sweet and closer to her own age.

'You're thinking of your cook again. I can tell by the look on your face.'

'I am not!'

It astounded her that he had read her thoughts, but she refused to feed his arrogance.

'He's too ordinary for you.'

'That's none of your business!'

Her face burned. She glanced swiftly over her shoulder. The Gates children were now all sound asleep and snuggled down under the tarpaulin covering, their faces smeared with the stickiness of jam and chocolate.

'Oh, I think it is. You've got too passionate a nature to end up with somebody like that. He's a cute guy – not that I would know that much about what a girl sees in a man, but I know what I see in a woman. And he's not brave enough for you. He'll let you down.'

'How can you say that?'

His eyes seemed to burrow into her mind. She turned away, unwilling for him to see that he had hit the mark.

Declan carried on blithely. 'Ed volunteered to be a cook not a soldier. He's got the kind of courage that opens a hamburger store, though not the kind that can start over when the going gets tough. You deserve better.' They stopped at a road junction to let a farm vehicle pass by in a cloud of smoke. He looked at her. 'You're what we call in the States a gutsy broad.'

Frances gaped. 'What does that mean?'

His smile was enough to make an igloo melt. 'It means that you were born brave. No matter what life throws at you, you'll win through. Trust me. I know this.'

Smitten by his smile and those roguish dark eyes, she found herself speechless. Unsure what else to do, she faced abruptly forward.

Once the tractor had passed, they pulled away. The ferry wasn't far now.

Declan resumed the topic of conversation. 'Do you want me to tell you what I see in you, Miss Frances Sweet, as a woman?'

Frances had mixed feelings about his question. On the one hand, she cringed at his impertinence and the uncertainty of what he might say. On the other, she adored the fact that he was referring to her as a woman – not a girl or a child!

'I suppose you're going to tell me anyway,' she snapped, her full lips pouting and her heart steeplechasing around her ribs.

'Now, let me see,' he said. Dark eyebrows frowned over his equally dark eyes.

Her attention was drawn to his hands. With easy confidence, he swung the steering wheel casually to right and left or held it firmly as he steered it straight ahead. Frances liked his hands. They were strong and tanned.

'Right. Now let me tell you what I know about you, Miss Frances Sweet. You're Ruby's cousin. Ruby has a married twin sister named Mary. These kind folk brought you up, but they're not your parents. You're the outsider, the waif brought in from the cold, but you've weathered storms and you'll weather plenty more . . .'

Frances turned her gaze to her own hands. 'I don't see . . .' She did not like the way he was relating details of her family and her life. The more he knew, the more he would want to know. She didn't know why she knew this, she just did.

'Let me finish,' he said, taking his hand from the steering wheel, patting the hand resting on her right leg. 'They took you in out of the kindness of their hearts and you feel you've got a lot to live up to. In fact, you really want to be like them, but you're not one of them and sometimes, just sometimes, you've a mind to find out who you really are. Especially now you're growing up and you're no longer a child. And I guess you would like to know where your mother is and why she let you down. I know that I would. There are rumours, and I guess you want to know about them too.'

Frances felt the force of his eyes burning into the side of her face. His assumption about her mother brought Mrs Powell's comments to mind. Only Pearl had been there when the old bitch had slandered her mother's memory. Had Pearl blabbed? Her face burned more intensely.

'Do you know Pearl?' Her tone was indignant.

'Should I? Oh, yes! I know who you mean. Ty's girl. I saw them together at the village dance. Right?'

'Yes.' Feeling a deep sense of panic, she turned to face him head on. 'What did she say to you?'

He shrugged. 'Nothing.'

'I don't believe you.'

A smile she could only describe as wickedly mischievous came to his face. 'She's a nice kid, but that's all she is. A kid, whereas you, well, I get the impression you're something else. That's why I've taken to you. I like Ruby, but we're too alike. She knows it too. We're not a long-term contract. Anyway, I get the impression her heart's with that guy out east. She's Ruby and, well, you're something else.'

'What does that mean? Me being something else?'

The air suddenly smelled of the salt-laden river. They were getting closer to the coast and the ferry. She wanted this out of the way before they got there.

'It means that you're nothing like your cousin. But let me tell you about me. I fully admit that I don't always say what people want me to say or act the way they want me to act. I realised that even before I turned down joining the family business. I'm not a store-man, same as everyone else. I'm me – something different – and I can't be anyone else. Neither can you. Accept how it is. We can never escape from who we are.'

Frances was panic-stricken. How did Declan know about her mother? She didn't think Ruby would have mentioned anything. But if her friend Pearl hadn't either, then . . . . . . Ty! Pearl's boyfriend.

'What did Ty tell you?'

He shook his head. 'It doesn't matter. Whatever your parents were, it doesn't mean to say that you will make the same mistakes that they made and you pretty certainly won't follow the same path in life. Things don't happen like that.'

Frances instantly felt uneasy. Whatever her mother was or wasn't, it was family business and should not be common knowledge. She had to challenge him.

'You know!'

'I do?'

Again that mocking amusement. Was he laughing at her, her predicament or her manner? She couldn't work him out.

'Yes. You know,' she said, adopting a malevolent glare.

Folding her arms over her chest, she continued to glare out of the window. The fact that Pearl had told Ty, who had in turn relayed the fact to Declan, was mortifying. Any light-hearted conversation she might have had with Declan O'Malley would not now happen, which seemed a great shame.

'You may recall I was close by when you and your friend were discussing a secret. It wasn't far to go from there to finding out what that secret was. Don't worry.' He patted her hand, which she promptly withdrew as though he'd burned her. 'It's safe with me and if at any time you want to unload more of it, feel free to do so.'

Frances sat unmoved, her face taut, her eyes wide and staring straight ahead.

'Ah! I can see from your stunning silence and your interest in the passing scenery that you're angry with me.'

If Frances had been made of metal, coal and smoke, she would well and truly have let out steam by now. Instead, she adopted a defensive tone of voice. 'I can't help thinking that you like upsetting me.'

'Hah!' He looked amused.

'Is that all you can say? Hah?'

75

'No point in saying anything else when the corners of a woman's mouth are downturned and she prefers the looks of a grey river to . . . Hey. That looks like the river we're looking for.'

To their right was the silvery grey expanse of the River Severn. A stone building, the tollhouse serving the crossing, stood solidly at the head of the slipway. A few farm vehicles including a tractor and khaki-coloured army trucks were waiting in the queue.

As the vehicle they were travelling in came to a halt, Frances remarked that it looked as though they might not be able to get on.

'We've booked a place. Of course we can get on. We just don't need anything holding us up. And nothing should.'

Roused from their sleep by the Jeep slowing down, rumblings of movement came from the children in the back.

Frances guessed what might come next. 'I wouldn't count on it.'

'I wanna wee!'

Her face broke into a knowing smile as other voices sounded from the rear of the Jeep. To her surprise, Declan refused them leave.

'Sorry, guys. You'll have to hold on until we're on board the ferry.'

'They'll never manage,' Frances protested.

'They'll have to,' Declan pronounced grimly. 'Hold on to your horses!'

He slammed his foot on to the gas. The Jeep skewed from one side of the road to the other, loose pebbles and dust flying out behind it.

The man taking the money for the ferry looked up, alarm registering on his face as the Jeep came skidding to a halt at the head of the queue.

'Churchill's children,' Declan shouted at the puzzled-looking man. 'I'm taking them to safety in Wales. Direct order.'

He held out a piece of paper that Frances had not seen up until now.

There was barely enough time for the man collecting the money to see exactly was on the paper before it was snatched swiftly back.

Declan headed for the front of the queue. Heads shook in astonishment as explanations travelled from the ticket collector to the waiting queue.

Once securely on board, Frances looked at him with an amazed look in her eyes and amusement rippling over her lips. 'Churchill's children?'

'Okay, I was a little generous with the truth.'

'It was a lie.'

'Okay. It was a lie. But don't you know that saying, darling? The end justifies the means.'

For a moment, the enigma that was Declan O'Malley was almost heroic. They were on board the ferry and, more than that, they were first in the queue to get off.

Face wreathed in smiles, Declan turned in his driving seat, his arm casually looped over the steering wheel.

'Okay, kids. Everybody out.' He then climbed out himself.

The eldest, a girl, groaned. 'Can't I stay here?'

'No.'

'I'm so very tired!'

The other kids having already got out, Declan reached in, pulled her into his arms and, swinging round, placed her feet firmly on the wooden deck of the river vessel.

'Nobody stays in the vehicle when we're crossing water. Anyway, I thought you all wanted to take a leak.'

'But I could sleep in there,' she groaned, her face creased with disenchantment.

Declan was unmoved. 'You could drown in there! Look at this thing. Look at that river. If an accident happened, where would you be? Asleep first. Dead later.'

The eldest Gates girl maintained her miserable countenance but did not attempt to get back into the vehicle.

'Right! Boys first!' Declan commanded.

'For what?'

Her question was taken by the stiff south-westerly blowing up the Bristol Channel. She watched as he proceeded to take the boys to where only an iron rail protected them from the water.

'This is where you pee.'

Frances covered her mouth with her hand to prevent herself from bursting out laughing. The two boys, and Declan, were standing in a row, their backs to her, all peeing over the side.

First to finish, Declan came back with a grin on his face. The boys remained peering over the side of the ferry, watching for signs of fish.

'Now the girls,' he said, his eyes meeting those of Frances.

'I can hold on,' said Frances.

Ellen Gates, the eldest girl, shook her head avidly, as embarrassed at the thought of it as Frances was. Little Maggie, the youngest, was whining, wanting to do what the boys had done because she just had to.

After setting her up on the rail, Frances held on to her until she'd been.

'Is there more water in the river now?' Maggie asked, her bright little eyes shining with interest, her white curls falling like a snowy avalanche from beneath her knitted beret.

'You mean now you've put some water in it?' Frances asked as she set Maggie back on the deck, pulled up her knickers and tugged down the hem of the little girl's coat so that it almost covered her grubby knees. 'You probably did, you know, and now the little fishes are swimming around in it!' The little girl giggled. 'Now go on. Go and play with your brothers.'

Declan came and stood beside her as they slid away from the bank. Due to the fast-running tide, the ferry headed upstream, the engines beating against the force of the water, causing it to be pushed back on to the course they needed to make the far bank.

'There's Wales,' said Frances to the children, whose faces had been pinched pink by the fresh wind. 'A land of mist and mountains.'

She went on to tell them more about the forest, the place where they were going.

'The Forest of Dean is in Gloucestershire. You'll love it. There are lots of trees to climb and flowers to pick, fish to take from the brooks, as well as rabbits and deer.'

Talking about the things she'd got up to herself when she had stayed there brought tears to her eyes. She'd loved her time in the forest and hoped they would love it too.

Declan turned to look at her. 'You make it sound like heaven – a heaven full of rabbits to be caught, trees to be climbed. They'll never want to go back to their mother.'

'They can do similar things in Oldland Common.'

'You know you don't believe that. They're entering something magical here. Their first time away from home, away from all they've ever known. It'll make them restless.'

He was standing with his legs slightly apart, braced against the movement of the ferry boat, eyes narrowed against the stiff breeze. A half-smile lifted one side of his mouth. His easy self-assurance was appealing and although she tried to drag her attention away, it wasn't easy. He was like a magnet and she couldn't help being attracted to him.

Looking towards the far shore helped her concentrate. 'We're almost there,' she breathed.

Locks of hair blew across her face along with the chill breeze and the tang of salty spray. 'Won't be long now,' she said brusquely. From now on, she would go all out to give the impression that she was looking forward to the end of the ferry trip. In one way she was. Ada might know how she could start looking for her mother. If she did then she wouldn't need to approach her uncle. Uncle Stan had been good to her and she had no wish to appear ungrateful.

Once the children were settled, she could have a quiet word with Ada and then she would head for home. Though heading back today meant having only Declan for company. Dismay and excitement vied for dominance. Excitement won.

There was a lot of engine noise and the shouts of men as hawsers were laid out on deck, the smaller berthing lines attached and ready to throw to the men waiting on the other side of the river.

Frances brushed her hair back from her face. Clouds lay like ruffled silk above the Welsh hills that rose behind the slipway at Bulwark, an English promontory on the Welsh side of the river.

'Get ready to disembark,' shouted the skipper.

'That means you,' Declan shouted to the five children.

It was early afternoon by the time they resumed their journey. Just before the road dropped into the Wye Valley, they pulled in so the kids could eat the lunches they'd brought with them – those who had any left, that was. Frances handed out more sandwiches to those whose rucksacks were empty. Declan handed out more chocolate bars, oranges, apples and bananas. The latter were looked on with awestruck interest; only the older children could remember ever having eaten a banana. Like onions, the banana had been an early casualty of the war.

'So how many kids do you want?' asked Declan as they set off again, instantly wiping the grin off her face.

'What sort of question is that?'

The Jeep bounded along the slipway and on to a narrow road.

Declan shrugged. 'A question I want an answer to. It strikes me that an only child is a lonely child and one with an inclination to surround herself with children.'

'I'll leave it to fate.'

'That's not a good idea,' said Declan, shaking his head. 'These things should be properly planned.'

Frances raised her eyebrows. 'Planned?'

'Sure. You have to be able to afford a family. That's my motto, my dear. I want every single one of my kids to go to college, or at least have the opportunity to go. So I'll plan how many I will have. And I won't have any of them running around in ragged trousers – or dresses – because I can't afford to clothe them properly. No sirree! My kids will be the best-dressed kids on the block! Or in the village. Just in case you don't know what I'm referring to.'

Bristling with indignation, Frances's response was as hot as her face. 'Mrs Gates does her best but her husband is away fighting. It's not easy for her.'

'I understand that.'

'You've got a bloody nerve, Yank!'

Those dark eyebrows rose in surprise. 'Do I?'

'You're implying that American children are better looked after than British children. That's what you mean, isn't it? That British children are scruffy and ill fed!'

'I didn't say that.'

'You did!'

'Only in a roundabout way. I said I would plan things. There's no way I would leave my wife with a bevy of kids, no matter what.'

Frances stiffened. Was he speaking from experience?

'Are you married?'

He threw back his head and laughed out loud. 'Oh, no! No, definitely, no. I've never been the marrying kind, honey, not yet, anyway. I fully admit that I love women, but whoever claps her saddle on me will have to be one hell of a special lady.'

'And you haven't met her yet.'

He looked straight ahead at the winding road as it dipped down into the valley. In the valley itself, the River Wye snaked its way through the thick foliage of deciduous trees. Although she wasn't sure what she wanted him to say, his lack of response ate into her patience.

At last she spat it out. 'Well?'

He raised one dark eyebrow. 'Now what do you want me to say, my pretty little English rose?' His smile was beguiling, cheeky and startlingly intent. That was when she knew he had said it on purpose, purely to feed her indignation.

'I just want you to tell me the truth. What else would I want?'

He shook his head. 'You're like all women. You want to be the one. It makes you feel special. The trouble is that once you've hog-tied me and made me your own, you'll expect me to conform to the norm, like all married men. You'll want me to mow the lawn, paint the house and mend the roof, play golf and go to church with you on Sunday.'

'I will not!'

His grin widened. 'There you are! My lady doth protest too much . . .Was it Shakespeare who said that?'

'I've no idea,' snapped Frances. It probably was but she had no intention of further enhancing his out-of-control ego!

Folding her arms she turned her head and stared unblinking out of the plastic window on her side of the Jeep. Declan O'Malley had a commanding presence. She couldn't think of him being *hog-tied*, as he put it, by anyone, though any woman would consider him a challenge. Was that what he was doing now, challenging her to rise to the bait? The trouble was she was sorely tempted, and even though she kept telling herself that Ed was in love with her, and if she really wanted to he would marry her, she also had to consider whether that was what she wanted.

Sensing she was backed into a corner, Declan changed tack. 'So tell me about this woman who's taking on all these kids.'

Frances willingly told him all she could, not missing out Ada's quirky behaviour and the way she looked at you, as though assessing every thought in your head.

'And she doesn't like being called Mrs Perkins. She prefers to be called Ada. Even her granddaughter calls her Ada.'

She went on to tell him that Ada's granddaughter was named Miriam and lived with her. 'Miriam doesn't get on with her mother, Mrs Powell, who runs the village shop.'

She considered there was no need to enlighten him further and say that Miriam's mother had kept her daughter a virtual prisoner in the living quarters behind the tiny village store. Poor Miriam. Frances had no doubt whatsoever that she was far happier wherever she was, and that whatever she was doing, she was happier than back in Oldland Common.

'I sense you're quite looking forward to seeing these women.'

'Yes. I am.'

They passed a pub, a railway station and headed off on a side road before reaching the Welsh town of Monmouth where, having crossed a bridge, they found themselves in England again, such were the convolutions of the land and the ancient border around here. There were no road signs to tell them where they were. Road and rail signs had all been taken down to confuse the enemy should they land. To find their way, Declan had brought a map and compass, and, of course, Frances could direct him to the right place.

He slid the map in front of the windscreen. 'Where now?'

'Take the next turning on the right.'

Eventually, they were bumping along on the track leading to Ada's cottage.

A spiral of smoke drifted lazily through the trees, the sight of it gladdening Frances's heart.

Ada's smokehouse was in operation, salmon probably, poached from the river and totally illegal. Not that the foresters would see it that way. They'd been living here for centuries. The fruits of the forest – and that included anything that swam in the river as well as what roamed or flew through the forest – was theirs by right.

Sunlight speared through a gap in the cloud, momentarily dappling the ground with diamonds of light. The track they'd bumped along widened into a clearing.

To her surprise, a group of people – adults and kids – stood around the cottage door, avidly looking in their direction.

The Jeep came to a halt. Frances got out and waved. 'Ada!'

Her heels sank into the soft ground as she ran to where Ada was standing with the others.

'Ada! It's lovely to see you.'

There were no hugs or shaking of hands: the sight of Ada's beaming face was enough acknowledgement that they were welcome.

She was greeted by the other people with Ada: two officials from the evacuee scheme, the local Methodist minister, the doctor and another man who she thought she recognised but couldn't quite place. She was slightly surprised that Miriam wasn't with them.

Ada instantly read the look on Frances's face. 'Miriam's gone. Ran away. Silly bitch!' Ada looked quite disgruntled about it.

'Where?'

'No idea.' Ada took her pipe from the corner of her mouth and spat on the ground. 'This lot are here to look the kids over.'

Those gathered eyed the tall American standing in the midst of the nervous-looking children.

'They're a great bunch and looking forward to staying with you all. Now who is going where? They're pretty tired. Hungry too,' said Declan.

Ada closed one eye, scrutinising him briefly before expounding the details.

'The girls are staying with me. The boys are going with Doctor Peters.'

Frances's attention fixed on the dark-haired man with the swarthy complexion. He was standing apart from everyone else but every now and then darted a furtive look in her direction.

She kept looking at him, keen to see his face more clearly; he seemed so familiar.

Nothing came to her. Taking advantage of the multiple conversations going on between Declan and the doctor, Frances bent Ada's ear.

'Who is he?' She nodded in the man's direction. 'That man over there. Do I know him?'

Ada lifted one half of her mouth in a knowing smile. 'Cast your mind back.'

Frances frowned. She did know him! She had seen him before.

There was no chance to speak to the man. Declan strode towards the doctor with his hand held out to Ada, the children, quiet now, following on behind like a gaggle of ducklings.

Frances fancied Ada was eyeing him too intensely, like she did when she read the tea leaves for people. Only Declan didn't drink tea. He drank coffee. Not that reading leaves, cards or a crystal ball had much to do with Ada's natural skills. Ada Perkins was good at weighing people up.

'What do you think of him?' she wanted to say to her. She wasn't sure when it had become so important to have Ada's opinion on the handsome American. Declan had made an impression on her that so far she'd kept well hidden.

She banished her flustered thoughts to explain to the children who would be staying where. 'You'll only be half a mile away from your sisters,' she explained to the boys.

The doctor told them they'd have to walk the half mile as he hadn't brought his car. Declan offered to give them a lift.

'It's a good vehicle for rough tracks,' he explained. 'Climb in, Doc. No point in walking when there's a ride on offer. Your kids will fit too.'

The Gates boys, tired now, clambered willingly into the back of the vehicle, along with the doctor's sons. The doctor himself climbed into the front seat.

The minister, who served on the evacuee committee, took his leave only after telling the children he would see them at Sunday School.

Frances, Ada, the three girls and the remaining man Frances thought she'd recognised, were left standing outside Ada's home.

The Jeep roared off in a flurry of dust. A doe hidden among the foliage was startled and disappeared.

Frances felt Ada nudge her side then heard her whisper, 'Mario. That man you keep staring at is Mario Lombardi.' Ada called to him. 'Mario. Come and say hello to Frances. While you're at it you can apologise for stealing her supper that day in the forest.'

The penny dropped. Frances gasped. 'The Italian! The one who stole the pigeon and the rabbit!'

Evacuated to live with Ada, Frances and her friends had been in the forest roasting trapped game over a fire of burning sticks. Living the life of a recluse in a nearby cave, Mario had waited until their backs were turned and stolen the food.

His voice broke into her musings. 'Miss Sweet. Thank you for past kindnesses.' There was something energetic about his eyes and also something kind and grateful.

'Take some fish with you,' Ada said to him now.

'Thank you.' He headed towards the smokehouse where sides of salmon and trout filled the air with smoky incense. The two women watched until the door to the smokehouse banged shut behind him.

'He doesn't say much,' explained Ada. 'I know nothing about his past, why he ended up living in the forest. Nobody does. They arrested him and locked him up at first, but when they found out how long he'd been living rough, he was given leave to work on the land if anyone would have him. I happened to grab him first. Right,' she said, turning to the three little girls who stood patiently, their carrier bags of belongings banging against their knees, 'time to come inside.'

Everyone trooped in. Despite all they'd eaten on the journey, Patricia's stomach rumbled on smelling whatever was bubbling away in a cast-iron pot on the old black range.

'Game stew,' said Ada, her fists on her hips and her gaze fixed on Ellen, the eldest of the Gates sisters. 'Up there for the three of you,' she said, pointing in the direction of the steep ladder that led up to a mezzanine level that was once a hayloft. 'Put your things away. There's water and a towel up there. Make sure you use it.'

Silently, the three girls climbed up the stairs, each clinging to their paper carrier bags, rucksacks and gas masks.

Feeling their apprehension as if it were her own, Frances called out to reassure them. 'I'll wait here to say goodbye before I go. Must say I wish I could stay and have supper with you. That stew smells delicious.'

Small smiles appeared on the nervous faces before they disappeared, off to explore their new surroundings.

When Frances became aware of Ada looking at her with narrowed eyes, she was the one who became nervous.

'That's a fine figure of a man you've got travelling with you.' Ada's words were simple, but spoken with intent.

Frances tossed her head. 'He certainly thinks he is.'

Ada closed one eye. 'You glow when he's close to you.'

Frances laughed lightly. 'How can you say that? We've hardly been close since we arrived and we've hardly spoken.'

A surgeon's scalpel couldn't be as incisive as the expression in Ada's eyes. Her looks were like fingers, reaching out and feeling the lumps and bumps in her mind.

'There's something about the pair of you.'

'Ada! He's old enough to be my father,' Frances said indignantly. Inside, she curled with pleasure.

'That's not true. Besides, sometimes we need the wisdom of older people in our lives. You were young when your father died.'

'That doesn't mean to say . . .'

Frances's voice trailed off. But then she realised this was her opportunity to ask Ada about her mother. 'Did you ever meet my mother? When you were visiting your family?' she asked at last. The words of Gertrude Powell, Ada's daughter, rang in her ears. *Whore! Slut!*

'Of course I did. Your mother was dizzy and weak. Loved men too much, but couldn't understand them. Couldn't read them. It helps if you can read the man you're married to. Your mother loved being loved, but wasn't much good at giving it out in return. She thought she did, but she didn't. Didn't really know what love was.'

The moment had come. Frances broached the subject of her mother's whereabouts.

'I don't suppose you know where she went, Ada? My mother? I can't remember much about her, but I want to see her. I want to know why she left me with Uncle Stan.'

Ada ambled over to give the stew a stir. Her back remained a broad barrier to conversation.

'I want to know, Ada. If you know where she is, please tell me.'

Ada looked at her over her shoulder. 'Reckon I might.'

'Can you tell me?'

Ada shook her head. 'No. I won't. It's for your uncle Stan to tell you.'

'But I—'

'I know,' said Ada, nodding her head. 'You don't want to appear ungrateful. Let me put it this way . . .' She turned to face Frances before carrying on. 'If you haven't asked your uncle by the time you're twenty-one, or if he hasn't told you by then, come back and I'll tell you where I heard she went.'

'That's unfair! Uncle Stan might die in the meantime. There's a war on. I might die! Please. I want to know.'

Ada reached for her pipe, seemed to consider lighting it, but then bit down on it with her yellowed teeth. 'Last I heard of her she was in Bristol. I don't know where. Your uncle Stan knows the rest and telling you is up to him.'

'But—'

Ada held up her hand. 'No more. That's an end to the subject.'

'Why do people run away?'

Ada shrugged and bit down on her pipe. 'For reasons they think are very important. They are – to them – but viewed from the outside, they're not always so weighty.'

'Did Miriam have an important reason to leave?'

Ada winced. 'I don't know. She never said.'

'I'm surprised she's gone. I'm sure she loved being here with you.'

She didn't ask whether Miriam had given birth to a baby. A bastard. Illegitimate. It might not be true, but the gossip in the village had suggested it was.

'Apparently, she didn't love it here quite enough.'

There was a hint of regret in Ada's voice. Frances guessed that she was hurting inside, but her attitude to life was pragmatic. In fact, she'd once told Frances that life was never fair, that children were only on loan, and that everyone had the right to live their lives as they pleased, without parents clinging on to them.

Frances thought back to the rumours about Miriam and the young curate back in Oldland. 'Did she have a sweetheart?'

'She was courted hereabouts.'

Ada's eyes seemed to shift sidelong, as though something or somebody outside had come into her line of vision. Frances could see nobody at first, then she saw Mario, a man of tanned Mediterranean features, his voice made more attractive by a romantic accent. In the absence of any other male company within half a mile, Miriam would have found him attractive.

'I go find another deer,' said Mario. 'I have gun.'

Ada nodded. 'He's a good hunter,' she confided to Frances.

'So Miriam was in love with Mario?'

'She thought so, but I don't think she could understand him. He's not the sort to settle down and raise a family, and that is what my granddaughter would like to do. It's babies she wants most of all, not men. Not really. She's like a bird, keen to build a nest and have chicks, but not lucky when it comes to the men in her life.'

Ada's comment about chicks scratched at a nerve. Miriam had once taken Charlie from his pushchair, though at first it was thought that he'd undone his harness and wandered. Frances had thought about it a lot since then and was convinced that he couldn't have done it by himself. Miriam had supposedly found him, but the Sweet family all suspected she'd taken him in the first place. Still, no harm done. At least they had got him back.

There was no point in mentioning their suspicions, not so long after the incident; to do so would only cause Ada unnecessary hurt and she didn't deserve that. Ada was odd but kind.

The sound of the Jeep returning preceded Declan's wide shoulders and impressive physique filling the doorway and blocking out the daylight.

'You'll be pleased to know that the boys have settled in. There's a stream at the end of the doctor's garden and he had the good sense to have two extra rods waiting for them along with a bucket of maggots. They settled down to it right away. I guessed they would.' He smiled at her and looked uncommonly pleased with himself.

'That's good.'

Frances knew instinctively that Declan would have done the same thing if the boys had been staying with him. Rather than let them miss their home and kick their heels with frustration, he would have prepared something that would occupy their minds – just as the doctor had done.

He took a deep breath as he came into the room. 'Something smells mighty good.'

'Game stew. I would offer you some, but I think you'd prefer to get going. Am I right?'

Ada looked deeply into his eyes; a lesser man would have winced, but not Declan.

'It's tempting,' he said, with a cheerful look on his face. 'In fact, it might not be a bad idea if we had a spoonful or two, enough to keep our strength up on the way back.'

Ada shook her head. Her smile was sardonic, her eyes as piercing as ever. 'A bowl and two spoons. That's all I can spare.'

They sat outside on a fallen tree trunk, the bowl of steaming stew between them. Ada excused herself, saying she had important things to do.

'This is cosy.' He said the word cosy in a way that almost made her blush, which was annoying. She'd promised herself that she wouldn't.

The sound of spoons rattling against china came from inside Ada's cottage. Not a word was being uttered by the hungry girls, and Frances knew that after the stew would come a slice of suet pudding, heavy as you like and dotted with homemade jam. Pots of jam lined one shelf of the dresser that served as Ada's storage space. She'd obviously collected a lot of berries during the last summer, as well as rhubarb and fruit given her in exchange for services rendered. Ada still made medicines from the plants she found in the forest. How Ada had got enough sugar to make the jam was another matter.

The time came to go.

'If we get a move on, we should be back before it gets dark,' said Declan. On seeing the look on her face, he gave a curt nod of his head. 'I'll stay out here while you say your goodbyes.' He grinned. 'Sure looks like I won't be lonely.'

Ushered outside, the three girls made a beeline for Declan. Amazingly, he had found more chocolate.

'Though not too much. I'm down to starvation rations,' he said to them. His laugh was infectious, deep as a gorge and flavoured like rum.

'I heard him say he'd stay outside while we said our goodbyes. That was thoughtful,' remarked Ada as she ferried empty dishes from table to sink.

'I suppose so.'

She stopped what she was doing and eyed Frances reflectively. 'There's no suppose about it. He's a good man, a strong man, protective, perhaps just the kind you need.'

Her directness took Frances by surprise. 'You feel it?'

Ada lifted her chin. 'More to the point, you feel it too. I can see it in your eyes.'

Frances recalled how some of the forest kids had told her that Ada Perkins was a witch. It was just something children said. Now she wasn't so sure.

'If Miriam does turn up, please give her my best wishes.'

'I will.'

'You must miss her.'

Ada looked sad. 'I do. I should have seen it coming.'

Ada Perkins had always presented a strong image, that of a woman who could cope with anything that was thrown at her. Now she looked smaller, somehow, less sure of the world than she used to be.

'I hope she does come back.'

Ada shook her head. 'I don't think she will.'

'Then I hope she finds happiness – wherever she is.'

'Never mind. You look to your own future, Frances Sweet. That's a charming man out there, one any woman would be proud to have on her arm.'

'I don't think . . .' began Frances, blushing to the roots of her hair.

'Don't think. Some men control their own destiny; others are controlled by it.' Ada's gaze met hers head on. 'That man out there is in charge of his destiny. He's the sort to take the world by its tail. Up to you whether you're up there with him.'

'An interesting woman,' Declan remarked on the journey home.

Frances had been thinking deep thoughts, some about her mother, and others about Miriam.

At the sound of his voice she turned and eyed the velvet black eyebrows, the tanned skin, the strong profile. Wrapped up in studying him, she made no comment.

He noticed and looked amused. 'Are you looking to eat me? I would have thought that game stew was more than enough to satisfy you. It certainly filled me up.'

The moment of admiring appraisal was gone. His cocky comment had once again annoyed her. 'Why ever would I want to eat you?'

'I intrigue you.'

That sideways glance, that simmering smile. Don't give in to his charms, she told herself. Convince him you're not impressed.

'You flatter yourself! Whatever would somebody of my age find intriguing about you?'

He gave no sign of being put out by her barbed comment.

'Oh, I think you're a girl who would have loved her father a lot if he'd been around a little longer, and figure somebody like me . . . Hey! What's the matter?' Declan pulled over on to a piece of solidly packed mud. He stopped the engine.

Frances couldn't help herself. Everything – seeing Ada again, Miriam running away just like her mother had done. Gertrude Powell saying her mother had been a slut. It was all too much. She just wanted to sob her heart out.

'Hey,' he said, his voice softer now. 'What's with you?'

Frances remained with her hands over her face as she shook her head. Her feelings were raw and torn already, even before he'd mentioned her father.

'Hey. I wouldn't have been that tough to eat. Though perhaps I might. Is that what this is? I might stick in your throat?'

He was trying to be humorous, but Frances just couldn't respond in the same light manner. She'd never felt so intensely about her parents when she was growing up, so why now?

If she hadn't been overcome with emotion, perhaps she would have backed away when he put his arm around her. But she didn't. Instead, she found herself burying her face in his shoulder, her eyes tightly closed.

Declan rested his chin on her head, his free hand stroking her hair.

'Frances, my sweet girl, I am a man who speaks his mind, or as you English would say, I do not mince my words. This means that I sometimes tread on the sensitive feelings of those more guarded than myself. I get the feeling that this is one of those times.'

He waited patiently until she came out from behind her hands. When she did, her eyes were very wide and at sight of them something in his expression changed.

'Okay. Okay.' He nodded his head and spoke more gently, no trace of sarcasm or humour. 'I see I need to eat humble pie. My profound apologies.'

He didn't rush her but waited for her to regain her self-control. Finally he said, 'Do you want to tell me what's upsetting you?'

'I wish I'd known my father better. You mentioning him and . . . everything . . . Worse was my mother running off and abandoning me.'

'Seems I put my big feet in it good and proper.' He sighed deeply. 'Do you want to tell me about it?'

'I've already told Ed about my dad dying and my mother not being around.' She didn't know why she said it, but sensed it wouldn't be long before Declan's usual manner dominated their conversations.

'So you told Ed? Well, I won't hold that against you.' He went quiet for a while. Frances got her handkerchief out of her pocket and blew her nose.

'And you heard it from Ty.'

He looked contrite. 'Men talk. I'm sorry.'

'It doesn't matter.'

'So you moved in with your cousins.'

Frances nodded. 'My mother left just after my father died. Uncle Stan brought me up.'

Declan nodded sagely. 'I see.' He paused again. 'You know, it's an old saying but a true one, that you can choose your friends but not your relatives. I guess that applies to parents too.'

'I can't remember her,' Frances blurted out. 'I think she looked something like me.'

She didn't add that her mother had worn red and had a reputation.

'No. She wasn't like you.' His voice was like a caress, soft and comforting.

Not sure she understood, Frances looked at him quizzically. 'How can you say that? You've never even met my mother!'

'You are you,' he said, pointing a finger so close to her nose it almost made her go cross-eyed. 'You're not your mother. You're a different person. You have some attributes inherited from your mother, but you also have a good dose from your father. That means you could be as much like your cousin Ruby or the married one; her name's Mary, right?'

Frances nodded.

'I've yet to meet her, though seeing as your cousins are twins, I reckon it's a case of meet one and you've met the other.'

'They're very alike,' said Frances, her voice more even. Declan doing all the talking made her feel less anxious.

'So! I could be seeing double! Any secrets as to how I can tell them apart?'

Frances smiled. 'Mary doesn't have the mole on her cheek that Ruby does.' She pointed to the very same spot on her own cheek.

'Oh, sure! I've noticed her beauty spot.'

He sat looking at her for a moment.

Frances looked away. She could cope with meeting those bewitching eyes for only so long. It was also an expedient time for changing the subject.

'I can't help wondering about Miriam, Ada's granddaughter, just going off like that. It sounds as though she might have had a crush on Mario. You know – the Italian who was there.' She said it blithely. Declan appeared to take it very seriously.

'A prisoner of war, I take it.'

'No, not exactly. He's lived in the forest for years and got arrested as an enemy alien. Then he was allowed his freedom as long as he did agricultural work of some description to anyone who wanted help. Ada nabbed him!'

'Nabbed him!' Declan laughed. 'I like that. Maybe I could get her a job in the US military police.'

Frances smiled. 'I can just see her wearing a white helmet. I'd dare anyone to call her a Snowdrop, though.'

They both laughed at the term given by the Americans to their military police on account of their white helmets.

'So do you think Miriam ran away because she was a woman scorned?'

'Miriam gets fond of people who don't get fond of her. She liked my cousin Charlie and he didn't want her either. She's not very pretty.'

'There's nothing like being blunt, my dear!' He took his arm from around her, settled both hands on the steering wheel and eyed the branches of trees hanging over a rough wooden fence.

'Well, Charlie was very handsome and fun to be around. I don't blame her for liking him.'

'You sound as though you were very fond of him. What was he like?'

'Charlie was lovely.'

'You're biased. He was a relative and as such . . .' He stopped abruptly, suddenly aware of what he had just said. 'He was Ruby's brother, the one who got torpedoed. I'm sorry. She did tell me.'

'Yes. He fell in love with a woman called Gilda. That's where little Charlie comes from. Gilda got killed in an air raid.'

'I recall Ruby saying something about it. I'm sorry, Frances. I shouldn't have mentioned it.' His hand covered hers.

Frances looked down at his hand, noting the dark hairs sprouting on the backs of the knuckles.

'I hope Miriam's all right. She's not always . . . well . . . you know . . . not all there.'

'It's us men,' said Declan, patting her hand. 'I've been told by more than one woman that I'm driving her crazy.'

'Are you making fun of me?'

'No,' he said, grinning at the bright young face beaming up at him and thinking how pretty she was. 'I wouldn't dare. You may be young, Frances Sweet, but you're very mature for your age.'

Rather than making her blush as a young girl to receive such flattery, she positively glowed.

Declan smiled at her and she smiled back.

'Besides cookie boy Ed, has anyone ever told you how pretty you are?'

'Some.'

'Only some? Never mind. There's plenty of time.'

'I'm sixteen next week. I'm having a party – well – it's at the village dance.'

'That's a bit unfair, making you have your birthday party on the same day as the village dance.'

That was pretty much how Frances felt about it when she learned she wasn't to be allowed a separate party, but her protests had fallen on deaf ears. She pouted at the thought of how superior Ruby had been on delivering her decision.

'There's a war on and we've got to make food stretch that bit further. And besides, everyone needs a bit of cheering up, what with all this fighting going on.'

There had been no point protesting any further. Ruby was immoveable once she'd made her mind up.

'Will you be there?' she asked him.

Declan grinned before preparing to carry on with their journey. 'I wouldn't miss it for the world!'

'Ruby will like it lots if you're there.' She said it reluctantly. In a way, she didn't want Ruby to be there. She wanted Declan to herself.

His eyes crinkled at the corners; his smile was close-lipped but heart-warming for all that.

'Never mind her liking it lots. How about you? Would you like it lots if I was there?'

She didn't blush when she looked into his face, but seeing as she felt no embarrassment, why should she?

'I would love you to be there!'

CHAPTER SEVEN

Ruby ticked off the food she'd need for her next demonstration. Satisfied she had everything she needed on her list, she then turned her attention to providing a small buffet for the dance at the village hall, as well as a birthday cake for her cousin Frances.

The dances attended by the soldiers from the US base were happening every month now and overall were good fun, though providing a small buffet could be quite hard work. Sourcing ingredients was the main problem. Luckily the Americans contributed generously, and although it had been suggested she leave everything to their very efficient catering corps, her pride wouldn't let her. Other women in the village thought the same way, stating their intention to bring along what they could. Nobody liked the thought of their friends and neighbours – or the visiting Yanks – regarding them as mean or too poor to contribute anything.

The cake was another matter. She'd carefully saved a quantity of dried fruit including cherries soaked in sherry, the latter courtesy of Bettina Hicks.

'I'm running low on brandy,' Bettina had apologised.

'Sherry will do very nicely,' Ruby had responded.

Frances was humming and smiling to herself.

Ruby had an inkling what – or rather who – was responsible for her happy mood. A boy, no doubt. Frances was of that age.

'So what's Ed buying you?'

Snatched from private thoughts, Frances looked up, her face a picture of innocence.

'I'm not sure. Stockings, I expect. Oh, and perhaps a bag of sugar. He knows we always need sugar.'

Ruby shook her head and smiled in that grown-up way that made Frances feel like a child again, as though she could read her thoughts. How surprised her cousin would be if she knew it wasn't Ed she was thinking about, but Declan. He'd made a big impression on her and although she'd been a little shy in his company at first, she'd warmed to him. And now he crept into her mind when she least expected it. It surprised her that nobody seemed to guess what was developing between them. Even Pearl was convinced Frances would end up with Ed Bergman, the young American cook.

On their last evening out, Pearl had asked her if she'd gone 'all the way'. Frances had told her to mind her own business.

'It'll be okay,' said Pearl. 'You can't get pregnant on your first time, everyone knows that.'

Frances wouldn't admit it to Pearl, but she was greatly relieved at this gem of information. After the last village dance, she and Ed had found a dark field screened by a hawthorn hedge.

Taking a leaf out of her friend Pearl's book, she'd given in to him. Perhaps she'd done it because Ed mentioned dying for his country at such a young age. Or it might have been down to getting a bit tipsy. Everyone said the time was getting close when the allied armies would invade Europe. Ed was so young, his face had turned so sad and she really had taken pity on him and done what she shouldn't have done. And now she was afraid, afraid of the consequences.

'Now we have to get married,' he'd told her.

Of course they did, but if Pearl were to be believed, it wouldn't be a shotgun affair. Pearl knew a lot more about sex than Frances so surely she was right to be reassured?

Yes. You'll marry Ed and live happily ever after, she thought to herself. Then Declan crept into her mind again, those dark eyes, that tanned face, the black hair so glossy and tight against his scalp. Ed was an immature boy in comparison to Declan.

'You sound happy,' said Ruby, eyeing her cousin curiously.

'I am happy. I love these dances. Love preparing the food for them too. And anyway, it is my birthday.'

'Sweet sixteen. Lucky you. Hopefully, we'll have enough food,' said Ruby. 'Those boys certainly know how to eat.'

'Ed said he could get you some extra sugar and also some coconut, oh and some tins of Spam for sandwiches. He'll bring doughnuts – you know how the Yanks love doughnuts – but he asked if you could make an apple pie. He reckons yours are the best.'

Ruby wasn't quite sure whether this was purely flattery on Ed's part. He was obviously very fond of her cousin and quite often went out of his way to ingratiate himself with her family by bringing along surplus supplies from his army kitchen. Ruby wondered if Ed was aware that he had a rival for Frances. Declan had made it clear he was interested in her cousin even if Ruby had told him she was too young.

At one time it seemed as though Ruby was the one that Declan was sweet on; not that she'd encouraged him. She liked him. There was no doubt of that. But getting serious about him was an entirely different matter. No matter how much she tried to push Johnnie Smith to the back of her mind, he refused to be side-lined.

Sometimes she thought Declan was only pretending to be serious. 'Once this war's over, we might make a go of a life together. Let's see how things go.'

At the time she'd laughed and asked him whether he was asking her to marry him or go into business together. He'd laughed too.

He'd once showed Ruby a picture of his folks standing outside their store and smiling proudly at the camera. That was before they'd died. She'd imagined a grocery store, but it was nothing like that. His parents looked very well off, his mother wearing a fur coat. There were more fur coats and dresses in the window display behind her. To Ruby's eyes it looked like a department store, like Coleman's in Bristol or Jolly's in Bath.

That was as far as things had got and somehow, just somehow, she wasn't sure whether he was being serious or not. His plans for the future varied from one meeting to another and he'd never been that fresh with her, certainly not for many weeks. At first she'd put it down to his concern about the invasion plans for Europe; they were bound to happen shortly. If he were at all serious about her, they would reunite after the war was over. What would happen then? Besides, Corporal Johnnie Smith might come home. She hoped he would. As an orphan, his life had not been easy. The army had become his home even before the outbreak of war.

Looking back on their time together, it seemed she had always known where she was with him, despite his acid wit, and the thought of him still brought a smile to her face.

Despite the desperate stories coming in from the Far East, she preferred to think that he was still alive. A lot of water had flowed under the bridge since she'd last seen him. There had been no commitment between them, no sweet words of love as such, just an understanding. Somehow their thoughts and their instincts seemed to meet on mutual territory, each complementing the other.

Suppressing a heartfelt sigh, she cast her mind back to the job in hand.

'Right, now let's see what we can put together for the buffet. How about rissoles? Small ones.'

Frances pulled a face.

'Not a good idea?'

'No. I mean, it's all right for us, but they're American . . .'

'I thought you said Ed was bringing doughnuts?'

'He is, but, well, couldn't we make something American?'

Ruby pulled a rueful expression. 'With the ingredients we can get, it isn't easy making something British, let alone something American. They're not on rations, well at least not in the same way we are.'

Frances was leaning back on the table. Although she was attempting to look interested, Ruby sensed she had something on her mind.

'What is it, Frances? And don't tell me it's nothing. I know you too well. Is it something to do with Ed?'

Frances sighed. She'd been thinking a lot about living in America. If she did marry Ed, then she'd have to move there. Declan threatened her thoughts again, but at least for the moment she pushed him to the back of her mind.

'I'd just like to make something American for the buffet.'

'I'm already baking an apple pie. That's as familiar to them as it is to us.'

'I know, but could we make something else too? Something to surprise him?'

Ruby was pleased that Frances wanted to impress Ed, a boy close to her own age. She'd been worried that Frances had her head turned by Declan. But on reflection, she had the oddest feeling it wasn't Ed that Frances was keen to impress.

Forcing the thought away, she pulled her attention back to the question of making a truly American dish for the next village dance.

'How about hamburgers?'

'Wow! Could we? The guys would be so surprised!'

'The guys? Not just Ed?'

'Well . . . yes . . . Ed and the guys. Can't leave anyone out.'

Ruby dismissed her misgivings regarding the attraction between Frances and Declan and thought how wonderful it was to be young and excited about impressing a young man with food. 'I think we can, though not with beef.'

It was disconcerting to see her cousin's enthusiasm change to suspicion. Like everyone else, she was getting used to making things that were similar to pre-war food though not using the same ingredients. Some were very successful. Others took more getting used to.

Food was an obsession with everybody. Make do and mend applied to clothes, shoes and home furnishings. With food it was a case of making do with what you could get hold of. The hamburgers were likely to be something of a challenge.

'What are you going to make them with?'

Ruby was still mulling it over, but was unwilling to let Frances know that.

'Well, let me think . . .' There was no denying that the older Frances got, the more astute she became. Ruby had been caught off guard, but needs must, so with quick thinking she managed to string out her words while thinking on her feet.

'There's no problem making the bread baps, and thanks to Dad and his garden, we have plenty of onions. . . . We'll also need salt, pepper, herbs . . .'

'I know all that, but what meat are you going to use?'

This was the question that Ruby had been dreading. 'I guess we'll have to see what I can get nearer to the date. Will that suit you, miss?"

Frances nodded, but there was something guarded in her expression. Ruby knew something else was going on behind those dark brown eyes and that baking had nothing to do with it.

'Are you worrying about the cake not being big enough?'

Frances shook her head. 'No. And anyway, it'll be small slices for friends only. No. It's not the cake.'

Ruby thought back to when she was Frances's age. That period between being an adolescent and true adulthood was not an easy time.

Feeling sudden empathy, she stopped what she was doing and placed her arm around her cousin's shoulders. 'So if it's not about the cake, what is it, Frances? Come on, you can tell me.'

Frances scraped a lock of hair back from her forehead. Her eyes were still downcast and she was sucking in her bottom lip, a habit she'd had all her life and a sign something was bothering her.

Might as well jump in with the obvious question. 'Is it Ed?' asked Ruby.

Frances shook her head. 'No. Ed's fine, but—'

'Nothing can be that bad that it makes you look as though you're sitting on a stool made of thistles. What is it? Come on, I'm your cousin. You can tell me.'

Her cousin's eyes flickered and she sucked in her cheeks before looking up into Ruby's face. 'It's that dress you gave me. The red one.'

Ruby drew in her chin and eyed her cousin cautiously. She was worried about a dress. Was that all? Inside she sighed with relief. 'You haven't ripped it, have you?'

'No. I took special care not to. It's a lovely dress.'

'Good. So what's wrong with it?' she asked.

Frances held her head to one side, her eyes looking dolefully up into those of her cousin. 'Is it true that red is the colour that whores wear?'

Ruby's jaw dropped. This was not at all what she'd been expecting. 'Frances Sweet, if you were younger, I would wash your mouth out with soap and water! That dress was mine. I wore it and I'm not a whore, am I?'

'I didn't mean that *you* were a whore.'

'Well, thank goodness for that! Where did you learn that word?'

Her initial suspicion was that it might have come from Ed, in which case she promised herself to have a stiff word with him. If she didn't then her father would, if he was told, that is. Her inclination was not to tell him.

Frances tossed her head and looked her in the eye. 'I'm not a child, Ruby,' she said in a matter-of-fact way. 'I do know what the word means. We do own a dictionary.'

The reference was unnerving, but Ruby was mature enough to maintain her equilibrium. Treat Frances as an adult. She really should have remembered that.

'I'm sorry, Frances. You're quite right. You are no longer a child, but you've still got a lot to learn about this world – and I don't want you picking up bad habits.'

'I won't.'

'Anyway, I don't see what the colour red has got to do with anything,' she said as confidently as she could. 'Cardinals wear red. They're churchmen,' she added, in case Frances wasn't aware of that.

'I know. And there are a lot of things that are good and are coloured red. Like birds. Robins, anyway.'

'That's right. Where did you get the idea that red was worn by women of that sort?'

Frances picked up a pencil and began to doodle at the top of one of the lists. 'Mrs Powell. It was a while back. We went into her shop. Pearl wanted a packet of . . . mints . . . yes. I think it was mints.' It was an outright lie, but Ruby would instantly point out that Pearl was too young to smoke, though many of her age and younger did. What they saw adults do, they also wanted to do.

As Ruby didn't seem to notice her hesitation, she soldiered on with her tale. 'Then Pearl asked me if her seams were straight and Mrs Powell saw I was wearing your red dress and said . . . like I just told you, she said that women . . . well . . . a certain kind of woman wore red.'

Ruby laughed. 'Mrs Powell? And all wicked old witches wear black just as she does! Take no notice of her. You know what she's like.'

Although her laughter died, Ruby couldn't keep the amusement from her voice. 'That woman belongs in the Dark Ages. She thinks everyone else is wicked and she's the most saintly person in the village. She's a witch. Perhaps we should think about burning her at the stake . . .' She stopped herself from uttering the avalanche of adjectives suiting Gertrude Powell. 'The names I could call her. I expect you could think of a few too . . .'

She'd expected Frances to join her with words and laughter, but Frances wasn't looking amused. Her expression was downcast as though her thoughts were dark and deeply buried. Something was troubling her. Regardless that her cousin might yet again object to being treated like a child, Ruby wanted to get to the bottom of this. She chose her words carefully. 'What else did she say, Frances?'

Frances stopped doodling on the precious notepaper. Once she'd stopped, Ruby took hold of it and placed it out of her reach. Paper was not easy to get hold of, nowadays. Norway, where most of the pulp had come from in pre-war days, had been overrun and was now behind enemy lines. Canada helped to fill the gap, but there were more important things to bring across the Atlantic than paper!

In the absence of something to scribble on, Frances tapped the end of the pencil against her teeth. Tap. Tap-tap.

Tap. Tap-tap. The unrelenting rhythm began to get on Ruby's nerves.

'That's enough!' Ruby snatched the pencil from her cousin's hand. 'What else did she say to you? Something nasty, no doubt! Come on, Frances. Tell me what she said. Whatever it was, it's obviously upset you.'

Pale pink lips pursed with reluctance, Frances sniffed, put the pencil down and raised her eyes.

'She said I was no better than my mother. That she'd worn red and was always a whore.'

Ruby felt as though the lining of her throat had thickened and all the words were stuck on her tongue. It came to her suddenly that Frances knew very little about her mother, which meant Mrs Powell's comment would have come as a terrible shock.

Partly our fault, she thought, especially Dad.

She tried to recall the last time Mildred Sweet had been mentioned in conversation, but couldn't think of one single time. Her character and manner were never referred to, neither was the way she dressed or the way she looked. Ruby herself couldn't recall what she looked like, simply because Uncle Sefton had never had too much to do with the bakery when he came back from the Great War. He and Mildred had lived on the other side of Bristol until his illness became so bad her father had insisted he move in with them. By that time, it was too late for him and there was little time to get to know Mildred any better before she'd run off.

'I think we've already decided that Mrs Powell doesn't know what she's talking about. Now let's get back to these hamburgers . . .'

'Was she a whore?' Her cousin's interruption was unwelcome but couldn't be ignored. Frances had a pained expression on her face.

'No. Of course not,' said Ruby, sounding more confident than she felt. 'She may not have been perfect, but then none of us are, and besides, she was your mother. That has to be all that matters.'

'Did she leave because she didn't love me?'

'She was devastated after the death of your father. Grief made her ill. People can get very ill when somebody they love dies. Something cracks inside of them.'

'Like a plate left too near the gas?'

'Something like that.'

Ruby had made it up. She really couldn't recall whether Mildred had become ill after Uncle Sefton's death, but took the view that the hurt Frances was feeling – thanks to Mrs Powell – had to be dealt with and healed. If it meant she had to lie, then so be it. The girl didn't deserve to be upset like this.

Frances moped over her food all through supper, and although Ruby was fully aware of her mood, Stan Sweet was otherwise engaged. There were so many things on his mind, everything in fact from how well his cabbages were growing, to facing his true feelings about Bettina Hicks. Everyone in the village knew he regularly frequented Stratham House, ostensibly to take care of her garden. He hated the idea that he and she being friends was the subject of idle gossip.

In his estimation, gossiping about respectable folks was something only the idle had time to do. He didn't hold with it himself and never gossiped about anyone. So far, any accusing eyes that had strayed his way had been soundly stared into silence. But he couldn't do it for ever.

Things were somewhat confused and dour at present, what with that and young Charlie a bit under the weather; plus Frances was growing fast, and becoming the spit of her mother.

If he had been able to read Frances's mind, he would know that she was still trying to figure out a way of finding the woman who'd abandoned her as a child.

Stan turned back to his grandson. 'Now come on, young man. You'll never grow big and strong like your granddad if you don't eat your dinner.'

Young Charlie leaned away from his grandfather and the food, grizzling and rubbing at his eyes. No matter what Stan did, Charlie shook his head and clamped his mouth shut.

'Just a bit,' said Stan, a spoonful of potato and minced rabbit just inches from Charlie's mouth.

Charlie brought his fists down from his eyes, held them tightly in front of his mouth and shook his head.

The spoon clattered as Stan let it fall on to the plate. He sighed heavily, his brow furrowed. 'Do you think he's sickening for something? He usually clears his plate, especially cottage pie.'

Ruby thought her father looked tired. If things weren't going one hundred per cent right, he worried. Charlie not eating his dinner was enough to give him a sleepless night. The little boy had been listless for two days now.

'He looks as though he might be sickening for something,' said Ruby as she began gathering up the empty plates. 'A new tooth coming through, I expect.'

She stopped behind Frances's chair, surprised to see that her food was hardly touched either. 'Don't you like my cottage pie?'

Frances shrugged. 'I'm not hungry.'

'In that case, you can wash up.'

Stan spoke sharply. 'Good food is not going to go to waste in this house. It can be reheated tomorrow, my girl.'

Frances didn't look up from her plate but continued to trail a fork through her food. She was thinking how difficult life had become and how different things might have been if her father had lived and her mother hadn't run off. They'd probably have been very happy together. She might even have had brothers and sisters. In the happy world she'd lost, she wouldn't have had to wear hand-me-down dresses, and perhaps even the war might never have happened.

Life was unfair and getting more so. On looking at Ruby, a wave of instant resentment swept over her. She didn't want to wash up, and what was more to the point, she resented Ruby telling her what to do.

Why was it that older people thought they could boss younger people around? What right did they have? And as for her uncle . . .

Stan was very strict on wasting food. 'And no apple pie for them who don't eat their main course.' Stan looked up at Ruby as an afterthought occurred to him. 'It is apple pie, isn't it?'

'It is.'

'I don't want any,' said Frances. She left the table without asking, went straight to the sink and began the dishes, if begrudgingly.

Stan Sweet placed both hands in the small of his back, stretching his muscles as he got up from the table. 'Come on, young man,' he said, looking down at Charlie. 'Time to brush your teeth and catch the train to toy town. Say goodnight to everyone.'

Charlie usually yelped with glee at Stan's terminology for going to sleep, but not tonight. Tonight he seemed grumpy and uninterested.

Stan frowned. 'You don't seem yourself, little lad. A good night's sleep might do the trick. Now come on. Kiss your Auntie Ruby and Auntie Frances goodnight.'

Both Ruby and Frances kissed the little boy goodnight.

Ruby smoothed Charlie's hair back from his hot little face and frowned. It could be just tiredness, but he could also have a temperature.

'Bunz is already up there,' she said to Charlie when he asked for the toy rabbit he had loved for most of his life.

The little boy rubbed his eyes but grizzled despairingly and failed to say goodnight to anyone.

Ruby continued to clear away the things from the table while Frances washed up in complete silence.

One sideways glance told her that Frances was still mulling on what had been said about her mother. She thought about her own mother, who had died when she and Mary were still babies. There were times when she'd wondered how different life might have been if she'd lived. How would I feel, she wondered, if my mother had abandoned me and was still alive somewhere?

Picking up a clean tea towel, Ruby joined Frances at the kitchen sink.

Keeping her voice low, Ruby said, 'Look, Frances, if there's anything I can do to help you find your mother, I will.'

Frances bit her lip and did not raise her eyes from the sink full of dishes.

'Uncle Stan won't like it if you do. He hated my mother.' Her tone was bitter.

Ruby opened her mouth to protest that it wasn't true, but stopped herself. On those rare occasions when her father had mentioned Mildred, it was never flattering. Sometimes he'd sounded as though he blamed her for his brother's death.

Ruby took a deep breath. 'My father loves you. Just remember that.'

'Not as much as he loves you!' Frances said petulantly. 'After all, you're a daughter. I'm only his niece!'

'That's silly.'

'Is it?'

Ruby bit her bottom lip and thought about what to say next. Nothing came immediately to mind. She reminded herself that her cousin was barely sixteen. Sixteen was an awkward age. Youth was a confusing time, a rickety bridge between childhood and adulthood. She'll get over it, she told herself. We all have to go through it.

Distraction came in the form of her father coming back downstairs wearing a worried frown.

'Dad, you look as though you've found sixpence and lost half a crown,' Ruby said laughingly.

'I think that boy might be sickening for something.'

Frances kept her head down as she shook the wetness from her hands. Ruby slowed in wiping the last plate.

'I must admit he does seem a bit hot,' she said, frowning. 'How about we call for the doctor?'

Stan rubbed at his face. He was feeling tired. Absorbed in worrying about his grandson, he failed to notice his niece's sullen mood.

'I don't know,' he said, rubbing the back of his neck. 'But it's not like the little lad not to eat.'

The dishes were finished and ready to be placed in the old Welsh dresser.

Ruby gave her father's arm a reassuring squeeze. 'Don't worry, Dad. Children get their moods, unless he just didn't like my cottage pie,' she said jokingly.

Her father gave a half-laugh. 'I don't believe he didn't like it. I liked it. I would even go so far as to say that your cottage pie is better than our Mary's – though don't ever tell her that, will you!'

Ruby smiled. 'It's a secret.'

Looking decidedly sullen, Frances took her leave and muttered that she was off to bed. Both her Uncle Stan and Ruby wished her goodnight.

Ruby waited for the door to close behind her cousin before turning to her father, impatient to broach the subject Frances was so obviously mooning about.

He was just reaching for his pipe, thinking he'd go out back and have a smoke before settling down with his newspaper, when he caught sight of his daughter's face.

'Something troubling you?'

'Dad, I need to talk to you about Frances.' She purposely lowered her voice until it was only just above a whisper. Frances might be loitering in the hallway and she didn't want to be overheard. After making sure the door was firmly shut, she went on to tell him what Mrs Powell had said and how upset Frances had been. 'I didn't know what to say.'

He shook his head and bit down on the stem of his unlit pipe. 'That bloody woman! And she calls herself a Christian? It's my opinion there are better Christians outside the church on a Sunday than there are in it!'

Ruby blanched at her father swearing. It wasn't often he did that.

Ruby's voice was soft when she told him, 'Frances was – is – very upset. She asked me whether her mother left because she didn't love her. And Mrs Powell told her that her mother had been a whore – that was the word she used. I tried to reassure her, but in all honesty, I'm in no position to say anything about her mother. I was younger than Frances is now when she left. I really don't remember much about her.'

Stan Sweet chewed his pipe stem thoughtfully, picked up the poker and thrust it into the coals burning in the hearth. For a moment, he stood there silently, watching flickers of flame lick around the hard nubs of coal.

Finally, once he'd dredged through his memories of those times, he sighed heavily and shook his head. 'The day was bound to come and I suppose it's only right she should want to find out more about her, even meet her face to face. I suppose I should have a talk with her.'

'I think you should. Is there anything I can say to help?' asked Ruby.

His expression was grim as he replaced the poker on to a companion set at the side of the fire.

'It's my fault. I kept putting off speaking to her about it, hoping, I suppose, that she'd forget she ever had a mother – silly, now I think of it, but there you are . . .'

'I would want to know.' Ruby's tone was sharp.

Her father's jaw tightened. His thoughts went back to days gone by. If only Sefton hadn't died. If only there had been no Great War. If only Mildred had been better than she was. There was, he reflected, a whole roomful of 'if only's.

He retreated from his thoughts to see Ruby eyeing him in the stiff manner Sarah used to adopt when he was procrastinating about something important.

'When are you going to tell her?' Her tone was similar. She was definitely her mother's daughter. 'It's her mother, Dad. She should have the right to make up her own mind about meeting her or not.'

'She's only a girl still – she's too young to know what she wants. I'll tell her when she's older, when she's twenty-one!'

His raised voice made Ruby jump. Like swearing, raising his voice wasn't something he did often.

'By then her mother might have moved on from wherever you think she may be at present – or is that what you're hoping for? It's not right, Dad. You have to give her the choice. She's almost sixteen. She's old enough.'

He turned and stared at the grate, his face taking on the glow of the coal fire as though the words he needed to say were dancing along with the flames.

'You're right. I can't put it off any longer. I'll choose my time, though. Certainly not right now. She's gone to bed and we all need to be up early in the morning. There's bread to be made and woe betide me if there's not enough to fill the shelves!'

Ruby stood silently, wondering at her father's reluctance. A man who had fought in the Great War, as it was now called, the one that had lasted from 1914 to 1918, nobody could say he was cowardly. However, it seemed to Ruby that in this instance he really did fear talking to his niece about her mother. Fancy that! He'd braved fighting a bloodthirsty army back then, but lacked the courage to talk to a young girl!

Cosy in her bed later that night, Ruby was just falling asleep when she heard an owl calling to its mate. She guessed the sound came from the old ruined barn on the opposite side of the road, its roof fallen in, two walls tumbled down and a forest of thistles hiding its broken foundations. Her eyes flickered open. The room was pitch black. She heard the bark of a fox then the screech of a rabbit. The fox had caught its supper.

That's when it came to her about the hamburgers. Rabbit hamburgers. Perhaps she should rename them bunny burgers. That's a good name, she decided. As good as sweets by the Sweets. Yes, she thought as she slowly drifted into sleep. Bunny burgers. That's what she'd make for Frances's birthday party. Hopefully the party would go some way to cheering her up.

Stan Sweet heard that same owl calling from the dilapidated wreck of the barn in the field at the top of Cowhorn Hill. The haunting sound drew him from his bed.

Maintaining blackout rules, he didn't switch the light on before drawing back the curtains.

Across the road, a black shape flexed its great dark wings as it set out for a night's hunting. A ragged cloud left the moon with enough light for him to pick out the black outlines of trees. The scene was one he never tired of, yet tonight he wasn't really seeing it. Tonight he was thinking of what Gertrude Powell had said to young Frances. The woman wasn't right in the head, but that was no excuse for interfering in other folks' business. Yes, Mildred had been less than a lady, but to upset a child – and he still thought of Frances as a child – was unforgiveable.

He resolved there and then that some time tomorrow he would speak to Frances about her mother, but first he would call in on Bettina Hicks, tell her what had occurred and ask her advice. He needed a woman's counsel and he still thought of Ruby as a girl. Bettina could sometimes see the better angle to take, though on this occasion he doubted it. There were other options, of course. He could go along and tackle Mrs Powell direct, but then what good would that do? The fact was that while Mildred wasn't a whore, she had been a good-time girl, probably still was. But how would Frances take the truth and was there anything he could do to help the situation?

Tomorrow, he thought, turning away from the window. Sleep on it and see how it looks tomorrow.

CHAPTER EIGHT

Early the following morning, Ruby got herself ready for her morning's work at a local factory. Yet another talk and baking demonstration was on the cards. The high spot would be mentioning bunny burgers, '*to impress our American allies*'.

Her father's voice interrupted her thoughts.

'Is young Charlie still in bed?' her father asked anxiously, his arms full of the bread he'd baked freshly that morning.

'Yes. I thought a good sleep might do him good.' She paused. 'You will let me know if he gets worse?'

Her father promised that he would. 'Try not to worry.'

It was easy to say, and although she would have preferred to stay home and look after her nephew, she had a job to do. Ruby loved her job, but today Charlie would be on her mind. She consoled herself with the fact that her father and her cousin Frances would be there to look after the little chap.

'Just keep an eye on him,' Ruby added.

'If he isn't any better after a good sleep, I'll call the doctor.'

Ruby frowned. 'I feel awful leaving you with the problem, but I've already promised . . .'

He waved a hand dismissively. 'I brought up three of you after your mother died. I know what to do. Anyway, Frances is here to run the shop so I can spend some time with the boy. You get on to your work. I'll pop up now and see how he is.'

At one time Ruby had disliked driving, but that was when she'd first started working for the Ministry of Food. Once Johnnie had gone away, she had taken the bull by the horns, slipped behind the wheel of the little black Austin and drove confidently to the various venues. As she hurtled along country lanes and wider roads, she would smile at the thought of Johnnie's cheeky ways and witty remarks, and how he never allowed her to get above her station. No airs and graces for him, she thought, smiling to herself. If there was a man to keep her feet firmly on the ground, John Smith was that man.

Hostile at first to what he regarded as non-essential war work, their relationship had not started well. After a while, once they'd got to know each other, he'd come round, especially after she'd involved him in her cooking demonstrations – much to his earlier reluctance to get involved.

At one point she'd forced him into an old-fashioned cross-over apron and got him to help her mixing and making dough. Amused at the sight of a man wearing a flowered apron over his khaki uniform, the women had laughed uproariously, his leg pulled mercilessly.

But that was before he'd gone away to serve in the Far East.

In the midst of mixing a bowl of dough or slicing up the ingredients for a meatless pie, she found herself glancing up at the audience and sometimes, just sometimes, thinking she saw him sitting there. On other occasions, she found herself surveying those standing against the walls of the church hall, factory canteen or social club, seeking the familiar sardonic smile, the craggy looks, the amusement simmering in his eyes.

Writing letter after letter, she'd kept him informed of what was happening in the village. She'd also sent him simple tips for eating in a country where rice was a staple.

The natives add spices to meat and fish for a very good reason: it hides the taste of bad food and also preserves it. Be careful what you eat! I hear people in the Far East are very partial to roast dog! Or even cat! Still, never mind their eating habits. How about I tell you of some of the recipes I've been given – well-meaning souls, but . . .

Listing some of the terrible recipes people had given her she hoped would raise his spirits, make him laugh despite whatever privations he was suffering. Some of the recipes were laugh-out-loud disgusting. She'd smiled the night before as she finished writing the latest letter on the flimsiest of paper. Terrible recipes to make him laugh out loud as well as heartfelt words about the ordinary things of home she thought he would be missing.

My dear John,

How do you fancy sheep's stomach stuffed with onions and squashed seagull? It was hard not to laugh out loud when the old man gave it to me. I had travelled all the way down to a village on the north Somerset coast – I can't say where – to give a cooking demonstration. The old man kept sheep and gathered berries from the hedge-rows. He said the bird had been run over by a military vehicle, but it was a big fat one with plenty of meat on its bones and that he never had been one to waste anything. I tried to appear interested but had already decided that seagull meat must taste a bit fishy, and that even in these times of scarce supply, mixing it with a sheep's stomach does not constitute a feast for the faint-hearted.

Charlie is growing and getting into mischief. I am so glad he came to us, especially for Dad's sake. It was hard to lose his only son.

Mary is in Lincolnshire with Michael. They have now had their first child, Beatrice. I'm desperate to see my new little niece, so is Dad for that matter. Two grandchildren. He talks about it as though nobody has ever had grandchildren before.

Frances is growing into a pretty girl and thinks herself grown up now that she's left school and helps in the shop. She has an American boyfriend whose name is Ed. I'm not sure where their relationship will go, perhaps nowhere. I know what I was like at that age. Love was wonderful – though on reflection it wasn't really love at all!

Just in case you're wondering, I do go out dancing and generally out and about, but there's nobody serious on the horizon. I'm too busy being the efficient employee of the Ministry of Food, besides taking care of Dad and the family.

I hope the recipe makes you laugh. I also hope you are faring well. I take the fact that I have received no replies to my letters means that no news really is good news.

Just to reassure you, I still think of that day when we picnicked at the railway station, the colour of the autumn leaves and the things we said. I shall always remember them. I hope you will too.

Love, Ruby.

She would post the letter on her way to the factory where today's demonstration would take place. Perhaps this time she might receive a reply. So far she'd had no news from him since the fall of Singapore. Was the Red Cross really doing its best? If they were, it didn't seem their efforts were hard enough.

Stan Sweet had counselled her not to give up hope but to take a pragmatic view.

'He may be in a place where there is no pillar-box on the street corner.' He said it good humouredly, but Ruby wasn't fooled. Rumours were circulating about the harsh treatment handed out to captives by the Japanese army. Nothing had been officially confirmed so she had to believe that was all they were – rumours. In the meantime, she had to get on with her life.

Declan O'Malley hovered in the background. She'd first met him one day when she'd been delivering bread to the home of Mrs Darwin-Kemp.

He'd struck her as officious, standing there like a solid wall between her and the larder. Despite or probably because he was a military policeman, he had the capacity to source food and luxury items that even Ed Bergman wasn't privy to. Nylon stockings were number one on his enticement list. So was tobacco, for which Stan Sweet was very grateful.

Ruby put on her smart three-quarter-length coat she had made from a creamy coloured blanket, teaming it with a cream skirt cut down from an old pair of cricket trousers. It was just a question of opening the stitching on the inner legs and sewing them together, trimming the lower part of the legs with a pair of sharp crimping sheers. The result was an ideal outfit for spring.

'I'd look like a tramp if I wasn't good with a needle and thread,' she muttered.

She stopped to admire her hat in the hallstand mirror. What wonders one could do with old bits and pieces! Feathers and stuffed birds had once decorated the broad-brimmed hat she wore – another item from Bettina Hicks's amazing collection of fabrics and old clothes.

Ruby sighed as she pulled on her gloves. It was difficult leaving her father to cope, and Frances didn't seem to have her wits about her at present.

Frances came through from the back, looking better than the night before, though Ruby sensed she was still harbouring questions about her mother.

'You look nice.'

'Thank you. Look at these,' said Ruby, raising her skirts so Frances could admire her stockings.

'From darling Declan, I suppose?'

'Of course.' Ruby paused, not quite understanding the condemnation in her cousin's voice. 'Don't you like Declan?' She hoped Frances still thought he was too old for her, though she had to admit that both young girls and women old enough to know better rarely failed to fall for him.

Frances shrugged as though she couldn't decide either way. 'He's okay.'

'Okay? Don't let Dad hear you say that. He doesn't like us talking American slang.'

'I might marry one, then I'll talk slang all the time.'

Ruby sighed. There was no point in arguing with Frances when she was in one of these moods.

'I'm off. I'll be back as soon as I can. And Frances . . .'

'Hmm?'

'Forget what Mrs Powell said. She's a wicked woman.'

Frances's lowered eyes hid her thoughts.

The smell of freshly baked bread permeated the morning air both inside and outside the grey stone building that was Sweets' Bakery. The bakery with its front shop, its gas-fired bread oven, and the family's living accommodation, was situated at the top of Cowhorn Hill in the village of Oldland Common just a few miles to the east of Bristol.

In times past, the village had been famous for producing shoes and boots for the Great War. There had once also been a thriving coal industry, but that was back in the nineteenth century. The coal seams were thought to have been the outcrop of the South Wales coal fields and as such were narrow and the access to the coal face no more than three feet high. Men had hacked at those faces with small pick axes and died young.

The village had fallen back to the way it used to be, farming being predominant, though of late some of the village had found jobs in munitions and further away at Fry's Chocolate Factory at Somerdale in Keynsham, thanks to a direct railway connection. Chocolate production had been reduced at the factory, Rolls Royce using the generous facilities to build Merlin engines for Spitfires and Hurricanes.

Today Ruby was giving a talk and demonstration at that very factory. Women who used to check chocolate for flaws in the finish now checked the small pieces that made up an aero engine. They were valued for their small fingers and sharp eyes.

Ruby admired them, swapping something so sweet for something so sinister. She could imagine what the place smelled of in peacetime – the sticky sugary smell of chocolate thick on the air. Now the air smelled of heavy oil.

The upturned faces in front of her looked tired. Some of them had red-rimmed eyes, either caused from working long hours or because they'd been crying. Each one of these women was likely to have family serving in one of the armed forces, either that or their loved ones, even themselves, spent time fire-watching or doing something else after working long hours in engineering factories, all turned over to produce armaments for the war effort.

'Right,' she said, pleased she'd been blessed with a resonant voice. 'Let's see what we can do about baking a cake without eggs. It's either that or think about the amazing tricks you can do with dried egg!'

There followed a ripple of laughter. Everyone, including herself, had suffered both failures and successes with the vagaries of powdered egg. Ruby always began the session in a fun way before going on to stress the importance of supporting the merchant navy in their efforts to feed the nation.

'But first, let's go through the basics. I have a list here kindly provided by Brown and Poulson – and it's not just about custard powder.'

Another titter of laughter. Everyone knew that Brown and Poulson made custard powder.

She held up the booklet in which was listed general advice and tips to help the housewife make do with the little she had available. She began reeling them off, though not without advising the women that there was a whole pile of leaflets waiting for them on the table on the way out.

'Number one, do not waste any scraps of raw or cooked fat. They can all be rendered down and the fat used for frying or baking. We all know how difficult it is to get hold of fat, sugar and eggs to bake a cake. Let's start with a recipe that does not call for eggs. Ladies – and those few gentlemen who are present – let me introduce you to the eggless cake!'

Murmurs of conversation trickled through the women assembled. Ruby read out the recipe before making it, though informed them that the recipe was contained in yet another leaflet they could take with them on their way out.

'Right,' she called out while enjoying the warmth of the oven behind her that some thoughtful soul had lit in anticipation of her using it. She announced each ingredient before adding it to the mixture. 'This is the recipe for eggless cake. No need to write it down. All the details are in one of the leaflets over there by the door.' Once the mixture was in the tin, she opened the oven door. 'Now! That looks good. Let's get it into the oven.'

The stove worked a treat, the audience clapped and Ruby felt tired but well satisfied. For just one final moment, her eyes yet again surveyed the crowded canteen. Some friendly faces smiled back at her, but most were talking among themselves. All the same she felt sure the demonstration had been a success.

The canteen manager wove his way through the crowd. Ruby stood there waiting for him to shake her hand. Instead, he ducked behind her and checked the gas taps.

'Can't be too careful,' he grumbled. It was obvious he thought these talks and demonstrations were a waste of time and considered the big gas stove his personal property.

Ignoring the man's rudeness, Ruby concentrated on packing up the items she'd used. She had suggested cutting the cakes up at the end of the demonstration to serve to the workers there and then, but Mr Gillespie, the canteen manager, intervened. 'Just leave them there. We'll cut them up and serve them for pudding tomorrow with custard – if we've got enough milk!'

Ruby gritted her teeth. 'This food belongs to the Ministry of Food. I can distribute it as I see fit.'

His rudeness persisted. 'Then they wouldn't want it wasted, would they!'

'Now look here!' She was just about to put him in his place, when another man came up behind her and spoke.

'Ruby?'

It was Andrew Sinclair. Andrew worked for the Ministry of Food and organised cookery demonstrations and talks on the wireless.

She wasn't that pleased to see him.

'Andrew. I wasn't expecting to see you here. Official business, is it?' Why was it her teeth ached when she spoke to him? He'd been sweet on Mary before she'd married Michael. Lately, he seemed to have transferred his affections to Ruby. Not that either one of them had ever encouraged him.

'Indeed it is, Miss Sweet, or may I call you Ruby, seeing as we have known each other for some time?'

'You've called me by my Christian name before, Andrew. Nothing's changed.'

He ignored the put-down. 'Can we talk?'

'Of course we can.'

He helped her pack everything up and for that she was grateful. He chatted as he packed, asking how the family was and outlining her timetable for the next fourteen days. However, he looked as though he had something else in mind. She waited for it to come.

'Now there's something very special I want to talk to you about. My mother has suggested you give a talk at the Dorchester to her ladies' circle. Some of them are ladies both in nature and in title. Do you think you could do that?'

'At the Dorchester?'

'Yes. Don't sound so surprised. My mother is very well connected.'

'I do hope you are not harbouring ulterior motives, Andrew.'

He gave a nervous laugh followed by an equally nervous cough. 'Of course not, dear lady. Of course not.'

Ruby prided herself on being able to read Andrew quite well. Her mind was working overtime. London was roughly halfway between Bristol and Scampton, where her sister lived. This might be a good opportunity to visit her sister, and she intended taking full advantage.

Pasting on her sweetest smile she said, 'That sounds very interesting, Andrew. How very clever of your mother to suggest it. I think it would be a very good idea indeed. Can I leave it with you to arrange the details? Though not yet. I have to check my timetable.'

Andrew beamed so broadly Ruby thought his face was going to burst like a balloon. 'Of course.'

'Then that's settled.'

'Can I give you a lift?'

'No. The Ministry have seen fit to provide me with an official car. Remember?'

He looked disappointed. 'Oh, yes. I forgot. My, my. Well aren't you the lucky one. You never used to like driving.'

'Needs must. Drivers are in short supply, nowadays. Most men are off fighting the enemy.'

Andrew, who she knew was definitely in the right age group, fidgeted briefly with his spectacles. 'Ah, yes. I wish I too could be there, but what with my sight and my flat feet. And Mother, of course. She would be terrified during a bombing raid without me around.'

'I dare say she would,' murmured Ruby.

Back to being his bumptious self, Andrew's dewy eyes peered at her through his glasses. 'And I suppose your Corporal Smith has let you down.'

Ruby gave him a fixed stare. 'Yes, if you can call being imprisoned in a Japanese prisoner of war camp letting me down. He is slightly indisposed,' she snapped.

'Ah. Yes. Yes.' He nodded three or four times but gave no sign of being at all put out by her attitude. 'So I can count on you to fulfil this very invaluable role at the Society of Titled Ladies?'

Was the man completely insensitive? Ruby sighed. She took it that the Titled Ladies he referred to would be very similar in status and attitude to Mrs Darwin-Kemp. Not her type of women at all. She much preferred the cheery women and girls working in the factories or doing their bit for the searchlight units. As for service women and nurses, well she had to take her hat off to them most of all. But this was England, and Andrew loomed over her like a small barrage balloon in a suit. Ruby sighed with resignation.

'As I've already said to you, let me know the details when you have them. In the meantime, you must excuse me. I've had a long day and wish to go home.'

He used one fingertip to push his spectacles more firmly on to the bridge of his nose. As he did so, she noticed he had beautifully polished nails, each one symmetrically cut.

I expect his mother insists, she thought to herself. Not wishing him to see her knowing smile, she turned away. As she did so, she wondered if his mother also still checked behind his ears!

That morning, after Ruby had left for that day's assignment, Stan Sweet was holding the fort in the bakery while Frances took young Charlie out in his pushchair. When the lad was on top form, he would walk anywhere, but as he was quite poorly at present, the old pushchair was heaved out.

Stan watched Frances bundle young Charlie in warm clothes and place him in his pushchair.

'He'll enjoy a bit of fresh air,' she said loftily.

Her manner was a bit more abrupt than usual, but on this occasion he did not reprimand her. She had a lot on her mind.

Whoever had coined the phrase about there being a spectre at the feast had surely been referring to his absent sister-in-law. He'd always thought good riddance to bad rubbish, but the ghost of Mildred Sweet was coming back to haunt him.

Perhaps it was cowardice, or merely compliance, but he still didn't consider it the right time to be tackling his niece with a few home truths about her mother. Neither was he ready to discuss Frances having a reunion with a woman who would only disappoint her. First thing first, he would have a chat with his dear friend Bettina.

'I need to call in on Mrs Hicks when you get back,' he said to Frances. 'So, don't be late.'

Frances, her full lips clenched in a tight line, muttered something almost inaudible that sounded like 'I won't be', though it could just as easily have been a tad cheekier. He couldn't be sure.

The shop door shut behind his niece and grandson, the sound reverberating slowly into silence, leaving only the resonant clunking of the oak wall clock's swinging brass pendulum.

Stan sighed, clenched his pipe firmly in his teeth but didn't light it. Most of his customers didn't mind the smell of his pipe, but in a bid to save tobacco, it had become a habit that he never smoked in the shop.

He stood behind the counter, surveying the shelves of bread, and the odd baked goods that Ruby still managed to make from whatever spare ingredients were to hand.

The brass bell above the shop door clanged as Mrs Martin came in carrying a sack. Her round face was red with exertion and she was puffing and panting as though she'd been running for a bus and had overtaken it in the effort.

'A leg of pork,' she confided swiftly without even saying hello. 'Too big for my oven, so if you could oblige, Stan, I'd much appreciate it. Our Joey's coming home on leave. He's bringing his girlfriend with him. Hope she ain't too stuck up. She'll have to take us as she finds us!'

Stan grabbed the sack from Mrs Martin before it dripped blood on his nice clean counter.

'Stuck up? Good grief, Lilly, has your boy found himself a duchess?'

'Not so far as I know. She's from up north. Liverpool, I think.'

'Then take it from me she's not likely to be stuck up. A lot of the girls up there are mill hands, hard-working girls without a stuck-up bone in their body.'

'Can you roast it in your bread oven overnight?' she whispered. At the same time she leaned forward while glancing nervously over her shoulder, despite there being no other customers at present in the bakery. 'And there's a bit of shoulder in there for you.'

Stan didn't need to be told that the pig had been born, reared, fattened and slaughtered without the knowledge of the Ministry of Agriculture. He used to keep a few pigs of his own, but the demands of the bakery, and the fact that his partner in pigs had been apprehended for trading on the black market, had recently put paid to his operation. The pigs had been disposed of. A shoulder of pork was worth the risk.

'Joey's been in Italy. He got wounded,' Mrs Martin continued.

'Nothing serious, I hope.'

'Nothing that won't mend. Got shot in the ankle.'

It crossed Stan's mind fleetingly that Joey might have caused the injury himself. He'd seen plenty of incidents on the Western Front, tired, homesick young men shooting themselves in the foot.

'Oh well,' said Stan, wisely preferring not to give voice to what he suspected. 'It'll do the lad good to be home.'

He might have learned more about what Joey had been up to, as well as further details of the girl he was bringing home with him, but the shop door swung open.

In a knee-jerk reaction, Stan let the sack fall to the floor behind the counter. Anticipating an official from the Ministry of Agriculture, Mrs Martin's ruddy face paled.

'My goodness, Lilly. You look as though you were expecting to see Jack the Ripper coming through this door.'

There was a distinct twinkle in the pale blue eyes of Bettina Hicks.

Relieved at the sight of her, Stan slapped his big palms on the counter. 'Bettina! Mrs Martin was just telling me that her Joey's been injured and is on his way home for some well-earned leave.'

No mention of the pig, but Stan went out of his way to exude a lot of enthusiasm for Mrs Martin's news. Actually, he wasn't sure whether he would recognise Joey by sight: Mrs Martin had a whole battalion of sons and almost as many daughters.

'That's wonderful,' said Bettina, her eyes sparkling and her pale pink lips curving into a smile. Anyone else might have asked for details, but there existed a distinct rapport between her and Stan Sweet: she could read his expressions just as easily as he could read hers. The finer points would be discussed in private.

Mrs Martin slapped a meaty hand against her thigh before adjusting her battered straw hat. 'Can't stand 'ere gossiping. I've a lot to do before our Joey gets back.'

'I'll have your special order ready for you first thing in the morning,' Stan called after her.

After she'd gone, Bettina looked at him and chuckled. 'I take it her special order is more than extra bread for Joey's return.'

'That's about right. How do you fancy coming round for a bit of roast pork on Sunday?'

'Enough for all of us?'

'I should think so!'

Stan's joviality was short-lived.

A small frown creased Bettina's smooth forehead.

'Something's wrong. What is it, Stan?'

He shook his head, looked beyond her to the shop door and suggested she come out back. 'I'll stick the kettle on.'

Leaning on the stick that helped support her right hip, though did little to alleviate the pain, Bettina followed him through.

On seeing she was having a bad day with her hip, he suggested she sit down while he made the tea. With a sigh of relief, his dear friend and confidante sank into one of the two armchairs placed on either side of the kitchen range.

After handing her a cup and saucer, he sat in the chair opposite her.

As she took a sip, Bettina scrutinised his face over the rim of her teacup. Sensing he had something serious to say, she kept silent while giving him time to gather his thoughts.

'It's our Frances. She's been asking questions about her mother. She wants to know where she is.'

'Oh. I see,' said Bettina, gently placing her cup back into its saucer. 'It was bound to happen sooner or later.'

Stan sighed. He'd heard this all before and said it himself a few times. 'I was hoping it wouldn't.'

'I don't think that was very realistic.'

Stan shook his head. 'I suppose not.'

'She's at the right age to become curious.'

'She might not have done if Mrs Powell hadn't thrown a few nasty comments at her.'

'Ah!' said Bettina with a deep nod of her head. 'Gertrude Powell. I might have guessed. If ever a woman was going to cast aspersions, it's her! What did she say exactly?'

As she awaited the details, she took another sip of her tea. Her eyes flickered with surprise as she studied Stan's face. His skin was a little greyer than usual and there were dark circles beneath his eyes.

'I've only got it second-hand from our Ruby but she said something to Frances along the lines of "your mother was a slut".'

'Not entirely untrue, but cruel to say such a thing to Frances.'

Stan looked a little taken aback at Bettina's honesty.

'You know it yourself, Stan,' she said quite abruptly in a bid to pre-empt any condemnation. 'Still, that's as may be. The poor girl must be terribly upset.'

'She is, and you know how it is at that age. One minute she's a child, and the next minute . . . Suddenly it seems the world and especially grown-ups are against you. I'm having trouble knowing what to do.'

Bettina looked down into her teacup, turning it slightly in the saucer so it made a tinkling sound. She had an inkling Stan was hiding something. 'Do you know where her mother is?' she asked pensively.

When Stan hung his head, Bettina immediately knew she'd guessed right.

'You do know.' She fixed him with a slightly accusing look.

He nodded. 'Yes. I do.'

'I won't ask you where she is,' Bettina said resolutely. 'All I will say is that you have no choice. Frances is at an age when she's searching for who she is. She wants to fit into the adult world, and in order to do that, she has to know where she comes from and why she's where she is.'

Just like Bettina to cut straight to the chase.

Stan eyed the handsome face of his dearest female friend and the serene expression in Bettina's powder-blue eyes. Like her eyes, she was soft, slightly fluffy but steadfast. He couldn't quite recall the exact colour of her hair when she was a girl, perhaps because he quite liked the colour it was now, gloriously pale grey and still swept up into the cottage loaf style of her youth.

Stan sighed. 'I don't relish talking to our Frances.'

'You don't have to relish it. It's your responsibility to do it.'

'You're right,' he said, nodding his head in agreement, though he still couldn't help feeling reluctant. 'I have to do it.'

'I saw Frances pushing Charlie up the High Street,' Bettina commented, changing the subject tactfully. 'I thought he didn't like being put in his pushchair any longer.'

'That's another worry. He's a bit out of sorts at present. We think he's teething, but we're not sure. I'll see how he is tonight and if there's no improvement, I'll take him to the morning surgery.'

'Poor little mite. Still, better to be safe than sorry.'

Her knees made a clicking sound as she got to her feet. Stan's knees made a similar sound when he got to his. They looked at each other and shook their heads.

'Sounds like we're two of a kind,' he said, with something close to a smile.

'Or at least our knees are,' exclaimed Bettina.

As he escorted her to the door she thought about their friendship and their past. They had known each other most of their lives, though she had only returned to the village a few years ago. In Stan's case, there was much pain in his past, what with the Great War, losing his wife Sarah, his brother and his son Charlie.

In Bettina's case, there was a secret she would take to her grave, involving an action she'd taken that she thought few people would understand. Now that her friendship with Stan had deepened, she sometimes considered unburdening herself to him, but so far had drawn back. Today she had come as close as she ever had to doing so, especially seeing as Gertrude Powell had been mentioned.

I'm a coward, she thought. Yet again I drew back, but I won't always. The day will come when I will whisper that secret into somebody's ear. But not now, not until the time is right.

Stan watched as Bettina made her way across the road. The day was fresh and the air smelled as though rain was imminent. Just right for the garden, Stan thought.

Bettina was almost lost to his sight, by which time he'd planned his jobs for the rest of the day. Stack earth around the spuds, fork the earth around the carrots and take a peek in the ramshackle greenhouse he'd built to see how the tomato plants were doing.

Just as he turned to go back into the shop, the sound of whistling made him pause. Melvyn Chance, the village postman, was striding along towards him, his face cheery and his baggy trousers flapping around his skinny legs.

Not only was Melvyn Chance the village postman, he was also their air-raid warden. The former occupation gave him some respectability and went a little way to blotting out his infamous past when he'd been a member of the National Socialist Party, its leader, Oswald Mosley, a great admirer of Adolf Hitler and the Nazi regime. Melvyn had resigned from the party just after war broke out, but no one had forgotten or forgiven his involvement with people who were now their enemies.

Melvyn smiled, though a wary look flickered in his eyes. 'Good morning, Mr Sweet.'

Stan grunted a response. As far as he was concerned, Melvyn Chance didn't deserve to be acknowledged. He for one had never forgiven him his nefarious allegiance.

Stan would never warm to Melvyn and never forget what he had once been. Melvyn was alive and kicking, but it was thanks to Hitler and the Nazis that his son, Charlie, was dead.

Stan snatched the post from Melvyn without a word of thanks. Melvyn, who knew better than to linger, dashed off. He didn't resume his whistling until he was posting letters through letterboxes a few houses along and beyond Stan's reach.

Stan scowled at Melvyn's retreating figure, the hunched shoulders, rounded body and stiffly striding legs. If it were down to him, the man would be locked up. Even if he hadn't been a member of Oswald Mosley's outfit, he would still have disliked him. A weasel born a weasel remained a weasel. That was his opinion.

Once back inside the shop, he glanced briefly at what he'd been given. There were the usual manila envelopes bulging with advice from the Ministry of Food and other official bodies.

It wasn't until he was back behind the counter and, there again, not until he had served a few customers, that he noticed the postcard that had slipped between the bulky envelopes. He frowned at it, noticing it was addressed to his daughter, Ruby. It was plain, grubby and stamped with the insignia of the Red Cross. A sudden roll of apprehension rumbled in his stomach. Official. Swiss postmark.

Switzerland! Never in his life had he received any item of mail from a foreign country. The feeling of apprehension rolled in his stomach even more determinedly than when he'd spotted the insignia of the Red Cross. Wasn't it based in that country?

His hand shook as he turned it over, saw the scribbled writing – in pencil by the look of it. In the lower right-hand corner he saw what looked like a reddish muddy-looking smudge. On closer examination, he deduced the convoluted lines of a thumbprint. The postcard was addressed to Ruby, though he couldn't help but read it. She wouldn't mind.

As he read the words, his eyes filled with moisture and it felt as though something sharp was stuck in his throat.

Dear Ruby. I am a prisoner of the Japanese but am being treated well. Love, Johnnie Smith.

CHAPTER NINE

That evening, the smell of cottage pie filled the kitchen. Frances had been careful to put it into the oven early enough so it would be ready to dish up by the time Ruby got in. The smell alone was enough to tell her it was ready, and anyway Ruby's instructions had been quite specific.

A blanket of heat reddened her face as she reached in with both hands. 'Stand back. It's piping hot.'

'I am stood back,' Stan grumbled, wondering when it was that he'd started taking orders from the younger members of his family. He purposely kept his attention fixed on what was happening around him, anything rather than let his gaze stray to the postcard from Switzerland, currently sitting behind the clock on the mantelpiece with the rest of the post. Get supper over first or nobody would eat a morsel.

Thrusting out her bottom lip, Frances blew upwards at the tress of dark hair falling over her forehead as she manoeuvred the pie dish on to the cast-iron trivet standing in the middle of the scrubbed pine kitchen table.

Stan Sweet stood silently studying her, thinking to himself that she'd suddenly grown up without him really noticing it. Dark hair and soft brown eyes, a girlish though developing figure. His head throbbed from the array of thoughts crashing through it – like dodgem cars at the fairground, bumping and banging and not really going anywhere. He felt exasperated, worried. Most of all he tried to recall the last time in his life when he'd felt as helpless as he did now. Ruby would welcome the postcard, but it said nothing, and in doing so said a lot. Reading it might worry her even more. As for Frances and her present mood . . .

The arrival of the postcard this morning only added to his feeling of helplessness. Although Johnnie had written that he was a prisoner of the Japanese and was being well treated, he couldn't shift the nagging doubt that things might not be that way at all. Johnnie would have said more. He was sure of it.

The sound of the small car chugging to a halt outside the shop door only served to make his thoughts rush around in his head at a greater speed than before. If anyone had said at the beginning of the war that his daughter Ruby would bear the burdens of this household with uncommon efficiency while holding down a very responsible war job, he would never have believed them.

Because it was too dark to go round the back of the bakery and into the kitchen, Ruby habitually came through the shop door, the old bell above it jangling as she opened it just enough to slip through before closing it behind her.

He made a mental note to silence that bell on a night so it wouldn't wake anybody up. Then he wondered why he should suddenly think of doing that. The answer came swiftly: because its jangling gets on your nerves. Since when had it affected him so badly?

Ruby's smiling face, flushed by the night air, appeared around the door. 'Oh, but it's good to be home.' With a determined grip on the handle, she closed the door firmly behind her.

Stan felt a clutch of nerves knot in his stomach. The postcard. He would have to tell her about the postcard, but dare he also tell her his thoughts on the message?

The first thing Ruby noticed was the pie and the bowl of carrots and swedes Frances had added to the table.

'That looks good.'

She did not notice the pensive look in her father's eyes. She was tired, hungry and very glad to be home.

Home wasn't just about warmth, good food and loving faces. Familiar things counted too, all contributing to what made a house – or even a bakery – a home.

Coals glowed in the grate of the old range, tapestry-covered cushions were plumped up in the fireside chairs, plates and cutlery gleamed with welcome: she relished them all.

Her first task on taking off her hat was to make a big fuss of Charlie. Although today had been enjoyable and well received by the factory workers, Charlie had never been far from her mind.

The little boy's bottom lip stayed petulantly thrust forward, his small knuckles rubbing at his eyes.

Face creased with concern, Ruby leaned over him. 'Charlie. Are you still not feeling well?'

For a moment he stopped grizzling as she stroked his hair back from his face.

'My beautiful boy. Your cheeks are very hot.' She frowned, certain he had a temperature.

'He won't eat,' said Frances. 'He hasn't had much to drink, either.'

With a pain in her heart, Ruby surveyed the dish of cottage pie, the ingredients well mashed up and set in front of him in his own little dish. She frowned as she ran the back of her fingers down his flushed cheeks. 'I hope it is just his teeth, though there's always something like measles and chickenpox going around.'

For a moment, the two cousins were silent with their own thoughts. Ruby was worried about Charlie more than she was about Frances. In fact, she felt resentment towards her cousin. Couldn't she have remained her old sweet, though slightly rebellious self for another year at least? Best of all, stay a child until the war was over?

Her resentment continued to simmer and might have stayed that way except that Frances was suddenly her old self again, asking her how her day had been.

'Fine,' Ruby replied, all signs of resentment kept firmly subdued. 'They were a nice crowd.' Funny, she thought. I'm getting so het up over Charlie and Frances, I'm forgetting about Andrew's offer and the possibility of seeing Mary sometime soon. On the drive home, Ruby had practised announcing that she was going to see Mary, thanks to an invitation from the Ministry of Food to go to London. Now didn't seem the right time to mention it.

Frances persisted in trying to persuade her young charge to eat. 'Come on, Charlie. It's lovely. See?' She pretended to taste the contents of the spoon before again proffering it to the little boy. The spoon was pushed away. The child continued to grizzle, rub his eyes and look increasingly red-faced.

'Perhaps he's just over tired,' said Stan Sweet. As a widower who had chosen to bring up his children all alone without the aid of a new wife, he prided himself on knowing as much about childish ailments as anybody. Thanks to his efforts, his children had turned out well and he was proud of them. His son Charlie had been the apple of his eye before he'd drowned courtesy of a German U-boat attack in the North Atlantic. Mary was married to Flight Officer Michael Dangerfield, and now had a little daughter. Ruby was a respected Home Front Economist. Even his brother's daughter, Frances, had turned out well. She was a bright girl and loved the baby, his grandson, with all her heart.

Ruby frowned. There was something about the way her father spoke that made her think he wasn't really stating what he was thinking or that there was something else on his mind. 'Let me feel his face again.'

She laid her hand on one cheek then the other. The little boy seemed to appreciate the coolness of her palm, quieting for a moment before she removed her hands and he began grizzling again.

Ruby looked at her father and knew immediately that he was as worried as she was. 'His cheeks do feel hot. Perhaps it's more than teething. Perhaps he's got a cold.'

Her father stared blankly, so immobile that she was half inclined to go over and shake him to make sure he hadn't turned to stone. Instead, she turned back to her nephew.

'Is that what it is, Charlie? A bit of a cold and those nasty teeth making it worse?'

Sighing, she clenched her hands in front of her, fingers tangled, and saw the deepness of her father's frown.

'I can't help thinking it's got worse,' she said to her father. 'I'm worried.'

'Maybe he's just teething. I remember his dad teething – cried the place down, he did . . .' But even as Stan said the words, he looked uncertain.

'Look, Dad. I think we should call the doctor. I'll pay if . . .'

Her father glared. 'Are you insinuating that I'm too mean to find the money for my own grandson?'

Ruby was taken aback. He wasn't a man for raising his voice to his children unless it was warranted. She wanted to shout at him that she had enough pressure on her without him yelling at her like that, but she had no wish to make the situation any worse than it already was.

Thrusting her jaw defiantly forward, she stated what her intention had been. 'There's no need to shout. I was just offering to pay for the doctor courtesy of the Ministry of Food. There's nothing wrong with that, is there?'

'So that's it! Just because the Ministry of Food pay you more than a hard-working man . . .'

'Dad! This is ridiculous!' She couldn't believe she was hearing this.

'A chit of a girl—'

'I am not a chit of a girl! I'm a grown woman!'

'I can pay!'

She knew there had been times when they were children that there hadn't always been enough money to pay for a doctor. Even now it wasn't easy.

'Dad, I know you can, and I think we should—'

Charlie began crying in earnest. Clutching his dish of untouched food with both hands, Frances looked from her cousin to her uncle.

'Do you two have to shout at each other? Can't you see you're upsetting the poor kid?'

'Less of that American slang in my house,' Stan shouted, half rising from his chair, one fist clenched as though he might lash out at her.

Frances couldn't believe what she was seeing and hearing. She slammed the dish on to the table. 'The sooner I leave this house the better!'

Ruby and her father stopped facing each other down and looked at her.

Frances was adamant. 'Don't look at me like that. I mean what I say. I am going! I promise you I am!'

'I'm sorry.' Ruby shook her head and blinked as though a light had suddenly been switched on.

Stan's stance and bad temper were unchanged. 'Then go if you want to go, you selfish little baggage! After all I've done for you.'

'Dad!' Ruby made a dash for Charlie. With all this noise going on, he should have been screaming at the top of his lungs. Instead, there was a wheezing sound from his throat, as though he were trying to catch his breath, as though he couldn't breathe.

With rising panic, she picked up the little boy, holding him so that his head lay on her shoulder.

'He's so hot. We have to get the doctor – now!'

Her father stared at her helplessly. Frances looked frightened, but also angry. Ruby knew that her cousin had meant what she'd said. She would leave home. But not yet, she prayed.

She rocked backwards and forwards in an effort to comfort Charlie and soothe the frightening sounds coming from his throat.

'Stay, for Charlie's sake,' she pleaded.

Frances had seemed puffed up with anger but appeared to deflate as the anger left her. 'I took him out in the pushchair today to give him some air. He fell asleep.'

'Well, that's something,' said Ruby. Nobody could now convince her that something serious wasn't wrong. Turbulent thoughts tumbled through her mind, and one thought above all others. 'Frances. Go ring for the doctor.'

Ruby glanced over her shoulder to where her father was now slumped in the fireside armchair, hands clasped in front of him and a grim look on his face.

He nodded at Frances. 'Ring for him.'

Frances dashed out into the hall, leaving the door swinging behind her.

Ruby cuddled the little boy. His lack of vitality worried her. Normally he would have responded to her open arms by stretching out his own.

Her father's voice trembled. 'Ruby, I don't want to lose my grandson.'

It occurred to Ruby that she'd never heard her father sounding so desperate. 'He won't die,' she exclaimed.

'Never mind putting the little lad to bed. Lie him down on the sofa.'

Ruby did as instructed and sat down next to Charlie. Stan got up and took off his knitted pullover, wrapping it around his grandson, tucking it in on both sides and around the little boy's feet.

The door banged open. Frances reappeared, her face flushed and beads of sweat on her forehead. 'He'll be on his way soon. He's out on call at the moment, but his wife said she'll tell him the minute he gets back.'

While Charlie snuffled and wheezed on the settee, his head resting against a cushion, Stan headed back to his armchair. Normally he settled himself comfortably into it, but tonight he perched on the edge, elbows between his knees, hands clasped tightly in front of him.

'Finish your supper, Frances, and then you go on up to bed. I'll do the dishes.'

'No! I won't! I can't eat. And I can't leave him!'

Stan took a deep breath. His gaze was steady and commanding. 'I think you should. The doctor might be a while in coming. We may have to take turns and it would help if you got some sleep so you can take over from us.'

Frances instantly regretted her terseness. 'Oh, I see what you mean.'

'We'll wake you,' Ruby added. 'When there's news.'

All signs of rebellion faded. Frances said goodnight, though softly, her voice not much more than a whisper.

Stan Sweet sat with bowed head, wishing the doctor would hurry. The slow ticking of the wall clock and Charlie's strangled breathing lay softly on the silence.

'I'll go wash up . . .'

In the process of rising from the sofa, Ruby noticed the look on her father's face. Fear gripped her heart.

'You don't think he's going to die, do you?' she asked, a jolt of cold horror welling up in her stomach.

'I hope not.'

The thoughts in his head weighed heavy, and rubbing at his forehead did nothing to relieve the pressure. There was so much going on in there, and going on in his life, their lives. 'Sit down. There's something I have to tell you.'

Feeling like winter inside, Ruby lowered herself back onto the sofa, nervously pushing a soft cushion aside with her elbow.

'What is it?'

She waited, fearing he was going to tell her something about Charlie that she didn't already know. His face was gaunt and pale. She tried to recall whether he'd looked so grim when she'd left the bakery this morning.

Her attention went back to her nephew, her brother's son, Charlie. His eyes were closed. His breathing was snatched and shallow. Her hands began to shake. How could she think of anyone or anything else when her nephew was gasping for breath?

She checked the clock. 'Where is the doctor? Come on, Dr Foster. Hurry up!'

The gaze of father and daughter met briefly. Stan turned his head to stare at the glowing coals in the old iron range.

'Ruby. I know you've written a lot of letters to Johnnie. Did you ever receive any replies?'

Ruby edged forward on the sofa until, like her father, she was perched on the edge of her seat. She strained to hear what he was saying. Her father struggled to his feet. She vaguely wondered when the strong physical presence she'd known all her life had visibly weakened. She swallowed. 'What is it?' It hurt to speak. It seemed to her that she'd swallowed a mouthful of burrs. Ordinarily, they attached themselves to clothes. Tonight it felt as though they had stuck in her throat.

He was standing by the mantelpiece, one arm resting along one end of it.

'It's only a card, Ruby. Nothing much at all and he isn't saying much . . . not that I meant to read it. But then, it's only a postcard.'

With a quick flick of his wrist, he brought out the card from behind the clock and gave it to her.

Ruby's hands trembled as she held the simple white postcard and read the address. Her heart trembling as much as her hands, she turned it over – and was sourly disappointed.

She read it again and again just in case she'd missed something. Nothing. All it said was that he was well and that the Japanese were treating him well. She frowned: so much for the rumours that the prisoners were being badly treated by their Japanese captors.

'It came through the Red Cross,' said her father, as though that might have some relevance as to why it was so short. 'I'd have mentioned it sooner but . . .' He motioned his head towards Charlie.

Ruby turned the card over to the address and then back to the message again. The words had the flavour of being written by somebody on holiday rather than in a prisoner of war camp somewhere in the Far East. She looked to see if there was something else. It wasn't like Johnnie to leave it at that. In the early days, when there had been letters, he'd always had a way of getting a message through despite army censors. Surely he would have done the same now if there were any truth in the wicked rumours they'd heard.

Nothing. Nothing at all. She was sorely disappointed. And then she saw it. A thumbprint. A sickening fear coiled like a snake in her stomach. The thumbprint was his. She knew it was his. He'd dipped it in mud, a dark reddish mud. But why mud?

She kept staring at it, trying to work out whether there was some hidden meaning. Mud and a thumbprint didn't really say anything to her, except that he might be knee deep in it. No. It was not quite the right colour for mud. Not quite . . . She narrowed her eyes in order to examine it more closely.

Her father fixed her with a steady gaze, aware that she was giving this card more than a cursory study. 'What is it?'

She heard the sudden sobriety in his voice, looked up and saw the way his brows had folded over the questioning look in his eyes.

She didn't need anyone to tell her that her own eyes were sparkling. Her heart raced with excitement as she glibly turned her suspicions into words. 'You know that Johnnie had a way of sending a message the authorities didn't always want sent?'

'You mean the censors.'

'That's right.' She looked down at the bottom right-hand corner of the card on the side where the message was written. 'There's a thumbprint. It has to be his. It looks like mud, but . . .'

Her father took the card from her shaking hands, took his spectacles from his breast pocket and scrutinised it just as closely as she had.

Holding it gingerly in the lower left-hand corner, he concentrated on the fingerprint, aware of the swirling lines that varied from one person to another.

Yes, she was right. He'd thought so earlier, too. It had to be Johnnie's fingerprint, but what was the point?

Then it hit him. *It looks like mud, but . . .*

She was asking him if she was right and that Corporal Smith had used a very specific medium for his fingerprint. He recalled the trenches of the Great War, the mixing of mud and the spilled blood of a lost generation.

'Blood,' he said, his fear-filled eyes meeting those of his daughter. 'Your Corporal Smith dipped his thumb in blood. I'm guessing it was his blood!'

CHAPTER TEN

'Has this child not been vaccinated?'

Dr Foster looked accusingly at Ruby and her father.

'Poking needles into a little lad?' said Stan. 'I hold no truck with that.'

'You're being ridiculous,' Dr Foster snapped. He placed his hands on either side of Charlie's throat. 'He has diphtheria. He has to go into hospital.'

'Hospital!'

'Can't you give him some medicine?'

On hearing Stan's comment, the doctor fixed him with a steely stare. 'I take it you want your grandson to live?'

Stan fell silent.

While waiting for the doctor, Ruby had tried soothing Charlie with songs and placing a cool compress on his hot little forehead. Nothing had worked.

Her father had stood over her the whole time, his face creased with worry, his throat pulsating as he attempted to swallow lumps of fear. His thoughts were easily read and touched her heart. He'd lost a son to a war; he did not wish to lose a grandson to an illness.

Dr Foster continued to glare at Stan. Ruby was surprised that he didn't glare back. Never before had she seen her father looking so intimidated.

'I'm not sure I agree with vaccination, Doctor . . .'

Judging by the doctor's red face, he was about to let off steam – and Stan was first in the firing line.

'Mr Sweet, there are some wonderful things happening in medicine that promise to make the world a healthier place for children to grow up in. You should have had your grandson vaccinated. Now! I have no more to say on the subject! This little boy is very sick. He has to go to hospital.'

His tone was brusque and his movements brisk.

Ruby watched as he placed a hand to either side of Charlie's neck. 'Swollen,' he said. 'Do you see?'

Ruby touched her throat in response to the sight of Charlie's thickened neck. He was sniffling and his nose was caking up with blood and debris.

A cold shiver ran through her. 'Doctor, will he live?' she asked bluntly.

Dr Foster, a man of around sixty years of age, had practised medicine in the village for most of his life. He was well respected and thought of as quite rich, mainly because he drove a car and had a telephone. Despite his years, he was interested in new developments, read scientific papers on medicine and improvements in surgery with great alacrity.

Wakened by the doctor's arrival, Frances had crept downstairs. Now she stood by dumbly while plans were made to take Charlie into hospital. She'd tried covering her ears to keep his crying at bay. She didn't want to believe he was ill. She wanted him to be back to his old self, chuckling and laughing, playing games with bits of wood and dirty puddles.

'No time to call an ambulance,' said the doctor, his mood and tone of voice as sombre as a church at midnight. 'Get his things together. I'll take him in my car. Which of you wants to go with him?'

153

Frances offered. 'I will—'

Brushing Frances aside, Stan Sweet decided otherwise. 'No. I'm his grandfather. It's my place to go with him.'

He didn't see the scowl on his niece's pretty face or the hurt look in her eyes. He wasn't to know that his brusque manner, born of extreme worry, had caused resentment. With steady advancement, her feeling of being an interloper in this family was growing.

Ruby and Frances stood at the shop door with their arms around each other, Frances crying softly.

'He will be all right, won't he? He won't die?'

Ruby gave her cousin a reassuring hug. 'No, of course he won't die!' Even to her own ears, she sounded more confident than she felt.

The hospital smelled of pristine things: antiseptic, starched uniforms and lavender polish. Every sound echoed from unadorned walls, and metal trays rattled on glass trolleys pushed by crisply attired nurses.

The hospital doctor told Stan that Charlie was a very poorly little boy.

To Stan those words were a stab to the heart. He'd lost a son. Surely he couldn't lose his grandson too?

Dr Foster informed him that he had to get back to the surgery. 'I've got another call to make tonight before I go to bed, so I have to get back. Do you want to come back with me?'

Stan shook his head. 'I'll stay here. The lad might wake up and ask for me.'

The doctor's square hand thudded on his shoulder. 'Do as you will, old friend. I'll be back to see Charlie tomorrow.'

Stan didn't see him go. The hospital doctor was just as old as Foster, a dishevelled band of white hair circling his pink scalp, his eyes peering through a pair of horn-rimmed glasses. Many old doctors had been dragged back from retirement, the younger doctors having been conscripted into the army.

He watched as the doctor's stethoscope dotted the soft flesh of Charlie's chest. The knife in his heart plunged deeper in response to the little lad's gasps for breath. The little boy's eyes were closed. His cheeks were flushed, his grizzling subsided.

'There's nothing you can do here, Mr Sweet,' said a gentle female voice.

'I don't care. I won't be moved!'

'Get some rest. I promise you we'll take good care of him.' The nurse who had spoken laid her hand lightly on his shoulder. 'I promise.'

Touched by the sincerity and sweetness of her voice, he looked up. She was a ward sister, probably in her early forties, in charge of a number of patients and junior nurses and normally a bossy type. He bit down on another acerbic response that he had no intention of leaving. That was his grandson lying there clinging on to life. He had to be with him – just in case.

Her eyes were brown and when she smiled her expression was kind. 'We will do everything for him we possibly can. You have to leave us to do our job. Do you know anyone with a telephone, or do you have a telephone box close by?'

'We've got our own. My daughter works for the Ministry of Food . . .' His voice trailed away. Why had he bothered to explain the reason he had a telephone when the majority of people did not?

'Could you give me the number?'

He nodded and gave her the telephone number of the bakery.

She wrote it down, then, taking hold of his elbow, purposefully escorted him to the door. Once that was in sight, she walked slightly behind him, one arm stretched out some distance behind his back.

Just in case I get stubborn and turn around, and run back to Charlie's bedside, he thought. As if she could stop me.

He wouldn't do that. She was right. It wasn't easy to leave but it made sense to leave little Charlie with the people who could save his life.

'We've had a number of cases locally,' she said to him when they reached the door. 'Not everyone seems to have heard of the vaccination programme. Diphtheria is an entirely preventable disease now, thanks to vaccination.'

'Some of them have heard but don't have the money to pay for it,' he couldn't help pointing out, even if he knew that he would pay all the money he had to see Charlie well.

Her gaze was steady. 'I understand.'

Stan stood in the open doorway wishing he hadn't allowed his fear of needles to affect his judgement regarding Charlie. 'How many of the cases you've had survived?'

'Quite a few.' She looked away. 'Now, do excuse me. I've a busy night ahead.'

The blackout blind was drawn first before she opened the door. Stan stepped outside. It was like leaving one black hole to be swiftly engulfed by another.

The night was black as coal. For a moment, he stood there, nose lifted like a dog sniffing the night air in an attempt to work out the way home. He started to walk, his hands in his pockets, his head bent. Not anticipating being turned out of the hospital to walk home, he had omitted to bring a torch. Not a light showed anywhere, though at least on the main roads he could follow the white lines painted along the pavement edges. Without those he could easily have tripped and broken his ankle. The painted pavement edges finally ran out, replaced by the grass verges of the country road that led home. He was in empty countryside.

It would have helped if there had been some traffic, but there wasn't any. Nobody drove out into the countryside at that time of night. There wasn't that much traffic around in the daytime either.

The sky was clear enough, but there was no moon. Living things scurried in the hedgerows; cows lowed from damp pasture and the leaves of oak, elm and ash rustled in the breeze.

Watching his step, Stan turned his coat collar up around his neck. The night air was mild and he sweated as he walked, but still he felt cold. Thinking the worst chilled him to the bone. Diphtheria! Why hadn't he listened to the doctor's earlier advice? Fancy ignoring it just because he'd hated receiving the sharp sting of a syringe back in the Great War. He couldn't even remember what it was for. TB? Typhoid? Smallpox?

Catching his foot in a rut, he stumbled, falling on to the banked-up hedgerow. He swore, got up and brushed himself off.

Finding his way home was never going to be easy, but somehow he instinctively felt he was going the right way. Like a pigeon, he thought, homing its way back to the loft where it lived. Yes. That's what I am. A homing pigeon.

The night was still and soundless and was easy to get used to. When he did hear a sound, it didn't quite register, not until it was close behind him. Not until it drew level did he recognise the vehicle for what it was.

'Hey, bud! Wanna lift?'

The hooded headlights of the American army vehicle threw dim circles of pale light. At road level they picked out the white line along the pavement. By their weak glow he could see the white star on the driver's door.

'On your way back to camp?' He guessed they were on their way to the camp at Siston Common.

'We sure are. Do you want a ride or not?'

'Don't mind if I do. I'd be grateful if you could drop me off on the main road before you turn up to your camp.'

'That's the plan, buddy. Climb in.'

He didn't know the three young men, at least he didn't think he did. They'd obviously been out on the town and had brought a bottle which they held up and offered to him.

'Have a drink, pop. Keep out the cold.'

At first Stan was disinclined, but what with the happenings of the night and his concern for Charlie, he accepted gladly, taking a generous swig.

The liquid was hot and raw on his throat, but enjoyable for all that. He exhaled a deep breath and wiped his mouth with the back of his hand. 'I could do with it. I don't mind telling you I've had one hell of a night.'

'So have we,' one of them chirped, sounding well and truly pleased with himself. 'We met some dames and—'

'Cut it out,' said one of them to his colleague. To Stan he said, 'Take no notice of him, pop. He's an innocent abroad. Never even met a dame before he came to these shores, I reckon. But let him ramble on and you'd think his name was Romeo not Rudolph!'

All three of the soldiers laughed and went on ribbing each other with regard to their sexual exploits, their drinking habits and other habits not mentionable in polite company.

Stan smiled to himself. The first company he'd met since leaving the hospital and they were talking like all soldiers do about drink and women. Nothing had changed much since he was a serving soldier.

Every now and again, one of them broke into song. Stan was in no mood to join in.

'So where have you been tonight, pop?' asked the driver.

'Been to a party, pop?' asked another.

Before he could stop himself, Stan told them about his grandson being ill and having to stay in hospital.

All three young men agreed that it was just too bad.

'So how come you're walking home, pop?'

He could have got irritated at being called 'pop', but they were young men and from another country. Pop was as good a name as any.

First he explained about the diphtheria. 'They refused to let me hang around so I started walking home. Unfortunately, I left my torch behind.'

'Torch?'

'Flashlight,' explained one of his colleagues. 'So where do you live?'

He told them he was the baker in the village of Oldland Common.

'Hey. That's a few miles further on from where we're stationed. We'll give you a lift.'

He thought about protesting but changed his mind. The young soldiers had warmed him up with their whisky and their easy friendliness. They were genuinely concerned and didn't mind him talking about his family and how he worried about them. Before long they were telling him about how they were worrying about their families and how their mothers, fathers, brothers and sisters wrote to them saying how proud they were of their being soldiers. Their mood turned sombre.

'Between the lines, we know they're worried but don't want us to know that.'

'Well, I for one don't intend getting my head blown off!' said the one whose name was Rudolph.

'Me neither. By the way, pop, my name's Chuck,' said the guy driving.

'Pleased to meet you, Chuck.'

'And I'm Joe,' added the third of the bunch.

Stan shook hands with all three, Chuck shoving his over his shoulder.

'So what are you boys going to do when the war is won?'

Chuck threw back his head and laughed. 'I'm gonna get through this war and go home to marry Maybelline and have a dozen children.'

'Does Maybelline know that?' asked Rudolph.

Chuck laughed. 'No. But she's easily persuaded.'

'I figure on becoming a boxer. Some kind of sport, anyway,' said Joe.

Rudolph said he had no plans. 'I just want to get through this. And then I promise you I'm never going abroad again!'

There was a lot of laughter, and although Stan didn't laugh as loudly as they did, he felt proud to be with them. He also hoped they would make it through the carnage and return home to have as many children as they liked.

CHAPTER ELEVEN

Half an hour after Charlie had left for the hospital, Ruby mounted the stairs to bed, insisting that Frances went too.

'I don't want to go. I want to stay up until Uncle Stan gets back.'

'He'd rather you went to bed at the proper time so that you can get up bright and early in the morning. The bakery needs to open in the morning, just like any other day.' Ruby's voice was stern, but underneath it all she was worried about her little nephew.

Frances followed her up the stairs, into their room and began to undress. 'I promised to teach Charlie to make daisy chains. Do you think he'll like that?'

'Why shouldn't he?' Ruby eased her feet out of her shoes. She didn't wear stockings except on special occasions, preferring to keep them for best. Wearing shoes without stockings had taken some getting used to, but the blisters were not as bad as they used to be.

When Frances slid her nightdress over her head, Ruby noticed how mature her body was becoming. She was filling out, getting curves. Frances sometimes acted very grown up. At other times she was still the tomboy she had always been.

Charlie was the light of Frances's life and she had always gone out of her way to entertain him. 'Charlie is such a love. I hope he's all right.'

She wanted to add *I hope he comes home*, but the words seemed to stick in her throat.

'He'll bounce back. He's a tough little boy,' Ruby remarked, not because she was one hundred per cent certain that he would, but to keep her deepest fears at bay.

Frances curled her arms around herself. 'He's such a sweet boy. Tough, as boys are, but on the other hand he does like running around fields and chasing butterflies and things.'

Unable to say anything without choking on the words, Ruby silently nodded her agreement. She also pinched at her nostrils in an effort to prevent the tears that threatened to pour down her face. She knew she wouldn't be able to sleep tonight for worrying. Her plan was to wait until Frances was asleep then go downstairs and put the loaves of bread in the oven ready for when the shop opened.

Throwing herself on to her bed and the patchwork quilt she'd made, she buried her cheek against the cool cotton of the pillowcase. Closing her eyes, she ran her hand over the many kinds of materials that made up the quilt, each piece representing a phase of her life.

The silkiest were those pieces left over from Mary's wedding dress, which had once been her mother's dress. A piece of red material, flowered blue and yellow and plain pieces represented dresses made for Sunday best and romper suits for Charlie, plus a dress for Frances.

Frances silently looked down at her nightdress. It had once belonged to Ruby and the pattern of scattered roses had faded over the years.

'I hate this nightdress. It's scruffy,' she said as she buttoned it up to the neck in a haphazard fashion. Thankfully it had never been cut down, hiding the new roundness that had come to her belly.

Preoccupied with the events of the evening and Charlie being rushed to hospital, Ruby failed to notice that anything was amiss.

'Frances! I don't want to hear it. Just get into bed and go to sleep!'

Frances slid thankfully beneath the bedclothes. 'You're not undressed.'

'I'm too tired,' Ruby snapped.

It was an expedient truth: she was tired but knew sleep would be elusive.

She heard Frances plumping up her pillows, lying first on one side then the other. Springs twanged and the cast-iron joints of the bed creaked against the bolts that held them in place. The metallic noise was accompanied by a series of sighs and a sob.

Guessing Frances would be tossing and turning all night, Ruby was unable to console her cousin. There was nothing she could say that would ease her pain, and anyway, she couldn't ease her own. Feeling drained and defeated, she closed her eyes and thought about Johnnie Smith. In one instant she cast her mind back to that day they'd made love, a time when neither of them had imagined him in prison thousands of miles from home.

Please God he gets through this.

For a time there was only the ticking of the alarm clock, before Frances spoke.

'Will Charlie die?'

Ruby's eyes flashed open. 'No! Of course not.' Ruby refused to admit it could happen. She would not admit it. 'Don't talk so silly! He'll get well. He'll be home soon.'

Her stomach churning with apprehension, she waited for Frances to raise another question. She wondered what time her father would be home. Perhaps not until breakfast time.

Ruby stared into the darkness, a thick, all-consuming darkness thanks to the lack of streetlights and the thickness of the blackout curtains. Closing her eyes took her halfway to sleep, and perhaps she might have had a short time of half-baked dreams.

Muffled sobs from the next bed drew her back to full wakefulness. Her heart went out to her young cousin. Frances had done her best to be brave, but no matter how much her cousin insisted she was an adult, Ruby believed she was still a child.

Her own eyes filled with tears. She bit her lip and choked back the sobs that threatened. We must be brave, she thought to herself, but knew she wouldn't be if she let Frances know that she was still awake and just as upset as she was. Somebody had to be strong.

Half an hour, perhaps more, and the sobbing had ceased, replaced by gentle breathing interspersed with a heartfelt sniff.

Unwilling to wake her cousin, Ruby slid quietly off the bed, her toes groping for her shoes. They had chunky heels and rubber soles. Noisy shoes. Fingers replaced toes. She found the worn leather around the heels that had caused her blisters. With a mind to the noise the mattress could make, she rose gently from the bed and with shoes in hand headed for the bedroom door.

The warmth of the bread oven met her halfway down the stairs. The oven was still warm from yesterday's bake. A flick of a switch and the gas pilot light would bring it into life for the loaves of bread waiting their turn to be baked.

Even though she was used to the smell of bread being baked, she never tired of its comforting smell. Today was different. Its rich aroma was unaltered, but the events of the evening before had changed everything.

Young Charlie was ill. She wouldn't feel comfortable until he was home again.

It was four in the morning and dawn was lighting the night sky to dark grey when the American army Jeep pulled up outside Sweets' Bakery. Stan alighted, the dawn light enough for him to see his way. Before leaving them, he thanked his new-found friends.

'It's much appreciated,' he added, just a little bit wobbly on his legs. 'That whisky was strong.'

'Irish whisky,' proclaimed Joe. 'Take care, old timer.'

Stan shook his head. The lad had called him old timer! They were right. He was – and just as a new day was breaking, that was exactly how he was feeling. Very tired, very worried and very old.

He told them to drop in whenever they were passing.

'Sure we will. What did you say your daughter's name was?'

The other guys laughed. Stan took it in good part but added, 'Excuse me, young man, but didn't you say you were getting married and having a dozen children when you get home?'

The young solider laughed and said he was glad to be reminded of it. 'Maybelline has one hell of a temper, pop. Thanks again for reminding me.'

On hearing the sound of a vehicle, Ruby had ventured into the shop, peering out from behind the closed blind, the shop black behind her. Motor vehicles were rare enough in the village, so to hear one at this time was even rarer. Although dawn was breaking, she refrained from turning the light on.

When she saw her father get out of the Jeep, she barely restrained herself from going out and demanding how Charlie was and where he was. She said nothing until her father was in the shop, the door shut tightly behind him.

'How is he?' Not wishing to wake Frances up, she kept her voice low.

"They'll let us know. I take it nobody's called?'

She shook her head. 'Nobody.'

Feeling a trifle disappointed, Stan removed his hat as he came inside.

Ruby locked and bolted the door behind him. It was still early and no customers were due until they opened at seven.

Stan threw his hat on to the counter, hung his head and sighed disconsolately. 'It's all my fault. I should have got him vaccinated.' He shook his head. 'Stupid, stupid, stupid.'

He would have repeated the same word a hundred times over, but Ruby touched his arm. 'Dad, you weren't to know.'

He looked down into her eyes, wondering when it was she'd grown to look like Sarah.

He sighed heavily. 'I should have paid when it was suggested and had him done. All this because I couldn't stand the sight of needles when I was in the army. Things have improved since then. Medicine has moved on and I was too pig-headed—'

'Dad! Stop it right now! Come on through to the kitchen. The kettle will have boiled by now.' Ruby was adamant, her voice fierce.

Obediently, hat retrieved from the counter, the brim rumpled beneath his firm grasp, he followed her into the kitchen.

He noticed the stiffness in her shoulders as she marched into the kitchen, the swift movements as she reached for the kettle, the teapot, the cups and the saucers.

'I see all the bread's in the oven.'

'It was my first priority.'

She did not report that she'd not slept all night. It was enough that she was here for him – that they were here for each other.

'I'm tired,' he said. 'I had to walk.'

'Why didn't you come home with Dr Foster?'

'He left before I wanted to. Said he had other patients to see.'

'I see you didn't walk all the way.'

'No. I did not.'

He slumped heavily down on to a kitchen chair and jerked his head in the direction of the front of the bakery and the road that passed its door.

'I was picked up by three young American soldiers. They were on their way back to Siston but took it into their heads to make a detour. I think they thought I was too old to be out by myself.'

Ruby stood with her back to the kitchen window, an aluminium teapot – one she hadn't given for scrap to make aeroplanes – clutched in her hands. 'It's a long way to walk. It was kind of them.'

Her father looked done in. His voice was low but steady. 'Yes. It was kind of them.'

His head drooped over his hands and his smile was sad and thoughtful. 'Young men full of bravado and out to have fun. I hope they survive the day when the allies retake Europe.' He shook his head. 'It won't be easy.'

'Drink your tea. I've put two sugars in it.'

'I'll drink this then help you finish the baking.'

'You're too late. I've already done it.'

Surprise shone through his tiredness.

Ruby took advantage of the situation. 'And here's some toast. Eat it up and drink your tea, then get up to bed. It's enough having Charlie being ill without having you poorly as well. I've got enough on my plate, thank you very much!'

Although taken aback by Ruby's manner, just for once Stan did as he was told. Once he'd obeyed orders, he took himself

167

upstairs, his limbs tired, his brain full of plans that included his grandson, once the boy was out of danger.

Despite his concern, despite his plans for the time when Charlie was home again, he fell asleep. In his dreams he was watching Charlie running through the long grass flying a kite. And then he was gone and the kite had turned into a Lancaster bomber and the sky was full of fire.

CHAPTER TWELVE

News of Charlie being whisked to hospital raced through the village like wildfire. No newspaper could spread the word as swiftly as the village gossips, and no matter what was going on in the world, local news took precedence over everything else. The shop had filled up quickly.

'It was just after midnight. The little'un, is it?'

Ruby ducked away from one customer, took the money, placed it in the cash register, her finger trembling as she stabbed a key. 'Here's your change.'

She took hold of the woman's hand and with the other one, poured the pennies into it.

The woman's face soured. 'Well, I never! In a bit of a rush this morning, aren't we?'

'Yes,' snapped Ruby, while moving swiftly on to the next customer.

'Are they here to buy bread or what?' muttered Frances, her face as creased as a crab apple through lack of sleep and bad temper.

Ruby sighed. She had to agree with her cousin. Their concern was appreciated, but attacking everything she did at speed helped her cope. Another customer. Another loaf of bread sold. They were knee-deep in customers.

Metal curlers rattled over foreheads. A few smoked, totally ignoring Stan's edict that the puffing of fags should be done outside the shop door. Shabby coats straining around broad bosoms, lips devoid of any artificial colouring pursed and puckered with hushed words, the women queuing exchanged information.

'It's Stan. Doing too much, that's what it is. What with running a business and taking care of a family, first his own babes and now his grandson.'

'There's a lot of stuff going round at the minute. Always is this time of year. My Betty had scarlet fever this time last year.'

'Mine had chicken pox.'

Feeling a bit left out, those at the back of the shop went on exchanging what information they had. A baby nestling in the crook of her arm, Mrs Gates proclaimed that she'd seen it with her own eyes. 'I saw Mr Sweet get in behind the little'un. I'm sure I did.'

Following the statement of somebody who appeared to have witnessed the arrival of the doctor, concern rumbled from one woman to another.

Ruby eyed them sardonically, her mouth set in a grim line.

'My youngest had mumps,' exclaimed one of the other women. 'Have your kids had mumps?'

'My kids are over in Wales,' said Mrs Gates. Mrs Gates had opted to leave them there for now.

'No, they're not,' declared Frances. 'They're in the Forest of Dean with Ada Perkins.'

Mrs Gates's face dropped.

'The Forest of Dean is in Gloucestershire, which is in England, not Wales,' stressed Frances, in no mood to be civil.

The woman was peeved. 'Sorry, I'm sure!'

Ruby was getting equally fed up, a factor partially fuelled by her anger.

'If you all must know,' she said, her tone as sharp as her actions, 'Charlie has been taken to hospital with suspected diphtheria.'

Once she'd properly confirmed the problem, sympathy was duly expressed, murmuring from one woman to another.

'I expect he'll be all right. All kids get something,' said Mrs Gates, who had six kids the last time they'd been together to be counted.

'They don't need to get diphtheria,' Ruby snapped as she took her place behind the counter, her eyes shining with missionary zeal. 'There's a vaccination available which means they don't get it. I would suggest all of you with children should look into it.'

A stony silence followed before the older women expressed their views; some were sensible views while others bordered on ignorance.

'I don't hold with it myself,' said Mrs Martin. 'I never lost any of my kids, and they caught just about everything.'

'Not all of us can be that lucky,' Ruby remarked.

Mrs Martin attempted a lofty expression that only served to make her look like one of the cows that deigns to go to the shed at milking time. 'Well, I don't hold with it.'

'It's not one of your kids in hospital!' Ruby shouted.

The women fell to silence at Ruby's raised voice. Even Frances looked surprised.

'Right,' stated Ruby, at last making the effort to calm down. 'Who's next?'

Bettina Hicks looked out of her door just after breakfast. The sight of a clear sky and the prospect of a warm day brought a smile to her face. Her joints weren't so stiff when the weather was dry. On a very good day she was even able to walk the length of the village without her stick.

Today, however, would not be one of those days. All she needed was a loaf of bread. She also needed to get out from within the four walls of Stratham House and find somebody to talk to.

Stan had come in the day before to turn the earth around the early runner beans, and she'd invited him around for tea this afternoon. A secretive smile danced lightly on to her lips. Not that they drank that much tea, much preferring a slice of cake with a glass of sherry. Her husband had laid down a considerable amount of wine and spirits before he'd died. Bettina had rarely indulged until Stan had come on the scene. Their conversations were always accompanied by a little tipple to 'warm the cockles of their hearts', as Stan was so fond of saying.

The sound of the birds in the trees gladdened her heart. Despite everything, they were nest building. Life went on, thank goodness. Birds of a feather flock together, like all those young men from all over the world flying together in the Royal Air Force.

The ringing of the telephone was as bad as seeing a magpie diving on a nesting sparrow. Bettina's lovely thoughts on the day were instantly blackened, almost as though a cloud had passed over the sun.

There were few telephones in the village, most people writing letters if they kept in contact with anyone at all. The doctor had one and so did the baker, the latter installed by the Ministry of Food.

Michael, Bettina's nephew, had persuaded her to have one so he could keep a better check on her now he was in England.

Back inside the house, her hand shook as she reached for the telephone. Was it Michael? She had considered urging him to get a desk job after his escapade with a burning Lancaster bomber but had held her tongue. Michael had warrior written all over him. He wouldn't thank her for her caution and would always do what he wanted.

Steeling herself to hear the worst, she brought the telephone slowly to her ear.

'Bettina? It's me. Ruby. Have you heard the news?'

Fear clutched at Bettina's heart. Ruby sounded anxious and very afraid.

'No. What is it? It's not Michael, is it? You haven't heard from Mary?'

'No. I haven't. It's Charlie. He was rushed to hospital last night with suspected diphtheria. Dad went with him and was dropped off at four this morning by some American GIs. After that he went up to bed, but he's not there now. I went up with a cuppa. You haven't seen him, have you?'

Bettina could hardly speak. Her mouth had turned quite dry, her tongue suddenly seeming to have swollen to twice its normal size.

'No. I haven't seen him,' she said at last. 'What did the hospital say?'

'Only that it would be some time before they could say for sure and that Dad should go home. He walked part of the way but was lucky some American soldiers were passing by in a Jeep and brought him home.'

Bettina felt a sinking feeling in the pit of her stomach. Charlie was such a darling little boy and the apple of his grandfather's eye. She forced herself to stop her voice from trembling. 'I haven't seen your father since yesterday.'

Ruby thanked her. Bettina put the telephone down. The ache in her joints seemed suddenly to come back with a vengeance. As pain gripped her knees and hips, she sank into a chair.

Diphtheria! She'd seen what it could do, the back of a child's throat thickening over, blocking the windpipe. The neck swelling until the outline of the jaw was barely discernible. And the deaths. Thinking back to times long gone, she most of all remembered the deaths. The majority had been children.

Stan must be very worried. A while back, he'd told her that the clinic in Warmley had sent him a letter inviting him to have Charlie vaccinated. There had been a fee, of course, not that Stan had objected to the cost. At least he could afford it. It was the thought of stabbing young Charlie with a needle that he'd baulked at.

This is no time to be tearful, thought Bettina, though her eyes moistened anyway. Her thoughts were many, but first and foremost she was feeling for Stan. Somehow she had to be strong for him, to reassure him that everything would be fine and that Charlie would pull through.

'Well. There's nothing to be done by sitting here,' she exclaimed.

Placing both hands on to the arms of the chair, she pushed herself up and headed for the hallstand. Her favourite coat, a pale grey-and-blue checked affair, was a little warm for the day, but there was no time to be lost searching for what might be more suitable. She had to find Stan. She had to help him through this, and she thought she knew where she would find him.

CHAPTER THIRTEEN

It was early for anyone to be in St Anne's churchyard, though the vicar, the Reverend James Johnson, had to admit that the colour of the sky, the smell of things growing and the chattering of the birds made the place more appealing than usual. It couldn't help but make everyone experiencing its delights feel glad to be alive. So far the only other person he could see was hunched over beside a headstone. He recognised the baker Stan Sweet.

'Good morning, Mr Sweet. Lovely day.'

The man kneeling on one leg beside the headstone failed to acknowledge him. Stan wasn't one to be rude. The vicar frowned, thought about greeting him again, but stopped himself. Sometimes people needed to be alone with their prayers, loved ones or thoughts without interference from anybody, even a vicar.

Reverend Johnson didn't mind being ignored. A priest should be sensitive to when people wanted the solace of a man of the cloth and when they wished to be solitary.

The reverend turned away, heading for the church door, where he was waylaid by another member of his congregation. His attention drawn to the village baker, he hadn't seen the other figure sitting in the church porch on a stone ledge. As he got closer, she stood up and nipped sharply in front of him.

'It's about the flower-arranging committee, Vicar. I'd like to apply to join it.'

The Reverend Johnson was lost for words. It wasn't that people volunteering to provide and arrange flowers weren't appreciated, it was just that he knew the other people on the committee wouldn't want Gertrude Powell among their number.

'Mrs Hellfire and Brimstone,' one of his parishioners had called her. He couldn't be drawn to comment one way or another, but judging by popular gossip, Mrs Powell spent more time inside church – and not just St Anne's – than he did.

However, he could hardly refuse her. All kinds of saints and sinners had to be tolerated. Not that he had ever analysed which category Mrs Powell fitted into. It was just that she was a little peculiar, though he saw her as a creature to be pitied rather than avoided.

He made a mental note to explain to the rest of the flower-arranging volunteers that they should open their hearts to Mrs Powell's odd ways.

'I dare say the other ladies will be pleased to have you join them,' he said, though he knew it was a white lie. The fact was he so hated for people to be disappointed or to feel themselves unwelcome.

'Right. I'll be along for the Tuesday meeting, then. I'll bring some flowers. Looks as though you could do with some fresh ones.'

It was cowardly not to stick up for the women who had gone out of their way to pick wild flowers for the church displays. Wild flowers were now the norm since most gardens had been turned over to growing vegetables.

Mrs Powell, her attire as black as the crows that preyed on the churchyard songbirds, stalked off, an unbending figure who had cast a shadow over the reverend's day.

He didn't feel happy until he was inside his church. After soundlessly saying a swift prayer, he made a mental note to be absent from the Tuesday meeting, citing a sick parishioner or the Sunday sermon as being in need of his urgent attention.

Gertrude Powell was feeling pleased with herself, smiling stiffly as she headed for home.

What did it matter that she lived alone? What did it matter that she had no close family to be responsible for now, and nobody she regarded as a friend? Spiritual satisfaction! That was the thing, though a few worldly things also satisfied her. She had her shop and soon she would have a valued position in the church. No more wild flowers and a few marguerites and marigolds brightening the darker corners of the church. Lilies were the thing, arum lilies especially that gave off funereal scents and reminded the sinners of this village that judgement day was at hand and they'd better not forget it.

It did not occur to her that since the outbreak of war few people grew flowers. As far as she was concerned, they were feeding their bodies and neglecting their souls. She, on the other hand, would not fall into Satan's trap. Food for the soul was far more important than food for the body.

Her triumphant mood might have continued if she hadn't seen a figure on the other side of the church gate, walking towards her. The woman was instantly recognisable from her pale blue coat and the fact that she walked with the aid of a stick.

Gertrude gritted her jaw. Today had been quite wonderful up until this moment. Since the time her daughter Miriam had left to live in the Forest of Dean with her grandmother, Gertrude had made efforts to avoid Bettina every time their paths had crossed. However, on this occasion there was no escape: the two of them must pass through the same gate.

On spying Gertrude, Bettina stopped and leaned on her stick on the other side of the gate. Her jaw tightened and her eyes, sparkling behind her spectacles, narrowed.

Gertrude Powell was far from being her favourite person. There never had been anything very amenable about her, and time had only made her more bitter, more eccentric in her beliefs.

Bettina braced herself for what might be coming. Gertrude couldn't help making snide comments. She tended to target some people in the village more than others. Bettina was one of them. She could make a comment first, of course, but she would not. Today was such a beautiful day – or had been until news of Charlie had ruined it. And now here was Gertrude to blacken the day further.

Let her cast the first stone . . .

Not today, Bettina decided. I will not be distracted or enraged by this stupid woman.

With her free hand, she pushed at the gate, resigned to her mission. It was Stan she was seeking, not an argument with this dreadful woman.

Gertrude's face visibly soured on sight of a woman she'd known since they were girls. Determined to get through this as quickly as possible, Bettina spoke first and even managed a weak smile. 'Good morning, Gertrude. Out enjoying the morning air, are you?'

Gertrude's thin lips tightened so much they almost disappeared. Her black eyes seemed to sink further into their deep hollows. 'This is the first time I've seen you near a church, let alone inside one,' she said, her voice full of malice.

Bettina threw back her head and laughed. 'At least the Good Lord isn't likely to grow tired of my company – unlike yours.'

Gertrude bristled with pent-up indignation, her inhaled breath hissing between her teeth. 'He wouldn't recognise you if you did visit! The Devil knows his own, Bettina Hicks! The Devil knows his own!'

Bettina shook her head. 'And the Devil finds a home in an empty heart, Gertrude. And your heart has been empty for years!'

Just for once, Gertrude Powell didn't have an answer. Bristling with indignation, her face like thunder, she stormed through the church gate and pushed rudely past Bettina. She was almost knocked over, but thanks to her walking stick regained her balance. Not without sympathy, she watched Gertrude march off. The woman Gertrude had grown into bore no relation to the girl she had once been. Bettina wondered at the happenings in the woman's life that had changed her into what she was today.

No matter, she thought to herself. You can't give solace or friendship to somebody resigned to being hostile.

Carefully picking her way over flagstones slippery with moss and heavy dew, she resumed her path.

Stan was exactly where she'd guessed he might be.

She paused at the sound of his voice, leaning on her stick and feeling something of an interloper. Her heart ached at the words and the sight of Stan Sweet, the man saying them.

'It's my fault, Sarah. It's my fault. I should have had him vaccinated. If anything happens, I don't think I can ever forgive myself.' Stan Sweet's voice trembled with emotion and he was clearly angry at his own stupidity. 'I hope to God he pulls through and I promise you, I really do, that I'll be going to church this Sunday. In fact, I'll go to church every Sunday for the rest of my life if he pulls through.'

On becoming aware that a shadow had suddenly fallen over the headstone, Stan looked up to see Bettina gazing down at him with sorrow-filled eyes.

'You know what's happened,' he stated in a flat tone.

Bettina took a deep breath and adopted the most confident of expressions. 'Ruby told me. She's looking for you. She was worried.'

'No need to be.' Stan shook his head. The words on his wife's tombstone glared at him. *Sarah, beloved wife* . . .

'I couldn't bear to see another stone saying "Charlie, beloved grandson",' he said to her.

'Oh, Stan,' said Bettina, her voice heavy with feeling. 'Don't talk that way. You won't have to bear it because it won't happen. Charlie will get better. He will come home. You have to believe that.'

'I should have been more sensible and less squeamish. I remember those bloody great needles they used to stick into us in the Great War. I saw more than one bloke faint right away. The medical officers had so many to do, they carried on regardless, stepping over the lads that had fainted.'

'Stan. That was a long time ago. They can work wonders nowadays.'

He nodded. 'I'm hoping they can. But what if it's too late? What if the stuff they can inject beforehand doesn't work after, once somebody's got diphtheria? What then?'

Bettina's heart ached for him. She had to do something to help, no matter how small an effort it might be.

'How about you take a walk up to the doctor's and ask him what his chances are? He'd know better than I would. I take it you haven't asked him directly.'

Stan shook his head.

'Has he dropped by to convey his fears?'

Stan shook his head again. 'No. Not since last night.'

'If the writing's on the wall, old Dr Foster comes calling beforehand – or didn't you know that?'

Of course he knew it. Everyone in the village knew it. Everyone knew it was bad news if one person had a visit from the doctor when they knew somebody living in that house was in hospital. Nobody went willingly into hospital, especially the old folk, who took the view that once inside they were unlikely to come out. But this was a small boy they were talking about.

It seemed her reassurance might have had some effect. Stan Sweet had broad, square shoulders. Bettina was familiar with them enough to know that some, though not all, of the tension had left them.

'I suppose I could,' he said.

'I'll walk up with you, if you like. Anyway, what have you got to lose? There's everything to gain.'

Bettina knew she'd got through to him when he patted his wife's headstone then gripped it so he could more easily get to his feet. 'See you again,' he said softly.

Although she loved him dearly, Bettina didn't feel jealous at Stan's show of affection for his dead wife. Too long in the tooth to feel that, she counselled herself. Besides, she felt for both of them. They'd been so happy together, a handsome pair who had deserved better luck than for Sarah to die so young, leaving her twin girls and her son in Stan's care.

She frowned as a thought suddenly occurred to her. 'Has anyone told Mary?'

Stan shook his head. 'Not yet. I suppose I'd better.'

'Though she mustn't come down, of course,' Bettina warned. 'Diphtheria is very contagious. We don't want Beatrice catching it,' Bettina reminded him. 'Now come on. I'm going with you to see the doctor.'

Bettina waited with Stan until Dr Foster was ready to see them. That morning's surgery wasn't too crowded, so they didn't have to wait long.

To her great relief, Stan didn't look quite so worried when he reappeared from his long talk with the doctor. Fortunately, there was nobody else in the surgery, nobody to ask about the doctor's late-night visit to the bakery.

Nobody to ask stupid questions, thought Bettina. What a relief!

'So what did he say?'

Stan heaved a big sigh. 'He said that Charlie's condition can be treated. He thinks they use the same substance to treat those with the disease as they use for the vaccination.'

'Well, that's a relief. I'm sure he'll be all right, Stan. We have to hope that is the case, and I'm sure it will be,' Bettina reassured, her blue eyes beaming at this lovely man who she might have married when she was younger. Water under the bridge now, of course.

Stan nodded but said nothing. He was clearly still anxious, but less than he had been. Bettina felt for him. He had the right to feel worried. I would if I were in the same boat, she thought. Still, we have to think positive, she told herself and stiffened her spine.

'Right,' she said, sounding as though she'd just made a momentous decision. 'We might as well part here, I suppose, unless you're coming round for a cup of tea.'

He shook his head. 'I'd better get back to the bakery. Ruby and Frances will be wondering where I've got to.'

'Do you want me to telephone Mary, or will you?'

'Thank you, but I think it's for me to call her, though I appreciate your offer. And I appreciate you suggesting I visit the doctor. He talked sense.'

His smile was full of tenderness and Bettina was touched, even more moved when he patted her shoulder, his hand lingering there, his face creased with emotion.

'My,' said Bettina, feeling herself blush. 'Go steady or you'll be kissing me before long!'

For a second, it seemed that he might kiss her, but both were too wrapped up in the problems of the moment. Everything stopped when family concerns were involved, and that included shows of affection.

Stan had always been the same. One thing at a time, and although he was very fond of Bettina, he would deny himself the pleasure of kissing her until he was sure Charlie was out of danger.

CHAPTER FOURTEEN

Mary threw herself into a bout of early morning baking. As the smell of cooking and the warmth of the old range filled the house, her spirits were lifted. If they hadn't been she would have shunned company, but as it was she felt in need of eating cake and drinking tea with a worthwhile companion. In that regard her satisfaction was complete when Barbara Kelly, wife of one of Michael's fellow air force officers, came to call. Once their babies were fed and sound asleep, they had time for girl talk.

Her pale blonde hair caught behind a girlish Alice band, Barbara was the most smartly groomed woman on the base, though she did like her food. She watched as Mary took a freshly baked loaf from the oven, the warm air rolling out with it and warming her feet.

'It smells lovely!'

'I've also made crumb cake.'

Barbara called at Woodbridge Cottage at least once a week, a sixth sense seeming to always pick the day when Mary was baking. Once whatever came out of the oven had cooled, Barbara would be offered a piece with a cup of tea.

Barbara leaned to one side so she could better see the crumb cake. She already knew that it was made from stale bread, currants or any other dried food Mary had to hand, as well as honey, a very small amount of sugar and whatever fats were available.

'I'm low on cinnamon so I added a little vanilla essence. I think it's worked,' said Mary. 'Let me know what you think.'

Once Barbara had taken the first bite, she confirmed that indeed the vanilla had worked.

'It's lovely. You really know how to make the best of things. For my part, I'll be glad when we can eat properly again. What I wouldn't give for some delicious preserves and a small jar of caviar from Fortnum and Mason. How simply divine that would be.'

Mary hid her smile. Barbara was a delightful friend but very much from a different world to the one Mary knew. Coming from a well-to-do family with an estate in Surrey and a villa in the South of France, she was used to good things. Even her clothes, bought before the war, still looked good simply because they were of superior quality. She'd paid a lot for them and they'd lasted well. However, when it came to cooking in general and baking in particular, Barbara didn't have a clue. Her family had had a live-in cook and a maid. She'd never even had to do her own ironing.

'I do have a woman coming in at present,' she'd previously told Mary, 'but she only does the most basic things. I've given up pressing my stockings just in case I get the iron too hot; stockings are such a luxury nowadays!'

Mary could hardly believe her ears that she really ironed her stockings but had made no comment.

Now Barbara accepted a second piece of cake. Mary suspected she wouldn't bother to cook when she got home that evening.

No matter the differences in their backgrounds, they were linked by the events of the present. Like Michael, Barbara's husband was involved in this very secret operation.

'You'll have to give us a talk sometime, seeing as you used to be a professional,' said Barbara, her mouth full of cake.

'It might be possible.'

It surprised Mary to be referred to as a professional, but on reflection she could see that she was. How odd that she'd never really thought of it before. No matter that she now had a husband and baby, she missed being a baking instructor. The thought of standing up in front of the air force wives was an attractive one.

'Oh. But I'd have to find someone to look after Beatrice.'

'I see no reason at all why you can't bring her along,' Barbara pointed out. 'In fact, we could all bring our children with us. It would be such fun! Something we've never done before.'

Barbara had two boys, Richard and William. She also had a nanny who looked after them when she wanted to arrange social events for air force wives.

'Have you any plans for this evening?' Mary asked her. She knew Barbara always had plans. She wasn't the sort who could happily stay at home.

Barbara sighed. 'Not really. I was invited to a bridge game but it's been called off. Gwen Younger had hoped to entice her husband home with a game, but he refused point blank. She said he was almost rude, reminding her he'd been in training for weeks and couldn't spare the time. She was in tears, of course. You know what she's like.'

Mary agreed that she knew what Gwen was like, and felt great sympathy for the girl. She was sensitive and desperately missing her husband.

Barbara, by comparison, was more happy go lucky; she was rarely depressed by anything, seemingly possessing the firm belief that nothing bad could happen to her husband. She also seemed to know everything that was going on at the base.

Mary wondered whether Barbara's husband was a little bit indiscreet, easily persuaded by Barbara's enticing laughter-filled voice.

'Of course, all us wives are aware that something important is in the offing, though we don't know all the details. If Hitler's spies were clever, they would be asking the wives what's going on. They wouldn't need any fifth columnists!'

Keeping her reservations about Barbara and Douglas Kelly's discretion to herself, Mary laughed. 'Spying on wives indeed. Whatever next!'

Barbara sipped her tea slowly between talking. Mary smiled into her own cup. Barbara was endeavouring to make the cake, the tea and the conversation last as long as possible so she wouldn't have to return to the house her parents had rented her in a pretty Lincolnshire village.

Mary wondered whether Barbara was merely lonely or wanted more cake. Eventually, she decided that Barbara was simply a social butterfly. She loved socialising and wasn't keen on being indoors all day. She even had a car, thanks to the wealth and generosity of her husband and her parents.

Barbara turned her handsome profile to look out of the cottage window across the flat farmland, the neat hedges and sprawling trees towards the hangars and stout brick buildings of RAF Scampton. Her features were incredibly refined and without blemish.

'I wonder what they're doing now,' Barbara whispered excitedly. 'They've been doing low-level flying in the Lake District. Did you know that?'

Mary saw the intriguing look on her face, heard the low whisper; all the trappings of telling a secret although pretending not to.

At mention of the Lake District, Mary thought of the book Michael had been reading over the past weeks and months.

It seemed that Douglas Kelly had told his wife far more than Michael had told her.

Mary had misgivings as she too regarded the wide fields of the Lincolnshire countryside. In the distance on the edge of the airstrip that was Scampton, a cluster of buildings crouched beyond the budding trees of early May.

She shuddered at the thought of what might be going on. After their early conversation, she had not pressed Michael on what he was up to or what might soon be happening. Yet, if she was honest, she had felt him distance himself from her. They were fine in bed, sex always bridging any awkward silences that Michael, at least, did not wish to be broken.

'I shouldn't have pressured Douglas into telling me,' said Barbara. 'I know it's wrong, but what's a girl to do? I need to be prepared just in case . . . well. You know . . .'

'I prefer not to think about it,' said Mary. A shiver of fear ran down her spine. The war would end one day and Michael would survive. She had to believe that.

By way of indicating that their afternoon tea was coming to an end, Mary began stacking the crockery.

'But what if something should happen?' Barbara's voice had not the hint of a waver in it. It was more as though she feared making plans for the future without her husband's stalwart presence, rather than fearing for his safety.

'Something has already happened to Michael,' Mary snapped. 'I don't want anything else happening to him.'

'Oh, I'm sorry, Mary. I didn't mean—'

'I know you didn't,' Mary cut across. At first she'd considered Barbara merely naive. Now she wasn't sure whether it was pure selfishness. A squawk sounded from the cot upstairs. The two women exchanged knowing smiles. Their female chat was at an end. The kids were awake.

* * *

Michael Dangerfield threw his flying gear into the small Ford he had traded in for the dark green sports car he'd used to love. But the Ford had plenty of room for a family. He already had one child and reckoned it was only a matter of time before he had a few more.

The thought of it made him smile. Fancy that, me a father! He stared at the aircraft hangers as he thought about how many children he and Mary might have in the course of time – as long as he survived, that was.

The station's ground crew controller held up a hand in acknowledgement.

'On your way home, Dangerfield?'

'Just to catch my breath.'

'Give your lovely wife my regards.'

Michael said that he would and turned back to his car, wishing it was bigger or that he was smaller. English cars were compact. He was not.

In the past, it had been a simple thing to reach for the door handle of the driver's door, drag it open. There had never been any need to consider how his hand might respond, or whether his legs might not bend to fit between the seat and the steering wheel. Everything happened automatically when you were young and fit. He was still young, but following the accident, not so fit.

He caught sight of himself in the chrome door handle. By virtue of the shape of it, the reflection of his face was distorted – totally distorted. Fear tempered with surprise suddenly gripped his heart.

Beads of sweat erupted on his forehead. A nervous tic – a recent development – flickered beneath his right eye.

It was broad daylight, yet his night-time dreams were suddenly with him.

In his dreams he was there again, the flames from the engine reaching towards him, causing him to wake up in a sweat.

The other men he spent time with back in the barracks really didn't notice – or chose not to notice. They'd all had nightmares. It was par for the course. At home he downed a few whiskies before going to bed, hoping he would drop into a dreamless sleep, though dream was hardly the right word for it. Anyway, he didn't want to disturb Mary. He didn't want her to know.

'Anything wrong?'

The station controller again.

Michael stared at his fingers. Why couldn't he open the car door? Why weren't his fingers responding to what he wanted to do?

Not having received a response, Rod Hadfield came over to check that he was all right.

'Having problems?'

Michael felt the other man's eyes studying his face before falling to his hands. He looked too and what he saw dismayed him.

The skin of his right hand had been taut since the accident. His fingers stiff – more like claws than fingers.

This was not the first time they'd let him down. Sometimes they seized into a tight clench without him being able to do a thing about it. So far his problem had not been noticed, and in time it might improve. The doctors had said so. It was just a case of hiding it until it did improve. But Rod Hadfield had seen. Rod Hadfield would tell.

always losses, always enemy fighters keen to shoot them down. All she hoped was that it wouldn't be Michael's plane. That he'd come home safe and sound.

For some time after the last Lancaster had flown over, she lay there staring at the ceiling, not daring to look at the window where a host of black shapes was diminishing into the eastern sky.

A shrill cry sounded from the cot. Mary sighed. The message was clear. Beatrice had woken for her supper.

Although she loved her to bits, Mary had learned quickly that dealing with a baby was hard work. At present she was still breastfeeding her small but demanding daughter and would be for a little longer. However, there was a brightly shining light at the end of the tunnel. The Ministry of Food had made National Dried Milk available to nursing mothers and those with toddlers. The attraction was obvious, but she'd vowed she would go on breastfeeding Beatrice until the baby demanded more than she could give. Once that happened, she'd resort to the tall white tins with the navy blue instructions printed on the sides. She'd also promised herself that once she stopped, she would take a leaf out of Barbara's book and find a nanny. Unlike Barbara, she would not resort to swanning around on the social circuit. She missed her job and had every intention of resuming her kitchen front duties as soon as possible.

'My darling daughter,' she said, leaning over the cot and gently stroking Beatrice's cheek. 'I wonder if you'd be so demanding if you had to go out shopping for your food.'

Hugging Beatrice close and trying not to show any sign of worry for her pilot father, Mary carried her downstairs.

She would have gone straight into the living room and unbuttoned her blouse, but the ringing of the telephone stopped her in her tracks. She went quickly instead to a long side table set against bumpy walls, its legs wobbling on the flagstone floor. A draught blew beneath the ill-fitting front door. She cuddled Beatrice closer.

The telephone had been silent all day, in fact for most of the week. It was par for the course, telephone lines being cut locally when a mass attack was about to take place. Surely it couldn't be Michael? Not yet. It was no time at all since she'd heard the planes go over.

Pushing her fear for her husband out of her mind, she answered the telephone.

'Mary! I've been trying to get hold of you all day. Is everything all right?'

A great tide of relief washed over her at her father's voice. 'I think the telephones have been down. I did try to ring a friend earlier but couldn't get through. The telephones seem to get cut off when there is – oh, and I shouldn't be talking about it. Careless talk and all that . . .'

She was about to laugh then thought better of it. It wasn't that funny. Careless talk could cost her husband his life. Besides, there had to be a very good reason why her father had telephoned. Like her sister, Ruby, and Frances, he preferred to write. There was an unspoken rule in their family that the telephone was only for emergencies.

'What is it? What's happened?'

There was a short silence. Mary feared the line might have gone dead again.

'Dad?'

'It's not good news, Mary.'

It was as though she was lying down in snow – her back was so terribly cold.

'It's Charlie. He's been rushed to hospital. We had to call the doctor out. If only I'd . . .'

Mary did not question what else he'd meant to say. It was enough to be told that her darling nephew was ill and in hospital.

'Diphtheria. We think we got it in time.'

'Diphtheria!' Mary echoed. 'That's terrible.' She cuddled her daughter closer. 'I suppose I'm not allowed to come down.'

'No. You're not. Not with little Beatrice to look out for. I'll keep you informed.'

'Of course. How awful. I hope he's all right.'

Beatrice protested with a fresh bout of crying when she suddenly held her closer.

Mary laid her head against that of her daughter. Was it selfish to be thankful it wasn't Beatrice? It probably was. But it wasn't Beatrice, thank God. Not that she didn't love her nephew, but she didn't know what she would do if it were her daughter who had been struck down. 'Poor Charlie. Let me know how he gets on.'

'I will, as soon as I know more. And how's my favourite granddaughter?'

'Hungry. She's just woken up and expected supper on demand.'

'That's good. Good,' he said again.

There was a silence. She sensed he wanted to ask her about Michael but was afraid to. He must have guessed from the pause in their conversation that she was troubled.

'Let me know as soon as you hear more,' she said to him.

'I will.'

Again the awkward silence. 'I won't ask where Michael is, but I hope he returns safely.'

'So do I,' said Mary, her mouth uncommonly dry. 'So do I.'

CHAPTER SIXTEEN

Frances shut the bedroom door quietly behind her. Ruby was downstairs in the shop, her uncle Stan was at the hospital. She'd asked if she could visit Charlie, but had been told she wasn't allowed.

'Close relatives only and no children,' Uncle Stan had said.

He failed to notice the dismay in her eyes. She couldn't decide if it was worse if he thought her a child or not even a close relative. 'I am not a child,' she'd muttered. Her uncle hadn't heard her. When she was younger, she'd sometimes felt invisible but had expected things to be different now she was a teenager. But nothing had changed; in fact, she sometimes felt that she was less important to the family now.

She'd tried explaining to Ed how she felt the night before, but he'd been drinking heavily and just laughed and told her she was great and that she was just imaging things.

'Live for today, honey. Tomorrow might never come.'

They left the pub where they'd been drinking at around ten o'clock, and once they were outside he kissed her.

'You do still love me, honey, don't you?'

She'd had too much to drink and although she'd resolved never to give in to him again, his remark about living today hit home. And anyway, she hadn't got pregnant the first time, and for some reason she chose to believe that she wouldn't get pregnant the second time.

The lane was dark. Nobody saw them and for one glorious moment it was as if there were only the two of them in the world. It was a snatched moment, intense and bittersweet. What did she care about the likes of Declan O'Malley? It was Ed who wanted her, Ed who was closer to her age.

'We'll get married when this war is over,' he whispered into her ear as he urinated in the bushes before doing up his trousers. 'We'll be together for the rest of our lives. How'd you like that?'

He'd followed his sweet words by regurgitating all the beer and food he'd eaten.

'Guess I had a drop too much to drink,' he said before being sick again.

Suddenly it hit Frances that there was no way she wanted to spend her life with a man who drank too much. How long before drunkenness became more prevalent than sweet words?

She'd stood there silently, discerning Ed's presence in the darkness and no longer wishing to be with him.

His beery breath fell over her. 'You okay?'

'I'm going home.'

'Fine. I'll drive you there.'

'No. I want to walk.'

She turned her back on him, stumbling over the uneven ground as she made her way up the lane. Home wasn't that far.

He followed her.

'Is something wrong?'

Hugging her coat around her, head bent, she let the words flow out. 'I can't go with you when the war's over, Ed. I belong here, with my family.'

'Are you giving me the brush off?'

He sounded surprised rather than hurt, after all Ed was a good looking boy who'd always done well with the girls.

'We're too young, Ed. And we're in the middle of a war. You'll go home and I'll stay here. The world will go back to the way it was.'

The Jeep he drove was there in front of them.

'Are you sure you want to walk?'

Frances kept walking. 'I'm sure,' she called over her shoulder. 'Goodnight, Ed.'

'You can't get pregnant the first time.' Pearl's voice was in her head, reassuring her. If only she'd stuck to that one time. She'd been lucky. What if she wasn't so lucky the second time?

She pushed the worrying thought from her mind. No matter what happened, she had no intention of marrying Ed Bergman. Tonight had been a big mistake. She realised now she'd been foolish to let him take advantage of her dejected mood. He hadn't really listened. She'd only thought he had. Only Declan O'Malley listened to her, and although their meetings only appeared to happen by chance, it was possible that Declan planned them. He'd never said so, but on reflection, why would he have been there at the bus stop on the day he knew she went into Kingswood? Even if it did strike her as odd that he always seemed to appear on the same day at the same time and in the same place, she didn't worry about it; in fact, she had thrilled at the sight of him.

'Come on, honey,' he said once she was comfortably seated beside him. 'Tell me the reason for the sour puss expression.'

She liked the way he spoke, though she knew he wasn't there to be serious, just to indulge her and try to cheer her up.

She had told him how she felt. 'I'm sixteen. I'm not a child any more. I wish people wouldn't treat me as though I was.'

'I hope you don't lodge me alongside them that do,' he'd said to her.

'No,' she'd said, after giving it some thought. 'I don't think you do.'

'Is Ruby acting like one of Cinderella's stepsisters? If she is, just tell her you've given up dressing in rags and sitting among the cinders.'

Being in Declan's company for just a few minutes was enough to make her feel happy again. She couldn't help laughing.

'You're a great girl,' he'd said to her. 'Anyway, won't be long now and you can make your own choices. Hey, there's nothing to stop you doing that right now, is there?'

She'd told him that she supposed there wasn't.

He'd stopped the car in the High Street. A few people looked their way, taking in the ruggedly handsome American military policeman and the beautiful young girl he was with. There was obviously years between their ages, but somehow they still looked as though they belonged to each other.

'So has young Ed asked to marry you yet?'

She had laughed at the sheer outrageousness of him asking. It wasn't the first time he'd asked and he already knew what her answer would be. Still he'd persisted.

'I've already told you. I can't marry yet. Not without my guardian's permission. Another thing I'm considered too young for!'

Her laughter had been as brittle as candy coating.

The day after seeing Ed for the last time, she was yet again standing at the bus queue when Declan came along in his Jeep.

'Jump in.'

She didn't wait to be asked twice. She needed his companionship, some reassurance that there was somebody there besides Ed Bergman.

'You look tired.'

'Thank you,' she said a little acidly.

'Too much work and too much having fun can catch up on you. How's the kid?'

'Charlie's still in hospital, but no worse.'

'How's your uncle? I understand he took it very badly.'

'He did. Charlie's the apple of his eye.'

Declan nodded sagely. 'I hope all goes well. I need to see the roses in your cheeks again, and if the family's well then I've no reason to worry about you.'

'You worry about me?' She couldn't help the surprise in her voice.

'Indeed I do. You're a kind of project of mine, a wild weed that will one day grow into a rose.'

Frances laughed.

'Seen our friend Ed of late?'

His question brought her up short. 'Yes. For the last time.'

'Any particular reason for that?'

His question unnerved her. 'We're finished.'

'I thought you two were madly in love.'

She felt her face warming. 'I don't think I told you that. We've grown apart. He's a sweet boy but not for me. Best to end it now before he goes away.'

'Is that so?'

Declan had a way of sounding amused that made her feel he knew she wasn't telling the truth.

He could also read expressions, or at least he could most certainly read hers. The last thing she wanted to do was to betray what she had done. Neither did she wish him to see how confused and despairing she was. It was Declan she had feelings for, but how to define those feelings: was he a friend? A lover? A father figure?

She felt so confused. Loving Declan the way she did was akin to hero worship. Sometimes he seemed far beyond her reach, a mature man not a boy – not like Ed. In his own way,

Ed loved her. She knew that, but no matter how hard she tried, she couldn't feel the way about him as she felt about Declan.

Despite the age difference and the short time they'd known each other, it was Declan she wanted. Why, oh why, had she been so rash as to give in to Ed not once, but twice? There might have been a chance of Declan being the man she would spend the rest of her life with, but what if she did become pregnant? Oh, how she wished she hadn't given in last night.

Taking Frances by surprise, Declan placed two fingers beneath her chin, gently turning her to face him.

'Take it from me, Frances. Ed is a nice guy, but you're both young. You've made the right decision. Don't marry him. Things will change between you once you start growing up. Marriages break up. You deserve somebody better.'

She shivered at the feel of his fingers on her chin: so warm, so firm. Their eyes locked together, neither wishing to break the hold in case the time wasn't right or something bad might happen if they discontinued.

'I can understand Ed wanting to marry you. If I was his age, I'd want to marry you too.'

'I don't think you're old,' she blurted out. 'I'd marry you.'

For a moment, he said not a word, an unreadable look flashing into his eyes before he took a deep breath and it was gone. 'Old enough. But I like what you say.'

He paused again, his eyes flickering as he studied her face. She loved it when he did that. It was as though he were touching her with his mind; impossible though it sounded, it felt real.

'Have you ever been in love?' The question seemed to lodge in his eyes.

'Well,' she said, 'have you?' She met his direct look with her own.

Fleetingly, it seemed as though he might admit that he had. Just when she thought she was going to hear something interesting, he threw back his head and laughed. 'Only a beautiful young woman with young men falling at her feet could ask a question like that.'

Frances frowned. 'Am I beautiful?'

She wanted him to say that she was. If he did, she would never forget him saying it, purely because nobody else had ever told her so. Even Ed had only ever told her she was pretty.

His smile was slow. His eyes twinkled. 'You know you are.'

She shook her head. 'No, I don't. But perhaps I do now. You still haven't told me whether you've ever been in love.'

He shrugged. 'I think you want to hear me say that I've never been in love until the moment I met you. If I did, it wouldn't be true.'

It was difficult not to let her true feelings flood over her face, so she turned away.

'I can see you're disappointed in me,' he said, that languid smile still on his tanned face. 'But that's the way I'm made. I speak the truth and if there's no truth to tell, I don't make it up.'

Frances looked down at her hands, feeling guilty she had not yet alighted from the Jeep. If she didn't hurry there would be no tea left to buy. Everything took so long nowadays.

'I have to go.'

'I think you should.'

There was something about his tone that made her want to see his expression, if only to confirm to herself that he wasn't making fun of her.

'Goodbye, Captain O'Malley.'

He raised one eyebrow. 'So formal?'

'We've only just become friends.'

'We might become much more. Who knows what the future may bring?'

His smile was sardonic. This was one of those times when he made her feel like a little girl.

'I don't know anything about you. You could already be married for all I know.'

His smile widened and he laughed. 'Remind me to tell you my life story some time. It includes the fact that I am very much a bachelor, though I quite like the thought of being married. Somebody warm lying beside me.' His honesty made her feel as though she were blushing from head to toe.

'I may wait around to take you home, though only if you want me to.'

She nodded before alighting. 'If you like.'

The queue for tea and sugar was long, just as she'd expected it to be. A hubbub of noise was going on around her, and yet she barely heard it. In her mind she was hearing Declan's voice and seeing those deep sea-green eyes. She couldn't believe he was merely a father figure to her. Although she could barely remember her father, she couldn't believe this feeling was the same as she'd felt for him. What she felt for Declan made her blush without warning. Dreaming of him in the middle of the night, she'd wake up tingling all over. He moved something in her, something that had never been moved before. So would he ever become something more to her? Her lover even?

With a pang of resolve, she promised herself that he would be. Wishing wasn't enough. Praying might be, though not in St Anne's or any of the other churches in and surrounding the village of Oldland Common.

Her thoughts were taken back to the magical time she'd spent in the Forest of Dean. The friends she'd made used to write prayers and place them into the trunks or between the roots of oak trees. She'd asked them why they did it. They'd told her the prayers were to the gods and goddesses of the woods.

'The old gods,' said Merlyn, one of the girls she'd befriended there.

The turmoil she felt inside made her feel both exuberant and sick, completely different to how she felt about Ed.

Ed! He'd be very hurt indeed if he knew that she fell asleep at night dreaming of Declan and not of him. But there was no comparison between the two of them; one was a grown man who made her feel more special than she'd ever felt in her life. Ed was just a boy, and anyway they were finished.

The conversation the previous evening had centred round Charlie being in hospital. Presuming Frances's silence was due to her worrying about Charlie, nobody asked her awkward questions or intruded into her thoughts.

Bettina Hicks came round to give comfort and talk about life in general. She helped herself to a slice of carrot cake freshly made that morning. 'With sugar in short supply, isn't it a good job carrots are so sweet?' she said after swallowing her first bite. 'Moist too.'

Frances managed to agree, although she thought the cake sickly, and anyway, she was wondering about Declan O'Malley; how did he really feel about her? Was he serious or just toying with her infatuation?

'How's that young man of yours?' Bettina asked.

The question took Frances by surprise. 'I don't have a young man.'

She went back to hemming the leg of a new pair of pyjama trousers Ruby had run up from one of her father's old pyjama jackets.

'Don't you? I must have been mistaken. What a shame. Never mind. No doubt it won't be long before you find yourself another sweetheart.'

'I don't know that I want one. I'm quite happy by myself,' Frances returned tersely. She couldn't help feeling awkward beneath Bettina Hicks's steady gaze.

'I'm not sure I believe you. Young people should enjoy themselves as often as they can. Best grab today in case tomorrow never comes. That's all we can do with life and more especially when there's a war going on. All we can do is pray.'

Frances thought of the times she'd been in church singing hymns and reciting the Lord's Prayer along with the rest of the congregation. No matter how she looked at it, she couldn't imagine the Christian god having much patience with something as trivial as a young girl's desire. He surely had more important things to worry about nowadays. Getting rid of Herr Hitler, the German Chancellor, had to be top priority.

Her ears pricked up when Ada Perkins was mentioned. Bettina Hicks was asking her about Miriam. 'I understand she's run away.'

Frances confirmed that this was so. 'Ada doesn't know where she's gone,' she added, glad of the change of subject matter.

Bettina shook her head. 'Ada must be worried sick.'

'I doubt it,' said Stan. 'She's got a different philosophy to the rest of us. If somebody wants to go off and live their own life, then so be it. Every fledgling has to fly the nest sometime.'

Bettina turned her pale blue eyes on Frances. 'So Ada's keeping well?'

'Yes. She's fine.'

The conversation and attention turned away from her. Uncle Stan reported on his latest conversation with Mary. 'Apparently something big is going down.'

Frances was no longer listening. Mention of Ada had opened a window in her mind.

At first she thought herself foolish to even think of doing what her friends over in the forest used to do when they wished for something in particular. By bedtime she had changed her mind.

Ruby did not come up to bed straight away, so Frances moved swiftly. Rummaging in the top drawer of the bow-fronted chest in which they kept just about everything, she found what she was looking for.

To her great relief, her old school exercise book had a plentiful supply of unused pages. She also had a very handsome fountain pen that she'd been given for Christmas, and there was a bottle of ink on the dressing table. A stool that fitted snugly underneath the dressing table was pulled out. The exercise book was opened at a blank page. The fountain pen was filled with ink from the bottle. She even had a piece of blotting paper just in case the pen dripped ink on to the polished surface.

With firm intent, she bent her head over the exercise book. Briefly she hesitated. Over in the Forest of Dean with her old friends, she'd written notes to the gods of the woods and hidden them in the hollows of old oak trees. Ada Perkins had also told her that the oak groves had been the temples of the old gods.

'The druids were their priests,' she'd told her. Frances had seen the other kids push notes into the hollows of trees. Sometimes their prayers were answered. They were mostly things to do with their families: a mother giving birth to her next baby without dying, a father finding a job before he drank them all into the workhouse – not that such things existed any longer.

As she thought about what to write, she looked out of the window over the back yard. Ruby had seen Miriam Powell, the granddaughter of Ada Perkins, stuffing written prayers into the gaps between the bricks of the old outhouse.

She could see the outhouse now from her bedroom window, its grimy bricks, the paint peeling from the door. It held an old-fashioned toilet, no longer used since a quarter of the back bedroom had been turned into an indoor bathroom. She wrinkled her nose at the thought of it. Perhaps the gods of the forest had been affronted by the use of an outside privy instead of a tree. It couldn't be right to do that, especially seeing as it housed the old smelly toilet and a whole lot of insects and spiders. It had to be a tree, more specifically an oak tree, a sacred oak tree in a sacred grove.

Frances thought about it. She certainly would not be doing as Miriam had done. Her only problem was finding a sacred oak hereabouts. There were plenty of other kinds of trees and even oak trees, but not circled in a grove as they were in the Forest of Dean.

Frances turned away from the scene outside the window, the rows of vegetables, the fruit trees now in blossom and the outhouse where gardening tools were now kept and strings of onions and leeks hung from the ceiling to dry.

Bending low over the book she began to write.

Dear lady of the forest, please bless my cousin Charlie. He's not a first cousin, only a second cousin, but I love him very dearly. Please do your best.

She signed it 'Frances Sweet' in a florid hand. She didn't usually try so hard to make her letters elaborate, but this was a special occasion demanding she take extra care.

Once the note was blotted, she folded it into four just as she'd seen the kids in the forest do. Now all she needed was an oak tree, and the only one she could think of was in the middle of a field up behind the abattoir. It wasn't a grove but it would have to do. She only hoped it had a nice hole in it where she could post her prayer. She would go there tomorrow.

Lying in her bed at Stratham House, Bettina tried counting sheep, but sleep eluded her. Was it her imagination or had she detected something different in Frances Sweet?

She sighed. She wasn't sure why the girl had said she had no sweetheart when Stan had told her about the American boy she was seeing. Frances wouldn't be the first girl to have fallen for a foreign soldier and would not be the last. What concerned her was that nobody else had noticed the change in her and nobody seemed to know about the American officer who picked her up from the bus stop. If they did, they were saying nothing. Of course, Ruby would say he was just a friend and so would Frances, for that matter. Still, it wasn't really any of her business.

Sighing, she turned over in bed, dragging one aching joint after another. In time she might mention it to Stan, but for now she would keep her mouth shut – just in case she was very much mistaken.

CHAPTER SEVENTEEN

Walking along West Street was not the smooth, straightforward affair Frances had expected. She chastised herself for forgetting that there would be more people around today because the bus would be running into Kingswood. There was a queue waiting outside the pub where the bus stopped and a few others on their way there.

Everyone was taking advantage of the prospect of shopping for things they couldn't get in the village store, their ration books clutched tightly in their hands.

One person after another asked her about Charlie.

'Is he better now? Whooping cough, was it?'

'No. It's diphtheria,' said Frances.

The women who asked were only being kind, but they couldn't help mentioning the ailments their own children had suffered from.

'Poor little mite. My Tommy had whooping cough back in January and for a while it was touch and go, but he pulled through. A right little fighter he is, and I wouldn't mind betting your Charlie's a fighter too.'

Frances paused only long enough to thank them and to explain that, no, she was not catching the bus. 'I'm just out for a walk.'

She was met with looks of disbelief. What was it about country people that they found it strange for people to just be out for a walk? Or was it purely her imagination that they thought it odd?

On glancing over her shoulder, she saw the way heads were drawn together while their eyes followed her progress. Yes. They thought her actions odd.

It might have been a clear walk from then on if she hadn't bumped into Mrs Martin coming the other way.

'Heard about your Charlie,' said Mrs Martin, who for some reason had a sheep on a lead and a hen tucked beneath her arm. 'Give your uncle Stan my best regards. T'would be a right shame if anything happened to little Charlie, bearing in mind he's got no dad and no mother either.'

Frances was desperate to ask why Mrs Martin had a sheep on a lead and a hen tucked beneath her arm, but the explanation came without her needing to ask.

'I'm just taking them out for an airing. Hens lay better if they have a change of scene now and again. As for Mavis here, well, she likes a nice walk too.

'I never knew that.'

'Well, you do now. Remember to give your uncle all the best for the little'un.'

Frances said that she would.

Two women talking either side of a hedge dividing their cottages nodded in her direction and asked after Charlie.

Frances told them he was as well as could be expected and soldiered on before they could ask her what she was up to.

Too engrossed in their previous conversation, they didn't bother.

Although Frances appreciated that they were all only being kind, her mission was to get to the top of the lane, climb over the gate and head for the oak tree.

The last person she'd expected to see was Mrs Powell. Miriam's mother was clothed in her usual black garb, her eyes like chips of coal in her washed-out face. Even at this distance – about fifty yards – Frances felt her legs go weak.

Frances crossed the road. She would cross back further along before heading up the lane to the field where a lone oak tree grew like a church spire in a flat desert.

To her astonishment, Mrs Powell crossed the road too. The woman wanted a confrontation! They were on a collision course!

Frances felt her heart race. A while back, at the time when baby Charlie had gone missing and been found with Miriam Powell, she'd cheeked Mrs Powell. Charlie had been found with Mrs Powell's daughter, Miriam, in a den built and added to by generations of children down on California Farm.

It was said at the time that Miriam was ill, and there were rumours she'd given birth to a child. Nobody was quite sure who the father was, though suspicion had fallen on a young Methodist minister who had promptly disappeared from the village.

Taking a deep breath, Frances prepared herself for what was to come. From a distance, it appeared that Mrs Powell had no features except for her coal-black eyes. Only on getting closer did her nose become more discernible, pointed and sharp as a bird about to attack a worm.

She hadn't been in Mrs Powell's shop with its dingy lighting and dusty shelves since the night the old witch had commented on her mother and her red dress. If there was something needed from Mrs Powell's shop, such as orange juice and cod liver oil for young Charlie, dropped off there by the district nurse, it was Ruby who fetched it.

Mrs Powell didn't dare ban Ruby from the shop. Ruby stuck up for herself and was not the kind of woman to be intimidated.

It made Frances smile to think of her standing her ground. If only she was here now.

The distance between them lessened. A few steps and they were face to face, the older woman barring her way forward.

Frances took a deep breath. 'Whatever you want to say, get it over with. I have things to do.'

Mrs Powell's eyes glittered. 'I hear the little boy is sick.'

Frances felt as though there was a constriction in her throat, similar to the time she had swallowed a gobstopper almost whole and thought she was dying. 'What's it to you?' She was purposely sharp.

'If he recovers, he'll need to eat only soft things: purées, soups and such like. Custard, of course. Rice pudding. I'm expecting some in. Bring your ration book and I'll have some ready for you. Good day.'

Her tone, her words and the way she strutted off were all sharply brusque.

Frances stared after her, feeling a great sense of relief. She'd expected some nasty remarks referring to the fact that Charlie had been born out of wedlock, the son of her dead cousin and a lovely lady whose husband had died at the hands of the Gestapo before the war had even begun.

Taking a deep breath, she hurried on, her footsteps lighter now, unaware that Gertrude Powell had stopped and was watching her walk away. Nor did she see the wicked smile on her thin lips. The smile was not for Frances, not really. Gertrude Powell had a score to settle with Bettina Hicks.

Gertrude walked on along West Street, heading for St Anne's at the bottom of the hill. Just as she'd expected, Stan was there, murmuring something above his wife's grave.

On hearing footsteps, he looked up. 'Gertrude. How are you?'

He brushed the knees of his corduroys as he got to his feet. He didn't like the woman, but he did pity her, and anyway it cost nothing to be polite.

Gertrude nodded at Sarah's tombstone. 'I wonder what she would say if she knew you and Bettina spent the odd night together.'

Stan knew she was insinuating they slept together, but controlled his anger. Gertrude wasn't quite all there. Reining in his anger, he delivered his words carefully.

'Mrs Hicks and I are good friends. We've known each other all our lives, just as we've both known you, Gertrude. So I'll thank you to mind your Ps and Qs.'

A malevolent blackness darkened Gertrude's eyes. 'You ought to ask her about that nephew of hers. Ask whose son Michael really is.'

She looked confused once the last sentence was out, as though she'd lost her train of thought. She'd been getting more and more like that nowadays.

The blackness faded from her eyes, replaced by the cloudiness of puzzlement.

'Must go. I've a wedding to plan.'

Stan shook his head as he watched her go. The last wedding Gertrude had planned was her own and that was years ago. Her more lucid moments were getting fewer. Gradually her mind was fading away.

Stan watched her go. Her comment about Mike Dangerfield had puzzled him. He reasoned it was just another of her wandering thoughts.

'Frances!'

Too wrapped up with thoughts of Mrs Powell, she hadn't seen the khaki-coloured vehicle coming along the road until it swung into the lane, stopping directly in front of her.

'Honey! Wanna lift?'

Most military policemen patrolled in twos. Why was it Declan O'Malley was always alone when she ran into him? She guessed he planned it that way. He had authority and, despite only recently being promoted to captain, even his superiors admired his common sense and pragmatism. Something lurched inside of her. Here she was off to post a note in an oak tree, and here he was, bold as brass and large as life. What with the note and him, it had to be an omen that she was doing the right thing.

'Where are you going?'

'Uncle Sam's got a running order with the farms around here. We need all the eggs we can buy.'

Dimples appeared on Frances's face. 'I thought the American army had tons of dried egg?'

His smile widened. 'The colonel likes boiled eggs. As I am sure you are aware, dried eggs are no good for that.'

Frances felt her cheeks warming.

He waved a hand at the vacant seat beside him. 'Well. Are you gonna get in?'

Frances looked up the length of the lane to the farm gate and the field beyond. A stiff breeze was blowing. The branches of the oak tree standing alone and proudly in the middle of the field barely moved.

Frances bit her lip. Would Declan think her foolish for what she was about to do? Perhaps if she didn't tell him the truth . . .

'Charlie's still in hospital.' Her voice was small.

She felt his eyes upon her, but didn't meet his look.

'Sorry to hear that, babe.'

'I wouldn't mind a lift.'

'I think I can manage that.'

'Will you wait for me here?'

'If that's what you want.'

Of course it was what she wanted!

She could tell he wanted to know what she was up to, but appreciated him not pressing her further.

'I won't be long.'

The Jeep was soon behind her, the gate to the field straight ahead.

A length of barbed wire had been wound around the gate catch because its fastening part was missing. The farmer had improvised, the barbed wire keeping it shut and thereby preventing anyone from opening it in the first place.

Used to clambering up apple trees, Frances put her foot on the bottom rung and climbed over in no time.

Once in the field, she ran through the long grass where cattle grazed. Over to her right, a herd of black and white Friesian cows clustered beneath the branches of trees overhanging the hedgerow.

Cows could be unpredictable and she'd always been wary of them. On this occasion, she regarded them with caution, but these were far enough off not to worry her.

The oak tree grew alone, dominating the flat field around it. Moss covered its exposed roots and yellow wild flowers bloomed in bunches where the grass ended and the moss began.

Frances hunkered down, her sharp eyes seeking a small crevice big enough to take her prayer. One place that looked promising proved to be too shallow; if a wind did get up, the piece of paper would be blown away. A hole behind a crooked root turned out to be just right, though not before she'd scraped at the earth with her bare fingers, reusing the loose earth to rebury it.

A shadow fell over her. 'Might I ask what you're doing?'

Startled, Frances sat back on her haunches and took a deep breath. This was the last thing she wanted. 'What are you doing here?'

Declan shrugged as he pushed his hands into his pocket.

'I figured that if you could climb that gate, then so could I, and that there had to be a reason for you climbing it. So I figured I had a reason too.'

'What reason?'

Yet again he was wearing that amused look that annoyed her, purely because it made her feel as though he knew her too well.

'I am of a curious disposition. That's why I became a policeman. I like to keep on top of what's going on.'

'There's nothing going on!'

He shook his head, the languid smile remaining. 'Oh, I think there is. So how about you tell me about it?'

His manner was exasperating. It was as though he was playing with her, seeing beneath her excuses and enjoying her discomfort. She didn't want him to know what she was doing in case he thought her a fool.

He came down to her level, elbows between bent knees, hands clasped in front of him. His shoulder was close to hers and she could feel his breath on her cheek.

'Is it a secret?' The way he said it made her feel her age and annoyed her even more.

'Yes! So don't ask me again. Okay?'

He looked suitably affronted though with the usual amusement. 'I respect secrets. Anyone who knows me will tell you that. As long as the secret is for a good cause. I've no respect for bad secrets.'

She got to her feet. 'It's a good secret, but that still doesn't mean I'm going to tell you what it is.'

He got to his feet. 'Your choice, honey.' He turned his attention towards the corner of the field. 'I don't suppose cows are anything to do with your secret?'

'I don't like them, but that's hardly a secret.'

His attention remained fixed on the corner of the field. 'Those cows look as though they're coming this way.'

Frances shook her head. 'You're pulling my leg.'

Declan grinned at her and held up his hands. 'I'm not pulling your leg at all. But, honey, those cows are definitely coming this way. Still, they're only cows and I guess if you don't hurt them, they won't hurt you – will they?'

Frances eyed the cows with alarm and then eyed him. 'I don't like cows. I got chased by one once.'

'Did it hurt you?'

'No. I climbed over a gate.'

He nodded and said that he understood. 'So you got out of the situation with no harm done.'

'Not exactly. I fell into . . . you know . . . a cow's pancake.'

Declan threw back his head and laughed. 'A rose by any other name should smell so sweet . . .'

'It's not funny!'

'Yes, it is. We could run?'

Wide-eyed, Frances assessed just how soon the cows would be with them while bearing in mind that she was wearing shoes with heels.

'No, we couldn't. I couldn't!'

Declan adopted a serious look, tilted his head back and looked up the expanse of the trunk to where fresh green leaves rustled around gnarled and twisted branches.

'Frances, my dear, you are less of a lady than other women that I know . . .'

'I beg your pardon!'

'No offence. Just what I'm about to suggest would not appeal to a shrinking violet.'

Frances folded her arms and glared at him. Never had she met someone who infuriated her and intrigued her in equal doses. She wanted to shout at him to go, but at the same time wanted him to stay.

'The cows are getting nearer. They're running!'

She gave a little squeal of alarm.

'Okay,' he said, his amusement undiminished, his stance as casual as you like. 'No running. No falling into cow dung. A girl should always smell of roses.'

'Stop that! Get me out of here!'

'Okay. How about we climb up this tree?'

Frances glanced from the cows to the branches and made an instant decision. Despite the heels on her shoes, she was up the trunk and sitting on the first branch in double quick time. On spotting what seemed an even wider perch on a higher branch, she moved across the trunk and upwards.

Declan's strong muscles made the job of climbing seem easy, his arms heaving him upwards, his strong legs propelling him from below. In no time he was sitting beside her.

'Whew,' he said, looking back down at the ground. 'That was quite a climb and that's quite a bunch of mean-looking cows.'

Frances burst out laughing.

'What's so funny?'

'You, sitting beside me in an oak tree; the big bad military policeman chased up here by a herd of cows.'

He jerked his head, an action of half-hearted agreement. 'As I said to you, that's a pretty mean-looking herd of cows. Just look at the way they're eyeing us. We're ripe material for tossing on their horns or chasing into the nearest pile of something smelling a lot less pleasant than roses.'

They both looked down at the black and white backs of the cows who had found their way across the field and were gathered at the base of the tree. One or two looked up, their jaws chewing impassively as though they were contemplating what to do next.

Declan pointed at one of them. 'I bet that one's named Gertrude.'

'Gertrude?'

'Yep. It's a fine name.'

Frances burst into laughter. 'I know someone named Gertrude.'

'Is she a cow?'

'I think some people call her that,' she spluttered as she attempted to control her laughter.

Even when the cows wandered off, they remained up the tree, neither speaking, both enjoying the view.

Frances sighed. 'I like it up here.'

'Is it your first time?'

'For climbing a tree? No.'

'That's not what I meant. I can see you can climb trees. I meant is it your first time up this particular tree?'

'Yes,' she said laughingly. 'Unless there was some time when I was small that I climbed up here, but I don't think so. I don't remember, anyway.'

Frances fell to silence and although Declan had a way with words, he too was keeping quiet, his eyes fixed on the roofs of village cottages.

She pointed towards the village. 'Those cottage roofs look like slabs of cake. What do you think?'

'Cake? I'm no expert on cake. Honey, you may not have noticed, but I'm a military policeman, not a chef.'

'I noticed.'

She was perched on the tree with her arms around her drawn-up knees. Declan had his arms outstretched, his strong hands holding on to the branches on either side of him.

'We could get down from this tree if we wanted to.'

Frances shook her head. 'I'm quite happy here.'

'The cows have gone home for milking.'

'It's not time to go home yet.'

'I've left my Jeep at the end of the lane.'

'Nobody's going to steal it. Everyone will know where it came from.'

'The colonel might want an omelette for his supper tonight.'

'Let him eat cake.'

'Cake? What's that got to do with anything?'

'A French queen once said that when she was told the peasants had no bread.'

'She obviously lacked tact.'

'I think so. She was guillotined.'

'A bit harsh just because she advised a change of diet.'

Frances smiled. The branch jiggled as the wind got up a bit.

Declan noticed. 'Are you okay there? It doesn't look too safe if you ask me.'

His arm snaked around her shoulders. She could have protested, but she liked the warmth of it, and the feeling of security it gave her.

'So did this queen bake cake?'

'No,' Frances replied laughingly. 'She had cooks galore to bake for her.'

Declan seemed to think about it for a minute before saying, 'I'd never hire a cook, mainly because in actual fact I consider myself a pretty good cook.'

She eyed him quizzically. 'So if your colonel asked you to bake him a cake, you would do it.'

'No problem!'

'I don't believe you.'

Declan nudged her forehead with his own, his eyes inches from hers, his nose and his lips so very close.

'Believe me, baby. Believe me!'

'I can bake a better cake than you – given the right ingredients.'

Declan burst out laughing.

'Are you challenging me?'

Her gaze travelled skywards as she thought about it.

'Yes,' she said, nodding. 'I think I am.'

Frances cocked her head to one side and stretched her legs. Declan attempted to do the same. Unfortunately, his legs were longer than hers.

'Whoa!' He grabbed the branches he'd been holding on to, his legs dangling either side of the branch. Pretending he'd lost his balance, he swung underneath it, holding on with his arms and legs.

'Hey! Get me up from here. I'm hanging upside down. Like a fruit bat, for God's sake!'

Frances burst out laughing. 'I can do that too!'

She did exactly that, swinging herself round and upside down so that she too was hanging from the tree, arms and legs wrapped around the branch. All the time she laughed and made fun of him.

'I'll get you,' he shouted to her.

She giggled and sidled out to the further reaches of the branch. In response, the branch, less thick now than the place where she'd been sitting, creaked and bent closer to the ground. The branch groaned again, bowing lower until its leafy ends were only six feet from the clumps of grass and yellow spring flowers spread like a carpet beneath her.

There was a cracking sound. Frances gasped. 'Whoops!'

The branch split but did not break. Taken by surprise, Frances lost her grip, yelled and fell.

She came to earth with a bump. The grass was damp, the earth soft. A few of the cows halted, turned their heads, their large brown eyes eyeing her curiously.

To her dismay, one cow, more inquisitive than the others, came all the way back. Its huge head hung over her, its warm breath falling on to her face.

'Help,' she said in a small voice. She kept her eyes on the cow, willing it to go away. The forest kids had told her it was possible to will animals to do what you wanted. It seemed cows were not one of those animals. This particular one didn't budge.

'Git! Git! Hey! Hey! Get out of here!'

Declan was down on the ground, waving his arms in an effort to shoo the cow away. As the cow turned, he slapped it on the rump then with both brawny hands gave it an almighty shove.

Message received and understood, the cow re-joined its companions. So much for willing it to leave, thought Frances.

Declan got down on to one knee and looked down to where she was sprawled. 'Are you okay?' There was no amusement in his eyes this time. No mocking overtone to his voice.

Breathless and bruised, Frances raised herself up on her elbows. Before she even looked at him let alone thanked him, she glanced towards the cows' retreating rumps.

'What did you do to them?'

His smile was all knowing and smug. 'Issued orders.'

'They're cows not GIs.'

'I can still issue them orders.'

Frances cooled her forehead with the back of her hand. 'I hate cows.'

'So you've told me.' He grinned. 'Are you going to get up or shall I come down there?'

'This is silly.'

'Okay. I'll come down there.'

He lay in the grass beside her.

She turned her head to face him and smiled. 'You have to fetch eggs.'

'Ah huh.'

'You'll get in trouble if you don't get back in time.'

'I'll risk it.'

She didn't believe that he would get in trouble. Declan was not just a man with authority over his subordinates; he was respected by his superiors.

She squinted against the brightness of the sky as she watched the clouds tumbling by like a flock of snowy white sheep.

Declan lay with his arms folded behind his head. 'Are you going to tell me what you're doing here?'

'Walking in the fresh air.'

'I mean the truth.'

Averting her eyes, she thought about whether she should tell him about the prayer. Would he think it childish or stupidly superstitious?

'Some of the guys at the base gave your uncle a lift home after he dropped your nephew at the hospital.'

She didn't correct him that Charlie wasn't her nephew. It really didn't matter. What did hit her was being reminded that Charlie was in hospital. Suddenly she didn't care what Declan thought of her.

'All right, I'll tell you. I wrote a prayer on a scrap of paper and posted it into a hole in the tree. I suppose you think it's stupid.'

He shook his head. 'Not at all. We all do whatever we think will help, no matter what other people think. Where did you get the idea?'

She told him she'd learned it from her friends in the Forest of Dean, and told him about Ada, Deacon, Ralphie, Merlyn and all her other friends.

'I don't want Charlie to die.'

She said it so suddenly that Declan jerked himself out of the grass and turned on to his side, his head resting on his hand. 'Is he likely to?'

'That's not the point. It's diphtheria. I should have noticed his swollen throat. Why didn't I notice?'

She felt Declan's eyes studying her face. 'You're fond of that little guy.'

'Yes.' Her voice was small. She blinked the moisture from her eyes.

He reached across and stroked her face. 'Are you certain you can bake a better cake than me?'

The swift switch from serious to trivial was typical of Declan. He tended to do that, one minute lively and funny, the next serious and focused on the job in hand.

'Yes.'

'Okay. So how about we have a little competition?'

She frowned when she turned her head to look at him. 'A baking competition?'

He nodded. 'Sure. There's a competition coming up at the village hall. A fund-raiser, I believe you call it. Part of it is a cake-making competition. It's not much in the way of prize money. Five shillings, I think, but that's not the point. It's a morale booster – that's what I've been told, anyway. So, how about it? Care to enter?'

'For five shillings?'

He grinned again. 'There's an extra prize. If I win, I get to kiss you, and if you win, you get to kiss me. Is it a deal?'

Her spirits were at rock bottom because of Charlie, but Declan dragged her back up again. She laughed at the prize he was offering.

'So whichever way, you'll be kissing me.'

'Isn't that good enough?'

She laughed. Of course it was.

'And then we get married.'

It took her completely by surprise when he bent over and kissed her on the mouth. She sprang up into a sitting position, her fingers covering her lips. They were tingling.

'You've never done that before,' she said through her fingers, her eyes round with surprise.

'It was bound to happen.'

He was right. It *was* bound to happen and had left her breathless.

Her head was spinning.

'Are you okay?'

'Just a bit dizzy. I got up too quickly. It makes you very dizzy if you do that, and—'

'Rest your head on my shoulder.'

She didn't resist when he placed his arm around her shoulders, his free hand cupping the side of her head, gently easing it on to his shoulder.

She closed her eyes. Enveloped by his arms and his body, she felt incredibly safe, incredibly calm.

'I guess I startled you. A guy of my age asking a girl like you to marry me is gonna startle a lot of folk, I shouldn't wonder.'

Behind her closed eyelids, Frances imagined her uncle's response. She was only sixteen years old. He would advise her to wait or find somebody of her own age. Ed would be his particular choice, and up until a couple of days ago she might have thought so too. But Declan was no longer just a friend. In her heart of hearts she'd always known that. The age difference had made her think it was impossible, but it wasn't impossible, not at all.

'Did you mean it?'

In the heart of his embrace, she rested her chin on her clenched fists.

'That I asked you to marry me? Sure I did. You don't have to answer right now, but . . .' Breaking the tight embrace, he held her at arm's length. She saw a frown creasing his fine forehead. 'I feel like a heel. A kid your age should be out of bounds . . .'

'Don't call me a kid! Never, ever call me a kid!'

Something she could only describe as admiration flashed in his eyes. 'You're not a kid. That's probably why I'm attracted to you. You're gutsy. Not afraid of anything.'

'They used to say I was a tomboy.'

Declan shook his head, his look intense. 'That's not the right word. You're independent, not sure where you're going but certain you'll get there – wherever it is. That's what happens when you've experienced disruption in your life. I should know.' The shine left his eyes and his mouth was set in a hard straight line. She knew then that he'd experienced much the same in his own life. There was a different man behind the tough exterior, one whose experiences matched hers.

'My parents were well set up, had a department store and money in the bank. Then they died and just like you, I was placed with an uncle along with my little sister. It was not a happy time. My uncle was distant – at least, that was the way it seemed to me.'

His eyes narrowed as he looked into the distance where trees dotted a faraway hill.

Frances waited with baited breath for him to continue.

He made no move to explain any further, but just carried on staring at nothing.

'What happened?'

Roused from his musings, his eyes narrowed. 'My uncle was a senior police officer.'

He leaned forward, his fingers interlocked around his bent knees and that faraway look in his eyes.

'Dear Uncle Chad! My aunt was a quiet woman who didn't say much and was closer to my sister than she was to me. Guys for guys, and girls for girls, I suppose. I was jealous of that. I figured it was my job to protect my sister, so sometimes I said and did things they didn't like. Then one day they weren't there any more. There was a shooting. Both my aunt and my sister got shot in a crossfire between police and the robbers. I blamed my uncle for it happening and stormed into my room, banged the door and stayed there. Later he came to my room and for the first time ever, hugged me. Then he cried on my shoulder. He explained that he'd wanted to be closer to me, but life was tough and he'd wanted to prepare me for that. I realised then just how much he'd loved us all. Later that night, he shot himself. That was when I decided to join the army and the military police. I wanted to distance myself from the other guys at the same time as being one of them. And, yeah, law and order had a lot to do with it.'

Frances said nothing, her big eyes fixed on this man who appealed to her far more than any younger man ever could. She reached out and touched his shoulder.

'Did you mean it?'

He turned his head. His expression was unreadable.

'About getting married?' He shook his head. 'How stupid was that?'

'Was it stupid?'

A sad smile came to his face. 'Spring and winter. That's what they'll say.'

'Possibly spring and summer, but not winter. Definitely not winter.'

His smile was slow and speculative, but the look in his eyes was decisive. He knew what would happen next and so did she.

He was gentle, just as she knew he would be, a warm tingle beginning at her lips, spreading down over her breasts with the touch of his hands. His fingers traced upwards inside her thighs, slowing at the very top, endlessly stroking before dipping into her.

She felt no apprehension, no fear of pain and no hesitation. He dipped his head between her thighs, drawing out a long exclamation of pleasure. She had never experienced anything like this. What she had done with Ed was nothing compared to this.

There was no pain. When he entered her, she was ready.

The sky seemed to spin, the earth heaved beneath her. And then she soared, feeling as though she were flying. Finally, when she could soar no higher, a shower of stars fell over her and she was swooping downwards, exhilarated, emotional and superbly satisfied.

Afterwards they lay in the grass, their bodies close and warm.

'I could lie here for ever,' Frances whispered.

'You mean you're no longer afraid of cows?'

Frances sat up abruptly. 'I forgot about them.'

The cows were gathered in a corner of the field around a water trough.

'I don't think they'll be troubling us again.'

He sat up, ran his hand along the nape of her neck and kissed her. 'So where were we? Oh, yes. I asked you to marry me.'

After all that they'd done today, this was the first time Frances had blushed.

'Yes. You did.'

'So?'

Overcome with massive apprehension, she was suddenly loath to give him an answer. In the meantime, she sought an excuse and easily found one.

'I can't give you an answer until I know that Charlie is all right. We're all very worried about him.'

His look was so intense she wondered whether he believed her. He hesitated before answering.

'I can wait. And he will be okay. I'm sure he will.'

They strolled back down the field, their clasped hands parting just before they climbed over the gate.

'No. I'll be the talk of the village,' said Frances when Declan suggested he would take her home.

He ran his hand down her arm. 'It's going to happen, you know.'

Her face was bright, her voice bubbled with laughter. 'Me becoming the talk of the village?'

'No. Us getting married.'

He gave her a final wave when he drove off.

She'd noticed nobody and considered herself unobserved, but then found out she was not.

'My, my. That's a fine-looking man. Just been in the field, have you? A favourite place that, for them up to no good!'

Of all the people to be observed by, it was Gertrude Powell, her face hard with malice.

'He's a friend of my cousin.' She barely kept the guilt from her face.

There was an odd smile on Gertrude's face and a mocking look in her eyes. She glanced tellingly towards the oak tree standing in the middle of the field.

'Seems to me that he's more of a friend to you than to your cousin. Much more than a friend!'

to himself, a grand bunch, though he'd still prefer not to be here.

Ruby and Frances had offered to visit too, but he'd spurned their offer. This was something he wanted to do by himself. If his son Charlie had lived, it would have been his prerogative. As it was, Stan felt an overwhelming duty to be where his son might have stood. Better still, it would have been wonderful to have him standing here beside him at this desperate time. Mutual support, that's what it would have been.

Sometimes, he felt alone in his concern for his grandson, although he knew that Mary, Frances and Ruby were all worried for Charlie. He felt something else, something deeper. It was to do with the fact that his only son had left him a grandson. The girls would go on to have their own children. They would be theirs and theirs alone. Mary already had Beatrice. But his grandson Charlie had nobody to stake a claim on him, which to Stan's mind made him all the more special and their relationship that much closer.

Once he'd finished his pipe, he knocked it against the grey stone the building was constructed from so the detritus of warm ash fell to the ground. A quick glance at the sky and he decided the fine morning wouldn't last. Rather than getting wet even before he started for home, he might as well get back in and wait. He had to be there – whatever happened.

The smell of antiseptic met him as he swung the door open. The wooden bench in the waiting area was set against the wall. It was hardly the most comfortable of perches, but he reckoned he'd get used to it no matter how long he had to sit there. The end justified the means, though he'd never foreseen that little saying applying to wooden benches!

He leaned forward, elbows on his knees, eyes staring at, though not really seeing, the brown linoleum, smelling the pristine sharpness of disinfectant without really thinking about it. He was in a world of his own, a world where his son Charlie was alive again and enjoying the novelty of having a son.

The sound of quick footsteps in stout shoes failed to rouse him from his thoughts. Neither did the swish of a starched uniform, not until the ward sister spoke to him.

'Mr Sweet?'

Unfolding his body, he looked up. On seeing her expression, cold fingers seemed to grab his heart, crushing the warmth and the life out of it.

He recognised her as the nurse who had ordered him to go home. Her expression had been different before; a little warmer, a little less officious.

He hoped that all she was going to tell him was that he should go home and stop getting in the way of them doing their job. Not that he was going to go home, no matter what she said.

'I'm not going. No matter what you say, unless you want to throw me out?'

Sister Parker's nose was long, her mouth naturally downturned at each end. 'You shouldn't be here,' she said brusquely.

'I'm not going!' he repeated firmly. He felt tired, heard the tremble of fatigue in his voice, felt the slight shivering that pre-empts utter exhaustion.

'I think you should, Mr Sweet. I came to tell you the antibiotics are working. Your grandson is recovering but he needs to rest. He's going to make a full recovery. I would suggest you come back tomorrow then we can discuss the prospect of him going home.'

Stan was speechless. He couldn't move. He just sat there staring up at her.

Sister Parker adopted a frosty, impatient look. 'Did you hear what I said, Mr Sweet?'

Stan rose swiftly to his feet and before the ward sister could make a move, he grabbed her shoulders and placed a smacker of a kiss on her cheek.

CHAPTER NINETEEN

With a heavy heart, Mary stared out of the window towards the airfield. That morning, she'd watched the bombers returning to base. Some were damaged, metal ripped aside as though it were not more than torn cotton or silk. She was too afraid to count them, to know for sure how many were missing. The news on the wireless had said a great blow had been dealt against the German Reich, though there had been losses. They had not said how many.

During her time living here, she'd developed a second instinct about numbers going out and how many of those aircraft had made it home. Today she knew beyond doubt that not everyone had come back – not yet, anyway.

There were always stragglers, aircraft damaged in operation, making their way back on one engine or with their fuselage so full of holes that the wind whistled in, blowing everything about – including the blood. Michael had told her how sometimes the crew got spattered with the blood of an injured colleague.

Since early morning, she'd been up, occupying herself around the house and trying not to look out of the window. The moment she heard a bomber fly over, she left what she was doing and ran to the window, and stared up at the sky. So far she hadn't seen the familiar number on Michael's aircraft. She feared that she had missed it while attending to the baby or other things. Deep inside, the fear that he had not yet returned refused to go away.

Brooding on her fear, she went on with the routine things in an efficient, though somewhat unfeeling manner: feeding Beatrice, washing dishes, getting out the Ewbank to sweep the rugs.

The Ewbank carpet sweeper clanged noisily as she pushed it to and fro. Every so often she stopped and cocked an ear, fearing its noise might drown out the sound of a returning engine. She couldn't bear to miss any of the returning planes if she could possibly avoid it.

At lunchtime she made herself a sandwich and a pot of tea. Eyeing the sandwiches with little interest, she poured herself a cup of tea. Occupying herself possessed her every waking moment. The precise way she set her cup and saucer on the table had become something of an art. No longer was it merely a case of setting them on the table. She was compelled to arrange them with nervous precision, the cup on the saucer, the saucer equidistant from the plate, the teaspoon set neatly in the saucer, the sandwiches placed spot on in the middle of the plate. Trivial things had never mattered before, but they did now.

Beatrice was sleeping after her feed. Mary checked how she was before switching on the wireless in time to catch the one o'clock news, which might give more information than the earlier bulletin.

'This is the BBC news read by Alan Baddel. In the early hours of this morning, a number of aircraft led by Wing Commander Guy Gibson, DFC, DSO and Bar, attacked a number of dams in the heart of the industrial Ruhr valley with great success. Two of the dams were destroyed. Eight of our aircraft are missing.'

*   *   *

Other news, other programmes, music and the all-pervasive advisory programmes created by some government department in the heart of Whitehall followed on from that stunning announcement. Not that Mary heard them. Neither did she hear Beatrice crying for her next feed or notice the passing of time in general.

Settling herself slowly in to an armchair, she sat stunned, not really seeing anything. Without her being aware of it, she drifted off somewhere frightening in her mind. Anyone seeing her would easily have thought she was made of wax. She was sitting forward, hands on her knees, shoulders tense. Leaning forward, unhearing, unseeing, with the exception of the telephone. Soon it would ring and then she would know. He was dead. Or missing. Or a prisoner of war!

She would welcome the last if it were true; at least he would be alive. But in the meantime, she sat waiting, hardly breathing as she waited for the telephone to ring.

Beatrice continued to cry, her small hands waving in the air, her strong legs kicking into the warm bedclothes she had so recently been snuggled into.

The child's cries were as unclear to her as the fuzzy sounds of a wireless when it wasn't properly tuned in to the station.

In her mind she attempted to face the likelihood that Michael wasn't coming home. According to the BBC, eight aircraft had been lost. It seemed likely that his plane had been one of them. None of the planes she'd seen fly overhead, back from the mission, had been his. She hadn't seen his identification number. Of course, she could be mistaken, but she'd identified his plane many times before. If he'd returned safely, he would have telephoned her. Perhaps he'd been too weary, or perhaps . . . he couldn't. He was dead. If he was dead, nobody had telephoned her to tell her the bad news.

Desperately, she searched for reassurance, telling herself there could be any number of reasons for her not having heard anything. Flight control may not have received a radio message. They may have received a radio message saying the plane had lost power and was limping home. Worse still, it might have ditched over enemy territory, which could mean he had crash landed and was dead or incarcerated until the war was over, if he had survived. She'd learned enough from Gilda Jacobsen, the mother of her nephew Charlie, to know that it was a regular occurrence for a prisoner to die at the hands of the Nazis.

Whatever had happened, it was not beyond reason that they were sparing her feelings.

The sudden ringing of the telephone coincided with her becoming aware of her daughter's crying. Her heart beating wildly, she pounced on it, though not before calling to Beatrice that Mummy would soon be there.

'Hello!'

'Mary! He's home! Charlie's home!'

She recognised her sister's voice. Half of her rejoiced. The other half was disappointed. She'd so wanted it to be Michael.

'Ruby. That's wonderful.' She forced herself to sound over the moon but it wasn't easy. Of course she was relieved. Charlie was home and had recovered from a dreadful disease.

As she listened to what Ruby was telling her, Beatrice's crying became more demanding.

'Sounds as though young Beatrice is screaming the place down,' said Ruby laughingly. 'What are you doing to her?'

'Nothing,' snapped Mary. 'She just needs feeding, that's all.'

'Oh.'

Mary caught the hint of disbelief in Ruby's voice. Only natural, of course, between twins who knew each other almost as well as they knew themselves and sensed when something was wrong.

'I'm sorry. I didn't mean to snap. I'm under a lot of strain at present.'

'Mary, I know that. We heard something about a big raid on the BBC this morning.'

Beatrice continued to cry. Ruby made no reference to her, her own feelings locked into those of her sister.

'Dad heard the news about the raid on the dams, too. We presumed Michael took part.' She paused. 'Are all the planes back?'

Mary held her breath for just a beat, enough for Ruby to comment again. 'Mary. You don't think they are, do you?'

Mary closed her eyes. Should she tell the truth or leave it until she knew for sure? She sighed deeply.

'I don't really know. Not yet. I'm so afraid . . .' She sucked in her lips and squeezed her eyes shut in an effort to keep her anguish – and the tears – at bay.

A few more minutes on the telephone and she would be bawling her eyes out. But she didn't get a chance. In the deepest depths of despair came the voice that changed everything.

'Hey! Hey! What's this baby screaming about?'

Receiver still clasped in her hand, Mary gasped. 'Michael!'

Michael's voice was followed by the sound of the front door slamming, announcing the unmistakeable arrival of her husband, breezing in like a hurricane. It always felt like that once he was home, both his presence and his physique seeming to fill the house.

She shouted into the telephone. 'He's fine! He's home!'

It was hard not to slam down the telephone straightaway and rush into his arms. 'Good news about Charlie,' she blurted. 'Love to everyone!'

Not for one minute did she consider her sister's reaction to her abrupt goodbye. Michael had been missing but now he was home! And Charlie was home too.

Mary stood immobile, hardly able to believe her eyes, her hand held to her open mouth.

Michael's broad shoulders and height filled the doorway. An odd thought came to her. Past residents of the cottage, long dead, of course, must have been a lot smaller than today if the cottage doors and ceiling heights were anything to go by. Her husband was jiggling his daughter up and down while she avidly sucked on his finger.

'I think this child's hungry.'

'You're home,' she said again, daring herself to believe it.

'I'm home.' There was something reserved about his smile, almost as though he were embarrassed to be there at all.

'I didn't see your plane go over. I mean, I saw it go out, but I didn't see it come back.'

A look of great sadness came to his face. He shook his head and the corners of his mouth turned down, all trace of a smile vanishing.

'It went down but I wasn't in it.' He heaved a big sigh. 'I've been grounded, at least for now. My fingers keep seizing up. A pilot needs two working hands to fly a plane. Flying with a gammy hand would put his own and his crew's lives at risk.'

'Grounded!' She repeated the word he had used, rolling the syllables over her tongue, at the same time thinking it was the most wonderful word she had ever said. 'I thought . . .'

Michael smiled down at his daughter, who was still doing her utmost to suck milk from his thumb. When he looked back again at Mary, his face clouded.

'The medical officer examined me. He said it could be some time before my hand returns to its normal flexibility, though there are no guarantees.' He shrugged. 'In the meantime, it's been suggested I take a job teaching the theory of flying to would-be pilots. It means a new posting, but hell, I suppose it's something.'

'And your plane? What happened?'

She already knew it had not returned, but she needed to know more.

'It crashed into a hill at the end of one of the dams they were trying to destroy. I suppose you heard it on the news.'

His gaze returned to his daughter, almost as though he was too ashamed to look his wife in the face. 'A lot of good men are dead. I should have been one of them,' he said quietly.

'Why didn't you let me know you weren't flying? I was so worried.'

'Nobody was allowed to leave the base. Everything about this raid was very hush-hush and top secret. Here. I think you'd better feed our daughter before she eats my thumb.'

Mary took the child from him, unbuttoned her blouse and sat down in her chair. Beatrice's rosebud mouth began sucking immediately she was put to her breast.

Overcome with emotion, Mary looked tearfully up at her husband. 'I'm so glad you're home.'

He put his arms around her, cocooning the baby between them. Beatrice carried on sucking. 'I'm glad to be home.'

He didn't need to say anything more to know that they were sharing the same thought, that there were a lot of other wives and girlfriends who would weep alone tonight.

CHAPTER TWENTY

By the time summer was in full bloom, Frances realised she was in love. Not only that but she was pregnant.

It had been over a month since her last period, but already she was feeling nauseous. Each morning she locked the bathroom door so she could be sick in private.

Gossip of who she was in love with was circulating the village, only to be expected seeing as she'd been seen on numerous occasions climbing into the passenger seat of Declan's Jeep. The gossip had not yet reached her uncle's ears, and Frances feared the moment when it did.

Preoccupied with her war work and with making sure Charlie was well looked after following his return from hospital, Ruby hadn't yet seemed to notice either the moony look in her cousin's eyes or the fact that she was declining her favourite meals.

To Frances's mind, everything hinged on getting married – as quickly as possible. The time had come to face her uncle Stan.

She stared out of her bedroom window, his response already in her mind. *He's too old for you.*

But Declan wasn't too old. He wanted to marry her and she wanted to marry him. Just one niggling fear lingered in her mind. What if Declan wasn't the father? What if the child had been conceived that last night in the lane with Ed Bergman?

The prospect of Declan not being the father made her desperate. She didn't want it to be Ed. Being unsure made the need to marry more urgent. She wanted getting wed done and dusted in double quick time. Never had she felt such urgency in her life, which in turn led to great concerns. What if Uncle Stan refused to give her permission to wed? What then?

The answer came swiftly. There was one other person who was able to give her consent. She would tell nobody about the prospect that she was pregnant until every avenue of opportunity was open to her. The only other person who could sign for her to wed was her mother. The prospect chilled her, but she was determined to face the woman who had abandoned her.

'I want to find my mother.'

Stan paused in the process of cleaning his pipe when Frances asked the question, his features abnormally still, almost as though he'd stopped breathing.

The prospect of facing her uncle had brooded with her for some while. It was early days but unless she suffered a miscarriage, she had to face the fact that she was pregnant and had to get married. Perhaps if Declan hadn't come along, she would have married Ed. Then it occurred to her it might not be Declan's baby. It might be Ed's.

Her problems loomed huge in front of her. The one thing she couldn't ignore was that it was Declan she wanted. She sighed. Getting pregnant and falling in love had changed everything. Childhood was well and truly left behind; womanhood was most definitely here. Declan was the cause of that, the man she gave herself up to with such unconcerned desire. She was still friends with Ed, but had distanced herself. He'd been hurt at first but there were other girls in the village and he had other things on his mind. Rumours were rife that this year was the one when the allied armies would retake the continent of Europe from the grip of the Nazis. Soon he would be posted and likely they would never see each other again.

'Soon you'll be off chasing the French girls, as well,' she'd said to him when he'd cornered her and asked her how she was. He hadn't denied that he would be.

'But I wondered about us . . . you know . . . after that time . . .'

'I'm fine. Let's just be friends.'

Ed had looked surprised but hadn't pestered her to resume their relationship. That in itself was a sign that he had accepted their romance was over. Declan had been right.

She drew her thoughts back to the task in hand. Never had this mattered to her so much.

Reading her uncle's thoughts was difficult at the best of times – more difficult now, with the closed expression on his face. Guessing at one of them, she said, 'It's not that I'm not grateful for all you've done. I just want to know why she ran away and left me after my dad died.'

She rested her hand on her stomach. Not for any conscious reason except as some kind of confirmation that she would never, ever leave a child high and dry.

Stan eyed the lovely young girl, wondering why he hadn't noticed how much she'd grown, how swiftly the child had become a woman. Like her mother, but not like her mother, the same confident tilt to the chin, but more serene, nowhere near as flighty.

Even before they'd married, he'd told his brother what he'd thought about Mildred, not that he'd taken any notice. His brother had been badly wounded during the Battle of Ypres back in 1914. Although it was the internal injuries that finally killed him, it was the physical scars he bore that affected his judgement.

'Look at me,' he'd said, coughing so harshly it was as if he was in danger of coughing his lungs up, before turning his head so that the scalded skin on the damaged side of his face was presented to his brother. 'There's not going to be too many women willing to put up with a bloke that looks like this."

Stan had admitted that Mildred appeared to be sweet enough, but would her kindness last? It looked as though she didn't have a penny or a relative in the world. It was hard to do it, but he had pointed out that she might just be marrying him for security.

'And who could blame her?' Sefton had responded. His smile had lifted the undamaged side of his face, giving him a sardonic look. 'I'll be giving her what she wants, and she'll make me believe that she loves me. It doesn't matter if she doesn't. We're both giving each other something we both need.'

At last Stan looked up at his young niece and said, 'Your mother was not my most favourite person.' He lowered his eyes to the task of cleaning out his pipe, as though doing that was more important. 'We didn't always get on. She wasn't like your father. She wasn't like you, either. I would advise that you leave her well alone.'

Frances felt her face growing hot. This was not what she wanted to hear. 'Whatever she is, she's still my mother,' she said, her tone of voice controlled but strident.

His eyebrows beetled above his nose and he looked at her with eyes that had sunk deeper in his head in recent years. There was kindness in them but also a look that hinted at deep thoughts laced with vivid memories.

As he straightened, he nodded affably, his brows going back to normal. 'I suppose you're right, but I really don't understand why you want to meet her. Why now? She left you . . .'

Frances broke across his statement with one of her own. 'I want to know why she abandoned me. I want to know why she didn't love me enough to stay!'

Stan was now in the process of refilling his pipe. Frances's outburst caused him to stop midway. 'I'm sorry. It's wrong for me just to look at her from my point of view. I wasn't thinking of you.'

Frances swallowed the web of nervousness that seemed to have been spun across her throat. 'Do you know where she is?'

Stan regarded her steadily. She couldn't know that Mildred had first been brought to the village by Gertrude Powell. For some reason he didn't know, Gertrude had taken the young and destitute Mildred under her wing. To Stan's eyes, Mildred, with her blousy figure and familiar way she looked at men – as though she could eat them whole – had not seemed the sort to fit into Gertrude's ideal of Christian womanhood. As it turned out, he'd been correct. Eventually, Gertrude Powell had concluded she had a cuckoo in the nest whose inclination was men rather than Bible studies. And Sefton had been the man Mildred set her cap at.

She'd got pregnant by his brother, got married and might have perhaps lived happily ever after if Sefton hadn't died when Frances was seven years old.

'I don't know for sure, but I had an address for her years back,' he said to her, reluctance hanging heavy in his voice.

Feeling a sense of destiny being fulfilled, he ambled over to the old roll-top desk where he kept family wills, property and insurance documents. The papers were in no particular order, in fact far from it; he could never bear to throw anything out, and anyway, paper was precious.

Beneath the rolled-up bundles, he brought out a small diary from a long time ago in which he'd jotted down useful addresses and the names of people he'd long since lost contact with. From the back of the diary he took out a small piece of paper.

There was a sad and apprehensive look in his eyes when he handed it to the lovely young girl whom he had brought up as his own.

'This is your mother's last known address. I would suggest you write first. Despite all your best intentions, Frances, I think turning up unannounced on her doorstep is not going to be favourably received. Write and tell her you're coming, make sure you know she's still there and plan a definite date and time, but be prepared: she might not want this.'

Frances felt herself filling up with a mixture of joy and gratitude. Her eyes brimmed with tears of happiness she could barely hold back. 'Uncle Stan! Thank you. Thank you so much!'

Throwing her arms around his neck, she buried her head in his shoulder, closed her eyes and breathed in the pungent smells of the garden and tobacco. No matter where she went in the world or what life threw at her, she would always relish that smell as that of security and love. Her uncle had always been there for her and somehow she couldn't help feeling just a little guilty that she was insisting on finding the mother who'd deserted her, the woman he so clearly disliked. The woman who, from the fragments of things told to her, might be willing to sign a consent form for her to marry the man she loved, the man who she could possibly dupe into believing that the child she was carrying was his.

CHAPTER TWENTY-ONE

Breakfast was over and Stan Sweet had gone across the village to tend to the garden at Stratham House on the day when Ruby finally tackled Frances about Declan O'Malley.

'Don't think I don't know about you and him,' she said to her. 'The whole village knows.'

Frances shrugged. 'If they're not talking about me, they'd be talking about somebody else. The village likes gossip.'

'You're being flippant.'

'Really? I thought I was being honest.'

Ruby wagged her finger and raised her voice. 'Now don't speak to me like that, young lady!'

Frances sighed and placed her hands on her hips while holding back her anger. 'Are you jealous?'

Ruby looked at her in amazement. 'Jealous? Why would I be jealous?'

Frances folded her arms and held her chin high and defiant. 'Because you wanted him for yourself.'

Ruby's jaw dropped. At first, it seemed she'd been about to voice a strong denial. Her open mouth finally closed and she chose her words more carefully. 'We were friends. We had a good time for a while. But that was all it was. We never got that serious. We didn't suit each other and we knew it. So you're wrong. I am not jealous. The plain fact is, Frances, I think he's too old for you.'

'I don't care!' Everything about Frances was defiant: her eyes blazed, her jaw was firm, her chin jutted forward.

'Look,' said Ruby, sighing as she pulled out a kitchen chair and sunk into it. She didn't consider herself the type to play big sister or be a mother figure; Mary was so much better at that. But Mary wasn't here. She was. 'He's much more mature than you. Yes, he's very masculine, handsome and all that, but you have to realise that he'll be off before very long and you'll never see him again. You're just a play thing to him—'

'No! You're wrong! He loves me and . . .' Frances took a deep breath. 'And I love him. We're going to get married—'

'He's asked you?' Ruby looked at her in disbelief. This was totally unexpected. Seduction had been her best guess, though on reflection she had to admit that Declan had always struck her as an honourable man.

Frances took a deep breath. 'Yes. He has. We're going to get married and have a house and children and everything, and there's nothing you can do about it.'

'Yes, there is. You're a minor. You have to have the consent of a parent or guardian before the age of twenty-one. Under the circumstances, I'm not sure my father will sign for you.'

'I know. Why do you suppose I'm so eager to find my mother?' Frances saw the look of comprehension on her cousin Ruby's face.

'So that's it. You want to find your mother and get her to sign for you!'

'That's my plan.'

'But Declan is—'

'Promise you won't tell Uncle Stan about Declan. I don't want him to know. Not yet. Not until I have my mother's signed consent.'

She wasn't certain Ruby would agree to keep her secret. Like her uncle, her cousin still regarded her as little more than a child.

She had thought this through so carefully and was adamant it would happen. Being the kind of woman she was, her mother would understand, she was sure of it.

It was clear from Ruby's hesitant response that her loyalties were divided. On the one hand, she loved her father and was unwilling to do anything to hurt him. On the other, the look on her cousin's face touched a chord within herself. If she were so in love with a man, what wouldn't she do to get him?

She thought of John Smith, a prisoner of war. What wouldn't she do to get him home?

Ruby looked down at her folded hands, her clean, neatly cut fingernails. She shook her head. 'I won't say a word about you and Declan. It won't come from me if he does find out.'

Frances voiced her appreciation. 'Not that I care what the small-minded of this village think of me, but I do care about Uncle Stan.'

Living in a village meant everyone knew everything about everyone else, and judged their neighbours by their behaviour, in effect what they saw on the surface.

'Then please don't hurt him,' Ruby pleaded, strain showing on her tired face. The sound of the telephone ringing came from the hallway. Feeling she could have run away there and then, Frances went to answer it. It was Mary.

'Frances! I wanted to know how Charlie is getting on.'

'Yes, he's doing well. Oh, Mary, I'm so glad we've got him back. I wish you were here so I could give you a big hug.'

'You sweet girl. I wish I was too. But there. I'm happy. Everything here is happy.'

'Shall I hand you over to Ruby?'

'Not yet. First tell me what you've been up to.'

Frances felt her reluctance to talk about her predicament and her life in general fall away. Mary had always been so understanding, replacing the mother she'd hardly known.

Frances's voice dropped to a whisper. 'Mary. I've got something to tell you, but you have to promise not to tell anyone else. It's a secret.'

Relieved that Michael was home, Mary was feeling much brighter than she had felt earlier that morning and cheerfully assured her cousin that, yes, she could keep a secret and that she wouldn't tell a living soul.

She waited while Frances took a deep breath. 'I'm in love with an American soldier called Declan and he's asked me to marry him.'

'So what did you say?' Mary asked.

'I told him he would have to wait until our Charlie was better. I couldn't possibly give him an answer until then.'

'So what did he say to that?'

'He was okay.'

'Okay?'

Mary was getting used to people saying okay, though she'd balked at it at first. People were readily accepting the Americans and their sayings and ways. They also had access to things that had been in short supply or virtually non-existent since the beginning of the war, nylon stockings and chocolate being top of the list.

'He says I'll have to make my mind up before the big invasion happens – you know – the invasion of Europe. He doesn't know when that's likely to be, but he thinks it will be pretty soon.'

Mary smiled into the telephone. 'Your sweetheart seems a knowledgeable young man. Is he an officer?'

'A captain.'

'My, my. At this rate you'll be getting married before Ruby!'

'It's possible. Though she has received a postcard from John Smith. It's got his thumbprint on it – in blood,' she added, and felt a little queasy

'I know. She told me. It's wonderful news, even though his captors didn't allow him to say much.'

'I know. All it said was that he's being treated well and is in good health. I think Johnnie is really clever. Fancy dipping his thumb into his blood and pressing it on the card! The moment she saw that, Ruby knew he was not being well cared for. All the same, we all hope he survives.'

Ruby came on the telephone and told Mary all that was happening as regards Charlie before going on to talk about the village in general.

'I think Bettina and Mrs Powell have had a bit of a row. Bettina used to be more or less in charge of flower-arranging at St Anne's. Mrs Powell has joined the group. Bettina isn't very happy at all. I don't know what it is with those two, but I think it's from years ago when they were young.'

Mary laughed. Bettina Hicks was Michael's aunt and it was in her garden that she and Michael had first met.

'I'm glad Michael's safe too,' Ruby said suddenly. 'You must have been worried.'

Mary's laughter died. 'I'm so relieved.' She went on to tell Ruby about his hands. 'He thinks he'll be posted somewhere else, though we don't know where.' She didn't mention the raid just in case somebody was listening. They were close to the airbase, after all, and there might very well be enemy collaborators. Anyway, Ruby had got all the details for public consumption from the BBC broadcast. Instead, she asked about Johnnie.

'At least he's alive.' Ruby's voice was sombre. 'I just hope he gets through it.'

'You really think the fingerprint was in blood?'

'Dad took it along to Dr Foster for a second opinion. He said it was. You know Johnnie; it was his little way of letting me know what's really going on. I don't think he did it to worry me . . .' She paused. 'He just wants me to know the truth of what's going on. I'm scared for him. Still, at least I've heard from him. Do you know, I used to hover near the letterbox for months in the hope that he'd write. I was becoming obsessive. Now I'm not so bad. It's Frances I'm worried about.'

'Is this all to do with her American soldier?' Mary asked. 'She is a bit young to be thinking of getting married, but she sounds like she's in love.'

Ruby sighed. 'I'm more worried about her wanting to find her mother.'

CHAPTER TWENTY-TWO

Each morning, following being sick in the lavatory bowl, Frances hovered around the house, flitting from making tea, breakfast and taking the bread through to the shop, listening for the sound of a letter dropping on to the coconut mat in the hallway.

'No breakfast again,' Ruby said to her.

'I'm not hungry.'

Seeing as she looked a picture of health, Ruby didn't press her.

Frances's ears had become fine-tuned to the sound of the letterbox. Sometimes when she was in the shop placing loaves on the shelves behind the counter, or displaying something to tempt a wartime palate, she would open the shop door having heard the postman's footsteps.

There were some days when she had failed to hear anything falling on to the front door mat. On those days, she would look up and down the street to see if the postman really had walked on by or was turning back ready to apologise that he'd made a mistake and there was something for her after all. He'd never done that yet.

Would her mother respond? There was no way of knowing.

She quite often felt Ruby's studied gaze. 'Nothing in the post?'

Frances sighed heavily as she did every day. 'No, Ruby. There's not.'

Every morning was a disappointment. Either there was no post at all, or nothing addressed to her.

Disregarding the pity in Ruby's pained expression, she clamped her mouth tightly shut. She had no wish to have trivial conversations about bread or the village or anything that didn't have a direct bearing on the letter to her mother.

She'd worded the letter carefully, not wanting to surprise her mother or blatantly accuse her of leaving her high and dry, a child alone in a big bad world. Would it have been so hard for her mother to have sent her a few words now and again?

Ruby was attempting to extricate a dollop of treacle from a spoon and on to the top of her porridge. 'What will you do if she does write?'

Frances didn't meet the enquiry in Ruby's eyes. 'Who's to say that she will? She never wrote to me in the past, not even to send me a birthday or Christmas card.' She frowned. Of late, the bitterness she felt at being abandoned as a child had ballooned into seething resentment and the frantic desire to have questions answered. 'I wonder why she ran off and why she didn't want me?' She'd only voiced those questions of late. Being a child had been comfortable; becoming an adult made the past more questionable.

'*We* wanted you,' Ruby exclaimed. Her expression was one of alarm.

Frances heaved another sigh.

Ruby raised her eyebrows and glanced sidelong at her suffering cousin. Yet another sigh? Goodness, sighing was actually becoming quite an art form on her cousin's part. Still, she thought, how would I feel if I were in her shoes?

'If your mother was alive and you had some idea where she was, what would you do?'

253

The question hit Ruby off balance. The answer was a foregone conclusion, though bearing in mind who she was speaking to and the circumstances thereof, she worded her response carefully. 'My mother's dead. So that's that.' She paused, imagining how things might have been if she'd lived.

'So how would you feel if my mother was your mother and had abandoned you? What would you do?'

Ruby had to concede that she would have endeavoured to find her, to face her and have her explain her actions.

'Exactly!' Frances exclaimed, satisfied that a fundamental point had been made. 'She could at least have said goodbye.'

It not being her nature to rub salt into an open wound, Ruby said no more. Although she maintained an aura of indifference, she understood the misgivings and obsessions of a young girl. That was me, she said to herself, not so long ago.

Frances stared out of the kitchen window as if the view contained a pretty garden rather than the vegetable field it had become. Before the war, there had been a vegetable patch at the end of the garden, but vegetables now filled the whole garden with the exception of the rose bush, Charles Stuart, bought for her cousin Charlie the Christmas before he was killed.

'You don't think I'll get a reply, do you?' Frances said suddenly. 'You think I'm just a silly child.'

Ruby felt a pang of remorse that she had used such words. Her cousin was at a sensitive age. 'No. I can imagine how you feel and I truly hope your letter touches a chord with your mother's landlady and that she replies soon.'

What she wanted to say was perhaps it might have been a good idea if she'd passed it to her to read first, just to make sure it sounded right.

'It was a good letter,' Frances stated, as though she'd read Ruby's mind. Yes, she could have had her check it, but it was *her* letter to *her* mother. Not only had she wished to keep it private, she'd wanted it personal, no other hand having touched it or eyes reading it.

The letter she'd sent had been carefully considered, though to the point. With meticulous precision, Frances had listed what her uncle had told her. Name, previous address, appearance, marital status, even to details of a coral necklace Mildred always wore. Stan Sweet thought the necklace had been bought overseas during the Great War, though he couldn't be sure.

'You'll know her by that alone,' he'd said to Frances.

She'd relayed that particular piece of information to the landlady at her mother's last known address. The letter had to come soon, but still she waited, heart racing like a greyhound at the prospect of seeing her mother again.

Two weeks of waiting finally paid off. On a cold summer morning, the postman paused at the front door so he could remove one knitted glove before rummaging around in his bag. Frances dashed out to the shop door and jerked it open.

'Well, that's jolly nice of you,' said the postman. 'Saves me bending down and shoving it through down there. Ever thought of getting it repositioned?'

Frances had no more liking for the postman than anyone else.

'I wasn't thinking of you bending down. I just want our post,' she said sharply. 'I'm waiting for a very important letter.'

Melvyn Chance smirked. She knew he was surmising she was awaiting a letter from a sweetheart but had no intention of confirming either way.

Two long weeks of waiting had passed since she'd written her letter; two weeks dwelling on whether she would receive a letter at all. It had also been two weeks of sensing that her waistline was expanding, if the waistbands of her skirts and dresses were anything to go by. She didn't want her cousin Ruby to notice what was up before she had a chance to put her plan into action.

However, it appeared she was in luck, and besides, she felt well and confident that everything would work out for the best. There was nothing to worry about. Only in the dead of night did fear clench at her stomach and the details of a frantically confusing dream drift back into her mind.

In the meantime, all that mattered was finding her mother, and at last she had a response.

Once she'd scanned the Bristol postmark, her heart quickened. If she was lucky, her mother might still be there at the address she'd given Uncle Stan some time ago.

Heart continuing to race like a steam train, Frances held the plain brown envelope in both hands. Eager to open it, though scared at what it might say, she willed her heart to cease its frantic rush. She must be calm – or as calm as she could be. She also wanted to read it by herself.

'I'm going into the kitchen. Will you be all right here in the shop?'

'I'm coming through too. My cup of tea is still sitting on the kitchen table and must be getting cold by now. We'll hear the bell if somebody comes into the shop.'

Frances knew better than to argue with her cousin. She could see by the look on Ruby's face that she was almost as curious as she was to know what was in the letter.

'She's had a reply,' Ruby said to her father, who only grunted and did his best to look uninterested. Inside he was seething. No matter Frances's feelings, he would never feel anything but condemnation for the likes of his sister-in-law. Not that Frances would listen. Not at present. But he would give it one more try. He had to get the message through to her.

Ruby pulled up a chair to the table. She gestured that Frances should do the same, but her cousin ignored her.

'Well, go on, you silly goose,' said Ruby, sipping her tea, eyes fixed on the letter.

Stan stayed silent, sitting in his favourite armchair, toasting his feet in front of the fire and pretending to read the paper. He flicked the page he was reading so it made a cracking sound, but he did not look up.

Ruby gave extra attention to scraping excess margarine from her toast. Not that it needed scraping off. It was just something to do while she waited to find out what the infamous Mildred had to say – if she was still at that address, of course.

Frances took a deep breath before taking a butter knife and running it along the seam of the envelope. With a steady hand, she brought out and unfolded the single sheet of paper within and began to read.

Her eyes skidded over the words. The strongest willpower in the world could not prevent her heart hammering.

Stan only glanced at her face. Ruby stayed fixed on it. Both could see that the letter was disappointing. Mildred Sweet was no longer at that address.

'She's not there.' Disappointed, Frances's face fell and her hands dropped into her lap.

'I did tell you it was years old,' said Stan from behind his newspaper. 'She's gone on to pastures new. Some other bloke that she's latched on to. Mildred always did like a bit of variety in her life. And I don't mean just with regard to location!'

Frances smarted at the harsh words. Her mother might be a tart, but she was still her mother.

Stan Sweet looked down to the empty breakfast plate sitting on his lap, as though, like Oliver Twist, he wanted more. But he didn't want more. It was on the tip of his tongue to say a lot more about his dead brother's wife but he made a big effort to control his expression. It wouldn't be fair to let Frances see how relieved he was feeling. He'd long entertained the opinion that his sister-in-law wasn't worth finding, and his opinion had not changed. He'd never forgiven her for the way she'd treated his brother, dallying with other men when Sefton was at death's door.

Guessing what he was thinking, Ruby frowned at him in reproach. Her father squirmed under the intensity of her warning look before retreating behind his newspaper. His plan to put his opinion of her mother to Frances broadly and simply was still on the cards. It had to be done, no matter how it might upset the girl.

Ruby squeezed her cousin's shoulder. Her voice was gentle. 'Didn't she leave any forwarding address?'

Frances shook her head, her eyes still fixed on the contents of the letter.

'Can I read it?' asked Ruby.

Frances shook her head. 'There's no point.'

Ruby placed an arm around her cousin's shoulder and gave her a hug. 'I'm so sorry, Frances. But still, perhaps it's all for the best.' She looked at her father, took in the headlines about rockets landing on London and suddenly saw red. This was not the time to hide behind a newspaper! 'Dad! Is there nothing you can say about it?'

With an air of reluctance, he came out from behind the glaring headlines, took off his spectacles and folded the newspaper into one hand. He sighed before saying, 'Frances, your mother's not the sort to stay in one place for long. She's like a butterfly, fluttering from place to place. That's the way 'she was and probably still is.' His face was like thunder. 'I'm telling you now, Frances. If you want to leave this house and go looking for that woman, then you're on your own! I'll wash my hands of you and you will not be welcome back!'

Frances winced.

Ruby could not believe her ears. 'Dad! You can't mean that!'

'Yes, I do. I'm putting my foot down on this matter.' His stance was rigid, his voice unkind.

Ruby stared at him, unable to recognise him as the man who had brought them up without a harsh word. And now this.

'Come on, Dad,' her voice was placating despite the anguished surprise seething within. 'My mother's dead and gone, but if she were still alive, I would be doing exactly the same as Frances. I would want to know where she was and if she was well. After all, it's only natural.'

'I call it ungrateful. I brought you up, Frances, not your mother. If you persist in going to find her, then I'm finished with you. I've made my mind up and that's an end to it.'

Although hurt by his words, Frances was adamant. 'I don't care what you think. I only know what I feel. I want to find her and that's it.'

Stan stood up and put his back to the fire, legs parted, fingers knotted behind him. All the hurt he'd felt at the time of his brother's death came flooding back. If there'd been no Great War, his brother would likely be here now. He might never have married Mildred and might never have been hurt by her. The wounds ran deep and Stan could not ignore them.

Ruby knew her father well. He'd been mother as well as father to her for many years, the unchanging lighthouse in the shifting sea of life. 'Dad, do you know where she might have gone?'

He remained unmoved.

Ruby tried again. 'Dad, Frances needs to know.'

'Even if I'm no longer welcome in this house,' added Frances.

Ruby looked at her cousin, suddenly alert to the fact that she *was* no longer a child. This was a brave new Frances, a young girl on the threshold of life who needed to know her mother in order to know herself.

'Please,' whispered Frances, turning the full force of her velvet brown eyes to him. 'If you know where she is . . .'

There was a guarded look in his eyes when he shook his head. 'No, I don't,' he said firmly. 'That was all the information I had. She left here. She didn't ever get in touch again, and that's an end to it! If you want to go searching for her, then go. But as I said, if you do go, then never darken my door again.'

'Dad! That's terrible!' Ruby was beside herself.

Frances eyed him more coolly. She glared at him, suddenly angry and wondering if she did in fact hate him. At this moment, it certainly felt that way.

Her anger came pouring out. 'She probably knew you didn't like her! That was why she ran away, wasn't it! Because you hated her!'

Alarmed at her outburst, Stan took a step back. As he did so, the corner of the newspaper he held in his right hand went too near the fire.

'Now look what you've done.' He was shouting at the top of his voice and at the same time attempting to beat out the flame on the top of the kitchen range. Deducing that his newspaper was beyond rescue, he crumpled it between both hands, opened the door of the range and threw it into the fire.

'There! Satisfied now?'

Her anger undiminished, Frances glared at him. He'd never shouted at her like that before. She felt as though he'd slapped both sides of her face.

Being threatened with banishment might have frightened some people, but not Frances. All Stan had done was make her angry and more determined to find her mother. There was always a way out, always an option to pursue. That was what Declan had told her.

'Never mind facing a problem head on. Take a side step. Sneak up from behind,' he had counselled.

Frances folded the letter up and slid it back into the envelope.

The silence in the room was deafening and outside wasn't much better. The feel of thunder was in the air. Clouds shielded the promising sun. The dull day and the difficult silence persisted.

Frances headed for the stairs. 'Well, at the moment there's nothing more to be done so I might as well go up and make the beds – while I'm still here.'

Ruby attempted to follow. 'I think I should go upstairs and give you a hand . . .'

Stan Sweet intervened. 'No. Leave her on her own for a while. Give her chance to get over it.'

Ruby wasn't so sure, though she certainly hoped so. She might have defied her father, but Charlie's behaviour intervened.

'Charlie!'

Ruby grabbed the spoon with which he was supposed to be eating his porridge. Instead, he was spooning it into his hair.

A jug of water was poured from the kitchen tap, an old towel borrowed from the bathroom, and a comb with big teeth borrowed from the top of her father's tallboy.

Ruby frowned. Frances had not confirmed the situation as regards her mother one way or another. 'I wonder what it says exactly in her letter. She didn't really say. Not really.'

Her father was surly. 'As long as it says Mildred isn't there, that's good enough for me.'

CHAPTER TWENTY-THREE

Upstairs in her room, Frances eyed the pink satin eiderdown that had slid from her bed during the night. It could stay on the floor until she'd read the letter for a second time. Never mind what her Uncle Stan thought or had said. Never mind that Ruby had taken her part. She was glad she had not divulged the contents of the letter. It was about her mother and thus very private.

Sitting herself down on the eiderdown's cool satin silkiness, she took the letter back out of the envelope. The thin paper rustled as she unfolded it. The words danced in front of her eyes.

Dear Miss Sweet,

In reply to your letter, I have to tell you that your mother did indeed reside at my boarding house some time ago, but then left to live with a friend in Cecil Street just around the corner. Her friend's name was Mr Mackenzie. I used to see her now and again, and when Mr Mackenzie died, she told me she had to get out of the house because his mother wouldn't have her there any longer. She moved out in a bit of a rush, leaving some of her things behind. Old Mrs Mackenzie, not allowing her over the threshold ever again, got in touch with me to fetch the few things she'd left there and

forward them on to her new address. I do have that
address somewhere. As soon as I find it, I'll send it to
you and I'll make a note if I hear anything of her in the
meantime.

    Yours sincerely,
    Mrs B Kepple,
    Sunshine Boarding House,
    77 Victoria Buildings,
    Stokes Croft,
    Bristol

Letter clutched in her hand, Frances stood up and grabbed the eiderdown, threw it on to the bed and slumped on to it full length, the satin cool against the heat of her cheek. She wanted to laugh, she wanted to cry, but most of all she wanted to get her hands on that information as quickly as possible. The best way to do that was not to wait for a letter to arrive, but to find Sunshine Boarding House and speak to Mrs Kepple direct. A little time was needed in which she could plan her escape – for escape it most certainly was. Despite any misgivings on anyone else's part, she was determined to do this.

The breeze coming in from the open window sent the familiar pink curtains billowing in. The colour almost matched the eiderdown. The walls were wallpapered, bunches of flowers scattered randomly in no particular pattern. All this she would leave behind if she went off to find her mother.

No matter the harshness of her uncle's words, and his statement that she would not be allowed to return, she would go. Her mind was made up. Besides, if he was this angry now, how would he be if he knew she was pregnant? How would her mother react?

She convinced herself that her mother would be over the moon, getting her daughter back and gaining a grandchild.

Somehow it seemed only right that her mother should know first before anyone else – including the baby's father.

Although Ruby appeared to be understanding of Frances's predicament, it was not possible for her to truly comprehend just how much finding her mother would mean to her. As she'd said to her uncle, it didn't matter what her mother had done, she was still blood of her blood, still her mother.

Holding the letter up over her head, she smiled as she re-read the address of Mrs Kepple's boarding house, where her mother had once stayed.

She smiled as she thought about what Declan would say. His gravelly tone was easily brought to mind.

'Get out there and do it.'

That was indeed what he would say.

Get out there and do it.

After carefully refolding the letter, she lay with her hands behind her head, staring at the ceiling. Some of the paint was flaking off. There were fine cracks in one corner, a fresh cobweb in another. None of it mattered. She'd leave it to Ruby to flick a feather duster at the cobweb. The cracks and the paint wouldn't be attended to until the war was over.

A plan began to form in her mind. It was no good telling her uncle that she had a definite lead to her mother's whereabouts. He'd made his feelings known in no uncertain terms: if she wanted her mother, then he considered her ungrateful. He might even forbid her to do what she intended doing, after all, she was only sixteen years of age. Nor would she tell Ruby.

Declan was the only person she could tell. She smiled at the thought of his face as he nodded approvingly, his deep eyes fixed on her as though she was the most delicious box of chocolates that had ever been.

He'd told her to follow her dream and she would do exactly that. She would run away and find Mrs Kepple, talk to her and then discover what her mother was like before going along to the address Mrs Kepple would give her. It would mean staying for one, perhaps two nights in Bristol. Declan would come with her! He would love to come with her. But first she had to get in touch with him.

Their meetings depended on a duty roster, a copy of which he'd given her a while ago.

'Just so you know where it's at.'

'Where it's at?' She'd laughed at some of his American slang.

She kept the duty roster in the drawer that also held her underwear, stockings – such as they were – and blouses.

'Same time, same day, same place.'

The time was always at two in the afternoon, on a Wednesday or a Friday. The place was the field at the top of Jarrow Lane, the place where they'd first made love.

As long as the weather was dry, their only company was the trees, the wide-open sky and the cows. Declan always brought a blanket if they were staying. Inclement weather meant a disused barn they'd found at the top of Tog Hill, halfway between Oldland Common and Siston.

Today was one of those days and she was feeling excited. Saying that she was going for a walk, she left the bakery heading for Jarrow Lane and the stile that had become her secret meeting place with the man she'd fallen in love with.

Wednesday, two o'clock, their usual time when he would drive along or, if he couldn't come, send a message.

Although she didn't own a watch, she could tell that roughly fifteen minutes had passed. Leaning against the gate behind her, she craned her neck so she could better see the end of the lane and the main road beyond that. The day was chilly so there was not a soul in sight. While waiting, she debated whether she should tell him she thought she might be pregnant. Only about six or seven weeks, but she felt different. Then there was the sickness. How long would that go on?

Still he hadn't come.

In an effort to see further, she clambered backwards on to the gate, finally sitting on the cross bar. Not that it achieved anything. There was no sign of him. No sign of anything, in fact.

Usually there were a few army vehicles passing by, but today there was nothing.

Half an hour or so went by, perhaps more. Finally, she conceded he wasn't coming. Gloomily she made her way back down the lane to the main road. She'd just got to the corner when she heard the unmistakeable sound of a motor vehicle.

Bursting with a new rush of happiness, she turned round. A Jeep was coming towards her at high speed, skidding to a halt just feet from where she was standing.

Ed Bergman gave her a perfunctory salute.

'Hi, Frances. How are you? Long time no see.'

His teeth shone white in his tanned face. He was chirpy, glad to see her. She guessed that he wasn't here by chance. She got straight to the point.

'Hello, Ed. Did Declan send you?'

He nodded. 'Captain O'Malley's compliments, but he has a prior engagement elsewhere.'

Frances picked up on the gloating tone, the message reluctantly delivered. She and Ed could have been closer, but once Declan O'Malley had put in an appearance, he didn't stand a chance.

It was pure instinct that she asked if he'd been posted.

'I'm not sure.'

Glowering at him, she folded her arms. 'What's that supposed to mean?'

'I mean I can't tell you where he's gone.'

His manner was casual and she couldn't help thinking he was enjoying having to give her the message. Ed Bergman had lost, Declan O'Malley had won, but today his win was hollow. He wasn't here. Ed Bergman was.

'So you don't know. Is it top secret?'

He shrugged and looked away. 'Could be. You know how it is.'

His grin was fetching and full of confidence. Yes. She knew how it was, all right.

A draught of air stirred the trees and sent her hair flying across her face. She eyed the oak while pushing her hair back from her face. The sight of the oak tree made her tingle.

'Fancy coming out with me this afternoon?'

She turned her head to look along the road, wishing that Declan would come driving along, tell Ed to skedaddle, and claim her for the rest of the day. If she did go with Ed he might think he could have what he'd had before. That alone did not make her feel nervous. Only a matter of days had passed between making love with Ed and making love with Declan. Declan didn't know about her condition, but she'd tell him soon and hope, just hope, that he would immediately assume it was his. Was that dishonest?

Again she looked up and down the main road through the village. There was no sign of any vehicle. Everything seemed strangely quiet.

'When will Declan be back?'

Ed made a snorting sound and didn't look too happy at being asked. 'I can't say.'

'Is it something to do with the invasion of Europe?'

She knew she'd hit the nail on the head when his cheeks turned as red as a girl's.

'No matter,' she said, holding up her hand, palm facing him. 'No need to answer. I think I already know.'

Declan had outlined reasons he might not turn up to meet her. The number one reason was the impending invasion of Europe.

'It's got to happen sooner or later,' he'd said to her. 'But, honey, never fear. I will return. Wait for me.'

Sooner rather than later, she thought to herself. In a sudden moment of comprehension, she rested her hand on her stomach. She began to walk away from the lane, the Jeep and the young GI who was fond of her.

'Hey! Frances! How about a date?'

She smiled at the way he'd asked his question, full of hope and flattery, but she didn't answer.

Her mind was made up. Before leaving home, she would give her uncle one last chance. She had a question to ask her uncle and although she had an inkling what his answer would be, she would still ask him to sign a document giving her permission to marry. It didn't matter too much if he refused. She now had another string to her bow. Mrs Kepple, her mother's ex-landlady, knew her mother's whereabouts. All she had to do was go to Bristol and find her.

She had enough savings to do that, and she would tell no one, not until she'd found her mother and told her that all was forgiven and that she wanted her to come home.

Your home or her home? asked the prickly voice in her head. She didn't know the answer to that.

CHAPTER TWENTY-FOUR

Ruby was getting a fish pie out of the oven when the phone rang for the third time that day.

'It's that creepy man again,' said Frances. 'Andrew Sinclair.'

Leaving the pie to cool on the window ledge, Ruby made her way out into the hall. She'd avoided Andrew throughout the time when Charlie was ill, deciding to postpone his suggestion that she give a series of talks and demonstrations to his mother's friends at a top-notch hotel in London. Andrew was persistent.

'Ruby! How are you?'

'Fine.'

'Everything's arranged. They want you next Wednesday.'

'Well, they can't have me.' To say that she was exasperated was putting it mildly. 'I've told you already, I have to wait until I'm sure my father and my cousin can cope with my nephew by themselves.'

'Ruby. You have to understand that they won't wait for ever.' He used a condescending tone as if she were a disobedient child.

'They might bloody well have to,' she snapped and slammed down the telephone.

Charlie had long been over his illness and was becoming quite a handful. Owing to the fact that Andrew had no sense of timing and not a clue about children, Ruby had continued to make the same excuses not to go to London, despite the fact that Charlie was perfectly well.

Anyway, Ruby was enjoying life and had just started dating yet another Polish flyer. 'It's not serious but I think it's the accent,' she said to Frances, whom she had started to confide in, Mary being too far away although she did write to her fairly regularly. There was always the telephone, of course, but it wasn't too reliable over a distance. Somebody said it was because the military had priority traffic. Chit-chats between families were low priority.

Once he'd mentioned that the allies had landed in France, Stan had spoken his thoughts about Ruby over his wife's gravestone.

'She goes out and enjoys herself with different blokes, but that's it. I asked her about Johnnie Smith. She told me that as long as there's no word otherwise, he's still alive. She's afraid that if she does get involved with somebody else, well then he'll die. It's superstitious nonsense, of course, but she's convinced that as long as she believes he's coming home, then he will.

'Mary is fine and so is baby Beatrice. Michael has got himself a position teaching new pilots the rudiments of flying. We're all grateful for that.

'Charlie is getting to be something of a handful, just like his father was . . .'

He did not mention Frances. The fact that she was so determined to find her mother stuck in his throat.

'You should go away and have some fun,' Frances suggested.

'Should I indeed?' Ruby was busy working on some recipes the Ministry of Food had asked her to test for usefulness. Some of the recipes had been forwarded by ordinary housewives keenly patriotic to do their bit. There was something very satisfying about rubbing fat into flour, feeling the crumbs of energising nourishment between her fingers. She made a point of rubbing the two ingredients together above the bowl and letting the mixture drop into the bowl. 'It takes in more air that way,' she'd explained to Frances.

Her thoughts far from cooking, Frances watched silently. 'Mary doesn't live very far from London,' she exclaimed while smearing fat around the edges of the baking tin that Ruby intended using.

'I'm not sure you're right. I think it's quite a way.'

'Actually, you're equidistant,' Frances said loftily. 'London is about halfway between the two of you.'

Ruby sighed, her flour-covered hands immobile as the facts outlined by her cousin sunk in. 'Ah! I forgot. You always were good at geography.' She stopped crumbling the mixture, an affectionate look in her eyes. 'I must admit I would love to see baby Beatrice.'

'If Mary came down to London, she could bring Beatrice that far, couldn't she?'

Ruby looked at her. 'Are you a mind reader?'

Frances looked nonchalant, that 'butter wouldn't melt in my mouth' look. 'It would be nice, though, wouldn't it?'

Ruby agreed that it would. She resumed rubbing the flour and fat between her fingers. 'I suppose you'd like to see the baby too.'

'No. I couldn't. I'd have to stay here while you were away, to look after Charlie and Uncle Stan and the bakery. You'd have to have a holiday from your cooking demonstrations – unless you did some in London.'

Ruby stopped rubbing the flour again and fixed her cousin with an enquiring frown. 'Have you been eavesdropping on my telephone conversations, young lady?'

'Andrew Sinclair said that he knew I was a good cook too and if I'd been old enough he'd invite me to London to give cooking demonstrations to very notable people – though I wouldn't mind if they weren't notable.'

Ruby eyed her in amazement. 'Andrew Sinclair asked that?'

Frances nodded. 'But I'm not old enough, am I, so I can't go. And you would come back just in time for the Fly the Flag Baking Competition. The money raised will go to the widows and orphans' fund. Did you know that?'

'I can't enter,' Ruby said. She would have loved to participate in the competition, but as a professional she was no longer eligible. She eyed Frances warily. Something was going on here. Not that Frances was likely to let on.

For the rest of the day, she thought about what her cousin had said. Frances was young and sometimes manipulative, but on this occasion what she'd suggested was highly attractive. Ruby missed her twin sister and desperately wanted to see the baby. Travelling in wartime from one side of the country to the other was difficult, to say the least. Trains were slow and loaded with essential traffic, mainly service personnel. Then there was the bakery and, as Frances had so rightly pointed out, her cookery demonstrations. Important war work. It was difficult enough to get a day off, let alone travel. On top of that, Mary was up there by herself and lived in constant fear that something bad would happen if her husband flew again. There was so much they needed to talk about, lots of reassurance to be given and confidences exchanged. Meeting up seemed a very good idea and if Andrew Sinclair could be persuaded, it was easily achievable. He had access to rail permits. He could also pass some of her baking demonstrations to other people.

It brought her great joy to imagine a reunion with her sister. She might have gone on day-dreaming if Frances hadn't suddenly dropped a bombshell.

Frances could no longer keep her secret to herself. She had to tell somebody and although she would have liked it to have been her mother, what if she never found her? What with Declan being away, Ruby was next in line.

'Ruby, I'm having a baby. I'm going to marry Declan, like I told you. I have to! I need your help to talk to Uncle Stan! I need his permission.'

CHAPTER TWENTY-FIVE

'No! And that's final!'

Her uncle's refusal to give her permission to marry was not a surprise, though it was a disappointment, one that simmered inside.

Stan Sweet had displayed a terrible show of temper, called her a slut and threatened to beat the man senseless when Frances had disclosed that she was pregnant.

'Taking advantage of a young girl! At his age! Just wait till I get my hands on him!'

She'd never seen him so angry, but Frances had never felt so brave, so sure of herself and what she wanted in life. 'You're too old to beat him, Uncle Stan. He's much fitter and stronger than you are.'

Her tone of voice was so calm, so matter of fact. Stan Sweet's jaw dropped as he stared at her in disbelief. The fact was he knew that for all his shouting, all his threats, she was quite right. He was an old man and the realisation shocked him.

Frances swallowed the suspicion that Ed Bergman could as likely be the father as Declan, though her uncle would probably have preferred it to be him, a man close to her own age.

She'd managed to get hold of Declan's whereabouts and sent him a note that the adjutant assured her would be passed on.

A brief note had come back that had made her heart sing. 'Marriage?' It was all it said but was enough to fill her with confidence and make her heart leap with joy.

Although the pair of them had set no definite date, she had determined to broach the subject. The air needed clearing. Her mind was set. If her uncle wouldn't give permission, then she had to find her mother, the only other person who could.

Perhaps she might have confided in Ruby about the child's paternity and asked her advice if her uncle hadn't angered her. What right did he have to shout at her like that, insisting that Declan was much too old for her? Worse still was his insinuation that she was no better than her mother, and she knew only too well what he thought of Mildred Sweet. Instead, she left the room, slamming the door shut behind her.

Her only regret was that the door slamming had awoken Charlie.

Ruby sighed. 'Dad. Will you reconsider? Think of Frances's reputation. Think of the child.'

Stan Sweet looked away, his hands clasped before him in front of the fire. His favourite chair suddenly seemed uncomfortable and he found it difficult to raise his head and look into his daughter's eyes. When had she become so confident, so much more a mature woman than the girl she used to be?

'I suppose I should,' he grumbled.

'Of course you should. Didn't women get pregnant before getting married in your day? Were things that much different last time we were at war?'

She couldn't be sure, but it seemed a faint blush came to her father's face. 'It's human nature. Anyway, I thought this Declan bloke was your man.'

Ruby shook her head. 'As I keep telling everybody, we're friends. Just friends.'

She didn't go into greater detail, how one night she'd sobbed on Declan's shoulders and told him about Johnnie Smith and what she thought he might be going through.

Johnnie might not be in her every thought, but he was still there, lingering in her heart.

'If you don't give her permission, she'll definitely go looking for someone who can.'

Her father looked sullen. He knew who she was referring to. If he didn't give permission, then Frances would most definitely go looking for her mother as she'd threatened.

Escaping her uncle's hostile response, Frances omitted to mention that Declan had been called away and that she suspected the invasion of Europe was imminent. Neither had she told him that she intended marrying Declan the moment he returned from his secret duty, regardless of whether he gave her permission to wed or not. It was more important than ever that she found her mother. Once she had that permission, then she was free to marry as long as Declan came home, and she hoped and prayed that he would, preferably before 'the big show', as the Americans called the offensive against the Third Reich.

Outside the warmth of the bakery, the village was dark, the night air chill and still. She had no particular destination in mind. All she wanted was time to think.

She shivered. If only she'd thought to grab a coat. It couldn't be helped. She had envisaged a scene and the consequences had set her mind on what she had to do next.

It was the height of summer and although the farmers would have preferred a series of sunny days, sunshine was still intermingled with bouts of heavy rain.

Having walked out her anger and sorted out her thoughts, she finally came to a halt outside the Dolphin pub. The big building rose stately and tall, visible even in the blank darkness of the blackout. There was no sound from within and no light showing. The pub had shut early.

The sound of a steam train blowing its whistle came from the direction of the railway station. Frances stood silently, imaging the clouds of smoke, the dusty smell of burning coal.

The railway stations were very busy nowadays, taking armaments from the industrial Midlands to the docks at Bristol. Rumour had it there were many ships waiting there to be loaded. Nobody knew for sure where they were headed, though it was whispered it had to be the south coast of England, anywhere from Dover down to Portsmouth.

The train would take her out of here, not to the south coast but as far as Bristol. That was where she wanted to be.

She thought of Declan's face when they met again, when she waved that important piece of paper in his face.

Her excitement bubbled over to such an extent that she almost ran back to the bakery with a mind to bursting in and telling her uncle that his permission wasn't needed. She was not so foolish as to do that. He might stop her from going to Bristol. She was underage. He could still stop her, make her a ward of court or something.

No. Her plan was her own and she would carry it through.

Mrs Kepple, the Bristol landlady, had told her in her letter that she knew her mother's whereabouts. She had just needed a bit of time to find the address.

She smiled at mental visions of how her mother would look, the smile on her face, the love in her eyes. Once the tears and regrets were over, her mother would confide in her as to the true reason she'd left, though Frances couldn't for the life of her imagine what that reason might be.

The sound of the train faded. The sound of her heartbeat seemed suddenly to fill her head. Tomorrow, having accepted

Andrew Sinclair's invitation to give a demonstration in the west end of London, Ruby was catching the train to London and would be gone for one week. Shortly after that, if Declan had not returned, Frances too would be on a train, though hers would go to Bristol.

CHAPTER TWENTY-SIX

Women with aloof expressions glided into the room at the Dorchester Hotel as though they owned it. The air smelled of flowers, though there were no displays in the room. Ruby concluded the strong perfume was emanating from the women themselves.

'Is everything to hand?'

Andrew Sinclair had stayed close by from the moment she'd arrived, hovering like a moth around a flame.

'Yes,' she replied brusquely. Full of his own self-importance, he appeared not to notice her attitude.

'My mother knows some very grand people,' he exclaimed, his face a bland repose of self-satisfaction.

Ruby had to admit that the ladies did indeed look rather grand with their fox furs, their fashionable hats and the way their nylons rustled when they crossed one leg over the other.

'Well, you seem to have taken my advice,' he murmured while casting his eyes over her notes and the ingredients she was using.

'I have.'

Andrew had suggested she give a talk and demonstrate suitable dishes for ladies who entertained.

'You can do that, can you not?'

She'd wanted to stamp on his foot and remind him that her remit was to help women feed families, not their guests. Before she'd actually gone ahead and done that, she reminded herself of the other reason for falling in with Andrew's plans; it was halfway to Lincolnshire and her sister Mary.

'I'm so glad you agreed to do this,' whispered Andrew, his breath smelling of mint sauce.

'It's a pleasure.'

She didn't add that her agreement was to her own advantage.

After waving to an elderly lady in the front row, presumably his mother, Andrew stepped forward, clapping his hands. 'Ladies! Can I have your full attention, please?'

His chin was held high, enabling him to look through his spectacles, which hovered on the bridge of his nose.

Following the introduction, which was followed by polite clapping, it was Ruby's turn to step forward.

'Ladies. Thank you for coming. My name is Ruby Sweet and I am here to talk about recipes for entertaining. I'm sure you will agree with me that catering for special occasions is not easy during war. However, may I remind you of the real reason I am here; entertaining friends, relatives and even VIPs is not really what this is all about. At the heart of it is winning this war. Brave men in ships have been burdened with the dangerous task of bringing food from across the sea. A lot of those men have lost their lives. My brother was one of them. It's down to you to set your selfish interests aside and think of the greater sacrifice that men in ships are making. Cast aside luxury ingredients. Make do with cheaper cuts of British reared meat. Bake simply, but bake well.'

Some of those attending the talk fidgeted uncomfortably; some murmured indignantly, some with surprise.

Andrew's jaw dropped. 'I say!'

For a moment, she thought she was about to get a warning about knowing her place and being courteous to her betters. He'd even given her a brief résumé of what to say, as if this was some kind of play and his was the script.

'For that reason, ladies, people from all walks of life, a large number with a weekly income of less than you spend on food in a day, have pared down their intake of food, making something from nothing, preserving, pickling and experimenting in order to conserve our food supplies. If the very poor can do without some very basic foods, then I'm sure you too can cut back.'

By the time she'd finished her opening gambit, the majority of superior expressions had been replaced by fervent attention, surprise, and guilt.

Remarks were hissed from pursed lips. Ruby carried on regardless.

'Let us begin with canapés. Pastry made from flour and rolled oats . . . fillings of sardine, puréed vegetables with added spice . . .'

Ruby warmed to her task, finding it rather amusing that some of the elegant ladies had brought their cooks with them. Not all, it seemed, had jumped ship and found work in a munitions factory.

Amazingly, a full-size gas stove had been manhandled into position behind her. Once her recipes were safely ensconced in baking tins, she placed them in the oven. Before very long the aroma of good things baking filled the air.

'Canapés are a fitting alternative to a three-, four- or five-course dinner,' she told them. 'We all have to make sacrifices,' she added after receiving one or two sour looks. They disappeared once she'd suggested soup or carrot and cucumber crudities with a spicy dip were a suitable starter for a proper dinner, while rabbit casserole with vegetables was ideal for a main course. 'I'm sure some of you must know people with country estates. Rabbits may be vermin to a farmer or gamekeeper, but they're as succulent as chicken and an economic alternative to more expensive game.'

As she made suggestions for dessert, which included every possible dish using apples, she went on to praise the delicacy that was egg custard made from dried egg.

At the end of it all, when Andrew asked the audience to put their hands together and applaud her presentation, she took the time to think of the contrast between these people, the lives they lived and those at the other end of the social scale.

A hubbub of cut-glass voices erupted as those at the back of the room threaded their way through the swathes of chairs to the exit.

A large number of them had tasted the canapés she'd passed round. Most had taken a copy of her recipe book, the latest thing she'd put together. Andrew had assisted.

'It should be published,' he'd told her.

She'd shaken her head at the time. 'Don't be silly.'

Much to her amazement, he had them printed courtesy of the Ministry of Food.

'Your work is vital, Miss Sweet. Absolutely vital.'

She thanked him, though a trifle tersely. Give Andrew an inch and there was no knowing what length he would stretch to.

'Though I really do think you should have kept to the script—'

'Andrew. Look at that table.'

She pointed. Only a few of her baking booklets were left on the table, which made her smile. It had given her great pleasure to see one after another being picked up by a group of kid-gloved ladies.

'Young lady!'

The woman who addressed her was the one Andrew had been waving to.

'My mother,' he said. His manner was deferential but also apprehensive. It turned out he had rights to be.

'Lillian Lavery-Sinclair. I'm Andrew's mother. Lavery was my maiden name. My son prefers not to use it. He says it's old-fashioned and too feminine, as though dropping it could make him more masculine than he actually is.' The look she gave her son verged on contempt.

Was it Ruby's imagination that Andrew's face flooded with colour?

His mother wore a pale mauve dress. Her fur jacket was mink. Her wrinkled lips were red. Ruby guessed that the fingers clothed in white gloves were stained with nicotine, judging by the woman's teeth.

Lillian Lavery-Sinclair fixed Ruby with a cold blue stare. 'I take it you've never been in service.' Her voice was sharp, her words clipped.

Ruby responded in the same clipped manner. 'No. I have not!'

'No. I thought not. Andrew has been very selective in what he tells me about you.'

'I can't understand why. I live in a small village and my father owns the local bakery, which was also where I was working prior to the war.'

Looking slightly embarrassed, Andrew intervened. 'Mother, this is hardly the time. Don't you have to meet your friends for tea at the Ritz?'

The hand he attempted to rest on her shoulder was brushed off.

'There's no point in going there. I can get tea here.'

'But your friends . . .'

Ruby sensed Andrew was doing his best to get rid of his mother. The old lady was having none of it.

The piercing eyes landed on Ruby again. 'I insist on you having tea with me, young lady.'

Andrew interrupted. 'Mother. Time is pressing. We really must be going . . .'

'I wasn't inviting you. I want to speak to this girl alone.'

Andrew looked as though she'd suggested something quite alien, something he feared.

Ruby smiled. A cup of tea with the old lady in the hallowed portals of the Dorchester was something she would never have experienced before the war. Blow Andrew. She had time before catching the train.

'I'd be delighted,' she said, picking up her handbag. 'As long as Andrew would be kind enough to pack up all the bits and pieces he supplied for my talk.'

'Of course he can,' snapped Mrs Lavery-Sinclair. With the air of somebody used to being obeyed, she slid her arm through Ruby's without it actually being offered.

Having the manner of somebody used only to having the best in life, she ordered that a table in a quiet corner should be allocated for their use. Ruby studied the woman sitting across the white tablecloth. Tea had been brought, two cubes of sugar per person and a small jug of milk. The cakes were of a superior quality, commensurate with its clientele.

'Before the war, there was a far greater variety.' Andrew's mother nodded at the cakes. Ruby counted four. 'They used to bring a three-tier cake stand, choux buns and cream cakes of every description. Now look at it.'

Ruby did look. 'I think they look quite good.'

Her companion raised a thin eyebrow. 'I suppose it depends what you're used to.'

'I suppose it does,' Ruby responded. She wondered at the woman's intention. She would not be servile, even if that's what was expected of her.

Holding her smallest finger aloft, Mrs Lavery-Sinclair eyed her over the top of her teacup, her lipstick leaving a smear of red on the rim.

Ruby took a bite. The cake was good. Andrew's mother crumbled a piece on her plate and didn't seem that bothered about eating.

The feeling that she was being studied made Ruby feel ill at ease.

'I hear you have a twin sister.'

Ruby confirmed that she did.

'And she's married to an air force pilot. A Canadian. Is that correct?'

'Yes.'

'And your father is a baker, you say. Is he a successful baker?'

'I think so.'

'And you met my son in Bristol.'

'Yes.'

'I worry about him when he's away from home. He's all I have since his father died. I look out for him and he looks out for me. Unlike his father, he's not the most masculine of men. You do realise that, don't you?'

Too many questions! Ruby sat back in her chair, her eyes narrowed. Being assessed as a woman was one thing, but feeling like a bug beneath a microscope was something else. She wasn't the sort to allow herself to be the subject of such scrutiny.

'Mrs Sinclair!' She purposely omitted the Lavery. 'What am I doing here?'

Both thin eyebrows now rose as though the question bordered on downright cheek. 'I thought the reason was obvious. You came here at my son's request.'

'I don't mean that. I mean why have you invited me to tea?'

Gloved fingers played with the cake crumbs as Andrew's mother considered her response. She didn't seem at all fazed by the question.

'Again, my dear, I think the reason is obvious. As Andrew's mother I have every right to know as much as possible about his fiancée . . .'

'Fiancée!'

It took all the self-control Ruby had not to burst out laughing, but after her exclamation, she found herself lost for words.

Mrs Lavery-Sinclair frowned. This was not the response she'd expected. For the first time since they'd met, she looked unsure of herself. Her thin lips moved almost imperceptibly as though she were chewing over something distasteful. 'You're not my son's fiancée?'

'I am most certainly not!'

'He led me to believe he'd asked you to marry him and that his proposal had been accepted.'

Ruby shook her head, her glossy brown hair dancing around at chin level. 'He's never asked me.'

'Hmm.' Andrew's mother visibly relaxed, her shoulders seeming to diminish beneath the weight of her mink stole. 'Good. When he does, I wish you to know that I would not approve of my son marrying you. Quite frankly, I think he can do better.'

'Quite frankly, I think I can do better too!'

At first Mrs Lavery-Sinclair looked surprised, arching her pencil-thin eyebrows as though she'd had something thrown into her face. Once that had passed she looked positively relieved.

'I'm so glad you understand,' she said after calling for the bill. 'Don't take it to heart that I don't want you to marry him. I suppose I'm just old-fashioned, but I know what I want in a daughter-in-law.'

Feeling likely to explode, Ruby got to her feet and picked up her handbag. 'I'm sorry. I have to go. Do tell Andrew I said goodbye. He was expecting me to come back later in the week, but I have other commitments. I hope he understands. Oh, and by the way, I already have a sweetheart interned in a Japanese prison camp. A brave man who really has served his country. Not a mummy's boy who stayed at home!'

A porter fetched the small suitcase she had left in his cubicle of an office. Face on fire, Ruby swept past the uniformed commissionaire at the entrance. The fresh air that hit her was welcome after the stifling interior of the Dorchester Hotel and Andrew's dreadful mother.

Her mood lightened as she headed for the train station; she even began swinging the suitcase as her steps quickened. She had a long journey ahead of her, but she didn't care. Mary was waiting for her – and baby Beatrice too – and they had lots to catch up on. One of the subjects of their conversation would be Andrew Sinclair. At the thought of him, Ruby finally laughed out loud.

'You sound 'appy,' said the man in the ticket kiosk.

Ruby's smile widened. 'I am.'

'Sounds as though you're in love and will be waltzing up the aisle in no time,' he chortled.

Ruby pulled a face and laughed. 'Far from it. I've just met his mother. I'm off to pastures new!'

CHAPTER TWENTY-SEVEN

It was early morning when Ruby had left home and ten o'clock at night when she finally arrived at her destination. The signs proclaiming the station's name had been removed at the outbreak of war so that if the enemy did land they wouldn't be able to work out where they were. The trouble was neither could anybody else. If the stationmaster hadn't been shouting it out at the top of his voice, she wouldn't have known where she was.

Her brother-in-law Michael waded through the crowds to get to her, took her luggage and led her outside to where he'd parked his little black Ford.

'It's compact, but useful,' he said to her. 'Also big enough to accommodate two children. We've decided to try for another one as soon as we can.'

'Michael, that's marvellous . . .'

Michael relayed all that had happened as far as he could.

'It's not going to be too long now before I'm back on Ops, at least that's what I'm hoping. Everyone thinks the big show is about to kick off.'

'I hope it's over soon,' said Ruby.

'Have you heard anything else from Johnnie? Mary told me about the postcard.'

'No. No, I haven't.'

She swallowed the lump in her throat. There had been nothing after that single postcard. Headlines of allied advances in the newspapers gave her hope. At home, in consideration of her feelings, Johnnie was rarely mentioned. There was every chance that he would come back, but equally there was every chance he might not. Keeping the thought of him bottled up inside was her way of dealing with the situation.

They travelled past fields, the vast sky an indigo backdrop to the flat black landscape.

She was welcomed by the smell of fresh baking as they entered the cottage.

'Duck,' said Michael before going through the door.

A pile of logs was glowing in the open hearth. Mary was standing by the vast inglenook, her face pink from the heat of the fire and baking. Beatrice was propped up in an armchair, giggling and kicking her legs.

'Mary!'

They fell into each other's arms and cried on each other's shoulders. The baby stilled and looked up at them with her big blue eyes, perhaps unsure as to why she was seeing two versions of her mother, both dressed differently but looking so alike.

Mary was desperate for news. 'There's so much to talk about. How's Dad? How's Charlie? How's Frances. How's—'

'One at a time!'

Ruby assured Mary that everyone was well. Charlie especially had recovered quickly from his illness.

'He's a typical rough-and-tumble little boy.'

Mindful not to hurt her brother-in-law's feelings, Ruby only glanced at Michael's face. Even so, she was sure she saw him wince before looking away. She felt for him – every man wanted a son – but perhaps this next baby would be a boy.

'And you're not engaged or anything,' Mary went on, excitement making her eyes sparkle. 'Last we talked I thought you were friendly with a military policeman.'

'He was a friend. That's all.'

She had considered mentioning Declan's relationship with Frances, but desisted; perhaps she might when Michael wasn't around. Neither did she mention Frances being pregnant. In time she would, but for now there were too many other things to discuss. Andrew Sinclair was one of them.

Beatrice had long been put to bed when Ruby told them what Andrew's mother had said. Everyone laughed but also felt sorry for him. Andrew was the way he was because of his mother's domination.

'Pity the wife, if he ever does get one,' commented Michael.

Mary began piling the dirty dinner plates. 'So how about you and your Corporal Smith, then? Clearly you're still carrying at torch for him. Are you going to marry him?'

Ruby looked down at the table.

'I fear looking into the future. I've had just one card. And that was from a prison camp.'

Mary sighed. 'He's tough. He'll survive. You just see if he doesn't.'

Ruby smiled sadly. 'Yes. Yes, he is.'

They washed the dishes between them, carrying on their conversation, chattering as if time and distance had never happened.

Once they were sitting comfortably in front of the crackling logs, breathing in the smell of apples, Michael brought drinks.

'Sherry. I'm afraid it's all we have. We need to visit Aunt Bettina before long for a re-stock.'

Ruby thanked him and, once he was holding a glass, suggested a toast. 'To the end of the war!'

'And to a growing family,' Michael added. 'Mary says just two, I suggested a lot more than that.'

'Six,' declared Mary. 'You said six!'

They all laughed.

'Hopefully, the war *will* be over by then,' stressed Ruby.

'Yes,' said Mary.

Ruby knew that the way her sister suddenly looked down at her feet was ominous. A quick glance at her brother-in-law confirmed something ominous there too.

'I expect you'll look for somewhere to settle once the war is over – somewhere nice where you can bring up a horde of children,' Ruby said laughingly.

Michael looked at her. 'Yes. That is exactly my intention. I've got the chance of a job in Canada. It's a good job and well paid.'

'You sound as though you've made up your mind.'

Of course he had, hence the look on her sister's face. She didn't need to be a mind reader to know that her sister didn't want to go to Canada.

It was at breakfast the next day, after Michael had left for the base, that her suspicion was confirmed.

Ruby took over spooning porridge into Beatrice's mouth while Mary rolled out the pastry for that evening's supper, mutton pie.

'What are you going to do?'

Mary shook her head. 'I don't want to go.'

'I didn't think you would.'

'Moving up here was bad enough.'

'It must have been difficult at first, though you seem content enough now.'

'Yes,' said Mary, her mouth tightening as she slammed the rolling pin down on to the pastry. 'Living here I can at least get on a train down to see my family, after the war, I mean. But

Canada . . .' Her arms slackened and her throat moved as she swallowed. A faraway look came to her eyes. 'Sometimes I wish I could turn back the clock . . .'

In the past, Ruby might have sided with her and said that of course she shouldn't go, but not now.

'Mary. What makes you think that your family – your old family – is going to remain in the same place they've lived all their life? It's all in the past. Frances is going to get married someday soon, and so am I, I hope. It's unlikely we'll remain where we are, and besides, we're your old family. You've got a new one now.'

'Someday soon?'

Ruby licked her lips. She hadn't meant to come out with it quite so swiftly.

'Frances is pregnant. She told us just before I left for London. That military policeman friend of mine.'

'Isn't he . . .?'

'Yes, a bit too old for her. Dad is livid and swears he won't sign for her to get married.'

'He has to,' Mary exclaimed sounding dismayed. 'Frances mentioned on the phone that an American soldier had asked her to marry him, but she said nothing about being pregnant. I didn't realise that the Declan she mentioned was your friend, either. What about the child? It's not an easy life for a child born out of wedlock.'

Ruby sighed. 'You try telling Dad that.'

Although she'd always been the gentler of the two, Mary adopted a determined stance. 'I will tell him. You can bet on it.'

'Anyway,' said Ruby, wishing to steer the conversation back to her sister's concern about leaving the country and her family behind. 'Would it really be so bad if you moved to Canada?'

'I suppose I would make new friends. I have here, though there's not many of us, and all air force wives. The rest of the time I'm here by myself. With Beatrice, of course. Writing letters is fine, but it's not the same as having somebody else to talk to.'

Ruby stood up and wound her arm around her sister's shoulder. 'You're a very lucky woman, Mary Dangerfield. You have a handsome husband who adores you and a lovely daughter. Your world is complete, whereas mine . . .' She sighed. 'I've got no husband and not even a sweetheart, really.' She stroked the imagined lines from the corners of her eyes at the same time peering at her reflection in the small mirror hanging to one side of the window. 'I'll probably end up an aged spinster! Then you'll feel lucky! Poor old Ruby, you'll say. A dried-up old spinster!'

Her humour worked, Mary's laughter attracting the curiosity of her small daughter.

'You'll be fine,' Mary said in a kindly manner. 'I envy you.'

The two sisters exchanged loving looks. Mary looked happier and more accepting. Ruby, although she smiled, knew what she'd stated was the absolute truth. There was no Mister Right dancing attendance on her and she'd feel a great emptiness inside until Johnnie came marching home – if he came marching home.

'I don't mind being a spinster,' she finally said. 'Anyway, I've got Charlie to look after.'

'And John Smith. He'll come home, Ruby. I'm sure he will.'

It was a couple of days later when Michael took her back to the station and the train to London. The journey across London to Paddington Station would be gruelling and she wouldn't arrive home until very late at night. The alternative would have been to stay in London overnight, but she didn't want to do that. She'd done her duty by speaking to the group at the Dorchester Hotel and did not wish to bump into either Andrew or his mother. Initially, Andrew lying to his mother had made her bristle. Now it made her laugh.

Michael was abnormally quiet all the way to the station. Ruby guessed the reason why.

'Don't worry, Michael. She will go to Canada with you. I'm sure she will.'

The suddenness of her comment caused him to veer towards the middle of the road. 'She told you?'

'Of course she told me. I'm her sister.' She smiled at him. 'Don't you two ever speak to each other?'

Michael kept his eyes on the road ahead, though it was totally empty, a narrow ribbon running between flat fields. Overhead, a single aircraft made its way across the sky.

'My fault. I've been a bit preoccupied of late trying to persuade the high command that I'm fit to fly. I want one last crack at the enemy before it's all over. Just one.'

'Haven't you done enough?'

He gave her a weak smile that tugged at her heartstrings. 'It may sound stupid, but I can't help feeling guilty. A lot of my old pals are dead. I'm still alive.'

'You shouldn't feel guilty about it.'

'So I'm told, but I can't help it.'

Ruby turned her head as though eyeing the endless landscape, purely so he wouldn't see the moistness in her eyes for all those boys, all those who would never have the choice between living in England and living in Canada.

Once her emotions were under control, she turned to him and smiled. 'Let me remind you that you're never going to be a concert pianist, thanks to your insistence on becoming an RAF pilot.'

At first he didn't see that she was being flippant.

'I never—'

Then the penny dropped. Smiling, he shook his head.

'You've made your sacrifice,' said Ruby, her tone turning more serious. 'You've sacrificed quite a lot and your beautiful wife and darling daughter would prefer that things went no further.'

He laughed again and for a moment she felt triumphant until the truth hit her that he would still go back into action if given the chance.

It was only two days following Ruby's return home that Frances went missing. She'd left a note.

Gone to find my mother.

CHAPTER TWENTY-EIGHT

The house had a bay window and a brass knocker.

Tilting her head back, Frances counted the windows: two on each floor and there were three storeys. The façade looked well maintained and the net curtains behind the gleaming windows were crisply white.

Taking a deep breath, Frances lifted the knocker and rapped sharply.

A sound of movement came from within before the door opened and an older woman with a round face and a ready smile stood there. 'Good morning. Can I help you?'

The woman's voice was high and squeaky and she had the comfortable look of a Beatrix Potter mouse.

'My name's Frances Sweet. I wrote to you asking for news of my mother, Mildred Sweet. She stayed with you for a while. You said you might be able to point me in the right direction.'

'Ah, yes. Do you wish to stay?'

Frances was immediately panic-stricken because she'd stupidly forgotten to ask in her letter whether she had a vacancy. 'Do you have a room?'

'As a matter of fact, you're in luck. Miss Scott moved out two days ago and I haven't got round to turning the sign over.'

With a nod of her dimpled chin, she indicated the *No Vacancies* sign in the ground-floor bay.

'Come in,' she added chirpily, opened the door wide then shut it firmly once Frances was inside. 'I presume you haven't eaten. You'll be wanting supper, won't you? Yes. Of course you will.'

She went on chattering, asking questions that she answered before Frances did.

Frances had arrived just as the night was drawing in and Mrs Kepple, the landlady, had already lit a fire in the front parlour. The smell of something hearty and warming came from the kitchen at the back of the house.

'Beef stew,' she said on hearing Frances's stomach rumbling. 'It smells wonderful.'

'And so it should,' said Mrs Kepple. She seemed a good-natured sort and jolly too, despite the man-sized fists that rested on her ample hips and the wrap-around apron straining at the seams over her belly. 'I put in plenty of dripping, enough meat to give it flavour, vegetables of every kind – including carrots – old Mr Dent, my greengrocer, was generous with the carrots this morning. And I added doughboys. I s'pose you'd call them dumplings, but my grandmother always called them doughboys so it's in me, so to speak . . . Doughboys was what they called the American soldiers back in the Great War.'

After Mrs Kepple finished describing tonight's stew in detail, she went on to the pudding she'd baked for afters. 'Suet pudding with treacle. I did put a few sultanas in it as well and I've got custard too for them that wants it . . .'

Frances refrained from interrupting. It seemed that when Mrs Kepple talked about food, there was no stopping her. She went over the ingredients and preparation of meals in great detail. Presumably the privations of the war had a lot to do with it. People did seem to think about food a lot more, not just longing for food no longer available, but also pondering how to make bland ingredients into filling and nourishing meals. Suet pudding and a stew with dumplings – or doughboys as Mrs Kepple put it – were a case in point. The landlady's eyes sparkled as she went over the details. Once that was out of the way she told her the price of the room. 'Just let me know how long you want it.'

The room she showed her into was at the back of the house. There was a bed, a chest of drawers and a washstand complete with jug and bowl. A clean towel was folded up beside it.

Mrs Kepple announced that the window overlooked the back garden. 'Not that you can see much at this time of night.'

Once her landlady had left the room, Frances sat down on the bed. There was no fire in the grate. Frances shivered, not just because the room was chillier than she was used to, but also her bedroom back home was warm thanks to the rising heat of the bread oven. Apprehension sat like a ball of knotted wire in her stomach. Sometime soon she would meet up with her mother, and the prospect was daunting.

That night at dinner, in the comparative warmth of the dining room, she only picked at the stew and hardly touched the dessert. The other guests, a gentleman named Mr Ford, a woman who looked to be in her fifties named Miss Standish, and a young woman named Emily Parkin who worked at Woolworths, were all nice enough.

The conversation was courteous but friendly and, thankfully, nobody asked her awkward questions.

She couldn't help thinking of her mother, more so when Mrs Kepple handed her a scrap of paper. 'That's where she's living. I'm sure she's still there.'

Having made enquiries of its location, she had decided to catch the early bus the following morning. She couldn't bear to wait longer than she needed.

Even though Miss Parkin ate up the food she'd left, Mrs Kepple looked quite hurt. 'Didn't you like my stew, Miss Sweet? Or my pudding?'

Frances apologised. 'I'm sorry. I'm not feeling very hungry after all, and anyway, Emily didn't let it go to waste.'

'Certainly not,' said Emily as she spooned the last spoonful of suet pudding into her mouth. 'I'm on my feet all day. I need plenty of nourishment.'

'Of course you do, dearie,' said Mrs Kepple, patting the plump young woman on the shoulder. 'Isn't it nice to see Woolworths and all the other shops getting back to normal? All we need now is for Germany and Japan to surrender and everyone will be back where they belong!'

Frances made her excuses and went up to bed. Before undressing, she cracked open the blackout curtain and looked out of the window. The moon was bright and the rooftops glistened with rain.

Everyone was saying that there would be a new beginning after the war, and this time the government would be held to it, not like in the last one when promises had been made and swiftly broken. This time the peace would be built to last and everyone would be happy.

It wasn't like Frances to be selfish, but in this instance, wanting to be permanently reunited with her mother was top of her list. She couldn't wait for it to happen.

CHAPTER TWENTY-NINE

The following morning, Frances found herself treading a narrow street lined on each side by shabby houses of ill-matched design, each one leaning against the other in mutual support. It occurred to Frances that even if the buildings survived the war, they might not survive much longer.

Strips of dry paint curled from a battered front door at the address she'd been given. Frances knocked tremulously, her heart in her throat. The sound of footsteps came from inside before the door squealed on stiff hinges as it was wrenched open.

Frances stared at the woman, not wanting to believe that she really was Mildred Sweet. She'd set her mother on a pedestal for so long. But on the opening of the door, the mother she'd always imagined had fallen from a great height.

How could this woman possibly be her mother? She was nothing like she remembered from her childhood. Her hair was dyed a peroxide blonde, her make-up far from subtle. She thought she recognised the full pouting lips as her own, though her mother's were plastered with bright red lipstick. The smell of face powder and cheap perfume was overpowering. She looked for the coral necklace but didn't see it.

Frances swallowed her disappointment and continued. 'I'm Frances. Frances Sweet. I-I'm your daughter.'

The woman stared at her with eyes as hard as dried peas.

'Frances.' She said it dully, without emotion or sign of recognition.

Frances nodded. 'Yes,' she said, her voice sounding small and anxious. 'I've brought you some things I thought you might like. There's tinned peaches, Spam, condensed milk, and fruit from the garden.' She'd used her own ration book for the tinned goods. 'Apples mostly. Oh, and some sugar and a jar of honey and also a jar of mixed fruit jam. I made it myself.'

The woman took the string bag from her, eyeing it in surprise and also eyeing the person that had brought it as if undecided as to whether she wished to admit her identity.

Could Frances be mistaken? Was this even her mother?

Frances tried again. 'You are Mildred Sweet, are you not?'

Swayed by the weight of the string bag into which she cast a covetous gaze, a loose-lipped smile exposed yellow teeth. She looked Frances up and down.

'It's Mildred Baxter now but . . . my, my! So this is my little girl! Why, Franny, haven't you grown!' She didn't sound terribly happy about it, just a little surprised and even a little anxious.

'My name is Frances.' Frances clenched her fists. This was not at all the welcome she'd expected.

Her mother's eyebrows, plucked to the skin and reinstituted with eyebrow pencil, arched and her mouth tightened as though tasting something bitter.

'It's just I don't like being called Franny. I prefer being called Frances.'

'Hmm.' Her mother eyed her disdainfully, obviously not happy with her daughter's response.

Despite her disappointment that her mother was hardly the icon she'd thought she was, Frances was feeling tired.

Yesterday's flight from home and the fact she'd hardly slept a wink the night before was beginning to have an effect.

'Do you think I could come in?' she began hesitantly. 'I have come a long way.'

Mildred Baxter, as she was now, frowned. She glanced nervously over her shoulder, chewing her lips as though considering the request. 'Well, I suppose it won't hurt, and seeing as you've come all this way. But not for long, mind you . . .' she added in a warning tone.

As she entered the dark passageway, the smell of a dirty house, mould and fungus growing in dark corners assaulted Frances's nose.

Her mother opened the first door they came to. 'We'd better go in here,' she whispered. 'Quickly,' she added, pushing Frances in front of her. Again she glanced along the passageway to where the gloom intensified. There was the faint smell of stale cooking and beer.

Once inside the room, Mildred took great care in closing the door quietly. Frances wondered if somebody else was in the house, somebody she didn't want to disturb.

'This is the parlour. Sorry it's a bit cold, but there's nothing I can do about that. I don't use it that often.'

Frances took in the sagging chairs, the dust, the cold ashes left in the fireplace from a heap of coals that she guessed had burned out months ago.

Suppressing a shiver – the room was so cold – she stood there in the middle of the room waiting for her mother to invite her to sit down.

'I can't ask you to stay. Not today,' her mother said nervously, her red lips spreading in a hard smile that held no welcome, no warmth at all. 'I've got company, you see, and Oswald, Oswald Baxter my, well, husband for want of a better word, he's not one for company. Likes to have me to himself, you might say.'

Frances felt almost sorry for her mother's attempt to sound jolly, as though she really believed what she was saying. The mother she'd envisaged had gone off to make her fortune before one day returning to collect her. They were supposed to live happily ever after. This was not the mother she'd hoped for.

There was nothing for it but to dive in at the deep end. 'Why did you leave me?'

The question resulted in a blank look as though it were totally beyond her mother's comprehension to give any sensible answer.

Frances tried again. 'You left me when my father died. I wanted to know why.'

Mildred blinked and pursed her lips. 'I made sure you were well cared for, didn't I? Stan Sweet's an old stuffed shirt, but he's got a good heart for all that. I knew he wouldn't see you out on the streets . . .'

Frances could hardly believe the blatant nonchalance of her mother's attitude. It angered her. 'That doesn't answer my question. You abandoned me and you never got in touch. Not once, not even to send me a birthday or Christmas card . . .'

'Now see here, young lady. Don't you dare raise your voice to me!'

In warning Frances to keep her voice down, Mildred had raised hers, the consequences of which seemed to unnerve her. There was fear in her eyes when she jerked her attention to the closed door, the tip of her tongue sliding over her moist lips.

Frances heard the sound of big feet plodding along the passageway.

'There,' her mother hissed, her face contorted with fear as she turned round to face her. 'Look what you've done now!'

The door flew open.

'You noisy cow! Can't a bloke get some bloody sleep around 'ere without you . . .' He stopped in mid-tirade, his eyes alighting on Frances. 'Who the bloody hell are you?'

The man's profanity was bad enough, but his appearance was worse. So was the stale smell of body odour. Oswald Baxter was big and bloated, flabby flesh pressing against a stained vest. Thankfully, he was wearing trousers, the braces straining over his shoulders so they left deep indents.

His face was red and his eyes were strange, one of them moving while the other stayed quite still. It occurred to her that it was made of glass. Hadn't her uncle Stan mentioned that some men blinded in one eye during the Great War had been issued with glass eyes?

Her mother stepped between Frances and the man she was currently living with. 'She's just going!' Her voice was loud but brittle. Frances sensed her fear.

The man pushed her out of the way, his face leering at Frances. 'Got a tongue in your 'ead?'

Frances was terrified, but she was good at hiding it. 'My name's Frances.'

'I don't care what your name is. Get out of my house. Now!'

To Mildred he said, 'I want my grub.'

'It's on the stove.'

'Well, that's a bloody change! You still 'ere,' he said to Frances. 'Out! Now!'

He pointed at the door. 'As for you, where's my breakfast? I won't ask again . . .'

Her mother cringed. 'I'm just going. Got a nice bit of bacon for your breakfast. It won't take long. I'll just see Frances out of the door . . .'

'I can see myself out,' said Frances. This woman who was supposed to be her mother was far from the image she'd had in her mind, but she couldn't help feeling sorry for her, even protective.

'Frances is a friend of a friend. She works in the NAAFI. See? Look what she's brought us!'

Mildred held up the string bag in which Frances had brought the precious gifts she'd so hoped would cement their reunion. She'd expected her mother to be pleased; she had not expected her to have to use the food to save her skin. Nor for her mother not to admit their relationship. Oswald looked a bully as well as a slob.

'Give it 'ere!'

He snatched the bag from her, opened it and peered in. Mildred took advantage of his inattention to move Frances towards the door.

'Lovely of you to have dropped in,' she said as they entered the passageway.

Frances felt the trembling of her mother's arm.

'Who is that man?' Frances whispered.

'Oswald, well, he's my husband,' she insisted.

Frances wasn't sure whether to believe her or not. There was something furtive in Mildred's eyes, like a cat that's swallowed the canary but has no intention of admitting to it. However, it was Mildred who adopted a protective pose, arm around Frances's shoulders as she guided her to the front door.

'Your husband? Shouldn't you get back in? He looks angry.'

'No! No! Of course not. His bark is worse than his bite. He won't mind waiting a minute extra for his breakfast,' said Mildred, her voice quivering with nerves, her smile forced.

Mildred leaned close, her voice lowered so Oswald wouldn't hear. 'I'll see you tomorrow at four o'clock in the Busy Bee Tearooms up in Old Market. It's where all the buses stop, them that don't go into the city centre, that is. I'll be knocking off work by then. Perhaps we can have a cup of tea together?'

'Yes,' said Frances, her heart full of longing. She so wanted to get to know her mother better, though not with the disgusting Oswald around.

'Right. See you tomorrow, then.'

The words were rushed before the door was slammed in her face. She loitered, hoping for another glimpse of that over-made-up face smiling at her from the window, perhaps waving affectionately. Her mother did not appear. Gone to dish up Oswald's grub, she thought.

She walked away feeling a mix of emotions. Her meeting with her mother had been a big disappointment. The house had smelled bad; the man her mother said was her husband smelled even worse.

Something inside her refused to believe that her mother's circumstances were of her own making. Things had not gone the way she had hoped. Her father dying hadn't helped, and all thanks to the Great War. If he hadn't sustained injuries in that war, then perhaps he might have not fallen ill and would still be alive. And her mother might never have left her.

She brightened up at the thought that the three of them might have stayed together as one happy family if it hadn't been for that war. In fact, she might have ended up with brothers or sisters of her own, not just cousins, if the first war had never happened.

CHAPTER THIRTY

The next morning, once everyone had left for their respective jobs and Mrs Kepple had gone shopping, Frances had a bath and took her time getting ready. Today she was taking tea with her mother and she badly wanted to make an impression.

It didn't really occur to her that the food she'd given her mother might have made more of an impact than she had. When it did occur to her, she swiftly pushed its implications to the back of her mind. That her mother was as preoccupied with food as Mrs Kepple, or perhaps needed it in order to placate the ugly man she was married to.

Mrs Kepple came back just before lunch, declaring that she had a nice cheese and onion pie in the oven for them.

Feeling guilty about not eating last evening's supper and having only eaten a bowl of porridge for breakfast, Frances said that she would like some. 'Though only a small portion,' she added. 'I wouldn't want to rob anyone else of your cooking.'

Mrs Kepple beamed broadly at the flattery bestowed on her. 'King Edward potatoes I used, got a few decent onions, chopped the lot up and cooked it all together. Salt, pepper and plenty of grated cheese. You'll love it once it's been under the grill, the top all crunchy and decorated with slices of tomatoes . . .'

Frances ate her fill and managed to clear her plate, but declined pudding. 'I'm off into town this afternoon. Will I be in time for the bus?'

She already knew what time bus she needed and that indeed she would be in time, but it didn't hurt to make Mrs Kepple feel she was helping.

By the time she arrived in town, her stomach was doing somersaults. Newspaper vendors were shouting about successes in Europe as the allies thrust onwards, gaining a bridgehead.

'Victory is in sight!'

And then Declan would return.

Just as an afterthought, she wandered into Woolworths. The back of the building was a bit battle-scarred, but not nearly as badly as the buildings at the end of the road which had been very badly bombed and would have to be replaced.

Everyone seemed to be busy and so many women seemed to be pregnant. She'd heard Bettina Hicks say there would be lots more babies born once the men were coming home.

She found Emily serving behind a big counter selling ribbons, cotton, knitting needles and balls of wool on one side, and stockings and scarves on the other.

'We've even got knicker elastic,' Emily exclaimed.

Frances blushed because she'd said it so loudly.

Different goods were for sale at each end of the rectangular counter, and although there wasn't much variety, Frances detected an eagerness to buy, understandable after years of there being less on offer than there was now.

Frances waved goodbye.

'Wait,' Emily called. She managed to get to the edge of the counter, lean over and speak to her. 'How about you come here to work? We're run off our feet.'

Frances bit her lip. She'd told everyone at the boarding house that she was here looking for a job. Only Mrs Kepple knew her true reason for being in Bristol, and she was keeping it to herself. Just her luck that somebody would take her at her word and offer her work.

'I'm not sure. Anyway, I'm off to see about one now.'

'Yeah? Where to?'

'The Busy Bee Tearooms. I've got to be there by four.'

It came out all in a rush. She hadn't meant for it to, but there was no going back.

Emily looked surprised and not terribly impressed at the news. 'That's in Old Market.'

Frances was suspicious of the way she said 'Old Market'. What did it mean? Was it a bit rough and ready up there?

'I think I might have a cup of tea while I'm there.'

A customer was calling for Emily's attention so there was no chance to discuss Frances's supposed appointment any further. Emily gave a brief wave before Frances lost herself in the crowd and headed for the rear exit out from the store.

There was also a lot of manual labour going on, the remains of buildings being pulled down to make way for new ones. There were no plans in place as to what those buildings would be, though Mrs Kepple had told her that it was rumoured a new shopping centre would rise from the area around Penn Street and Fairfax Street, all the way up to the Horsefair. The medieval heart of the city had borne the brunt of the bombing. It was somehow fitting that a shopping centre would rise on a site named after a medieval horse fair.

On her way to Old Market, she paused to window shop. Not all the shops were open, some still boarded up after their windows had been blown out during bombing raids.

By the time she got to Old Market, she wished she'd eaten more lunch. Her stomach was rumbling, though it wouldn't have surprised her if it were due to apprehension as much as it was to hunger.

Old Market was crammed full with double-decker green buses that had replaced the trams after bombs had destroyed the rails at the beginning of the war. As fast as one bus pulled out at a bus stop, another pulled in.

Conductors hung from the rear platform, ringing the bell and shouting out, 'Move further down the bus, please!', and 'Plenty of room on top!'

Frances swallowed her nervousness before hurrying across the wide expanse where a street market had thrived many hundreds of years before. Now there were just buses.

'Hello, love,' somebody shouted. Another conductor whistled and made an obscene remark.

Frances felt her face reddening. No wonder Emily had turned up her nose. Old Market was a minefield of saucy bus drivers and conductors. The conductresses wore trousers and turbans and didn't look friendly.

The Busy Bee had a small frontage squashed between an old pub named The Stag and Hounds and a shop advertising handmade corsets.

Frances pushed open the door to be met with the smell of cigarette smoke, the clinking of teacups and the stickiness of toasted teacakes and iced buns. She found a table squashed up in the far corner, from where she had a good view of the door. Her heart was beating like a drum. People were looking at her. Did they know why she was here? Could they see the reason etched on her brow?

A waitress asked to take her order.

'Tea and an iced bun, please.'

She doubted the iced bun would be a patch on those they made at the bakery, but she had to have something to help fill the nervous void in her stomach. A little food might stop her heart from racing.

The windows of the teashop were misted up, thanks to the cigarette smoke and condensation from the giant tea urns sitting on the counter. The other tables were mostly taken up with bus drivers and conductors, some of the latter being female. All of them blew smoke into the air, a cigarette held lazily in yellow stained fingers, eyes narrowed, lips pursed in readiness to take their next puff.

The eyes of the men left her to go back to their newspapers or conversations with others of their like.

Frances breathed a sigh of relief, confident now that they wouldn't bother her. After she'd paid the waitress, she sipped at her tea and chewed on a sliver of bun.

Just for a moment, she dropped her eyes to the consistency of the bun. It felt dry beneath her fingers and dry in her mouth and the icing was watery and not properly set.

A draught of fresh air sent the cigarette smoke twirling like dancers as the door opened.

She'd prepared herself for meeting her mother again. What she hadn't prepared for was the uniform, the masculine jacket and trousers, the white-blonde hair tucked beneath a plaid headscarf tied turban style. Her make-up seemed more heavily applied than yesterday and a cigarette dangled from one corner of her crimson lips.

'All right, Joan?' she called to the last woman to shift her gaze from Frances's face.

'I'm okay, Mildred. How's the old man?'

'Same as ever,' Mildred replied.

Frances continued to stare, and this time not just at the powdered face, the rouged cheeks, the petulant mouth smothered in lipstick. Her mother had not warned her that she was a bus conductress, one of the women who shouted at people to move down the bus, swung around the bar on the platform at the end, ringing the bell, shouting at people in a nasally, nicotine voice! She could hardly believe it. There she was wearing her mannish uniform, a ticket machine hanging heavily at the end of a long leather strap around her neck.

She nodded as she sat down on the other side of the table to her daughter.

A waitress asked her what she wanted.

'Cup of tea and a toasted tea cake, love,' said Mildred. Immediately following the woman taking her order, Mildred took the cigarette stub from her mouth and ground it into an ashtray. She got out a packet of Woodbines and selected one, tapping it on the table between them before placing it between her lips.

'I don't suppose you've got a light, have you?'

Frances shook her head. She didn't smoke but saying so was blocked by her surprise and feeling of apprehension.

Mildred turned to the man behind her. 'Got a light, Arthur?'

The man took out a lighter from a ragged leather case. The flame flared into life momentarily until a red glow appeared.

'So,' said Mildred, turning back to face Frances. 'How come you're here in Bristol? Why ain't you at school?'

Frances paused before responding. Was it her imagination or had her mother's accent altered since yesterday. Alone in the front room, she'd spoken without a significant accent. Now, in the company of bus crews and the people in the tearoom, her accent was more noticeable, as though she was trying to fit in with the people around her.

It had also surprised her that her mother thought she was still at school. As her mother, surely she should know that.

'Well?' said her mother. She sounded annoyed that Frances hadn't answered straightaway. 'Are you going to tell me why you're here and not at school?'

'I'm sixteen. I've left school. I work in the bakery.'

'Do you, now?' A surprised and oddly speculative look crept over her mother's features.

'And I look after Charlie. He's cousin Charlie's boy. Cousin Charlie's ship got torpedoed. Charlie got killed and the baby's mother died in an air raid.'

Mildred nodded. 'That's a shame.' Her eyes were stone hard and didn't leave her daughter's face.

Frances felt uncomfortable. Neither meeting with her mother had been terribly positive. It came to her that she didn't know her mother at all.

'I didn't know that. I expect old Stan's a bit upset. Still, he's got his daughters to look after things.'

'Mary's married. There's only Ruby left. And me.'

'I dare say she'll leave and get married too before very long. I dare say you will too. You're pretty. Just like I was at your age.' A look of regret flashed over her mother's face but vanished quickly. 'Still – that's all in the past. It's the present that matters – that and the future.'

Uncomfortable with the way her mother was looking at her, Frances fidgeted in her chair. 'I suppose it is.'

'So what do you want to know?' demanded her mother. The hard look was back.

Frances felt flustered. Her mother hadn't sounded so hard yesterday and it frightened her. Sensing the time was not right, she dismissed the idea of asking her to sign a consent form that would allow her to marry Declan.

Taking her courage in both hands, Frances asked for the second time, 'Why did you leave me?'

Mildred considered her answer as she stirred her tea. The teaspoon at last tinkled into the saucer.

'I thought you might ask me that again.' Placing both hands around the warm cup, she leaned forward. Her gaze remained fixed on the teacup. 'I was young and romantic. Only eighteen when I had you; did you know that?'

Frances did not. She shook her head.

'I was born poor but didn't want to stay poor. Sefton, your dad, offered to marry me and I jumped at the offer. Who wouldn't? I was honest with him. I told him I didn't love him. Who would? His legs were shattered, he could barely breathe and he still suffered from war wounds to his face and body. He just wanted company and somebody to make him feel normal. That's all. So he provided for me and I gave him what I could. When he died, well, everything changed. I had a bit of money saved and I was free. Better off than I'd ever been in my life. And I was still young.'

Frances sucked in her lips. This was all news to her and she feared what she might hear next.

'Sefton Sweet, your husband. He was my dad, wasn't he?'

Mildred looked at her blankly. Frances spotted the bruise beneath one eye. Oswald. It was no surprise.

Mildred stubbed out her cigarette in a plain metal ashtray. 'What do you take me for? Of course he was!'

Her tone was abrupt, so swiftly rendered that Frances was inclined to think she wasn't telling the truth or at least couldn't know for sure.

'I knew old Stan would look after you. He's always been a soft touch as far as children are concerned.' A cloud of smoke blew down her nostrils and from her mouth as she turned away.

Frances felt sick. She looked down at her hands, thinking that the good person in all this was her uncle. And she'd wronged him, shouted at him and showed resentment at being a part of his family. On reflection, she'd actually resented not being his daughter, though she realised now that she'd never felt that growing up, only recently.

Her mother interrupted her thoughts. 'So you work in the bakery and look after the little boy. I bet old Stan don't pay you much for that.'

Frances shrugged. 'He pays me what he can and I don't have to give over anything for housekeeping. It's just for me.'

Mildred flicked more of the cigarette into the tin ashtray. Eyelashes thick with mascara swooped downwards before swooping up again, her lips curving tightly over teeth yellowed by nicotine.

'You could earn a lot more in a factory,' she said, more brightly now. 'Like Wills's for instance. They pay well and you get free fags at the end of the week.'

Frances shook her head. 'I don't want to work in a cigarette factory. And I don't like the smell of tobacco.'

Her mother took one long drag of her cigarette then stubbed it out in the ashtray. 'You should have said so. Not normal, though, is it? I mean, everybody smokes. It's only natural. Anyway, if you don't want them I could have them.'

Frances failed to see what was natural about it, but didn't comment.

Her mother tried again. 'Or there's Robinson's, where they make paper bags. You could work there, though the money ain't as good as making cigarettes or cigars. How about Fry's or Carson's? You like chocolate, don't you?'

Frances agreed that she did like chocolate.

'And they give you free chocolates. Brown bags at the end of the week full of them that ain't quite perfect.'

Neither are you, Frances thought to herself. More importantly, she wondered what had attracted her mother to the life she was living – and that man – Oswald.

'It sounds nice.'

She had to admit even to herself that the prospect of getting free chocolates after the deprivations of the last few years was very attractive.

Mildred smiled. 'Very nice. Lots of chocolates and a lot more money than you're earning now. Tell you what,' she said, leaning forward, her accent disappearing as her voice dropped to little more than a whisper. 'We could both work there. What do you think of that? Mother and daughter earning lots of money, living together and eating chocolates all day!' She laughed. 'Now wouldn't that be nice?'

The apprehension Frances had felt lessened. Suddenly it no longer mattered that her mother was far from being the tragic widow desperate to make her own way in the world and come back for her abandoned child once she was rich and secure. The fact that she wanted them to be together more or less came down to the same thing, didn't it? Being together made up for everything: her mother loved her.

'It sounds a good idea but . . .' Frances sucked her bottom lip into her mouth. She was thinking of what Uncle Stan would say. She was also thinking of little Charlie. She would miss him. So far, she hadn't mentioned that she was having a baby. What would her mother say about that? she wondered.

'You could visit your uncle and that lot any time you liked,' her mother added, as if reading her thoughts. 'You'd certainly have enough for the bus fare. After all, you'd be earning decent money,' her mother hissed, keeping her voice down and leaning close so nobody else could hear. 'It won't be easy. Nobody said it would be, giving up your life with them that raised you, and leaving the lad, of course, but it won't be easy for me either. This isn't a bad job. But I'm willing to do it if it makes you happy.'

Her red lips broke into a smile as she laid her nicotine-stained fingers over her daughter's hand. Her mother's touch ignited an electric shock that ran all the way up Frances's arm. It was accompanied by a great surge of emotion welling up inside her. Her mother really did want her with her. Why else would she be willing to leave her job on the buses to work in a chocolate factory with her?'

'Tell you what,' said her mother, leaning even closer. 'How about we go out there now and take a look? Out to Somerdale. It's at a place called Keynsham and surrounded by green fields. Do you fancy that?'

Frances nodded fervently before wondering how they would get there.

'It just so happens,' whispered her mother, 'that I'm on the Keynsham run! No need for a ticket. You just get on board and if an inspector does get on to check the tickets, I'll tell him who you are. Anyway,' she said with an airy uplifting of her chin. 'I know Sid Chalmers. Me and him used to be close, once upon a time.' Regret for what might have been flashed in her eyes then was gone. 'Well? What do you reckon?'

Frances felt sick. This was not at all the woman she'd imagined her mother to be. That woman had gone away to make a fortune before claiming her. She had not expected her to be quite like this and hadn't accounted for somebody like Oswald. How could she live with a man like that?

Her thoughts were in turmoil. A chasm a mile wide existed between them. The warmth of Uncle Stan and the bakery was calling her. She had to go back. She had to put her trust in him to assist her in her hour of need, and somehow she knew he would.

*　　*　　*

Mildred Baxter, who had once been Mrs Mildred Sweet, rubbed at the bruise on her cheekbone. A dash of powder and rouge had done wonders to hide it, but the soreness prevailed. Her mouth was set in a grimace until Frances turned and waved to her. Mildred waved back, her grimace widening into a smile.

'See you soon, love,' she called out.

The driver of the bus on which Mildred was the conductress had willingly dropped the girl off at the bus stop closest to Mrs Kepple's boarding house. He grinned at Mildred knowingly and winked. Mildred winked back, signalling that it had been a free ride that might shortly get paid in kind. Sid Chalmers, the ticket inspector, hadn't got on the bus this evening, so there'd been no need to explain to him that she had a daughter. Yet another man she'd had a physical liaison with. He had a wife. He would do what she wanted and keep his mouth shut.

Mildred was pleased with herself. She hummed a happy tune as she collected her stuff from the locker room and prepared to go home.

Home! The thought of going back to Oswald and that gloomy place in Montpelier caused the bruise beneath her eye to throb painfully.

She'd been planning to leave him for some time, but circumstances were not in her favour. Men had always been her key to changing her life. If you fluttered your eyelashes and made them feel special, they were stupid enough to do anything for you. Sid Chalmers, the ticket inspector, had seemed for a time to be just that. His wife was an invalid and he'd told Mildred he was unhappy in his marriage. When the chips were down and she'd tried to persuade him to run off with her, he'd swiftly changed his tune.

There had been other men, but her looks were fading. There were younger, more attractive women with persuasive powers every bit as good as hers.

Your day is done, she thought to herself. The trouble was that her wages as a conductress wasn't enough for rent, food and everything else. A woman didn't make as much money as a man, even in comparable jobs. The male conductors earned more than the women, even though they were all doing the same job and working the same hours. It wasn't fair, but that was the way things were.

Frances turning up had altered things. The girl was pretty and capable of earning good money.

Mildred smiled to herself. It had been so easy to persuade her daughter that she was determined to make a new start. And indeed I am, she thought as she went out of the door and across Old Market to catch the bus that would take her home. Two wages were needed to make that new start, her wage as well as the wage her daughter would bring in.

If she played her cards right, the money Frances earned would mostly go to her. Young girls were malleable and she'd seen the longing in her daughter's eyes. She wanted a mother and she would give everything to have one. Mildred would see that indeed she would give everything, and she would take it.

Leaving Oswald and setting up a new life depended on her daughter earning that extra wage.

Once she was indoors, and after checking Oswald wasn't home, she poured herself a glass of sherry and toasted her future. If she couldn't take advantage of men's desire any longer, then she would take advantage of her daughter.

Mrs Kepple was very understanding of Frances's situation and even helped her pack.

'She wasn't quite up to the mark, was she, my pet?'

Frances shook her head. 'I think I made a mistake.'

'And you feel such a fool.'

'More than that. I feel cruel. What is it they say? The other man's grass is always greener.'

'And you don't know what you have until it's gone,' stated Mrs Kepple with a resolute jerk of her bristled chin.

Not mentioning getting married to her mother had been an easy decision to make. Neither had she mentioned her delicate condition, which she doubted her mother would welcome.

She was swift in telling Mrs Kepple that she was leaving. 'I want to go home.'

Mrs Kepple beamed. 'Home is where the heart is.'

Frances had to concede that she was right.

She got a lift to the tramway centre – which of course no longer catered to tramways, but the name had stuck. The lift was with Mrs Kepple's taxi driver son, who had a tin leg after coming back from the war.

The single-decker country bus only ran three days a week and then only intermittently but it was cheaper than the train. She was just in time to catch the last one home.

Mrs Kepple gave her a big hug. 'Having met your mother and having her as a guest for a while, I'm sure you're doing the right thing, my dear.'

Frances didn't ask what her mother's shortcomings had been when she'd stayed with Mrs Kepple. She didn't need to.

She smiled. 'I'm sure I'm doing the right thing too.'

CHAPTER THIRTY-ONE

Hi to the child of the forest. This note is short but sweet and I shouldn't be sending it at all. Everything is top secret nowadays. I'll see you when I see you. Don't lose hope. Don't lose trust. Be assured I will stand by you.

Be with you soon. Declan O'Malley

Even if he hadn't signed it, Frances would have known who it was from. Nobody wrote in the way that Declan did.

There'd been no recriminations when she'd got home. Her uncle hadn't said 'I told you so' though his taciturn demeanour conveyed he was still not pleased about her being pregnant.

'I'm just glad *you're* back, sweetheart,' said Stan. 'Charlie's missed you.'

Up in their shared bedroom, Ruby helped her unpack. 'Another baby in the house.' She sighed and shook her head. 'The more the merrier.'

Frances took a deep breath. 'I might not be living here when he's born.'

'How far gone are you?'

'It's been about two months since I last had my monthly.'

Ruby took a moment to place things in the top drawer of the chest they shared and did a quick calculation in her head. The baby would be born some time in the New Year.

'It's Declan's, isn't it?'

Frances sat down on the bed, her head bent, her clasped hands resting on her knees. 'I think so.'

Hearing the helplessness in her voice, Ruby sat down beside her. 'You think it might be Ed's?'

'It wasn't that long before. He was drunk. I was a bit tipsy too and feeling bitter about my mother and what Mrs Powell said about her. For a moment, I thought I may as well follow in her footsteps.'

'Frances! How could you think such a thing? You're nothing like your mother. You're *you*. Frances Sweet.'

Frances kept her head down, her eyes scrutinising her clasped hands. 'Should I tell Declan that it might be Ed's? What do you think?'

Ruby bit her lip. Frances had not been a virgin when she'd gone with Declan, but did that really matter nowadays? The fact was it might matter to him. Some men were like that. The truth was she didn't know what to say, though in all honesty she would do what women had done for generations. She'd keep mum!

'Look. Just think about it. You'll know the right thing to do when the time comes.'

'Do you really think so?'

Ruby looked into her cousin's upturned face. This kid needed reassurance.

'You won't be the first one who fails to be a virgin on her wedding day.'

Frances smiled. 'Thank you, Ruby. You've made me feel better.'

Ruby gave her a hug. 'I'm glad you're back. I've got a lot of catching up to do with my work for the Ministry of Food. I need help and you're it.'

Frances said she would be glad to help.

The welcome home was better than Frances had expected or felt she deserved. For the first time, she felt part of this grand plan to help the nation feed itself. Ruby even persuaded Andrew to pay her on a part-time basis. No mention was made to him of Frances's condition.

Bettina Hicks helped the wounds heal with an impromptu visit and a half bottle of brandy.

'To toast an ongoing victory through Europe,' she declared. They all raised their glasses to that.

It's said that into every life a little rain must fall. Frances was filled with happiness that her uncle was going to sign the form giving her permission to marry Declan O'Malley. She'd written to Declan and he'd suggested September.

The bombshell was brought to them by his commanding officer. The moment he walked into their living room, his cap under his arm and a grim expression on his face, they knew that something was wrong.

Stan felt his stomach churn on seeing the frightened look on Frances's face.

The officer, Colonel Marks, turned a letter over in his hand before handing it over.

'O'Malley was picked to go on a secret mission in order to gather information prior to the invasion of Europe. The plane he was in was shot down. I can't tell you where he is, of course. All I can say is that we've lost contact with him. But he's well trained. He knows what's coming and that it's best to lie low for the time being. I'm sure you'll understand, and please, please don't give up hope.'

After he'd gone, they all fell to silence. Frances's hands were trembling. Ruby patted her on the shoulder.

'I'm sure he'll be all right.'

Stan Sweet was oddly quiet. 'Does Declan speak any foreign language?'

His question came right out of the blue.

Frances tried to think, but it was Ruby who answered.

'I think he said his mother was German and he could speak the language.' She frowned, not sure what her father was thinking.

Stan Sweet looked from his daughter to his niece. 'I think he was lying. He told you both he was military police. I think he was military intelligence.' He looked at Frances. 'Prepare yourself for a long wait.'

CHAPTER THIRTY-TWO

May 1945: Victory in Europe

Church bells rang out the news of the German surrender, people danced in the street, and a bonfire sent sparks exploding into the sky.

'It's over! He'll be home,' shouted Frances, her voice quaking with a mixture of laughter and relief. 'Germany's surrendered!'

Stan declined going along to witness the village bonfire, get drunk and eat jacket potatoes pulled directly from the fire.

Instead, he went down to the graveyard that evening, keen to impart everything that had occurred in recent months to his darling departed wife.

The air was balmy and the summer bees were already buzzing in and out of the wildflowers.

His joints creaked as he knelt down beside his wife's tombstone. 'I'm getting older, Sarah my love, but I'm still here.' He sighed as he readjusted his arm to rest more comfortably. 'There's a lot of young men who are not.'

He bowed his head in respect to those who would never come home, including Charlie.

'You may recall I told you some time back that Sefton's girl, Frances, now has a child of her own. Her name's Daisy.

She's a bonny little thing. We're awaiting word that her father has survived and is going to do the honourable thing. He's an American officer, military intelligence and right in the thick of it, from what I can see. It's been hard for him to get away from the conflict, but we're fairly certain he's alive and he has promised Frances they'll marry the moment he can get to England. He's quite a bit older than her but she's adamant that he'll come back. I hope she's right for her sake and that of the little one. Children born out of wedlock have never had it easy. And you know what the village is like – even if they'll never say anything to my face. Anyway, the Germans have surrendered so we're hoping he'll soon be in touch. Ruby is still waiting to hear from that young man who used to drive her around. We won't know much about him until the Japanese surrender, and so far they're showing no sign of doing that. In the meantime, she's busying herself with her job and Frances is helping her. But of course that's all coming to an end. Things are less stiff and serious now, so much so that they take Charlie and Daisy with them . . .'

The road they needed to take was blocked with people in uniform and the ominous presence of an army vehicle marked 'Bomb Disposal'.

'Sorry. You can't go down 'ere, love. There's an unexploded thousand pounder down 'ere. You'll have to go up Fairfax Street and bear left from there.'

Ruby sighed resignedly and thanked the man. It wasn't his fault that the Germans had dropped a bomb that hadn't exploded, or that it hadn't been detected soon after it fell that night back in 1940 when the heart had been ripped out of the city. Not that their surroundings were much improved on the route he'd suggested.

Ruined buildings lined their route, stairs precariously clinging to exposed walls climbing to non-existent upper floors, blackened facades fronting bombed-out and empty interiors.

Ruby and Frances eyed the sad scene with utmost dismay, Frances with Daisy in her arms and hugging Charlie to her side. The last thing she wanted was for him to see the grim reality of this war. Buildings that had survived centuries of other wars, other catastrophes, had been totally destroyed back in '40 and '41. She was no expert but judged it would be some time before new buildings would grow from the ashes of the old.

'We're half an hour late,' muttered Ruby as she eyed the assembled crowd. It was probably a bit more than that and the crowd would be impatient. Whether she liked it or not, Ruby's talk and demonstration would be as much about entertainment as information on struggling along on meagre rations.

Shops with patched-up windows attracted long queues. Half the time, people weren't entirely sure what they were queuing for, but joined the long line of people in the hope of ending up with something worthwhile, perhaps liver, onions, or tins of meat brought in by merchant ships from the other side of the Atlantic. There were also rumoured to be extra rations in order that people could celebrate the final victory. Everyone was planning street parties. Today Ruby's demonstration was about sandwiches, cakes and as many sweet-tasting delicacies as possible.

The van with the drop-down side was already in situ. To Ruby's surprise, Andrew Sinclair was standing there beside it. On seeing them arrive, he pulled back the cuff of his jacket to peer at his wristwatch, a smart affair with an ivory face and a strap made of crocodile skin.

I could do without you being here, thought Ruby. The fact that he'd lied to his mother about their relationship was not her concern and she never mentioned it. So far neither had he.

Everything was ready for her. Not only had he let down the drop-down side, thus forming a counter, he had also fired up the gas ring and got out what he thought were the things she might need today.

After making sure that Frances was coping with the children, Ruby turned her attention to the crowd that had gathered. She pasted on a hasty smile, the straw hamper bumping against her side before Andrew took it from her. Once that was gone, she addressed the crowd. 'Sorry for being a bit late. There was an unexploded bomb and we were diverted.'

There were only a few half-baked grumbles. Most people had learned to accept the shortages, the delays and the fact that things were not so dependable as before the war.

'Oh, well. At least you're here now, love and that's all that matters.'

The speaker was a pink-faced woman with china-blue eyes and a hat that sat on her head as flat as a pancake. Only the addition of a limp feather sticking from one side marked it out as a hat at all.

She noticed her tilting her head to one side, peering enquiringly at Frances.

'Here,' she suddenly exclaimed. 'Is that you, young Frances? Well, I never.'

It was Mrs Kepple, the woman who took in lodgers and had been instrumental in reuniting Frances with her mother. To her credit, she had also been partially instrumental in reuniting Frances with Ruby and her uncle.

'I knew she was a bad 'un, that Mildred Sweet,' she'd said to them.

Ruby headed swiftly for Andrew Sinclair before Mrs Kepple repeated her comments all over again in the midst of these people.

'I've got everything ready for you,' said Andrew.

He stroked his moustache, a vague smile on his lips.

Ruby thanked him brusquely, immersing herself in the rest of the preparations – a good enough excuse not to be alone with him for too long. She was also thankful that Frances was helping out today, even though her help was somewhat curtailed by Charlie's company.

Once Charlie held a piece of bread and jam in his clenched fist, he sat down on one of the steps leading up into the side entry of the van, chewing slowly and contentedly. Daisy was fast asleep. He promised to keep an eye on her.

'Ladies!' Ruby cried out at last once everything was done. 'Today I am going to make a chocolate cake, an ideal confection for little Johnnie's birthday or a special Sunday tea, and perfect for a street party.'

Everyone's ears pricked up at the magic word. Chocolate was the ultimate luxury and so lacking in this wartime world, even in its aftermath. Ruby knew when she'd concocted the recipe that she was on to a winner.

'The great thing about this cake is that it needs no baking, though you do have to plan your ingredients beforehand. Number one, breadcrumbs. Save every stale slice days before making it. The ingredients are as follows:

'Eight ounces of breadcrumbs, two ounces of margarine or butter – if you should be so lucky! Two ounces of sugar, two tablespoons of golden syrup or honey, three ounces of cocoa powder – or some real chocolate – courtesy of a friendly ally.' A titter of subdued laughter ran through the crowd. The Americans had real chocolate.

'If you don't have an American friend or prefer free stockings to chocolate, then cocoa powder will have to do. All you do is to melt your margarine, sugar and syrup or honey in a saucepan then stir in the breadcrumbs and cocoa powder.'

As she talked she lined a sandwich tin using the paper greased with a pat of margarine, glancing up every so often to add some pearl of wisdom, studying the upturned faces, taking a second glance at a man in uniform, glancing swiftly away because it wasn't Johnnie. It couldn't be Johnnie.

She went on to outline another recipe for chocolate cake, this time using flour. The chocolate icing she'd devised was based yet again on margarine and golden syrup, though here again she referred to the likelihood of knowing a generous American and using real chocolate.

By the end of the session, the smell of chocolate was getting to her. So was the look on Andrew Sinclair's face. When was it he'd switched his desire to her from her sister? It didn't matter. What did matter was keeping her job for now and having him pay Frances for helping out.

Frances had the job of circulating with the chocolate cake that, although it hadn't stood for long enough, was now cut into pieces. It wasn't long before there were only crumbs remaining, and even these were picked up on the ends of wet fingers and sucked greedily into hungry mouths.

'Lovely talk, my dear.' Ruby was washing and packing things away, Andrew hovering at her shoulder and yet again urging her to consider an appointment in London. 'It could lead to great things.'

'I might not want great things. I might be quite happy with little things,' she said quite testily. Not that Andrew seemed to notice. He had a knack of not hearing anything hostile to his attentions, or at least that was the way it seemed to her.

Mrs Kepple was a welcome diversion. She was very appreciative of the talk.

'How lovely of you to say so,' said Ruby.

Andrew looked quite astounded when she handed him the tea towel and the plate she'd been wiping. There was a bowlful of washing up still to do, enough to keep him out of her hair for a while.

'Not that it weren't something that I didn't already know,' stated Mrs Kepple, her head nodding in time with her words.

Ruby's attention kept being drawn to the feather fluttering like a trapped blackbird with each nod of Mrs Kepple's head.

'Baking is all very well, my dear, but it's the main courses I concentrate on. I have my lodgers to think about, tough men some of them doing tough jobs. And ladies, of course, but even ladies work in factories nowadays.'

'Of course they do.' Ruby tried to say more, but when Mrs Kepple was holding forth, even Churchill couldn't have got a word in edgeways.

'It's this snoek that's a challenge,' said Mrs Kepple. 'Not a bad fish, I dare say, but it does need a little bit of something to make it more tasty. I add tripe and onions myself.'

'Really? How interesting.'

The great thing about living in the country was that fresh food, although in short supply, was still obtainable. Not for them the long queues for fresh produce as were seen in the city.

'I add just a little marge and a drop of milk. The fish and the tripe add the rest.'

To Ruby's ears it sounded revolting, but she smiled and intimated that she would love the recipe if she'd like to send it to her sometime – and instantly regretted it.

'No need. I've got it here.'

Mrs Kepple pulled out a crumpled envelope from her pocket. Unfolding it took some time, the envelope having been folded numerous times until it was no more than two inches square.

Unseen by Mrs Kepple, Ruby slipped a sidelong smile at Frances. Frances merely grimaced and pulled a long- suffering face.

'There you are,' exclaimed Mrs Kepple once the scribbled recipe was in view. 'It's all yours to do with as you please.'

Hesitant but smiling, Ruby took the proffered scrap of paper. 'Thank you. I'm sure it will come in useful.'

'I bet the little'un 'ere will love it. Yours, is he?'

Ruby shook her head. 'No. He's my nephew, and the little girl is my niece – Frances's baby, in fact.'

Smiling affectionately, Mrs Kepple ruffled Charlie's dark curls and cooed over little Daisy, tactfully not asking if Frances was married.

'Charlie is my brother's son,' Ruby explained. 'Both his parents are dead. My brother's ship was torpedoed and Charlie's mother was killed in a bombing raid on London.'

'That's terrible, but that's war for you. But there you are. Come to think of it, I've got a mother and baby staying with me too. She was staying with her grandmother over the Welsh side of the Severn, but she's come 'ere to wait for the baby's father to come home. Baby is as good as gold – not a peep out of it. Not sure whether they're married or not,' she said, her voice low and secretive. 'But there. Never mind. Live and let live, I always say. Is your baby's father away fighting?' she asked Frances.

'Yes. But he will be back soon,' Frances said defiantly. Her pride wouldn't allow her to admit that Mrs Kepple's reference to the young woman staying with her was unsettling. Declan had told her he loved her. Of course he would come back.

Charlie began rubbing his eyes, the usual prelude to tiredness. As if that wasn't enough, Daisy began to cry.

'Time we were going. They're both tired,' said Frances. 'It's been a long day.'

Mrs Kepple remained chirpy. 'Tell you what, me dear. How about you come and have a cup of tea with me? I can find the little boy a slice of jam tart.' She bent down so her cheerful face was level with that of Charlie. 'You'd like that, wouldn't you?'

Charlie, one fist still clenched at the corner of his right eye, gave a cautious nod. He didn't know who this cherry-faced woman was, but she had mentioned something about a jam tart. Charlie loved jam.

Although she too was invited, Ruby declined the offer, citing the fact that she had to clear up. She also wanted to stress to Andrew once and for all that she wasn't interested in him and neither was she interested in transferring to London.

'You go,' she said to Frances. 'I'll keep Daisy with me. She's not due for a feed yet, but Charlie is tired and hungry. He's only a small boy with short legs, after all.'

'And a very deep stomach,' Frances added with a grin.

Resigned to yet again entering Mrs Kepple's house, and feeling a little tired herself, Frances accompanied Mrs Kepple to the tall terraced house with the bay window.

An aspidistra now occupied prime position in the front window, replacing the necessity for net curtains.

'All living things need light,' Mrs Kepple had pronounced. Frances had presumed she meant just plants, though on reflection decided that people needed light too. Nobody liked winter because it was dark. Everyone preferred lighter nights so it stood to reason they also preferred lighter rooms.

'I expect Miriam will be home too,' said Mrs Kepple.

'Miriam?'

'Yes. That's her name. Mrs Miriam Charles.'

Frances felt a grabbing feeling inside, what Ada Perkins would call a premonition.

Mrs Kepple prattled on with what she knew about Mrs Charles. The young woman had been living with her grandmother in the Forest of Dean. Her name was Miriam and she had a child. More tellingly, she'd said that the young woman's name was Mrs Miriam Charles.

A clammy feeling erupted on her forehead and the hairs on the back of her neck pricked upright. Miriam. A grandmother in the Forest of Dean, a baby and the name Charles. Her brother's name. Or was there really a Mr Charles?

She swiped her free hand across her forehead. It came back damp with perspiration.

Mrs Kepple noticed that something was wrong. 'Are you all right, dearie?'

Frances managed a reassuring smile. 'A little dizzy spell, though nothing to worry about. It's gone now.'

The outer door was wide open. The inner door, with its upper panel of jewel-like blue and red glass, was closed. There would be no need to unlock it. Mrs Kepple pushed it open.

Frances stared straight ahead as she entered the familiar house, her hand firmly grasping Charlie's.

Frances had not suspected that when Miriam had left her grandmother's home, she had come to Bristol. To her knowledge, Ada had not written to Uncle Stan, and she probably would have done, just to keep him informed. Nobody would have known whether Ada Perkins, Miriam's grandmother, had written to Miriam's mother. Ada's daughter, Gertrude, had washed her hands of her daughter, a fact she retold to everyone in the village.

'My daughter is a slut,' she'd told them.

She'd not gone into further detail but there had been a rumour that Miriam had got pregnant by a visiting Methodist minister. Sometime later she disappeared then reappeared in the village with no sign of being pregnant. And now she was here? With a baby? Frances could hardly believe it.

Mrs Kepple began taking off her hat and coat on her way to the kitchen. Frances followed, Charlie just behind her asking when he was likely to get his jam tart.

His shrill little voice rang out along the passageway with its bumpy floors and scattered rugs. 'Strawberry jam or plum jam?'

'Plum,' exclaimed Mrs Kepple, both arms raised in the process of taking off her hat. 'Take a seat, dearie. Oh, look. The kettle's already on. I expect Miriam saw us coming. Hang on and I'll give her a shout.'

Her small feet padded over the scattered rugs, the loose floorboards creaking with each step. Frances watched her go, a small gripe in her stomach.

'Charlie have more?'

Charlie wasn't exactly asking for another jam tart, but actively taking one from the plate on the table.

'You already have,' Frances said with a sense of defeat. Charlie had a habit of taking before asking. She presumed he would grow out of it, though what did it matter if he didn't?

Mrs Kepple was already on her way back along the passageway, a cheery smile on her face. 'She's put the baby down for a sleep. She'll be down shortly.'

The lid on the kettle began to lift with the pressure of the steam rising upwards. A stream of it puffed from the long spout. Frances offered to make it. 'You put your feet up. And take your coat off.'

'Oh dear,' said Mrs Kepple, looking down at the front of her coat. 'I didn't realise I still had it on.'

Frances's heart began to thud at the sound of footsteps coming down the stairs and along the passageway.

The young woman in the doorway appeared dumbstruck. 'Frances!'

Miriam's face was more animated than Frances had ever seen it. Once she'd got over the initial shock, she gave Frances a hug and tousled Charlie's shock of black hair.

'You are so like your daddy,' she said to him, and Frances noticed a wistful look in her eyes.

For his part, Charlie looked up at her with wary amazement. He was too young to remember her as the lady who'd taken him from his pushchair and down into the woods at California Farm. None of the family now believed that he'd simply wandered off. Miriam's behaviour both at that time and after had made them believe otherwise.

'I bet you didn't know I'd left the forest,' Miriam exclaimed, her staring eyes touched with a brilliance that wasn't quite sane.

Frances was unnerved. Her tone was sceptical. 'No. I didn't even know you were married.'

'He's in the navy! He's a sailor! Just like Charlie was.'

'A merchant seaman? Like Charlie?'

'That's right. Not a sailor, a merchant seaman. That's it.'

'Would anyone else like a jam tart?' Mrs Kepple poured the tea and pushed the plate of jam tarts into the middle of the table. Charlie helped himself to a third one. Frances apologised and told him to put it back. Her attention kept going back to Miriam. Something was very wrong here. She didn't seem sure whether her husband was a sailor or a merchant seaman – and there was definitely a difference. Perhaps she didn't know who the father was.

Mrs Kepple's voice regarding Charlie and the jam tarts interrupted her thoughts.

'Don't worry, me dear. He's welcome to it. I got a nice tin of jam from my shopkeeper. It had no label on it so he said I had to take pot luck. I tell you, I was lucky to get it. Once the word got round, the queue was a mile long!'

She chuckled amiably and so did Charlie, his face beaming with pleasure.

Although she smiled and talked pleasantly to Miriam, Frances couldn't shift the feeling of unease. She felt extremely uncomfortable. There was something brittle about Miriam's brightness, every so often her gaze shifting away, anywhere but looking at Frances. It was as though all that she was saying had been carefully rehearsed, like the words and actions in a play. Not real but a façade, like the grim old buildings with nothing behind them.

Hiding her concerns, Frances adopted a happy face. 'So what's your baby's name?'

'Charlotte Louise Charles. Her father's name is Charles. Not Charles Charles,' she said with a light laugh. 'His name is Deacon Charles.'

'Oh. That's nice.'

Frances didn't think it was nice at all. Charlotte was the female form of Charles and it just seemed too much of a coincidence that Miriam's husband's name was Deacon Charles. Not only was it her dead cousin's name, as well as that of his son, but she'd said that his first name was Deacon.

'So where did you meet him, this Deacon Charles?'

'Coleford. I got a job there in a shop and his family lived nearby.'

Frances dipped her head to her tea, sipping it as she thought it through. The only Deacon she knew on the other side of the Severn Bridge had been her favourite boy from the moment she'd moved there. Could Miriam really have married him? She wasn't sure, but she couldn't recall whether his surname had been Charles. She certainly didn't think so.

'So where is he at present?'

'Here. In Bristol. Or at least he will be shortly. That's why I'm here. I'm waiting for the war to end and him to come home. It won't be long now. I'm sure it won't.' Her eyes were oddly bright, her voice brisk.

'I hope you're right,' returned Frances.

'I reckon so,' said Mrs Kepple, who was now busily stirring a saucepan. Whatever was in the saucepan smelled extremely appetising.

Under the pretence of sipping tea, Frances studied Miriam's appearance. She was wearing the same old black coat she'd used to wear when she accompanied her mother to church. Did her mother know about the marriage and the baby? Somehow she doubted it. Somehow she couldn't believe that Miriam was married or had a baby. Curiosity scratched at her mind. Miriam. A baby. A husband. It was the existence of the baby that intrigued her most of all.

'I've got a baby too. Her name's Daisy. Her father's American.'

'Oh really,' said Miriam, all unsuspecting.

'Do you think I could take a peep at your baby? I promise not to wake her.'

Miriam's expression was hesitant, as though frozen in a sudden blast of cold air. Frances presumed she would say no. She was proved wrong.

'Yes. Of course you can. But we'll have to be quiet and Charlie will have to stay down here. I don't want him to wake her.'

'Of course not.'

Mrs Kepple immediately offered to keep an eye on Charlie while the two young women headed for the stairs that were half-hidden behind a draped velvet curtain that Mrs Kepple had put there to keep the draught from coming down.

Frances recognised Miriam's room as being the same one she had occupied when she'd stayed here.

The baby was sound asleep, tucked up in a blanket on the bed. Her face was sickly pale, the lips almost waxen.

Sickening fear closed like a cold fist around Frances's heart. Miriam hovered behind her, close to her shoulder.

Miriam gave a little laugh. 'She's always asleep. Never a murmur.'

Frances moved slowly, her legs unsteady. Suddenly it seemed such a long way to the bedroom door, but she had to make it. She had to raise the alarm. The baby was dead.

'I'd better see how Charlie is before he eats any more of Mrs Kepple's jam tarts.' She kept her voice as steady as she could.

Seemingly oblivious to the true state of her baby, Miriam hung over the bundle, her fingers tucking the blanket more firmly around the ashen face. 'I would let Charlie see my baby, but she needs her sleep.'

The stairs seemed to loom up to meet her as Frances stumbled swiftly down them. Mrs Kepple was waiting at the bottom, wiping the jam from Charlie's sticky fingers.

'Mrs Kepple, have you ever seen Miriam's baby? Have you held her?'

Mrs Kepple frowned. 'No, Miriam seems quite particular, keeps herself to herself.'

Frances took a deep breath and relayed her fears. 'It's dead!'

Mrs Kepple looked dumbfounded. 'You're sure?'

Frances couldn't stop shaking. 'She always wanted a baby.'

Mrs Kepple touched her hand. 'Let me go up and take a look. I'll insist this time. Tell you what: I've just made a cuppa so why don't you sit down with a brew and I'll take one up to her.'

Mrs Kepple sounded incredibly calm, though her hand shook a little.

Frances sat there trying not to feel nauseous. A dead baby! Lifeless!

Mrs Kepple came back down soon after with a tight smile on her face.

'Don't worry, dear. It's not a real baby. It's a doll.' She shook her head. 'Poor thing. Fancy playing pretend at her age.'

CHAPTER THIRTY-THREE

October 1945

While Charlie chased the last lingering butterflies and picked wild flowers, Stan Sweet knelt beside his wife's grave. He didn't come here so often nowadays, what with Ruby being so busy, little Daisy and his young grandson making demands on the time of all of them. But today he felt more elated than he'd felt for a long time.

Resting his clasped hands on his knee, almost as though he were praying, he began telling Sarah the great news.

'So the war is finally over. The Japanese have surrendered. They've paid a terrible price for entering the war, but I'll leave the whys and the wherefores to the historians. The thing that causes my heart to soar is that Johnnie Smith has been released from a Japanese prisoner of war camp. He wrote to our Ruby and she's going down to meet him.'

Swallowing the lump of emotion rising in his throat, he raised his eyes, blinking away the tears as he regarded the branches of old trees creaking in the breeze. Like my joints, he thought to himself.

On clearing his throat, he put his thoughts into words, words he had not said to Ruby.

'I did think for a while that she was going to marry one of her Polish pilots, but she didn't. Still, I'm glad she didn't. If she had, it would have meant her going with him when he went back to his own country. I don't think I would have been able to stand that. As it is . . .' He smiled, his chest seeming to swell with great joy as well as a lungful of fresh air. 'We weren't sure Johnnie was still alive. During all that time he was imprisoned, we only received one card from him. I suspect he won't be in the best of health. Our Ruby knows that, but she's a different girl from the one she was when this war began. I know she'll cope, no matter how bad he is.'

Masses of people had gathered to watch the fifteen-thousand-ton ship *Chetril* berth at Southampton. She had sailed all the way from Rangoon, in India, through the Suez Canal into Cairo, Malta, Lisbon and finally Southampton.

A breathless excitement hung in the air, but also anticipation. Although the men coming home had received medical attention back in Rangoon, rumours were rife that their health had been badly affected by the long years of imprisonment and that starvation, brutality and disease had all taken their toll.

Ruby had dressed carefully in a navy blue coat and a wide-brimmed hat. The dress beneath her coat was blue with white polka dots. Her gloves were white, the same as her shoes and her handbag.

The excitement running through the open-ended shed where embarkation would take place was palpable. Flags and bunting hung from every available rafter and beam, fluttering brightly and lifting the gloom of the October day.

Ruby had the oddest feeling that she was made of glass, brittle and likely to break into a thousand pieces at any given moment. She hadn't been nearly so nervous when she'd caught the train at first light this morning; in fact, she'd been quite pragmatic and confident, rehearsing in her mind what she would say to him and what he would say to her: witty, sharply humorous things.

By the time the train had idled through Blandford Forum, the excitement that had begun in her stomach had travelled up to her throat. Her mouth had turned dry at the thought of seeing John again after so long. Would he have changed that much? Well, of course he will have, you silly goose! she told herself. He's been a prisoner of war since the fall of Singapore.

In her mind she'd pictured him as he used to be, the sardonic grin, the fair skin and the mockery in his eyes when going out of his way to annoy her. He'd enjoyed annoying her and in turn she'd enjoyed giving him as good as she got. They were so similar like that in wanting to knock sparks off each other.

In the meantime, she felt like a sardine, one of many in a very small can. People were heaving and jostling in all directions, straining against the metal barriers brought in to keep them beyond the place where the ship's hawsers, the heavy ropes used for mooring, would be thrown on to the quay.

A woman brushed against her, apologised and moved away dabbing at her eyes. 'Oh, my,' she was saying to herself. 'Oh, my.' She wore an expression of intense nervousness, biting her bottom lip or the thumb that was buried deep into her cotton handkerchief.

It wasn't until there was a little space between them that Ruby noticed that the woman was heavily pregnant. Of course, it was possible that she was here to meet her brother or even her father or other relative. But it could equally be a long-lost husband. Unlike the German camps, few letters had got out of the Japanese camps; neither had lists of internees drawn up by the International Red Cross or the Vatican, both of whom had done their best to find out who was dead and who was alive. Missing presumed dead, presumed prisoner, missing in action: the terminology was short and sharp. The years had gone by, three years since Singapore fell. Letters written but never replied to. What else could a woman do except presume that her man was dead, that she was free to remarry or live as best she could without him? Some had clung on to hope; some had cut their losses and found happiness elsewhere.

Ruby briefly thought of how the man would react once he saw the clear evidence that his wife had strayed. She found herself hoping that the woman still loved her husband, at least then there was a chance of reconciliation. She chose to believe it were so, otherwise the woman would not have been here to greet him, would she?

The sound of ships horns sounded from Southampton Water, heralding the arrival of the *Chetril*, the ship carrying the men imprisoned by the Japanese Empire, a country now occupied by the victorious allied forces.

It sounded as though every ship, boat and even the ferries that crossed to the Isle of Wight were saluting the arrival of the troop ship and the men Lord Mountbatten had called 'the forgotten army'.

For a moment, Ruby thought she was looking at a huge grey wall gradually closing in from the seaward side of the dockyard shed. The smell of oil-filled exhaust and the sound of the ship's engines and that of the tugboats filled the air.

A great roar of applause went up from the waiting throng as the gangplank was heaved up to the ship's side and an army of men, who had seemed to be just lurking around, unmistakably German or Italian prisoners of war, went into action, handballing kitbags and other luggage at the same time as the first men began to walk down the gangplank.

Tables had been set out immediately in front of the gangplank where stern-looking ladies and bespectacled gentlemen sat complacently until reams of paper were placed in front of them, lists of the very particular passengers the ship had brought home.

Somebody nudged Ruby's arm. 'If he don't come looking like a lost dog down that gangplank, you can ask them sitting there if he were definitely on board. That's why they're there – in case the men don't recognise us or we don't recognise them. It's been a long time, me ducks, ain't it!'

The woman who had relayed this advice wore a hat that looked as though it had been sat on. But her eyes twinkled with joy. Judging by the few iron grey curls showing from beneath her hat, she was waiting for her son.

Ruby nodded, smiled but found she couldn't say a word. Her mouth had been dry enough before; now it felt as though her throat had closed up.

Finally, she found her voice. 'I thought I'd know what to say, but now . . .'

The woman, her chin just about reaching Ruby's shoulder, nudged her again.

'Don't you worry, my lovely! You and your young man won't need words. I'm right, ain't I? It is your sweetheart you're waiting for?'

Ruby responded that indeed it was.

'Guessed it,' said the woman. The way she chuckled and winked made Ruby blush.

The men continued to pour down the gangplank, like an unending tide of ragged scarecrows. Not that their clothes were tattered and torn, more that their clothes hung on their bodies as though they were made of twigs with very little flesh at all.

On seeing those first men alighting from the ship, Ruby felt a great tide of emotion sweep over her. They were so thin, their skin tautly stretched over faces that had only a short time ago been so young. They looked like men grown old before their time.

At first she told herself she was mistaken. "No. It's just an illusion.'

Various excuses came to mind, such as the possibility that a few had been very ill and that was why they looked like nothing much more than walking skeletons.

As the unloading continued, she reached a very much more startling conclusion.

With the exception of the ship's crew, the men unloading the kitbags, and the sudden appearance of medical staff helping the more disabled down the gangplank, all the returning men snaking down on to the quay were alarmingly thin.

More and more poured off the ship like a tumbling torrent. Excited chatter, shrieks of delight, tears, the crying of children, some quite terrified of a father they barely remembered, a father whose body had been better covered with flesh and without the intense haunted expression that these men had.

Ruby held on to the top of her hat as she craned her neck and scanned the surging tide of men. There were so many; not only that, she couldn't help allowing her gaze to settle on the haggard appearance of one man, the staring eyes of another, the injured, the disabled, the men with bandaged heads, truncated limbs . . .

A cold shiver ran down her spine. What if Johnnie was injured? Could she cope with that? She thought she could but didn't know for sure.

The telegram he'd sent had mentioned little more than the name of the ship and the estimated time of arrival. It had been sent on US army services notepaper and had been terse and to the point. At the time, she'd thought it all he needed to say: he was coming home. He expected her to be here. That was all there was to it. Had she been right to believe that? After all, she'd had just the one postcard from him during his period in captivity. So why a telegram? Why not a decent-length letter telling her what he'd been through and his plans for the future, his future, their future?

It seemed to take hours, but eventually the tide of abused humanity being unloaded dwindled to a trickle.

A feeling of the utmost disquiet flooded over Ruby even though her eyes still searched the remaining men coming ashore, most of whom were sick and being assisted.

The crowd that had surged forward to welcome their men home was slowly dissipating. A few women, including the pregnant woman she'd spoken to earlier, stood asking the people with the lists to check and double check why their men were not on board.

'My dear,' she heard one of the women at the tables say to the woman expecting a baby. Placing a reassuring hand on the young woman's shoulder, she got to her feet, her voice dropping to not much more than a whisper. 'I'm sorry.'

Ruby saw the young woman's shoulders slump before she turned away. Ruby caught her eye.

'Your husband. Is he not coming home?'

The young woman's eyes were tear-filled. She shook her head. 'He embarked on the ship but died on his way over. They brought his body back. I have to make funeral arrangements.'

She looked down at the ground, her hand on her belly. A furtive, sad smile chanced on her lips then was gone. 'Who'd have thought it? There was I worrying myself sick about explaining what had happened, and there was him lying dead on board. Two days ago, they told me.'

She bit her bottom lip as she had earlier, though this time it wasn't because she was feeling nervous, almost terrified at having to explain herself, but because she was disappointed.

'This war,' said Ruby, shaking her head. 'Is there anything I can do to help?'

The young woman shook her head. The handkerchief she'd dabbed her eyes with was screwed up in her fist. 'I'll just go ahead and have the baby.'

'Is there somebody else? I mean, the baby's father . . .?'

She shook her head, at the same time averting her eyes. 'No. I didn't see who it was . . .'

Ruby sensed her shame and was about to ask her whether she'd told the police that she'd been raped, but didn't get the chance. As though suddenly aware she was telling her troubles to a stranger, the woman excused herself and hurried off. Ruby watched her go, thinking that not all the casualties of war happened on the battlefronts.

'Can I help you?'

It was one of the women sitting at the table. Ruby was aware of the ship's manifest in front of her. In peacetime, a manifest listed the cargo on board a ship. At the end of a war, on this particular ship, it listed the names of men.

'Corporal John Smith,' said Ruby, her heart in her mouth. An expensive tortoiseshell fountain pen clenched between finger and thumb traversed the first sheet of paper, then the next, the next and the next. Finally she shook her head before suddenly saying, 'Ah, yes.' She looked over her shoulder at the gangplank and the tall metal side of the ship. 'It doesn't seem as though he was on board.'

'Who are you looking for, Mrs Risdon?' said one of the bespectacled gentleman sitting along from her.

'A Corporal John Smith. The only one I have here has been ticked off as having disembarked.'

'That's right,' said the man. 'His wife enquired what deck he was on and precisely what time he was getting off.' He jerked his head up. 'Are you another relative?'

Speechless, Ruby stared at him. 'His wife? You must be mistaken.' She almost burst out laughing in disbelief. Johnnie didn't have a wife. He didn't have any family. He didn't have anybody – except her!

She heard the woman say something about her being rude as she rushed away. Married? John was married?

Why had she come? She felt her face reddening and her eyes smarting as she headed for the exit and the railway station. Johnnie had lied to her! She'd thought he was different from the other men she'd known. Apparently he was not.

Memories of the short time she'd had with him came back in drifts of doubt. There had been occasions when he'd been apart from her for quite a while, times when she'd had to use another driver or drive herself. His excuses for those occasions had been offhand, either because he couldn't be bothered to talk about them, or because he didn't want to own up to anything. They'd always been about the army wanting him to be somewhere else, driving important people around. Damn him! He'd lied. He'd gone home to be with the family he said he didn't have.

Tears threatened, but she steeled herself to keep them at bay. She wouldn't break down. She had to be strong and on this occasion for nobody else except herself. An aura of aloof indifference always helped at times like these. All the same, she couldn't help feeling humiliated.

At the back of her mind, the spectre of her first serious beau, Gareth Stead, loomed sneering and large. When he'd let her down, she'd vowed never to get involved with anyone ever again. To a great extent she'd succeeded in that, at least of late. There had been a Polish flyer, Ivan Bronowski, whom she'd dallied with, but she'd found out he was married. It hadn't really occurred to her at the time that she was waiting for Johnnie to come marching home, like the song said, but the fact was that she had waited for him. He had never fawned over her or told her how much he loved her, or even attempted to like dancing just because she did. He had always been his own man with his own opinions – not always ones she'd agreed with – but something about his challenging manner had met something similar in her.

His features, as well as his attitude, were still easily called to mind.

She didn't stop hurrying until she was finally on the platform where the train would pull in to take her home, or at least as far as Bristol. From there she would get a branch line train to Oldland Common Halt. On checking with a porter, she was told she had at least two hours to wait.

'The war might be over, but we've a long way to go until we get back to normal,' he said to her in a sullen voice.

Waiting gave her time to think and try to lick her wounds. Every thought was accompanied with a vision of Johnnie, his sharp features and mocking eyes, the half-sneer on his lips that it seemed at times he was trying to control. Over a period of time, she'd reached the conclusion that he'd wanted to smile at her and declare how much he cared, but had held himself back. It seemed that she'd been wrong. Could it really be that he was married, and that was the reason he'd held back? Men would do anything to get their own way. She'd said so herself, but still she found it hard to believe.

There was the moment in the field close to the railway station, of course, but that was the only time they had allowed their physical desires to get the better of them.

By the time she was on the train heading north, she had still not come to terms with how she really felt. The carriage was crowded and she found herself squashed into a corner, surrounded mostly by demobbed service personnel and those still in uniform, all intense and overly happy, laughing, singing and talking as though they hadn't done any of it for years.

For the most part, Ruby kept to herself, occupied with her own thoughts. Anger and affection seemed to be fighting a pitched battle inside her head. She wanted to scream; she wanted to cry. She also wondered whether she should have waited, perhaps got those people to recheck their lists.

'Cheer up, love. It might never happen.'

The naval rating had dancing eyes and wide wet lips. She could tell he was a bit tipsy and trying to get even tipsier, if the beer bottle he had in his hand was anything to go by.

Ruby merely smiled at him and looked out of the window at the fields, cows and cottages huddled around a village church. She didn't want to get into conversation with anyone, least of all a single man looking for fun following his time at war.

'Oh dear. Looks as though it already has happened. Is that right, love?'

Even though her ignoring him had bordered on rudeness, he wasn't put off. A few people got off at the next station, leaving room for him to move closer. It didn't help trying to move closer to the window. He found space to sit beside her. His boozy breath was close at hand.

He took a swig from his beer before trying his luck. 'Are you spoken for, sweetheart?'

'Yes. I am.'

'Just my luck. All the prettiest girls are.'

She didn't look at him. At this moment in time, she was thinking she never wanted to look at another man again.

To her great relief, her would-be beau got off the train at Taunton, his place taken by yet more service personnel, soldiers mostly and as tipsy as the sailor. Those that were sober sat gazing out at the passing scenery, their eyes glistening with emotion. They were the lucky ones, the men who had made it: they were still alive.

When they finally arrived at Bristol, Temple Meads Station was as busy, if not busier, than the other stations where men had alighted and got on the train, all eager to be on their way home.

Vast clouds of steam from the locomotive billowed upwards to the glass roof where, trapped, it promptly billowed its way back down again.

Masses of people alighted from the long line of railway carriages and Ruby was jostled and pushed from all sides.

Women waiting on the platform shrieked, cried and shouted before throwing their arms around their loved one's neck. Everywhere among that heap of humanity were islands of couples hugging each other more tightly than they were ever likely to again.

For the rest of their lives, they would remember this bittersweet moment. From this time onwards, they would attempt to rebuild their lives, even though deep down they knew nothing would ever be the same again. Ruby wished she was one of them whose life would be changed for ever, but Johnnie wasn't here. He belonged to somebody else.

CHAPTER THIRTY-FOUR

Frances admired the wedding band on her finger. Declan had kept his promise.

She'd been honest with him and told him about Ed, how he'd been drunk and how she'd been feeling very down. Declan was uncommonly casual about the child's likely paternity.

'Honey, there's a war on. Nothing is the same as it is in peacetime. The rules no longer apply. There's a new set and we take them as we can.'

Ed Bergman had been involved in a manoeuvre off the south coast. In heavy seas and a squalling wind, a number of young men had lost their lives. Ed Bergman, handed a gun and turfed out of the cookhouse, was one of them.

She and Declan had finally married between him coming back from Europe and being posted to the Pacific. In between times, they had also created another child. After she'd got over the surprise – Daisy was still not yet two – Frances was adamant it would be another girl. There was no doubt the child would be born in the United States. Arrangements were in hand for her to sail across in the *Queen Mary* to New York, where they would start a new life together.

Daisy was asleep and Frances was talking to her bump.

'I bet you're hungry. How about we eat the rest of the scones your auntie Ruby made yesterday?' She cocked her head sideways as though listening for the baby's reply. 'Okay,' she said finally. 'I'll put the kettle on and we'll finish them up.'

'Are you talking to yourself again?'

Her uncle Stan brought the smell of earth in from the garden, even though he'd left his wellington boots outside. Charlie tagged behind his grandfather as he always did, the toes of his socks – unpicked from a cardigan and knitted to fit him – were wet so made a slapping noise with each step he took.

'No, of course not,' Frances said loftily. 'I'm talking to Vivien.'

Her uncle raised his eyebrows in disbelief. 'I take it that will be the name of the new baby.'

'That's right.' She took the scones from the tin they'd been stored in and placed them on a plate. The plate had a large chip, but it was pretty and by far her favourite.

The whole family knew that Frances was into the habit of talking to the unborn child. 'She hears everything I say,' Frances stated.

They also knew that she'd named the child after Vivien Leigh, the actress who had played Scarlett O'Hara in the film *Gone with the Wind*.

Frances had been so struck with the film that she'd gone to see it three times, each time awestruck by everything about it.

Ruby had questioned why not name the baby Scarlett. Frances had laughed out loud and shook her head as though Ruby just wasn't thinking straight.

'I can't call her that! It's not a real name. It's made up.'

Ruby had also pointed out that the baby might be a boy. 'I presume that if it is a boy, you're more likely to call him Clark rather than Rhett.'

Frances had wrinkled her nose. 'No. I don't like either of those. I think if it is a boy I will call him Ashley. I quite like that name. But there, it doesn't really matter. It's a girl. I know it's another girl.'

Charlie's fingers gripped the edge of the table. His brown eyes followed each scone as it travelled from the tin to the plate. 'Charlie have cake?'

Once all the scones were on the plate, his eyes never strayed from them.

Frances smiled at him. 'Would Charlie like a cake after I've cut it in half and spread it with butter and jam?'

A wide smile spread across the little boy's face when he nodded.

'Then you shall have one!'

Uncle Stan pulled out a chair and sat down, beaming with pleasure at his grandson. The little lad was growing fast, chatting nineteen to the dozen and trotting along behind his granddad no matter where he went. He often wondered how things would have been if the war had never happened, if Hitler had not risen to power in Europe and everyone had stayed in the place they knew as home. Charlie, his son, young Charlie's father, would never have met Charlie's mother. There would have been no young Charlie, unless his son had married in the village, then perhaps he would have had a host of grandchildren. Michael, Mary's husband, a pilot in the Canadian Air Force, would never have been transferred to the Royal Air Force. They too would never have met. As for Frances, well, it was unfortunate that Declan O'Malley had been posted to the Pacific, though he assured her he was on his way home.

Up until the Japanese surrender, Frances had feared for his life. But all that was over now, and even though she hadn't heard from him in a while, she refused to believe that he'd been in many battles and would die now – right at the end of the war.

Frances was glad to be reconciled with her uncle. Of her mother there was no trace.

'Never mind, love. You've got your own family now,' Stan had said to her.

At one time, he would have run her down, constantly referring to her chasing after anything in trousers. Frances wondered at his calmer behaviour. She was not to know that Mildred had been in contact, asking after Frances.

She'd telephoned from a public telephone box, the pennies dropping into the box with a metallic noise as she outlined her rights.

Once Stan had told her that Frances would be unable to work because she was expecting, the telephone was put down. Mildred hadn't wanted her daughter when she was a child, and she certainly didn't want the burden of a grandchild!

'I know you of old and you're unchanged,' he'd said to the woman who now called herself Mrs Baxter.

Now, Stan noticed the smug expression on Frances's face and felt instant apprehension.

'Do you mind telling me what you're smiling about?' he asked.

Frances's thick eyelashes swept down over her eyes. He'd always been of the opinion that she only did that when she had a secret that pleased her greatly and that she had no intention of sharing.

'It's a secret.'

Stan sighed. 'I should have known.'

'I'll tell you as soon as Ruby gets home. I think she'll be pleased.' A sudden thought seemed to strike the smile from her face. 'Well, I think she will, though not when she first gets home. I expect she'll be tired and probably annoyed.'

'I expect she will,' said Stan as he reached for his cup of tea.

There was no doubt in Stan's mind that his daughter would be dog tired. Johnnie would be too, poor sod, after all those years of privation.

His thoughts went back to his daughter. All the way to Southampton to meet a man she hadn't seen for three years. He wondered where they would go once they'd met up. No doubt they'd make arrangements to meet again, unless Johnnie came back here. They'd put him up somewhere, even over at Bettina's.

'I think Ruby will miss working for the Ministry of Food,' Frances declared suddenly.

Alarmed by the comment, in case Ruby might reconsider moving out of the village, Stan told Frances in no uncertain terms that she hadn't been laid off from her war work just yet.

'And then we've got a Christmas party to arrange. Never mind the big cities having street parties; the whole village will be along to have a Christmas party, what with everyone being demobbed.'

'We've already had a village party.'

It was true. The whole village had gone as wild as the rest of the country when Germany then Japan had finally surrendered. It was all over at long last. People couldn't stop celebrating, such was their sense of relief. Declan had been freed and paid a flying visit, enough time to get married and make her pregnant again.

She looked up at the clock. 'Ruby should be home soon. I think I fancy a walk to the station to greet the pair of them,' said Frances. 'Can you keep an eye on Daisy, please, Uncle Stan?'

Busily slicing another scone and smothering it with jam and cream for his grandson, Stan raised no objection.

The night air was sharp with the promise of frost, but Frances had wrapped up warm and sang to herself and her unborn child as she tramped up the road towards the hump-backed bridge and down the steps leading down to the station platform.

Frost was beginning to spangle in tiny crystals all over the platform. During the blackout they wouldn't have been noticeable, but the lights had been switched back on. It didn't matter that the station was poorly lit; there was enough to mirror the star-laden sky.

Seeing as there was nobody else around, Frances resumed talking to the bump that would shortly be gone once the baby was born.

'Vivien, I do hope you'll like your name. I wish you could say that you do out loud, but of course that's not possible. I mentioned it to your sister, Daisy. She thinks it's a lovely name. So does your father.'

Not for the first time, she felt a movement beneath the touch of her hand, a small hand or foot, or perhaps something else, rearranging itself.

Frances smiled. 'Yes. I think you do like it, don't you?'

The train station was like a lighthouse in their midst, the place where everyone set out from and everyone returned to. The smell of coal dust mixed with steam made the air smell different here and stayed in the nostrils.

Ruby emerged from the cloud of steam, an indistinct figure that gradually solidified, as though she'd been formed from the steam itself.

Frances looked for Johnnie. There was no one. Her cousin was alone. 'Where is he?' she shouted.

Ruby shrugged her shoulders. 'Not with me.'

Her manner was such that Frances took the hint that she did not wish to discuss Johnnie any further.

'Come on,' she said, head down and striding resolutely up the gradient to the main road. 'Let's get home.'

They walked in silence. Frances was desperate to know what had happened, but didn't dare ask. Ruby was brooding on something. Perhaps in time she might tell what that something was.

A single streetlight on the opposite side of the road to the bakery glimmered uncertainly. All the same its glow represented the end of war and the beginning of peace. It was the first time it had been lit since 1939.

At first it seemed like an apparition, a greyish form parked outside the bakery, the streetlight picking out the single white star on its side. An empty Jeep. Nobody in it.

Frances's pace quickened. 'Declan! He's here! And I thought he meant we'd meet up in America!'

Ruby urged caution, hugging her cousin's arm to prevent her from racing off and being disappointed. 'You don't know for sure.'

Frances's response was swift and sharp, though she knew what Ruby was insinuating: that somebody had come to tell her he wasn't coming back. But she knew he was. She refused to believe any differently.

'Yes it is! It's him!'

Giving the shop door a good push, Frances flew in, the doorbell clanging as though it hung on a fire engine and the house was on fire.

'Declan!'

He was leaner, his face more lined and browner, but it was him. He was back and holding Daisy with one arm as though she were no weight at all.

Frances threw herself into his free arm.

'You said . . . what are you doing here . . .?'

'I said I would come home for good before very long.'

'But you said . . .'

'This has always been your home, and if it's your home it's also mine. We won't leave it entirely behind. Ever! I had to pay my respects to your uncle and the rest of your family. I'm not a callous man.' Declan kissed the top of her head.

Stan Sweet turned to face the fire and Ruby swiped a tear from the corner of her eye.

'I'm off again shortly, but we won't be apart for long. There's a ship leaving Southampton in two weeks. You're on it. My oldest friend will be waiting for you at the other end. But first we've got a wedding to go to. I think I've got the job of best man. Am I right?'

A man with hollow cheeks and sunken eyes sat silently in one of the armchairs, his hands folded listlessly in his lap.

Johnnie Smith was home.

'Where's Ruby?' Declan said.

'Gone to see how Mrs Powell is coping. She's given up the shop, not so much out of forgiveness for her daughter, more out of shame. She feels she can no longer hold her head up in the village. I think Ruby's words of comfort will be ungratefully received.'

'I'll tell you later,' said Frances, when Declan frowned questioningly.

On her return, Ruby uttered a small cry, standing in the doorway too shocked to move.

Although her driver had never been a big man, there was far less of him now. He had a haunted look in his eyes which for all that stared brightly from a sunburned face, the skin taut across his cheekbones, his hair kissed to lemon brightness by the hot Asian sun.

His body was overly lean, far more so than when he had left for Singapore before he'd been starved, before he'd been beaten and left to wander around in rags.

He smiled at her. 'I'm sorry about my teeth.'

At first she didn't understand what he meant, not until he smiled a little wider and she saw the gaps in his gums, luckily mostly his molars, his front teeth having miraculously survived.

She stood there unmoving, feeling incredibly empty, as though all her blood along with her emotions had flowed out of her.

'They told me your wife had fetched you. I thought . . . I thought . . .'

She couldn't go on.

He shook his head. 'I told you before. I've got nobody. But John Smith is a pretty common name. I recall somebody telling me there were three John Smith's on board, but that one of them had been taken ill at the last minute. Malaria, I think he said.' He shook his head again. 'That's one thing you can get plenty of in the Far East.' He held up a package. 'I brought you silk.'

Pushing his hands down on the chair arms, he got to his feet. He smiled weakly, as though it took all his strength as indeed it did. Then he picked up the parcel again and held it out.

Ruby took the package, her hands trembling as she did so. 'Thank you.'

'I brought back sacks of food too. Tinned stuff mostly. We were given a pick of it at the American base. They shipped it in as fast as they could before any more of us dropped dead. They dropped supplies too during those last months. I don't know what we would have done if they hadn't . . . we couldn't have taken . . .'

Suddenly his knees crumpled.

'Johnnie!'

With Declan's help, Stan Sweet was able to get Johnnie upstairs to bed. Light as a feather, he thought to himself, and felt a terrible sadness that a young man should have gone through such torture.

For a while, he and Declan stood at the foot of the bed, watching Johnnie's head twitch against the pillows.

'Like carrying a child,' murmured Stan.

'No weight at all,' agreed Declan.

Stan turned round to see Ruby and Frances standing by the door. Ruby came into the room and stood between them. Frances hung on to Declan's arm.

'He's been through hell,' Stan said softly.

Ruby nodded.

'So,' he said, eyeing his daughter with one eyebrow lifted, the quizzical look that he always adopted before asking a typically awkward question. 'Are you going to stand by him, or dash off to pastures new?'

Ruby knew her father wanted an answer as much for himself as for Johnnie. 'Home is where the heart is, Dad. Johnnie deserves to be looked after and I'm glad I waited for him.'

'And I've got a secret,' said Frances, smiling in the way she had when she was a child.

Stan laughed softly. 'What? Another one?'

'Mary telephoned to say that Michael's been offered a position as an engineer at the aircraft works in Filton.'

'That's good,' said Stan nodding without stopping. 'That's very good.'

'But I'll still be going to America,' she added.

Stan glanced at Declan then at her. 'That's good too. I think you're in good hands.'

* * *

The following morning, Stan walked down to the churchyard, his grandson's small fist clenched in his much larger one.

The first mists of November 1945 were curling around the naked branches of the trees and misting the outlines of the gravestones and the church itself.

Charlie had brought his own small trowel with him and began digging around the edge of his grandmother's grave.

Stan leaned on the tombstone with one hand, reluctant to take up his usual kneeling position.

'My knees aren't so good today,' he said out loud. 'But there, Sarah, I'm not so young as I used to be, though I still remember how I was, how we were.'

He smiled at the memories before his thoughts turned serious again.

'Another war over. At long last. It looks as though it's our Frances who'll be moving overseas with that American of hers. Mary's husband did consider going back to Canada but has decided otherwise. I know it's selfish, but I'm hoping they'll come back here to the village. Michael has a great affection for Bettina Hicks. He's like a son to her, far more so than her own son, who's failed to put in an appearance for the duration. Bettina adores him. Understandable, I suppose. He's unaware that his real father was Bettina's husband. You know how it was. Dangerfield was injured and unable to father a child, and Bettina gave her blessing for her own husband to save the day.' He shook his head forlornly. 'Such is the nature of war. As for our Ruby, well . . .' He took a deep breath, which helped restrain the sigh that heaved his broad chest. 'Johnnie has come home. She's adamant she won't leave him. I've no doubt they're going to get married, though it could take a while before Johnnie is fully recovered. He was talking to me about opening up a garage in the village or over in Longwell Green. He reckons the demand for cars and for repairing them is bound to grow. He could be right. Anyway, I wish him all the best. I trust you do too. In the meantime, it's good to have everybody home.'

He found himself breathing slowly, as though both he and the whole world had taken a step backwards into a peaceful past. He thought about all the people over the centuries laid to rest in the churchyard and how they too had had their problems, their losses, their children and their wars.

For just a moment, it felt as though the years since Sarah died had never happened. He was back there again, invigorated and full of joy and also great peace. He hadn't felt like that for a very long time.

The breeze and mist seemed suddenly to combine to send the branches of the oak trees creaking as though speaking in a low crackly voice. Just for a second, he thought they were words, not the trees speaking, but Sarah's words. *Home Sweet Home*. He smiled. The world was at peace and his family were home.

Recipes

EGGLESS CAKE

- 14 oz flour
- 2 oz cornflour
- 8 oz currants
- 4 oz mixed peel (chopped)
- 8 oz sultanas
- ¼ teaspoon salt
- ½ lb brown sugar
- 1 teaspoon mixed spice
- 1 teaspoon bicarbonate of soda
- 8 oz dripping or margarine
- Milk
- 1 tablespoon vinegar

Sift the flours, salt and spice together. Rub in the fat, add the fruit and sugar, mix well together. Dissolve the soda in a little milk, add the vinegar and sufficient milk to mix to a fairly stiff consistency. Put into a greased 2 lb tin and bake for about 2 hours in a slow oven. Regulo 3. (The old gas thermal measure.) Temperature: 175°C/350°F.

HONEY SCONES

- ½ lb plain flour
- 6 oz wholemeal flour
- 2 teaspoons baking powder
- 2 oz cornflour
- 3 oz margarine
- ½ teaspoon salt
- 2 tablespoons honey
- Milk

Sift the flours, cornflour and salt together. Rub in the fat lightly, add the raising agent. Dissolve the honey in a little milk, and mix all to a fairly soft dough, adding more milk as required. Turn on to a floured board, roll out to about ¼ inch thickness, cut into rounds and bake in a hot oven for 10-15 minutes. Regulo 8. (The old gas thermal measure.) Temperature: 250°C/475°F.

TREACLE SCONES

- 1 lb plain flour
- 1 oz margarine
- ½ teaspoon baking powder
- 2 tablespoons black treacle
- 1 teaspoon cream of tartar
- Milk — about ¼ pint
- ½ teaspoon mixed spice

Sieve all the dry ingredients together. Rub in the fat. Make a well in the centre, add treacle and enough milk, about ¼ pint, to make a firm dough. Turn on to a floured board, roll out to about ¼ inch thickness, cut into rounds and bake for about 15 minutes in a hot oven. Regulo 7. Temperature: 250°C/475°F.

CUT AND COME AGAIN CAKE

- 14 oz flour
- 2 oz cornflour
- Pinch of salt
- 1 teaspoon mixed spice
- 6 oz margarine
- ½ lb brown sugar
- ¼ lb sultanas
- ½ lb currants
- ¼ lb mixed peel chopped finely
- 1 tablespoon marmalade
- 1 teaspoon bicarbonate of soda
- 1 egg
- Milk

Sift the flour, cornflour, salt and spice together. Rub in the fat. Add the fruit, sugar and marmalade. Dissolve the soda in a little milk, and add with the beaten egg and sufficient milk to make a fairly stiff consistency. Put into a greased tin and bake for 2-2½ hours in a moderate oven. Regulo 4. Temperature: 190°C/375°F.

SPOON CAKE

- 7 tablespoons plain flour
- 2 tablespoons sultanas
- 1 oz cornflour
- 1 tablespoon chopped candied peel
- 1 tablespoon self-raising flour or 1 teaspoon baking powder
- ½ teaspoon mixed spice
- 4 oz margarine or dripping
- 1 egg
- 4 tablespoons sugar
- 3–4 tablespoons milk
- 2 tablespoons currants

Sift flours and spice together, rub in the fat, add all dry ingredients. Mix to a fairly stiff consistency with the beaten egg and milk. Turn into a greased tin and bake for about 1½ hours in a moderate oven. Regulo 3. (175°C)

DATE COOKIES

- 3 oz chopped dates
- 4 oz wholemeal flour
- 2 oz sugar
- 2 oz cornflour
- Little milk
- 2 oz plain flour
- 2 oz melted margarine
- 1 oz Raisley or 3 level teaspoons baking powder

Sieve the flours and baking powder together. Add the chopped dates and sugar. Mix to a fairly stiff consistency with the melted fat and milk. Put into greased bun tins and bake for about 15 minutes in a moderately hot oven. Regulo 6. Temperature: 220°C/425°F.

HISTORICAL NOTE

The Dambuster Raid occurred in the third week of May 1943. 'Geoff' was the code name of Professor Barnes Wallis, the inventor of the bouncing bomb.

Wing Commander Guy Gibson led the fleet of Lancaster bombers setting off from Scampton airbase in Lincolnshire.

Also by Lizzie Lane:

A WARTIME WIFE

Trapped in a marriage to the wrong man . . .

Struggling to make ends meet, Mary Anne Randall is offered no help by her drunk and abusive husband. A pawnbroking business run from the wash house at the back of her home is the only way she can hope to keep her three kids fed and clothed.

But, as storm clouds gather over Europe, can Mary Anne break free from her loveless marriage for what might be a last chance at love . . .?

EBURY
PRESS

Also by Lizzie Lane:

A WARTIME FAMILY

Mary Anne's story continues . . .

A scandalous woman?

Having left her abusive husband for very good reasons,
Mary Anne Randall finds herself judged harshly by her
neighbours, especially after she has the courage to risk
a second chance at happiness.

But with the only man she has ever loved away fighting,
Mary Anne is less concerned by her tarnished reputation
than with keeping her children safe, as the bombs fall
on Bristol – all too close to home.

EBURY
PRESS